VOL (2) [PRICE ~~ONE SHILLING~~ 6 D

EDWIN J. BRETT'S JACK HARKAWAY AND HIS SON'S ADVENTURES ROUND THE WORLD.

EDWIN J. BRETT,
"BOYS OF ENGLAND" OFFICE.
173, FLEET STREET
AND ALL BOOKSELLERS.

HARKAWAY SERIES VOL.

GIVEN AWAY WITH No. 3]   [OF JACK HARKAWAY AND HIS SONS ADVENTURES ROUND THE WORLD.

YOUNG JACK HARKAWAY AND HIS MONKEY SETTLING THE DISPUTE BETWEEN THE TWO NIGGERS, SUNDAY AND MONDAY.

JACK HARKAWAY

AND HIS SON'S

Adventures Round the World.

BEAUTIFULLY ILLUSTRATED.

• VOLUME I. •

LONDON:
"BOYS OF ENGLAND" OFFICE, 173, FLEET STREET, E.C.,
AND ALL BOOKSELLERS.

EDWIN J. BRETT'S

JACK HARKAWAY
AND HIS SON'S
ADVENTURES ROUND THE WORLD.

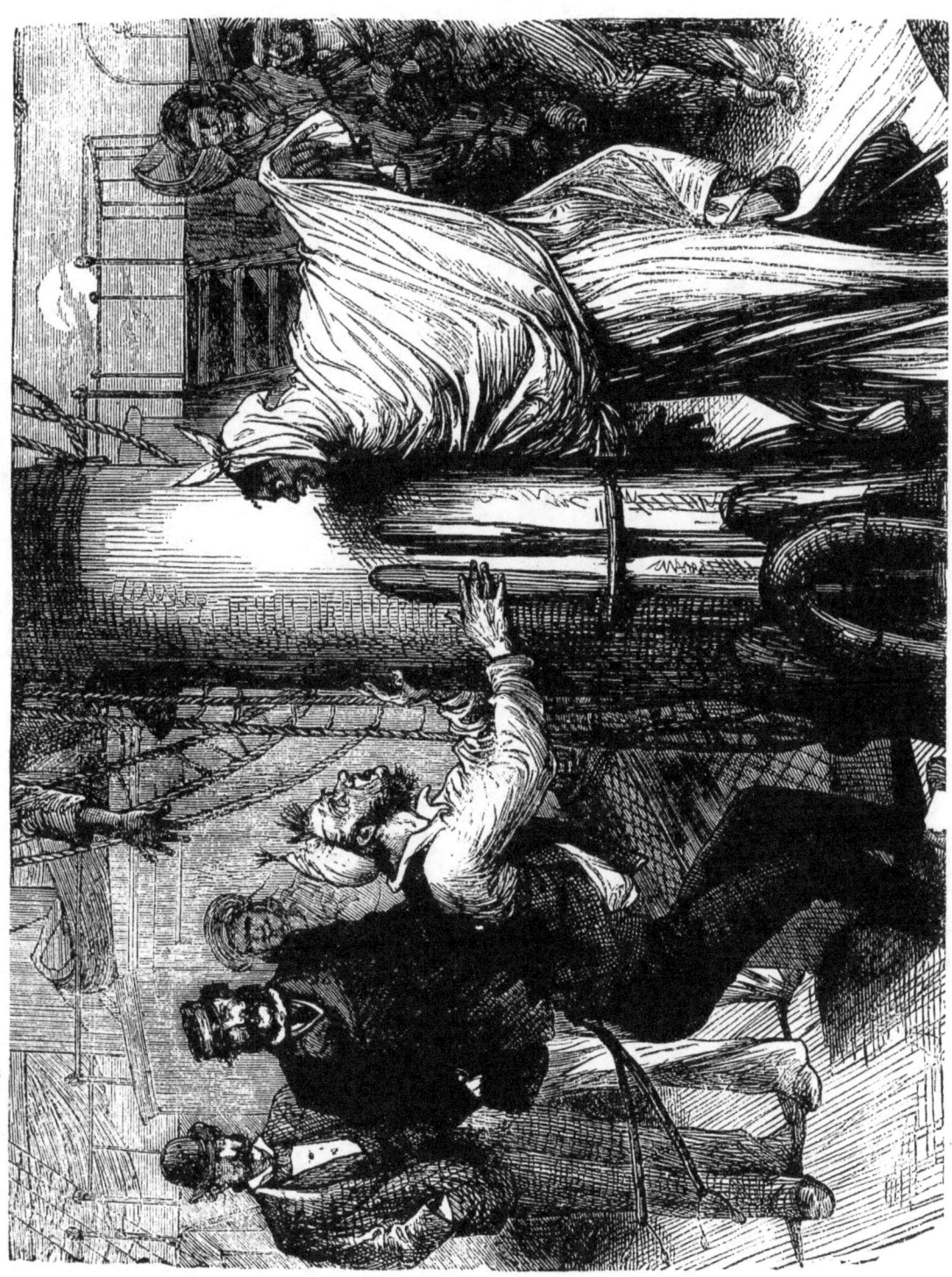

"'I'LL HAVE YOU,' SAID THE SPECTRE TO MOLE, 'COME TO MY ARMS.'"

NO. 1 {No. 2 Presented GRATIS With This Number.}   PRICE ONE HALFPENNY.
[PUBLISHED EVERY TUESDAY.]

With This Number is Presented Gratis a Splendid Coloured Picture.

JACK HARKAWAY AND HIS SON'S ADVENTURES

ROUND THE WORLD.

CHAPTER I.

JACK COMES INTO AN INHERITANCE, AND DETERMINES TO TRAVEL ONCE MORE.

You who have followed Jack Harkaway's progress at school and Oxford, on sea and land, at home and abroad, have seen how brave he was in boyhood, and noble in his manhood.

Jack Harkaway's life glided on smoothly enough for some years.

But life is made up of joys and sorrows —of smiles and tears.

When our Jack's son was just turned twelve years old, a great and unexpected sorrow came upon him and his family. His father fell ill.

The family doctor was called in and consulted by Jack with some eagerness, for the old gentleman's complaint had puzzled them.

"If you can tell us what's the matter with my poor governor," said Jack, "we shall look upon you as a wonder."

"Why so?"

"Because it has bothered us all."

"What are the symptoms?" demanded Doctor Purcell.

"That is difficult to answer."

"Indeed?"

"There are no painful symptoms."

"Doesn't he complain of anything?"

"Lassitude, weakness, dizziness in the head."

"Well," said Doctor Purcell, smiling, "these are symptoms; that is what I asked you for."

"Well," returned Jack, "go now and see the governor."

The doctor was very grave and full of anxiety on his return to Jack.

Jack saw there was something wrong.

"Doctor," he said, with great anxiety, "what is the matter?"

Doctor Purcell made no reply.

He shook his head.

"Is my father ill?"

"He is, indeed."

"Good Heaven, doctor, you frighten me!" exclaimed Jack; "not seriously?"

"He has not twelve hours to live."

The words struck Jack Harkaway to the very heart like a knife.

"This is indeed sad tidings, doctor," he cried, sinking into a chair.

The doctor did not interrupt Jack's sorrow.

He knew he would be calmer afterwards.

And Jack stood in need of all his calmness for what he had to go through.

"Your father wants you," said the doctor; "some matters of business are troubling him, that is very evident."

"What is it in particular that worries him?"

"He wants to make his will."

"He must not trouble about that."

"Just what I said," returned Doctor Purcell. "He wants to leave you everything—now you, as his only child, must inherit all if he dies intestate."

Jack's father was, as the doctor said, at the point of death.

He was also, it is true, troubling himself about his worldly affairs.

The trouble on his mind at that dreadful time was concerning some property he possessed in the island of Cuba.

Now the estate, from which he had derived for a long while a very considerable income, had lost two-thirds of its value of late.

The civil war which raged for so long in that unhappy island depreciated every property and ruined many landed proprietors.

The Cuban agent (a gentleman owning the high-sounding name of Don José Serrano D'Acquila), was killed in a skirmish during the early part of the civil war, and then the collection of Harkaway's quarterly moneys fell into the hands of a stranger called Ostano.

Ostano left the island, it appeared, for political reasons.

Since his departure no news had been received of him.

The matter, it is true, was urgent, but it caused his son no little pain to see his father trouble about it at such a time.

It would indeed have been the same had their bread depended upon it.

Jack mounted to his father's room, and then he was infinitely shocked to see how fatally near the last moment was.

He was, in fact, already wandering in his mind.

Doctor Purcell followed closely upon Jack's footsteps, and catching his eye in the looking glass facing the door as they entered, he held up his hand with a warning gesture.

"Silence!"

In the sick chamber, every movement of the medical man is watched in the deepest anxiety.

Jack felt that the dire calamity was approaching fast.

In less than one short hour all would be over

He scarcely wanted Doctor Purcell to tell him this, as the fatal truth was written in his father's face.

* * * * *

"Jack, my son," said the dying man, in a faint voice.

"Here, sir."

And Jack turned away to conceal his emotion.

The sufferer stretched forth his hand, but not in the direction of his son.

His sight was gone.

Jack saw it, and he took his father's hand in his.

"My poor boy," said the dying man, "I am going to leave you soon."

"You mustn't grieve for me, my son," said the dying man; "keep your strength for awhile. This is the great ordeal in life, Jack, but it will soon be over."

Jack was silent. The words of the dying man seemed to thrill him.

They struck like a death knell upon his ear.

"I want to know that you and my dear grandson, my little Jack, are well provided for."

"We are indeed."

"But can be better."

"We have all that we can possibly desire in the world, dear father."

"But there is that rich Cuban property—your birthright, John."

"Do not trouble about it, sir."

"But you must see after it, do you hear me, Jack?"

"I hear you, sir."

"And my commands are that you see after your property."

"I will obey you, sir."

There was a ring of sadness in Jack's tone as he spoke.

"It is not for myself, John, I speak. You have a son, God bless him!"

"Amen," said Jack, piously.

"He is good, and will be a brave boy. He has been a great comfort to me, and reminds me of you, Jack, when his age."

"He is wild and thoughtless, sir," said Jack; "but, believe me, he is a true Boy of England, has a good heart, and loves you tenderly."

"I know it well," retorted the dying man; "but I would not have him shocked by what is about to happen. He is too young; it comes quite soon enough upon you. Let us keep him from the presence of death as long as possible; keep my death from him at first and then break it as gently as you possibly can."

A big lump rose in his throat.

The tears swelled up into his eyes.

"Farewell, dear Jack," said the dying man, in mournful accents.

But his son could not reply.

A silent pressure of that clammy hand was his sole response.

They remained thus for several minutes in silence.

Presently the pressure of the father's hand relaxed. The son looked up.

Then he gave a cry of mingled grief and awe. All was over; Jack's father was dead.

"Come," said Doctor Purcell, placing his arm in Jack's, and leading him gently away, "come and speak to your son, young Jack Harkaway."

CHAPTER II.

COMMENCEMENT OF NEW ADVENTURES.

Now we have to step over a certain lapse of time.

Jack Harkaway bore in mind the injunctions of his dying father.

The Cuban property was in urgent need of personal supervision, and so Jack determined to cross the Atlantic and rout out the necessary information for himself.

But a certain difficulty presented itself.

Emily would not hear of her husband leaving her and young Jack, and so it fell out that a pleasure party was organised.

Dick Harvey would not hear of his friends leaving England without him.

"What shall I do, Jack?" he exclaimed, when first the subject was broached. "I'm not going to mope away here all alone."

"But I must go," urged Jack.

"So shall I."

"What, to America and Cuba?"

"Of course; or round the world, if you wish."

"You don't mean it?"

"Don't I? You'll see; where you go I'll go, unless you've turned sneak in your old age, and want to throw over your pals, unless you have got altogether sick of me."

"None of your chaff," returned Jack Harkaway. "If you will stick to me, we will yet see more sport and adventure, and, if fate bids it, die together, old boy."

Young Jack, of course, was to be one of the party, and, although small in years, he proved to be big in action.

Consequently his tutor, our old friend Isaac Mole, was bound to accompany them.

Our old friend Monday was in great form, making the preparations for the voyage.

He was the major domo of the Harkaway household, and as Dick Harvey was wont to say, "he didn't forget to let the people know it. Oh, dear, no!"

"America and Cuba," said Monday, with enthusiasm. "Dat's bery much magnificent. I shall be one big man there."

"Magnificent," iterated Dick Harvey; "that's not the word; it's gollopshus."

Monday, according to custom, ran after his dictionary and referred; but much to his disappointment, he failed to find the signification of Dick's adjective.

As for Mr. Mole, his delight took the most extravagant form.

"Cross the Atlantic," he said, in ecstasy. "It will seem quite like old times."

"You'll go, then?" demanded young Jack, anxiously.

"Go, of course I will; splice my jib-boom."

Young Jack was rather alarmed at his tutor's oath.

"What's that?" he asked.

"Which?"

"Splice your what-d'ye-call-it?"

"Oh, that's merely a nautical habit of mine. I feel like an old salt again, directly I hear them talk of the sea."

"And does that make you say splice your—your jibboom?"

"Yes, that's it," said Mr. Mole.

"Curious language, you seafaring folks have," remarked young Jack.

"Very. But very characteristic and significant."

"No doubt, sir."

Mr. Mole walked up the room, turning an imaginary quid, and hitching his trousers up, after the fashion of nautical men on the stage.

Young Jack watched his tutor in considerable curiosity.

"Is there anything the matter, sir?" he demanded.

"No; why?"

"Because you keep doing that, sir," said Jack junior, pointing to Mr. Mole's nautical manœuvres.

"My sailor habits," returned Mr. Mole, blandly; "we term that, technically, hoisting our slacks."

"Slacks?"

"Yes, slacks, the nautical for continuations."

"Good gracious!"

"Very singular expressions, are they not?"

"Very."

"Yes; we old tars can't get out of these habits; that especially is a trick common to all of us."

"Which?"

"Hitching."

"Itching?" said young Jack, slily. "It looks more like scratching; I thought you'd got a flea."

Mr. Mole gave his pupil a very sharp look at this reply. It sounded like his father's old impudent style.

But young Jack looked as demure as a school-girl, so Mr. Mole took it for sheer innocence.

"You are every inch a sailor, Mr. Mole, I see," said young Jack, when they were fairly on board ship.

"There's no denying that," replied the modest tutor.

"You share all the good qualities of a true British tar," said young Jack, piling it up for the fun of the thing, to see how far Mr. Mole's brag and mendacity would carry him, "all of them."

"And some of their weaknesses," said Mr. Mole.

"Rum, for instance?"

"I won't deny that I like a little rum," replied Mr. Mole, "a very little."

"Of course. And your pigtail?"

"Well," replied Mr. Mole, "I will confess that I like a bit for the tooth."

"And you like rats aboard ship?"

"Eh! what?—rats! Well, I can't say that I do."

"Oh, but no sailor would go to sea in a ship that hadn't rats, I've heard."

"No more would I," said Mr. Mole. "No more would I."

"Of course not," said young Jack; "you are so superstitious, you seafaring men."

"That we are."

"And afraid of ghosts?"

"Eh? No, no," said Mr. Mole, "not afraid of ghosts."

"Oh, you must be," pursued young Jack.

"Not I; in fact," said Mr. Mole, "that is the only characteristic which I do not share with mariners."

"You don't believe in supernatural things, then?"

"Not I."

"Sailors always do."

"I know that," said Mr. Mole, "but I was always of too dare-devil a character for that. Indeed, I believe that if I saw the old gentleman himself, it wouldn't alarm me."

"Lor', sir!"

And young Jack pretended to be woefully afraid at the bare mention of the evil one.

As young Jack was going aft, Ben Hawser accosted him.

"Beg your pardon, Master Jack," said the honest tar, "would you like to see Nero?"

"Is he a Newfoundland?" asked young Jack:

"Lord bless your heart, no, sir," replied the sailor; "Nero's a monkey."

"A monkey?"

"Yes, a fine fellow, and as harmless as a child; only they won't let me set him loose."

"Why not?"

"The passengers would not like it.

Nero was a full-grown chimpanzee, standing over four feet high.

A square-shouldered, thick-set monkey, that looked like a stunted man.

He was as strong as he was lithe and agile, and although full of tricks, when at liberty he was not vicious.

He was kept in a large cage like a horse-box, with a grated door, where he had just enough room to move about, but no more.

"Nero," said Ben Hawser, opening the door, " I've brought your prog."

The monkey grinned.

Evidently he was not sorry to be at feeding time again.

"Poor Nero," said his master, " tip us your fin."

The monkey shook hands in the most natural way in the world.

"Now shake hands with Master Jack."

Never was such an intelligent chimpanzee.

He held out his paw immediately, and made friends with our young hero.

"Up here, Nero," said Ben.

Nero leaped out of his cage, and with a hop was on Ben Hawser's shoulders.

" Up! T'other way up!"

In an instant Nero was standing on his head on Ben's, balancing himself as cleverly as a trained acrobat.

" Down."

Nero dropped to the deck.

" Over—turn!"

Nero threw a back somersault, and then a succession of what professional tumblers call flip flaps, concluding with a bow that would not have disgraced a real ring master in a real circus.

Jack was delighted, and he patted and caressed the chimpanzee, while the latter grinned, showing at once his teeth and his satisfaction.

" Can he do anything else?"

" Lots of tricks," replied Ben Hawser, " Would you like to see some more?"

" That I should."

" Then here goes—stop," he added, sinking his voice ; " here comes the captain, and I shall get into trouble."

CHAPTER III.

WESTWARD HO!

" WHAT are you up to, Hawser?" said the captain, approaching.

" Only showing Master Jack the monkey, your honour," answered Ben Hawser.

" And what does Master Jack think of the monkey?"

Jack answered with enthusiasm—

" Nero's a splendid fellow! I should like to have Nero more than all the world."

" What would you do with Nero if you had him?" asked the captain, smiling.

" Why, to begin with," answered young Jack, promptly, " I would make him frighten old Mole out of his skin."

" Ah, but we can't let him loose," said the captain, laughing, " for Ben Hawser has brought it specially to sell to Mr. Jamrach, the great dealer in London."

" But he could sell it to me instead," urged Jack. " Why not?"

" Because it is a very rare and costly kind of chimpanzee, and Mr. Jamrach is to pay goodness knows how much for it."

" My father can pay more," said young Jack, proudly.

" Perhaps—but he will have to pay a good stiff sum, for the carriage of Master Nero will have cost Ben Hawser something. Mr. Jamrach offered him eighty pounds. Ben didn't think it enough, and so he brought it away again. The great dealer sent an offer after him, but it was too late ; the ' Prospero' had started, and so Nero has to make another voyage before he claims his master."

" My father will give a good deal more, I know," said Jack. " But you will let Nero out, captain?"

The skipper paused.

" What do you say, Ben?"

" There's no danger, your honour."

" Sure?"

" Sartin."

" Then I think that—but what do you want with him out at large?"

" Why," said young Jack, chuckling, " old Mole was bragging to me that he's not afraid of ghosts, and I should like to send Nero down dressed up when he's asleep, and pay him out."

The captain shook his head and tried to look serious.

"I'm afraid you're very like your father, Master Jack," he said.

"Thank you, sir."

"I mean that you are an incorrigible practical joker."

"Mr. Mole is fair game, I think, sir," said young Jack.

"Well, that is true, perhaps, but I can't be a party to such pranks upon the passengers on board my ship."

And so saying he turned to walk away.

"But may I let out the monkey?" asked Jack.

"Well," replied the captain, with a smile, "I can't recognise any such thing; only I shan't know, of course, who has let Nero out—of course."

"Oh, of course," said Ben Hawser, looking inexpressibly artful, and putting his finger to his nose.

*   *   *   *   *

Well, Ben Hawser and young Jack together got Nero out, and dressed him in a night shirt that reached to his heels and a frilled night-cap that an old woman on board ship lent them.

And then everything was prepared for their plot.

It was evening by this time, and the moon had risen, so that the hour was all that could be desired for the business before them.

Now young Jack and his accomplice Ben Hawser had said little or nothing about their plot, yet somehow it got whispered all over the ship, and by the time that all was ripe for the worrying of poor old Mole, there was a goodly audience assembled about the deck near the tutor's cabin.

There was a window or ventilator in the roof of Mole's cabin just over his berth, through which young Jack spoke an impressive address to the tutor.

It was groaned through a big speaking trumpet, which lent a sepulchral tone to the awful message.

Mr. Mole had imbibed freely that evening, and he went to bed rather earlier than usual, as he found some difficulty in keeping his sea legs.

The worthy tutor, when he retired to rest promptly upon his libations, dreamed invariably.

This night his visions were of a most horrible nature.

He thought that his brace of wives from the island of Limbi had brought their offspring, two lots of twins, who had grown to young men and women, and the whole six of them were dancing a diabolical cancan round his bed.

He tried hard to chivey them off, but tried in vain.

He half aroused himself in his efforts.

"Isaac Mole! Isaac Mole!" cried a solemn voice.

He sat upright in his berth, and listened.

"Who calls?" he asked, in a sort of nervous tremolo.

"Isaac Mole! Isaac Mole," repeated the same unearthly voice, "prepare! prepare!"

"Oh, Lord!" cried the tutor, aghast. "For what?"

"For the return of the wife you have so cruelly deserted."

And this was followed by a dismal groan.

Poor Mole felt alarmed then.

But it was nothing to the fear he experienced the next moment, when he heard a faint scratching noise in the corner of the cabin.

He stared in that direction, and—oh, horror!—something white moved.

He turned all over goose flesh.

An awful sensation.

A creepy, crawly feeling came over him.

A white thing in the corner rose up, and assumed a female form.

At the same time the sepulchral voice before heard exclaimed—

"Isaac Mole, you do not fear ghosts? You do not believe that we departed people revisit the earth?"

"Oh, yes! oh, yes!" groaned Mole.

And he tried to cover his head over.

But the ghost made a leap—it was a wonderfully nimble ghost—on to Mr. Mole's bed, and sat grinning at him.

He looked up aghast.

He never forgot the horrible phantom that sat before him.

The face of the spectre was black and hirsute, and while, to all appearance, it was the shade of his late wife, the face was that of the prince of darkness himself.

"Mole! Mole!"

"Oh!" groaned the wretched tutor.

"Do you believe in ghosts now?"

"Of course I do."

"And fear them?"

"Oh, yes, yes!"

"And you'll never brag again to your pupil?"

"Never, never."

"Swear."

"I do, I do. Oh, Lord, have mercy upon me," groaned the unhappy Mole.

The ghost of the late Mrs. Mole made a tug at the coverlet, and dragged it away from Mole's face.

The tutor could bear no more.

He leapt from the bed.

Over went the ghost of the late Mrs. Mole in a most undignified scramble.

Her night-dress flew up, and then—oh, terror!—his worst fears were realised.

He saw a long tail.

It was fortunate that Mr. Mole had gone to bed in his trousers, for he ran up the ladder on deck with one despairing cry, quite heedless of the fact that his braces were flying behind him, and that he wore his nightcap.

"Murder! murder!" yelled the wretched Mole, as he flew up, the ghost after him, close at his heels.

More terrors awaited the tutor on deck.

A long, lank figure, draped in a dismal shroud, beneath which appeared two wooden legs, leaned against the mainmast, evidently waiting for its victim.

Mole drew up short in his wild rush.

This was a colossal ghost, and it towered threateningly over Mole.

Mole gave a cry, and darted back to the ladder, but he heard the first ghost clattering up in pursuit.

What was to be done?

"I'll have you," said the colossal spectre, bending over him. "Come to my arms."

And its two arms opened wide to embrace him.

"Oh, mercy!" gasped Mole.

And then he dodged his long, spectral visitor round the mainmast.

An exciting chase now ensued.

The long ghost appeared slightly weak-kneed, like very many lanky people, and could not get along as nimbly as Mole, but this was counterbalanced in a certain measure by his great length of reach.

First one way and then the other went Mole.

And, while they were dodging in this way, Mole fancied that he perceived spectral forms filling the air in all directions, and the most unearthly cries smote upon his terror-stricken ears.

It never occurred to him that these cries came from human throats; aye, and familiar ones too.

And this for the simple reason that during the whole scene the skipper and Jack Harkaway, senior, and Harvey and a lot of the crew were standing by, convulsed with laughter.

The little black ghost with the tail now joined its lanky brother, and poor Mole was hard put to it.

He kept the mainmast well between him and the enemy for awhile, but suddenly a new foe sprang up in his rear.

A black hand reached down from the cross-tree, beneath which he stood, and grabbed his cotton nightcap.

Mole looked up.

"Oh, mercies!" he gasped, "Beelzebub himself."

A black face, white teeth, and big, glistening eyes were peering down upon him from above.

A demoniacal chuckle came from that huge mouth.

Mole shivered from head to foot.

"By golly, I've got um," said a voice, which sounded most diabolical in Mole's ears.

To casual listeners it would have borne a very striking resemblance to Monday's voice.

Mole dodged again, gave a wild, unearthly yell, and dashed to the cabin stairs.

Down he went, all of a scramble, dashed to the door, and leaned panting up against it.

In this position he remained until morning dawned.

*   *   *   *   *

The ghost of the late Mrs. Mole grew skittish, upon which Ben Hawser laid her without bell or book, but simply took off her nightcap and nightgown, and revealed Nero the chimpanzee beneath.

The black ghost aloft dropped off the crosstree on deck, and helped the colossal ghost to disrobe.

And when this was done, the colossal ghost looked more like young Jack Harkaway on stilts than anyone you can imagine.

*   *   *   *   *

Do you think Mr. Mole was cured of bragging?

Not he.

Young Jack woke him up in the morning, and inquired if he had slept well.

"Pretty well," he answered, coolly.

"I fancied I heard you cry out," said young Jack.

"Not I," said Mole, stoutly.

A merry twinkle in young Jack's eye half betrayed him, and Mr. Mole being pretty ready, said—

"I fancied that some of the crew were up to their tricks with me, so I ran up on deck to punish them. Your father," he added, changing the subject abruptly, "your father will tell you that I was always an intrepid sailor."

"Indeed?"

"Yes."

"Well, I should never have thought it, sir."

"Why not?"

"I should not have thought you were able to give your mind to such trivial matters."

Mr. Mole was flattered at this.

In his enthusiasm, he was apt to deviate a good deal from the strict truth.

But he had one peculiarity in his deviations.

He repeated the same lie so often, and with such relish, that at length, like the Gascons, he believed it himself.

Jack strolled up on deck, where his son was talking with Mr. Mole.

The latter appealed to him at once for confirmation of his audacious fibs.

"An intrepid sailor!" ejaculated Jack senior.

"Yes; was I not?"

Young Jack winked at his father, as much as to say, "Don't spoil sport, dad."

So Jack senior fell into the fun of the thing at once.

"Of course you were, Mr. Mole."

"Dare-devil fellow, wasn't I?"

"By jingo, you were."

"The first up the rigging?"

"Like a monkey."

"Egad, I was," said Mr. Mole, quite delighted. "No lubber's hole for me."

"No," said Jack Harkaway, "that's true enough; you never crept through the lubber's hole;" then he added to himself, "for I'm hanged if ever you got within ten feet of it."

But alas for the mutability of human affairs!

Alas for the weakness of the human stomach!

They were not three days afloat, when poor Mr. Mole fell woefully seasick.

He kept to his berth for three days and nights, moaning piteously, and only imploring them at painful intervals to pitch him overboard.

Dick Harvey and young Jack could not quite forgive him for his crammers.

It is not quite the generous thing to hit a man when he is down; but they determined to have some fun with him.

So they went to his berth.

Mr. Mole looked precious queer.

His eyes were a deep yellow, and his skin had assumed a ghastly, greenish tint.

"I hope you are better by this time, sir," said young Jack.

Mr. Mole groaned.

"I'm half dead."

"Dear me!" said Dick, appearing to take it literally; "I shouldn't have thought it."

"I wish I was thrown overboard," said Mr. Mole again.

"Mr. Mole," said Harvey, in a voice of sham solemnity, "I've come to gratify you."

"Me?" groaned Mole, piteously. "You can't do it."

"I can."

"How?"

"In your only desire."

"Rubbish!" snapped up the suffering tutor. "I have only one wish."

"What is it?"

"To be thrown overboard; I wish I'd the strength to jump."

"It shall be done," said Dick, with a very serious air.

"What?"

Mole did not think that he had heard aright.

"You shall be thrown overboard," repeated Dick, seriously. "You shall, if you wish it, become food for the little fishes."

His former pupil's manner fixed Mr. Mole's attention in spite of himself, and it had at the same time a very excellent effect for the moment.

It made him forget his sea-sickness.

"Oh! I wish I was a fish with a great, big tail," sang young Jack.

"Harvey, and you, young Jack," said Mr. Mole, with another groan, "it is very indelicate to joke over a man who is half dead."

"Quite right," said Harvey, seriously. "It is very. I hope no one has ventured to take such a liberty, Mr. Mole, in my absence."

Mole roared.

He bounced upright in his berth, and in so doing he bumped his head against the beam just above.

"I mean you," he cried, rubbing his hurt.

"Me?"

"Yes, you."

"I assure you I'm not joking," said Harvey, gravely; "seeing that you were very seriously ill, I made up my mind that anything that lay in my power to gratify you should be done."

"Well?"

"Well, you expressed a wish."

"I didn't. Nothing but pitching me overboard to put an end to my misery."

Dick pressed Mr. Mole's hand with silent warmth.

"It shall be done."

Mr. Mole was staggered.

His jaw dropped, and he stared aghast at Dick.

But Harvey kept his countenance wonderfully well.

"What do you mean?"

"That you shall be thrown over, or rather that you shall be lowered decently, and with all the respect that is due to you, Mr. Mole."

"What!" almost shrieked poor Mole, "thrown overboard?"

"Yes."

"Alive?"

"Yes."

"It would be murder."

"Not if it is your own request."

"But—"

"Trust in me, my dear friend," said Dick, in a voice seemingly broken with grief. "I heard you ask it so often, that knowing you to be a man who weighs his words well before uttering them, I determined you should be obeyed."

"You did?" gasped Mole.

"Yes."

"But the captain would never allow it," urged the tutor.

"Yes, he would."

"Then he's a murderer, an assassin, nothing better."

"No, he's not. I knew he would refuse if I told him the truth, so I said that you had a bad attack of yellow fever."

"The devil you did!"

"Yes," said Harvey, complacently, as if conscious that he was rendering Mole a great service, "and after much persuasion he consented."

"The villain!"

"But only with the greatest reluctance, after young Jack had explained your bad case."

"The young monster!"

"Yes, yes; I have carried out all the arrangements in a way that will be most satisfactory to you."

"Harvey, dear Harvey!"

Dick took no notice, but went on, apparently not hearing the reproachful tone in which old Mole spoke.

"We will leave you now, Mr. Mole," said Harvey, "to compose yourself. Jack."

"Yes, Mr. Harvey."

"Say good-bye for ever to Mr. Mole."

"Yes, sir."

"It is the last time you will see him."

Jack junior hid his face in his handkerchief, as if sobbing convulsively.

In reality he could not control his laughter any longer, such a comical picture did his tutor present.

Fright of the most exaggerated character was depicted in his face, and his head hid in a cotton handkerchief, presented the look of a practical joker's ghost, with a dash of the scarecrow about it.

"Good-bye, Mr. M — M — Mole," sobbed young Jack, behind his handkerchief.

"Jack, my own dear young Jack, don't leave me!"

But Jack affected not to hear.

He dared not show his face, so he moved towards the companion ladder.

Harvey pushed him up the ladder first, for fear of spoiling sport, as he termed it, and as he followed, he turned to deliver this parting shot at the terrified Mole.

"Compose your mind if you can."

"Come back," gasped Mole. "Harvey, I say, come back; do, please, come back to your old, old Mole."

"Your last wishes shall be obeyed, trust me for that——"

"Will you listen to me?"

"I am going to send down some of the crew with a hammock."

Mole half sprang from his berth.

"What for?"

"To sew you up in before you become the poor victim of the wandering fishy tribe," replied Harvey.

"Oh! horror," cried Mole.

"Yes," said Harvey, nodding his head with great seriousness. "The time is quite propitious; no one's about. We shall sew a twenty-four pound shot at your feet, and down you'll go like a stone."

"But I won't," roared Mole, thoroughly aroused now; "I say I——"

"You must."

"I won't, I——"

"But you must; you'd float else, and then you'd be snapped up by the shoal of sharks and torn piecemeal."

"Oh! oh! oh!"

Harvey was pitiless.

"Yes, sewn up in a nice hammock with a twenty-four pound shot, and then I shall have at least the consolation of knowing that I have done all that could be done to make the last moments of my old friend and tutor comfortable."

He went up on deck.

The groan of anguish of poor Mole followed him up the companion ladder.

"Isn't he in a state, Mr. Harvey?" said young Jack.

"He is," said Dick, "and serve him right for telling such crammers. Take warning, Jack, and be truthful yourself."

Dick hadn't done with him yet.

He called two of the sailors.

"Can you take a hammock down to the gentleman in the cabin?"

"Mr. Mole, sir?"

"Yes."

"Aye, aye, yer honour."

"Very good; two of you carry it down, and make as little noise as you can."

"What are we to do with it?" demanded the sailor.

"Mr. Mole wants it slung, I think," answered Harvey.

"Can't sleep in his berth, I suppose, your honour?"

"That's it."

"Don't wonder at it. A hammock all the world over for me."

"You are right, shipmate," answered Harvey; "down with you, and inform Mr. Mole that you have a very large needle and strong thread with you."

The hammock was brought, and down they stepped gingerly, so as to make as little noise as possible.

Harvey and young Jack anxiously watched the result from aloft. They had not long to wait.

Mole no sooner caught sight of the hammock than, with a mighty roar, he sprang bodily out of his berth, to which he had retired, dressed in shirt and trousers, and overturning the basin that stood at hand, seized a chair, with which he struck wildly at them.

"Stand off!"

"Your honour!" exclaimed the amazed tar. "What's up?—we have got a good hammock for you, and a large needle and strong thread."

"Sew me up, would you?"

"Do what?"

"Sew me up—twenty-four pound shot, eh?"

"I beg your honour's pardon," said one of the sailors, approaching.

Mole flourished his chair menacingly.

The sailor stepped back.

"I'll brain the first man that comes near me," cried Mole, excitedly. "Murder me, would you?—sew me up, would you?"

The sailors could only interpret his wild gestures in one way.

They made sure he was mad.

So they tried to soothe and coax him into quietness.

"Come, come, your honour," said one of them, "let's help you back into your berth. Here's the needle."

"Keep off!" shouted Mole.

"Or into your hammock."

"Ha!"

"Yes," remarked the honest sailor; "you sink down in a hammock quite nice."

"You ruffian!" cried the unhappy Mole.

He lowered his chair for a moment, and they pounced upon him.

And then followed a desperate struggle.

Up and down they went, all over the cabin, while Harvey and young Jack looked on in high glee from the companion ladder.

"We've got the twenty-four pound shot," said Harvey. Mole yelled again.

"What say, your honour?" asked one of the sailors.

Mole took advantage to spring up and seize the chair again.

As the sailors retreated, Mole grew valiant and rushed at them. So one of the tars tripped him up, and they made their escape on deck.

"Please, your honour," said one of them, coming after Jack Harkaway the elder, "he's clean gone."

"He—who?"

"Mr. Mole."

"What has happened to him?"

"He's lost his head, your honour," said the sailor; "as daft as he can be. By Neptune! here he comes like a mad bull. Clear the decks and make room for him. Oh! here's some sport for us."

CHAPTER IV.

THE PERILS OF THE OCEAN.

THE next moment Mole rushed on deck, still waving round his head the chair he had taken to protect himself.

The sailors now thought Mole quite mad, and Ben Hawser, seeing the confusion all were in, called his monkey Nero.

"At him, Nero," he said.

The monkey, seeming to understand what his master meant, made a dash at Mr. Mole, and butting him suddenly in the centre of his body, he sent him back into his cabin quicker than he expected.

Mr. Mole grew better next morning.

He was not troubled with sea sickness any more that voyage.

"Strange you should have been so ill, Mr. Mole," said young Jack, who soon descended to his tutor's cabin.

"Very," said Mr. Mole.

"So sea sick."

"What, Jack?"

"Sea sick, sir, for such a daring old tar as you."

"You don't suppose it was sea sickness, do you, Jack?" said Mr. Mole.

"It looked like it."

"You were never more mistaken, then, let me tell you."

"Dear me!"

"Yes, my dear boy, it was change of air, nothing more."

"Indeed."

"Though that wouldn't have proved much if it had really been sea sickness, for many bold sailors have been known to be sea sick every voyage at the start."

"You don't say so!"

"I do, though. Nelson was always sick, so I've heard."

"Why, then, it is rather a thing to be proud of than not."

"If you choose to look at it in that light," said Mr. Mole. "But of course," he added, modestly, "I don't think of comparing myself to a Nelson."

Just then Jack Harkaway the elder and Harvey stepped up.

They heard the last words.

"Really, Mr. Mole," said Harkaway, "you are such a bashful man."

"So very retiring and diffident," said Harvey.

"For such an intrepid sailor," added Jack.

"Such a daring seaman," continued Harvey.

Mr. Mole hung his head like a young lady when her beauty is being too openly praised.

"Really, gentlemen, gentlemen," he said, "you overpower me. 'Pon my life, I never—really, now."

"The captain would be happy to profit by a hint or two from you on the management of the ship."

"I scarcely think that," murmured the blushing Mole.

And then he swelled up a bit, and put in a modest word or two for himself.

"The handling of the ship never possessed the same charm for me since I had to take the command in the thick of the hottest fight you ever heard of."

"What?" exclaimed Dick Harvey, astounded.

"I say that navigating a ship in a mere gale is child's play to an old sea lion who has commanded when the vessel has been hulled—raked fore and aft by two Malay pirates."

It took his hearers' breath away.

Mr. Mole could pitch the hatchet better than most men, but they never even heard him venture on such a piece of audacity as this.

The worthy tutor thought that they were lost in admiration, so he piled it on.

"Yes," he said, "I sighted the gun myself that sank one of the scoundrels' ships."

"Oh, you did?"

"Yes," said Mole, complacently; "and blew the next one up, and damme! we boarded the third."

"Come, I say, Mr. Mole," said Jack, "gently does it. You said there were only two ships."

"Three—three!"

"You said two," persisted Jack Harkaway.

"My good friend," said Mr. Mole, "you did not hear aright, or you have been indulging in strong waters."

"Hang it, I say——"

"Go on, Mr. Mole," said young Jack, who was enjoying the fun mightily.

"We boarded the third," said Mr. Mole. "I cut down six of the Malays with one stroke of my cutlass."

Dick groaned.

But Mr. Mole continued, not at all disconcerted.

"I broke my cutlass over one of them—they have such thick skulls—and then I went in at them with my fists. Hang me if they didn't go down like skittles! I made a 'royal' every go, as I'm a sinner. I distributed black eyes amongst eight and thirty of them—eight and thirty! I stood them in a row after the fight and counted them."

The listeners groaned altogether at this.

It was too much even to make young Jack laugh.

"Our victory was complete," said Mr. Mole. in conclusion; "but ever since that day, I never can relish a fight if I have anything less than six to tackle at once."

"Well, I'm blowed!" ejaculated Dick:

"The fourth ship of the pirate fleet sheered off when the captain saw me pointing one of our big guns."

"Here comes the Prince of Limbi," said Jack Harkaway; "it's quite a relief."

"I wonder the lies don't choke him," said Dick Harvey.

"Mr. Harkaway, sir," said Monday. coming up at this moment.

"What now, old friend?" said Jack.

Monday pointed up to the sky and shook his head.

"Queer weather."

"Benighted savage," said Mr. Mole, "the weather was never more beautiful."

He was right.

At present it was calm and serene enough.

For a sailor afloat almost too serene, for the roughest gales but too often follow such weather.

The day was declining; the sunset was, in truth, very beautiful.

But suddenly a heavy bank of thick, inky clouds appeared upon the horizon, ready to receive the blood-red sun as it dropped lower and lower.

Monday's quick eye had been the first to detect this.

The Prince of Limbi (as they often used to call Monday in joke) had learned to be weather-wise from his earliest childhood.

Monday had barely spoken when the black clouds seemed to shoot up and darken the whole sky.

Prompt action was wanted now.

"Queer weather this, Mr. Harkaway," said the captain, as Jack approached.

"It will be queerer before long, captain," answered Jack. "I've been in this kind of weather more than once, and the gale will be on us soon."

"What would you do?" demanded the captain.

"Take in the topsail, stow away all spare hampers, and look smart out after your crockery, for the squall will be on us in a brace of shakes."

The captain was rather astounded to hear a landsman speak like this.

A sudden gust of wind sent the ship on to her beam ends.

Then a vivid flash of lightning illumined the horizon from east to west.

This was followed by a deafening peal of thunder.

"In with the topsail!" roared the captain.

But the tempest drowned his voice.

Young Jack stood near his father, and he looked earnestly up into his face, asking, as plainly as words could have done, if he should go. There was no time for thought.

Young Jack took permission, seeing his father irresolute, and made a lurch at the rigging, just as Dick Harvey, Monday and a brave-looking sailor made for the same point.

But the youngster was the nimblest of the three.

Like his father, young Jack Harkaway was no milksop.

He was captain of his gymnasium, and he climbed like a monkey.

It was fearful work.

The lightning lighted up the scene with vivid flashes and showed the four climbers mounting the rigging.

Their progress was watched by all in breathless interest.

The sail for a moment hung loosely, and then, suddenly bellying out, it caught young Jack a fearful blow that half stunned him.

It would have been all over with him then, but for Monday.

The faithful black's stalwart arm was there, and it pinned the boy to the rigging until he could recover his breath.

They then began to gather in the canvas as fast as they could.

But suddenly a rope by which the sailor was holding parted in his hand, and down he went into the raging waves. It was impossible to save him, nor had they a moment to spare for useless regrets.

Unless the sail was instantly secured, the ship would be lost.

In a short time their task was done.

A second more, however, and the wind burst upon the straining vessel from the opposite quarter, taking her all aback and throwing her upon her beam ends again. The man at the wheel was blown overboard.

A minute more, one despairing cry, heard even above the roar of the tempest, and another unhappy man had gone down for ever.

This same lurch sent Mole and several of the crew flying into the lee-scuppers, where a desperate struggle ensued in their endeavours to extricate themselves.

Mole, finding himself in a pool of water, fancied he was overboard; so according to custom in the presence of danger, he shut his eyes and struck out, meaning to swim for life.

But in striking out he punched two of the sailors, who, in spite of the confusion, instinctively punched back.

Now, sailors have hard knuckles, and poor Mole's nose and eyes suffered in consequence.

Meanwhile the three friends in the rigging passed an anxious time.

"Master Jack," said Monday.

"Jack," said Harvey.

"All right," answered Jack, quite reassured at hearing their voices.

So sudden and so violent had been the gale, and so dense was the darkness, that each feared for the safety of the other two.

They dreaded to find their companions had been blown off the yards into the boiling sea, like the brave seaman who had mounted the rigging with them.

The lightning still played about the ship, and the peals of thunder were deafening and incessant.

Jack Harkaway watched for an instant to see that his boy was safe and near his two faithful friends.

Then with a murmur of gratitude, he turned to see where he could be of any use.

His quick eye detected the vacated wheel, and by clutching by the rigging, he made for the spot.

Holding on by one hand, he lashed himself to the wheel with the other, for he found a length of line attached to it.

The poor helmsman, an experienced mariner, had foreseen his danger, and was providing against it, when the violent lurch cast him overboard to a watery grave.

Two brave men had gone down in the storm.

"Take in every bit of canvas!" cried the captain. "Square the yards."

The crew, recovered from their momentary confusion, flew about their work with a will.

Jack Harkaway put the helm hard up.

Then every bit of canvas was taken in with great rapidity, young Jack lending such assistance that the crew were amazed.

It did them a very material service.

Every man on board endeavoured to rival the lad, who had upon such short notice become so thorough and so daring a seaman.

They put the ship before the wind, and away she scudded at a rate that was truly amazing, under bare poles.

The rain came down. First in big drops like crown pieces, then in a heavy shower.

The floodgates of the heavens appeared to be suddenly opened to deluge the earth, sea and land.

And thus the storm raged in unabated fury for several hours.

But the longest lane must have a turning, the longest day must come to an end.

At length the fury of the tempest was spent.

The wind lulled.

The boiling sea calmed down.

And the good ship "Prospero" was brought through one of the greatest perils she had ever encountered.

CHAPTER V.

HIGH JINKS ON BOARD.

"ALL hands on deck!"

"Aye, aye, sir!"

All hands were piped up.

Then, when all the crew had mustered according to orders, the captain sent a messenger for Mr. and Mrs. Harkaway, young Jack, Harvey, and Monday.

"I hope there's nothing wrong," said Jack Harkaway the elder.

"There can be nothing," said his wife. "Where is Jack?"

"Here, mamma," said her son, appearing at the cabin door.

"What's the matter?"

"I can't say," replied the boy. "The crew have all been called upon deck."

Harvey, who was reading in a corner, looked up.

"It's all right, I suppose," he said, "unless the captain's jealous."

"What of?"

"You, for helping him as you did. There are some rum people in the world."

"Let's go up."

"You're sure the captain asked for me to go up too?" said Emily.

"Sartin, marm," replied the sailor; "he mentioned Mrs. Harkaway in particler."

"It's all right, then," said Jack; "we will come up at once."

Up they all went together, and were received by the captain and the chief officers of the "Prospero" with bows and much ceremony, mingled with great cordiality.

"I hope I have not put you to any inconvenience?"

"None whatever, Captain Rudd," replied Jack; "not the least."

"I've got a duty to perform," said the skipper, "and I shall not feel that I have done it until I have thanked you before all the crew for saving our ship."

Jack was staggered.

"You exaggerate our services, Captain Rudd," he said.

"Devil a bit," retorted the captain, "asking your pardon, madam," he added, bowing to Mrs. Harkaway.

"I see him lashed to the wheel, I did, your honour," said one of the crew, "and steering away like a regular A. B."

"And it was these three gallant people who scrambled up the rigging to reef the topsail when many a sailor might have feared to go."

"Young Jack was foremost," said Harvey, pushing the boy forward.

The captain took young Jack's hand and shook it heartily.

"I'd give a trifle if you were my son," said he, earnestly. "Master Jack Harkaway has helped to save the ship. So hark you, my men, give him a good old English cheer."

"Hooray!"

"A LOUD REPORT, AND TORO THE BRIGAND'S HAT WAS FLYING OFF."

"Stop!" cried Captain Rudd. "Take your time from me—hip—hip—hip——"

"Hooray!"

A deafening cheer came from the united throats of the crew of the "Prospero."

It was a comical thing to see the way young Jack took it.

Like his father, Jack junior was not usually wanting in brass, but this ovation took all his pluck away.

He slunk back by his mother.

Mrs. Harkaway was blushing with pride all the while.

"You must say something, Jack," whispered his father. "You thank them."

"Do it for me," pleaded the bashful young Jack.

"You have taken my boy's breath away," said Jack Harkaway, addressing the captain and crew; "he is not in the habit of being praised so lavishly for doing his duty. I am a happy man this day to hear your cheers for my boy. I want him to be brought up no milksop, but this honour has come earlier upon him than I ever hoped for. I feel prouder than I can express that he should have earned such cheers as yours upon the sea in the profession to which I had at one time devoted my life."

"Damme!" cried Captain Rudd— "asking your pardon, madam—if I didn't know it."

"Every inch a sailor," cried one of the crew.

"Let's give him a cheer, boys," suggested a third enthusiast.

They did, too.

Cheer after cheer rang out, while Jack stood bowing his acknowledgments.

When they dropped off, young Jack stepped forward.

"It was through Monday that I kept up," he said.

"No, no, Mast' Jack," said the faithful Limbian.

"Indeed it was."

Jack the elder stepped up to Monday and took the worthy fellow by the hand.

"Monday," he said, with great warmth, "you have acted nobly to our boy, and made us all love you more than ever."

"Oh, by golly, Mast' Jack," cried Monday, "you pile um on rather too thick, make this poor chile feel precious uncomf'able."

"You'll make poor old Monday blush," said Dick Harvey.

"You're an incorrigible joker," said Jack, who couldn't help laughing himself.

"Here's one more, then, for the black prince," cried the enthusiastic sailor before mentioned.

"Take the time from me."

"One—two—three! Hip—hip—hip——"

"Hurrah!"

Captain Rudd came up to Monday and shook him heartily by the hand.

"I am proud to shake hands, Mr. Monday," said the skipper. "I never met a bolder heart under black skin or white skin."

Another ringing cheer greeted the captain's short but earnest speech.

"Now," said Dick Harvey, going forward, "it's my turn to palaver."

"Hear! hear!"

"I'm not going to say that I am accustomed to public speaking——"

"No need to," said Jack senior; "any fool can see that."

This caused a laugh.

"That's why you perceived it so readily," retorted Harvey.

A loud laugh rewarded this piece of impudence.

"Go on."

"Speak on, sir," from the crew.

"I was going to observe," said Dick, with his sham-serious look, that told his friends who knew him that he was bent upon foolery, "that notwithstanding the late inclement weather and the price of coals, whereas, as we might say in a manner of speaking and so forth, that in my humble estimation, in spite of whatever my friend with the red nose may say to the contrary, I may reiterate, without repetition or circumlocution, my decided and emphatic opinion that any stick is good enough to beat a dog with, and that it is a poor beast which never rejoiceth, so that, all things considered, we may rest assured that our worthy and loved friend Mr. Mole has a pair of splendid black eyes!"

Here the mischievous Dick pointed suddenly to the cabin stairs.

All eyes turned in that direction at once.

There stood Mr. Mole with his cotton

night-cap on, his damaged nose plastered up, and his eyes as black as sloes.

This was the result of his scramble in the lee scuppers.

He did not know at first that he was observed, not having rightly heard Harvey's concluding words.

Dick profited by this, you may be sure.

"Now then, shipmates," he said, "three cheers for Mr. Mole's black peepers !"

"One—two—three—hooray !"

Mr. Mole saw it now.

He stepped hurriedly back, and in so doing he missed his footing, and went bump, bump, bump down to the bottom of the companion ladder, whence he scrambled into his berth, and was seen no more that day.

"And now," said Dick, "one word more. I want Captain Rudd to let me stand you as many cans of grog as you can take without losing your sea legs, to drink the health of our friend here, young Jack Harkaway !"

The skipper gave his consent readily enough. And Dick gave his money.

There were high jinks that day on board the good ship "Prospero."

Dick Harvey played the fiddle in a way that made the sailors all but worship him, and young Jack danced a college hornpipe with such a rattle that every man's feet were seen upon the go.

On board the good ship "Prospero" were two passengers who made themselves very agreeable.

These gentlemen were entered upon the passenger list as Mr. Percival and Henry Webb.

Mr. Webb was a very simple young man, with long fair hair and spectacles.

His hair and whiskers were of a peculiar vegetable tint, and among the crew he was never spoken of by his name, but as "Carrots."

A very odd young man was he, and his chief characteristic was an unmeaning grin, which caused the sailors to christen him "Soft Tommy."

He was apparently a young man of weak intellect.

Indeed, so it was understood on board, and Mr. Percival was tacitly set down as his keeper.

But Mr. Webb's softness was like the peculiarities of Hamlet in the play ; there was method in his madness.

Mr. Isaac Mole cultivated the acquaintance of these two of his fellow passengers, and in his fashion made himself very agreeable to them.

"Your illness doesn't affect your strength," said Mole, with a patronising air.

"Oh, it does, though," replied Mr. Webb, with a grin. " I'm as weak as a rat."

"How very odd," said Mr. Mole.

"Very ; isn't it ?"

"I've always noticed," said Mr. Mole, addressing Mr. Percival mysteriously, "that people who are weak here "—tapping his forehead—" are singularly muscular."

"You must be very muscular, then," said the weak-witted passenger.

"Well," said Mr. Mole, feeling his biceps, "not to say muscular."

"Oh, you are."

"I'm not to say feeble."

"You look like an athlete," said Mr. Percival. "Doesn't he ?"

"That he does," returned the weak-witted Webb.

"A sort of gladiator."

Mr. Webb grinned.

"I should think you excelled in gymnastic exercises," said Mr. Percival.

"I could always hold my own."

"And handle your fives well ?"

"I don't quite understand," said Mr. Mole.

"This sort of thing."

And Mr. Webb sparred idiotically, punching wildly at an imaginary enemy.

"Have you ever had the gloves on ?" said Mr. Mole, elevating his eyebrows in some surprise.

"Never."

Mr. Mole grew very much anecdotal at this.

"When I was a younger man, I was considered good," he said.

"Indeed ?"

"That I was."

"I suppose among private people only ?" said Mr. Percival.

"Well, no ; not altogether," said Mr. Mole.

"Indeed ?"

The apparent interest of Silly Webb and his keeper encouraged Mr. Mole to recitals of his prowess, which rather astonished his hearers.

" You may have heard of Tom Sayers," said Mr. Mole, " a professional boxer ?"

" Oh, yes."

" Champion of England, wasn't he ?" added Mr. Percival.

" He was. Well," said Mr. Mole, modestly, " Tom Sayers used to say that I was the quickest member he ever tackled. One, two, three ; pom, pom, pom."

And here he sparred round and fibbed away as though he had got an adversary in chancery.

The two fellow passengers gave a sort of moan of admiration at Mr. Mole's style and finish.

" You used to give it to Tom Sayers ?" said Silly Webb.

" Tom Sayers was very clever with the gloves," said Mr. Mole, " but he used to lose his temper, because he never could touch me."

" You don't mean it ?"

" Yes, I do, though," said Mr. Mole, encouraged by the evident impression he had made. " ' Now look here, Mr. Mole,' Tom used to say, ' play light.' "

" You used to punish him, then ?"

" Sometimes I used to hammer him a bit ; but I must do him the justice to say that he took his punishment very quietly ; in fact, he was rather afraid of me."

Silly Webb laughed with delight.

" I shouldn't like to put up my fists to you, Mr. Mole," he said.

" Why not ?" asked Mr. Mole, with conscious pride.

" You frighten me so."

" I'm not very dangerous," said Mr. Mole, modestly.

" And would you show me how to fight, just a little ?"

" If Mr. Percival likes."

Mr. Webb looked towards his keeper for consent, but not quite as vacantly as usual.

There almost appeared a twinkle of merry devilment there which looked very different to his accustomed vacant stare.

" Be careful," said Mr. Percival, smiling.

" All right."

" And play light," said his keeper, with emphasis.

" You hear that, Mr. Mole ?" remarked Silly Webb.

" I hear," replied Mr. Mole, with his patronising air ; " but I almost thought " —and here he chuckled quietly—" that Mr. Percival meant it for you."

Then they began to spar.

Poor Silly Webb stood up, facing the redoubtable Mole as though he feared every moment to receive a taste of that horseplay which, according to Mr. Mole, had been so liberally dealt out to poor Tom Sayers.

Mr. Mole stood up with his legs wide apart, like Mr. Pickwick going down the slide. In other respects, his attitude was not bad.

He kept his left well out, and his guard high.

But Silly Webb still persisted in revolving his arms like a girl does, when she is pretending to spar.

" Not like that," said Mr. Mole ; " this way. There ; keep your body well back and hit with your——"

Crack !

Silly Webb dropped him an unexpected stinger upon the chest, which made him cough and splutter in a remarkable way, considering the apparent weakness of the demented creature.

" Dear me !" said Mr. Mole. " How very odd that you should have touched me !"

The weak-witted one went off again whirligigging his arms in the same feminine attitude of pugilism.

Crack ! crack !

All of a sudden Mr. Mole got it again ; but this time it was a brace of smart slaps in the face, that seemed to knock his head on one side.

" That is a London ' postman's knock,' " said Silly Webb.

" Most extraordinary !" said poor Mole, blinking, and rubbing his damaged parts.

" Very," said Mr. Percival ; " and yet I have often seen it before."

" Seen what ?"

" That sort of thing."

" What, this ?" asked Silly Webb.

And off he went sparring again at Mole, who stepped out of the way of mischief very nimbly.

" No ; a thoroughly scientific boxer dodged and surprised by a man who did not know how to hold up his hands decently."

" So have I," said Mr. Mole, breathing hard.

" Indeed !"

" Oh, yes," said Mr. Mole. " You may have heard of Heenan ?"

" That fought Morrisey ?"

" Yes. Well, you'd hardly believe that, although I used to give him many a drubbing——"

" You did ?"

" Many and many a drubbing, he positively used to touch me now and again."

His hearers held up their hands in amazement.

" Never !"

" Fact, I assure you," said Mr. Mole, modestly; " but then I used to let him have it very severely after."

" Let us have another turn, please, Mr. Mole," said Silly Webb.

" Very good," said Mole; " but mind I don't hurt you."

And then, as they stepped forward again, Mole, who was smarting from the taps he had received, made a sudden effort to drop one into his " pupil."

Silly Webb guarded the blow, and quick as lightning popped in two smart smacks upon Mole's cheeks again.

" Come, I say !" cried Mole, " you should not do that so quick."

" All right, Mr. Mole."

And Silly Webb dropped them in then just where he pleased.

" One !" he cried out, landing a stinger in the ribs.

" Oh !" cried Mole.

" Two !"

This was dropped heavily upon the muscle of the right arm, and it made poor Mole sing out.

" Three !" cried Silly Webb, laughing; " now for the bread basket."

It was most remarkable how straight from the shoulder Silly Webb hit this time.

It doubled Mr. Mole up, but Silly Webb peppered him about the face and head generally so sharply now, that he soon knocked him straight again.

" One !" cried Silly Webb, popping them in now rapidly, " two—three—four —five—six—seven—eight, and a good one for——"

" Murder ! murder !" cried Mole.

He didn't wait for nine.

The number eight was such a stinger on the nose, that he saw Fourth of July fireworks, and could not stand any more.

Still crying out " Murder !" he bolted off as if the devil was at his heels, while the other two dropped into a seat, and rolled about laughing until the tears came into their eyes.

" What fun !" cried Percival.

" Didn't he run !"

" And howl !"

" By jingo, he did."

" But don't you think he may begin to have doubts ?"

" Of what ?"

" Of us and whom we are."

" Yes, we have a desperate game to play here, and we must be cautious."

" If our character and calling were once known, we should find it more difficult to catch our men, they both being desperate ruffians."

" Yes, and our instructions seem to imply that the lives of Harkaway and his friends may be sacrificed."

" Well, then, let caution be our password," said the two strange men, clasping each other's hands.

*   *   *   *   *

Two days later. Time, five a.m.

Young Jack Harkaway stood upon deck beside the look-out man.

He had a reason for this early rising.

One of the crew had told him that they would in all probability sight land this day.

Dick Harvey had a very fine gold watch—a repeater, which he had frequently promised young Jack.

Dick had made a stipulation with young Jack that he should have it if he should be the first to sight land.

" You promise, Mr. Harvey."

" Yes."

" Mind, I shall keep you to it."

" All right, my hearty," said Dick, laughing.

" Lend me your glass ?" said young Jack to the look-out man, " and I'll give you some baccy."

" I'll lend you my glass, Master Jack," said the sailor, " without any bribery ?"

" But you won't refuse the baccy," said young Jack, slily.

" Not if it would offend you, young gentleman."

" Then it would."

So the tobacco and glass at once changed hands.

Jack raised the glass to his eye.

In a minute he gave a loud shout of exultation.

"Hurrah! I've done it!"

"What?"

"I'm first," answered young Jack, springing down. And seizing a speaking trumpet, he shouted in Harvey's ear—

"Land ahead, your honour!"

CHAPTER VI.

LAND AGAIN.

"BRAVO, young Jack," cried Harvey; "you have sharp eyes, and have won the wager."

Soon after this all on board sighted land.

When the good ship "Prospero" heaved to, the custom-house officers came on board.

Mr. Mole perceived them in the boat, so he hurried on deck. He was determined to show them what a man could do by reading.

He had picked up his notions of American idioms in English novels, and polished himself off with a digest of the American humorists.

Artemus Ward, Bret Harte, Orpheus C. Kerr, and the like, were his masters.

"Harkaway," said Mr. Mole, with conscious pride, "it has been my happy lot in bygone years to teach——"

"My young ideas how to shoot," interrupted Jack; "yes, that's true."

"It is never too late to learn."

"True."

"This journey is destined to prove a source of wonderful information to us."

"I hope so."

"I know so," said Mr. Mole, emphatically, "if we know how to sift the pure metal of instruction from the quartz of generalities."

"Quarts of generalities?" echoed Jack, shamming stupidity; "quarts is a liquid measure."

"Quartz," corrected Mr. Mole. "A figure of speech. I will explain."

"No, pray don't," said Jack.

"Nay, but I will," said Mr. Mole, misinterpreting Jack's interruption. "I will address these officers coming on board."

Jack walked away.

"I think old Mole is more cracked than ever," he said.

Mr. Mole put himself in the way of the customs officers as they mounted the ship's side and gained the deck.

"Good day, boss," said he to the foremost of the officers.

The officer stared.

"I beg your pardon."

"No offence," said Mole, graciously. "You come to examine the luggage?"

The officer nodded assent.

At the same time his manner showed some surprise at the address of the passenger.

"You do—of course," said Mr. Mole, looking round to Jack as if to say, "What do you think of my penetration?"

"Not very difficult to guess," said the officer, smiling.

"No, boss—go it, my hunky boy."

"What?"

The customs officer stared at Mole.

As for Jack, he was not a whit less surprised than the new comer. But Mole was not at all disconcerted.

He took it all as a compliment.

He imagined that the slangy locutions he had read in the American novels published in Cockayne, and the curious phraseology of Artemus Ward, were fair samples of American conversation.

Poor Mole!

He little thought that the Americans, as a rule, speak the mother tongue with more purity of idiom and accent than two-thirds of Britishers.

Jack felt rather ashamed of Mole, so he fell back and joined Harvey, who was bringing young Jack forward.

"Poor old Mole has been indulging again," he said.

"Has he? That's too bad."

"Yes, and his weakness has assumed a new phase."

"What is it?"

"He's taken to talking slang."

"Slang?   Poor old fellow!"

"Yes."

"Never!"

"Yes; and what's more, he seems proud of it."

"The deuce he does!"

"Well, he just now spoke to the customs officer who boarded us as 'boss,' and called him ' my hunky boy.' I felt quite ashamed, for the officer was evidently a thorough gentleman."

"He must have thought old Mole daft."

"Wouldn't be far out."

A few moments later, the officer took advantage of the captain's presence to express his opinion pretty freely.

"He is not dangerous, I suppose, captain?"

"Who?"

"That poor old fellow," said the officer, lowering his voice and pointing to Mole.

"Dangerous?" said the captain, with a puzzled laugh. "He dangerous?—not he."

"He ought to be kept away, though,' said the officer. "Let his keeper stay beside him.   He is certainly wrong."

"Wrong!   What in?"

"The upper storey."

"You think so?"

"It's a fact."

Mole heard this, and then for the first time he began to suspect that all was not quite right.

So he moved away.

But he didn't guess at the truth.

"This is a mixed nation," he said to himself; "and no doubt this officer is not a native, probably an Englishman."

While the preparations continued for going ashore, Harvey got Mr. Mole into a corner and questioned him if the officer understood him.

"You shall soon have an opportunity of gratifying your reasonable curiosity," answered Mr. Mole, with conscious pride.

Dick foresaw a joke might be got out of this vanity of old Mole's, and he was never one to spoil sport.

CHAPTER VII.

STRANGE GUESTS AT THE HOTEL.

JACK and his friends took a handsome set of rooms for their party at the best hotel, one of the largest in the town.

As soon as they were settled down, Dick and Jack got Mr. Mole aside, and began a little lark of their own.

"You had better order dinner, Mr. Mole," said Jack.

"I?" said Mr. Mole, in some surprise.

"Yes, you had better do it."

"You know how to talk to them better than we do," suggested Dick, slily.

"Well, well," returned Mr. Mole, "perhaps there is something in that."

So they called the waiter.

Mr. Mole referred a little anxiously to a sort of dictionary he carried, and then he opened fire on the waiter.

"Wall, stranger, we should like a meal, some. What provender ken you propose?"

"Provender?" said the waiter. "Meal, sir?—dinner, sir?"

"Yes, siree," returned Mr. Mole, watching the effect of his technicalities upon his former pupils. "Provender, dinner; that's so."

"Oh! indeed, sir."

He was a well-trained waiter, and he did not dare to laugh.

Neither Jack nor Harvey showed the faintest signs of a smile, so he was forced to take it all in sober earnest.

"Clear soup, fish," repeated Mole, after the waiter, "boiled turkey. I reckon that they are average fixin's."

"Yes, sir, just so."

"But I guess you have a tall thing in feeds denominated about these parts as pumpkin pie, with a modicum of apple sass."

"Pumpkin pie, sir?"

"That's so, sireebob."

The waiter was staggered.

This was the lowest slang of New York, and had long since grown stale.

He could not naturally understand such language from people who gave every outward appearance of high respectability.

"You seem surprised," said Mole, gravely construing the waiter's looks after his own fashion.

"I, sir; no, sir."

"But you see we Britishers lick creation in taste."

"Yes, sir," stammered the waiter, scarcely knowing whether to be flattered by the visitor's condescension or not.

"I for one," continued Mole, in the same lofty strain, "play second fiddle to no breathing cuss in belly culture. I'm known, in point of fact, as the all-fired snorter of gastronomy."

Harvey and Jack could no longer contain themselves.

They burst into a boisterous fit of laughter, during which the waiter made off in a rage.

He was puzzled all through this singular interview.

Now he had, he thought, discovered the key to it all.

The clerical-looking old gentleman was making a laughing stock of him.

"He's getting at me," said the indignant waiter, who was born within sound of Bow Bells, it would appear. "I ain't a-going to stand still for a psalm-smiting old buffer like that to guy me."

Jack and Harvey laughed until the tears ran down their cheeks.

"You had better dry up, Mole."

"Sir, I shall not dry up."

"Yes," said Harvey; "hold your tongue."

"I'd have you know," began Mole, loftily, "that I——"

"Don't bother!" interrupted Jack, impatiently. "Enough's as good as a feast, and you'll spoil our grub if you're not quiet."

"Harkaway!"

"Be quiet, Mole."

"What do you mean?"

"Why, that you are making a fool of yourself. Don't you see that the waiter looks on you as a madman?"

"I see nothing of the kind. He is stricken with surprise at my great knowledge of this country."

"Very well. keep your eyes shut," retorted Harkaway, growing vexed with the gnawings of hunger; "only don't spoil our dinner now you've had your say out, so please shut up."

Mr. Mole was dumbfounded—shut up.

He made a faint remonstrance, but finding it was of no avail, he very wisely held his peace.

"The table d'hôte is on now, sir," said the Cockney waiter.

"Very well."

"Will you join it?"

"What do you think, Dick?"

"As you please."

"Let's ask Emily. Hilda is yet too unwell to meet company."

The table d'hôte was composed of a mixture of most of the nations of both continents, Europe and America.

There were French, English, Americans, Spaniards, Italians, German, Dutch, Russians, Cubans, Mexicans, Portuguese, and Danes.

Opposite the Harkaway party sat one or two very remarkable-looking persons.

One was a middle-aged man, with a handsome face and fine military presence.

A fine old veteran, who had faced the battle and the breeze often enough.

Then, next him, sat a man in a fur-collared coat, who was an Armenian, and reputed to be enormously rich; a very peculiar-looking man, with a beard like Pharaoh in the pictures.

And then there was a sailor-like man, who had a peculiar cast of countenance, and an uneasy, roving expression, that made you uncomfortable at sitting beside him. He was a one-armed man.

He had a manner of regarding everybody, the first time that he saw them, as though he instinctively regarded them as enemies.

Dick Harvey called the waiter, and made a few inquiries.

"That gentleman with the Persian turban is enormously rich, sir," said the Cockney waiter, confidentially; "he's got whole pints of diamonds; and that one there, with only one arm——"

"Ha!" said Dick, with a start, "how hard he's looking this way."

"I don't like him; I hope he has not overheard," said the waiter. "Perhaps he knows you, sir."

Indeed, it would almost have looked like it, for the subject of their remarks was staring at them with all his eyes.

And very remarkable eyes they were, too; deeply sunken, black as sloes, and glistening like brilliants from the depths of their sockets.

Suddenly he perceived that his fixed gaze was evidently attracting notice.

So he turned to his right-hand neighbour, and was immediately buried in a deeply interesting conversation.

"Do you see that man?" asked Dick to Mr. Mole, pointing to the one-armed man.

"Yes."

"When he's not looking, watch him."

"What for?"

"To let me hear if you remember him."

Mr. Mole walked round the room, and tried to get a better view of the person in question.

But he could not manage it, for every time that he moved, down went the stranger's head.

The one-armed man was a very singular-looking person.

A restless-eyed man, who never by any chance looked you fairly in the face.

His companion was noticeable from his huge person.

He stood considerably over six feet in height, and he was more than proportionately broad across the shoulders.

His head was round, and was covered with flaxen woolly curls; yet the beard he wore was black.

It would almost appear that he dyed his hair.

Evidently, this mammoth man had very weak eyes, for he wore blue spectacles.

The one-armed warrior led his companion downstairs to the smoking saloon.

It was empty.

He gave a sharp glance round, and ascertained that they were alone.

"Come here," said he, in a voice of authority, to his giant companion. "Now, tell me, did you see them?"

"I do not understand you, signor."

"You keep neither your eyes nor your ears open," said his superior, angrily.

"What mean you?"

"Had you only looked across the table, you would have seen faces you know but too well."

"Whose—whose?" cried the giant, impatiently. "Why, in the fiend's name, do you speak in riddles? Do you laugh at me?"

"I'm in no humour for laughing," retorted the other. "He was there, facing you."

The giant stared at his friend.

"He! Who?"

"Who but the man of all others that I loathe and abhor, the bane of my life —Harkaway, whose life shall yet be in my grasp?"

The giant started.

"If you are correct in your man, this hand shall help you, even if he had a thousand lives."

And the giant clenched his big hand fiercely.

"It is true; and all our old enemies are with him—Harvey, the black, and the drunken old tutor, Mole."

"And I failed to see them, all through these accursed spectacles which you insist upon my wearing; they blind me as effectually as my poor old comrade Barboni."

"Stop that; none of your reminiscences; they are not of the most agreeable."

"But tell me, did they know you?"

"No."

"Or me?"

"I think not," was the reply. "Harvey—curse him!—stared as though he remembered me, but he was not sure."

"I wish I had seen him," said the giant, apparently subduing his fierce emotions by a powerful effort. "Once let me close upon him or his friend Harkaway—aye, or any of his accursed crew—and if I let them escape me, may I die upon the wheel. I'll not be blinded!" he added, passionately, tearing off his spectacles. "I shall be caught like a rat in a trap."

And when the blue glasses were away, his fierce black eyes lit up his face, and showed how moved the man was with passion.

"Well done, Redgrave! well done!" said his companion, with a sneer. "Well done! Play the fool, indulge your melodramatic bravado, if you like, and mount the scaffold."

"Silence!" thundered the other, menacingly.

But his companion was not easily alarmed.

"Do it as much as you like," he said, "if it pleases you to risk your life; it makes me sick. I don't care that while you are with me you should blow the whole game and let them recognise me, Mr. Redgrave."

"I am Toro, the brigand," interrupted the giant.

"Hush!" exclaimed the other, in alarm.

"I'll not hush, Hunston," thundered the robber Toro; "I'll not be badgered and bullied any longer by you. I'll have this Harkaway's life for causing the destruction of our band in Naples!"

"Bah!"

"I will, I say; and his boy's too!"

"Now you are talking more like common sense," said Hunston, with a vicious smile. "Kill Harkaway, and there's an end to everything. Kill his boy, if you like, and let the father know that the brat died in slow torture, and then you earn a noble vengeance."

"Right," said Toro; "right, Hunston."

"Hush; sink the name, I tell you. Look, I think we are watched."

Hunston suddenly perceived, for the first time, they were not alone.

The curtains, which shut the verandah off from the smoking-room, were drawn aside, and two men entered.

They were Silly Webb and his keeper.

CHAPTER VIII.

PLOTS AND COUNTERPLOTS.

"COME along, please," said Silly Webb.

"I'm coming."

And then Mr. Percival stopped short, apparently only just noticing that they were not the only persons present.

"Hush, Mr. Webb," he said. "Don't you see those gentlemen?"

Toro the brigand stepped up to Mr. Webb, and confronted him with a fierce air.

"How long have you been listening behind the curtains?" he demanded, menacingly.

"Listening?"

"Aye, listening."

"Dear me!" said Mr. Webb; "what a very singular remark to make."

Toro clutched him savagely by the arm.

"Don't attempt to play the fool with me," he cried, raising his big fist.

It was strange to see with what seeming ease the supposed feeble Webb threw the giant suddenly off.

"Don't you get up to tricks," he said.

"What?" thundered Toro.

He advanced again upon Silly Webb.

But Mr. Percival stepped between them.

"Stand back," he cried.

Then, after looking fixedly at Toro for a moment, he said, coolly—

"Pray, don't be so violent, my good sir; moderate your anger, and don't excite my patient."

"Patient?" echoed Hunston "Your patient?"

"Yes; can't you see?"

Then he tapped his forehead significantly with his forefinger.

"Cracked," whispered Hunston; "oh, I see. Poor devil!"

"Well, he's weak," responded Mr. Percival, "and I can't have him excited, for he is very dangerous."

"Dangerous, the deuce!"

"And if he were to bite——"

"You don't mean——"

"Indeed, I do," replied Mr. Percival. "I've known two men to get hydrophobia as surely from him as if he were a mad dog."

They fell back.

Even the fearless Toro felt uncomfortable at this.

Such is the very natural horror of hydrophobia.

"Excuse my excitable friend," said Hunston. "He actually fancied you were listening behind the curtain."

The other laughed.

"Oh! dear, no! we were taking the air upon the balcony—nothing more. It was a whim of my patient's; and we are obliged to humour him, you know."

"Of course."

They passed out of the room, and as Webb neared Toro, he gave a sudden start as though about to spring and bite, whereupon the giant jumped back affrightedly.

He would not mind the biggest enemy you could pit him against, but the fancied risk of hydrophobia frightened him.

Webb and Percival went up to their rooms.

"What do you think of the two beauties we have just left?" asked Percival.

"I thing they are desperate men, and we must put Harkaway and his party on their guard."

"How?"

"By an anonymous letter to them. But we have probably missed the pigeon and shot the crow this journey."

"How?"

"Why, by dropping on to Hunston and his blackguard pal, when we were on the hunt after Emmerson the murderer."

"Still we must look after Harkaway and his son's safety."

"We must, and promptly, too, for Emmerson, although a thief, a forger, a murderer, is not, in point of fact, a greater villain than Hunston. He will have to be looked after first, and then——"

"But how about Mr. Harkaway and his party?"

"They are in danger, no doubt; great danger."

"From Hunston?"

"Yes; and from his colossal friend too."

"Well, I should be sorry for my part to see harm come to them, for they appear very decent people, and young Jack seems a brave and jolly lad. But what can we do?"

"Warn them."

"And betray ourselves? Impossible!"

"Why?"

"Nothing must be done by us which would in any way risk the keeping up of the strictest incognito. Emmerson, the man we are after, is as keen a blade as you will meet with, and after taking the trouble to disguise ourselves and ship in false names, it will not do to risk blowing the whole game because we have fallen across these people."

"True."

"Then I see no way."

"I do. Drop them an anonymous letter to put them on their guard."

"That's the notion, and it shall be done forthwith; it is our duty to save their lives if possible."

*   *   *   *   *

Meanwhile Hunston paced up and down the smoking saloon in the greatest excitement.

"This puts an end to my little Cuban business," he said to Toro.

"Why the end?" demanded the burly giant.

"It is this that has brought Harkaway out, depend upon it."

"Perhaps."

"I feel sure of it."

"Ha! you have so long enjoyed the property that you begin to regard it as your own for ever and ever."

"True; and shall I now be cheated out of it?"

"Never; you must keep it, for it will supply us both with money."

"So say I; but saying is not enough —we must act—aye, and that promptly, too, or this income, already reduced to one-third of its original value through the insurrection, will glide from our hands altogether."

"What's to be done?"

"Let us think."

Toro paced the room impatiently, while Hunston sat upon a couch in silent meditation.

Presently Toro stopped short, and said, abruptly—

"If Harkaway died suddenly, what then?"

"Useless."

"Why?"

"Worse than useless," returned Hunston.

"What do you mean?"

"Simply this," replied Hunston: "the day that Jack Harkaway died, the property would pass to the next of kin, and the agency would pass to other hands than those of Ostani, the secretary of the late lamented Don José."

Toro burst into a loud fit of laughter.

"Poor Don José!"

"Aye; poor Don José!" chimed in Hunston. "His connection with me, when I took the false name of Ostani, was not fortunate for him."

And they both laughed in chorus at it as a capital joke.

The Cuban agent of Harkaway's father had some years before made Hunston's acquaintance.

Thinking him a political refugee, he had taken him to his heart.

But soon the agent died in a way that was as mysterious as it was sudden.

The papers which were found after the

Cuban gentleman's death appointed Ostani his successor in the management of Mr. Harkaway's property.

So far Hunston had triumphed.

How long his success was to last remains to be seen.

"I have it," said Toro, presently, sending his huge fist on the table with a force that nearly split it in two.

"What?"

"Harkaway's life must be taken, and that quickly."

"No, his boy must die."

"What do you mean?"

"Mean?" echoed Hunston, fiercely. "Why, this; we must spare Harkaway's life, but we can torture him through this brat—this boy of his. Yes, yes, Toro, kill the brat when you can."

"It shall be done."

"Aye; and so all purposes are served. We shall be secure, and when the boy is dead, we will condemn the hated Harkaway to a living death, as our prisoner. What think you, Toro?"

And Hunston's eyes sparkled with vicious hate.

"You agree to my proposal, and will be guided by me?"

"Yes," said Toro.

"Your hand upon it?"

"There."

And this brace of worthies shook hands with as much fervour as two thoroughly honest men might have done.

The door just then opened, and a negro servant entered the smoking saloon.

"Is dar one of you gemmen as calls himself Webb?" he asked.

"No," said Toro.

"Get out," added the other.

The coloured gentleman's dignity was touched.

So he pretended not to hear, or not to understand the insolent command, but looked about the room for something which was apparently rather difficult to find.

"Go."

It was Hunston who spoke.

The negro still looked on; but his search was just as unproductive as before.

"Get out," thundered the irritable giant, "before I break your neck."

And then, without so much as allowing the negro the bare time to obey, he seized him by the nape of the neck with one hand, and thumped his woolly head with the other.

A nigger's head is proverbially thick, but the giant's hand came like a battering ram against it, and it made him wink again.

"Oho!" yelled the negro. "Murder! murder!"

Toro was just in the humour for brutality, so he clouted away merrily.

The negro yelled.

But the harder the poor wretch cried, the harder the brutal Toro hit.

The negro wriggled and struggled, and, suddenly jerking himself free, he butted with his head, and catching the doughty giant in the pit of the stomach, sent him staggering back, gasping.

Toro was only staggered for one instant, however. Then he rushed wildly at the negro, full of murderous intent.

Had he caught the black man then, it would have gone hard with him.

But the nigger dodged him nimbly enough.

Twice he eluded his pursuer cleverly, but a third time Hunston stopped him, and Toro, throwing out his brawny arms, caught him in a regular bear hug.

He did not hit this time.

He only squeezed.

The negro yelled, "Oho, massa! massa!" and then gasped.

Suddenly a loud voice at Toro's elbow exclaimed—

"Stop that!"

Toro looked sharply round.

It was Harkaway who stood before him.

"What are you about?" said Jack, sternly. "Do you want to murder the man?"

"Be off," retorted Toro. "You, above all others, should not interfere. If you are wise, go!"

"Oho!" cried the unhappy negro. "Murder!"

The giant gave him another squeeze.

"Will you desist?" cried Jack Harkaway, all his old pluck mounting to his brave heart.

"No," cried the giant, fiercely.

"I shall strike if you do not, so I warn you."

Toro's only reply was to squeeze again, eliciting a groan of anguish from the miserable negro.

Harkaway clenched his fists, and dashing forward, gave Toro two fearful blows upon the chest.

The disguised brigand staggered back.

The negro, freed by the act, jumped behind Harkaway.

The giant, recovering almost immediately from the shock, made a rush at Harkaway. Our old friend Jack stood well prepared.

But the noise had brought a number of people to the saloon, and Hunston, stepping in before his burly comrade, seized him by the arm and gave him a timely word of warning.

"Fool!" he said, in a low voice, "would you ruin all? Come with me, or all will be lost."

So saying, he half dragged, half coaxed the brigand Toro out of the room.

CHAPTER IX.

INTRODUCES CÆSAR HANNIBAL AUGUSTUS CONSTANTINE JEX.

THE skirmish in the smoking saloon created quite a sensation.

Most of the people applauded Jack Harkaway for his defence of the negro, but not all.

The Americans and the English present were delighted with Harkaway, for they could but admire the courage of the man in attacking such a huge ruffian as Toro.

But the Cubans present—several—condemned him for taking the part.

Conscious, however, of having only done his duty, this did not affect Harkaway.

As for the poor negro, his gratitude took the most extravagant and grotesque forms.

He could not sufficiently acknowledge the goodness of his champion.

"I'm berry much 'fraid," he said, "dat man'll look out for you, sar, and give you 'toko,' sar."

"You have nothing to fear for me," returned Jack Harkaway. "I can take care of myself, and give him in return what you call 'toko.'"

"Golly, massa, dat you can. I hope you give him one—two for him nob next time," said the negro.

"You keep out of his way, though," said Harkaway.

"You make him smell agony, massa," laughed the negro. "My! what a big crack you did gib him!"

"I hope so."

"Dat's so," responded the negro.

"Hurt him, think?"

"Not berry much like—only nearly killed him."

"I don't think that—not that I should mind a great deal," said Harkaway; "it would be ridding the world of a murderous ruffian."

Dick Harvey just then came in with a letter in his hand.

"Well, Dick," said Jack, "what's the matter? Have you heard of the row?"

A few words of explanation ensued.

"Just my luck," said Harvey, "I always manage to drop in after the opera is over."

"No matter this time, Dick," said Harkaway, smiling.

"And so this is the darkey?" added Harvey.

The nigger swelled up like a pouter pigeon, and expanded his chest.

"I am de pusson ob colour," he said, with withering emphasis.

"Just so."

"De obligated indiwiddle," added he.

"And what," asked Dick, "what may be the name of de obligated indiwiddle? Let's hear it, old man."

"My name, sar, am Cæsar Hannibal Augustus Constantine Jex."

"Phew!" cried Dick, laughing, "that's a snorter."

He thought then, for the first time, of the letter which he brought in his hand.

"Your American friends have found you out soon, Jack," he said.

"Why?"

"A letter for you."

"You don't say so?"

"I do, though, and here it is."

"Strange," said Harkaway, musingly: "I know no one here, nor do I know the writing even. I wonder who it can be from."

Dick laughed.

" You are like Dundreary, I suppose."

" I—why ?"

" Because you can set all wondering at rest in a crack, if you open the letter."

Harkaway smiled.

He opened the letter and glanced carelessly over it.

But his attention was fixed at once in a way he certainly had not counted upon.

Dick Harvey watched his friend's face anxiously.

" Is there anything wrong, Harkaway ?" he asked.

" Well, I hardly know; but you are certainly very wrong."

" How ?"

" Why, I've read the letter, and am still wondering who it can be from."

" Why ?"

" Because," said Harkaway, " there is no signature."

" Anonymous ?"

" Yes."

Dick made a grimace.

"Nasty, ugly things anonymous letters."

" They are," said Harkaway, seriously, " and this one is not less ugly or less nasty then the rest of them."

He handed it to Harvey, who ran his eye rapidly down it. He was not less astonished than Harkaway had been.

This was the letter which occasioned so much surprise and uneasiness.

" *Be on your guard. You are in great danger here from an old and much-to-be-dreaded enemy. Hunston and a creature of his you well know are in the hotel under assumed names.*

" *Be on your guard night and day. The writer of this is not able to see you personally, as it is of vital importance that he should remain unknown. Yet do not neglect this warning, and again I say, be on your guard night and day.*"

" What do you think of that ?" asked Harvey.

" I scarcely know what to think," was the reply.

" Do you believe it possible, Jack ?"

Harkaway paused to reflect before replying.

" I should say, Harvey," he answered, " that it was very improbable if it were argued upon reasoning grounds solely, but yet——"

" Yet you believe it ?"

" Well, I do."

" And so do I."

" I'm not a superstitious man, Dick," said Harkaway, " but then I am half inclined to believe that there is a kind of fatality in our running foul of this Hunston at every turn !"

" True."

" How wonderfully his life has been mixed up in our career."

" Wonderfully indeed," replied Harvey.

" Dick, we must not neglect this warning. It may be some trick; there may not be the slightest foundation of truth in the whole history; but still we must consider it for safety as being as true as gospel."

" Just my opinion," said Harvey; " forewarned, forearmed."

CHAPTER X.

HUNSTON dragged his burly companion by sheer force along the passages of the hotel up to their own apartments.

Then, once in, he slammed to the door, locked it, and withdrew the key.

" Are you mad, Toro ?" he exclaimed, passionately. " Are you a fool, thus to bring down the eyes of the whole house upon us, when everything depends upon our lying snug ?"

The giant gave a grunt of impatience.

" Don't talk to me," he said. " Are we children, to be thus badgered and beaten and insulted ?"

" You provoked it," said Hunston.

" Why does he always spring up in our path to gibe and twit us with his success in all he does or touches ? I tell you, Hunston," he cried, with a passionate oath, " I shall never rest until I have had Harkaway's hated throat in my clutches, until I have felt him wriggling here in my grip, and pressed the life slowly out of him."

Hunston laughed scornfully at this outburst.

"Words, words," he said. "Kill him if you can, but don't brag too soon."

"I'll do it," returned the giant, sharply. "I'll do it."

"Not here."

"And why not?"

"Because I order you not to attempt it."

"You? Bah!"

"Yes, I, and beware how you would cross me," said Hunston.

"Cease your idle threats with me," said Toro; "you know that I value them not."

"You want to quarrel with me, then?"

"Quarrel? Not I, indeed, only have a care how far you go with me, for though I am a patient man——"

"You?" laughed Hunston, derisively, "you a patient man? Rubbish!"

Toro, goaded to fury by the other's sneers and taunts, sprang upon him, and seized him in his powerful grip by the throat.

Hunston never uttered a word of remonstrance.

He simply drew from the inner pocket of his waistcoat a long, slender stiletto, and glided it with a sharp motion through the fleshy part of his assailant's arm.

Toro yelled. It seared him like a red-hot iron.

He stepped back, and clapped his hand to the wounded part.

"A blight upon you!" he cried; "you have stabbed me."

"A mere prick," said Hunston, coolly; "let it warn you."

Toro looked dangerous.

"Be advised," said Hunston, menacingly.

Toro stepped after him, holding his bleeding arm.

Hunston retreated a step, and stood on guard.

"The next time I strike, it shall be at your heart," he said, as quietly as before.

The brigand Toro stopped short.

There was a quiet intensity in the other's manner, which told the giant that he would keep his word.

Toro was no coward, but his courage was of that kind which cannot bear to face danger with the same deliberation as the scoundrel Hunston would.

So he grumbled and growled, and growled again, and finally swallowed his wrath.

Hunston knew better than anyone with whom he had to deal.

He watched Toro for a moment, and then put by his stiletto.

"Let me bandage your arm," he said.

Toro made no answer, but sullenly bared the wounded part.

Then Hunston bathed it with a handkerchief, and bound it tightly up.

"It is idle for us to quarrel, you see,' said Hunston.

"It is no fault of mine."

"Nor of mine."

"Why——" began Toro, in a loud voice.

"There, there," interrupted Hunston, impatiently, "we are recommencing, it appears to me."

The giant gave a sullen growl.

But you could see, however, by the workings of his face what a struggle it cost him to subdue his fury.

"Toro, my friend," said Hunston, when the arm was finished, "I must say a word or two to you seriously."

"Say on."

"If we are to continue together, you will have to control that temper of yours, for you will ruin both of us otherwise."

"I?"

"Yes, you."

"Would you have me submit tamely to his insults and blows?"

"For awhile."

"I cannot."

"You must. You will if you are wise."

"Never."

"Not if I show you how to repay him, to have your vengeance upon him and his, all at one blow, and to make a rich booty by it at the same time?"

"How?" demanded the ex-brigand, eagerly.

His eyes sparkled like diamonds at the thought.

"I will tell you. To-night, when all the house is wrapt in sleep, we will—hush!"

"What is it?"

Hunston pointed to the room door significantly.

"There's no one there," said Toro, eagerly; "go on."

YOUNG JACK HARKAWAY.

EMILY, YOUNG JACK HARKAWAY'S MOTHER.

JACK HARKAWAY, YOUNG JACK'S FATHER.

DICK HARVEY, JACK HARKAWAY'S FRIEND.

"HARKAWAY STOOD BRAVELY AT BAY."

Hunston resumed in a low voice.

What he had to impart was evidently of a nature to interest and excite his hearer rarely.

Toro's fierce eyes gleamed, and his face flushed again.

"It shall be done," he cried, with an oath; "it shall be done."

"You are right."

"And this night, too."

"This very night. Hush!"

The door moved.

Hunston stepped very nimbly and noiselessly to it, then tore it suddenly open, discovering a man stooping to pick something off the floor.

"Ah!" ejaculated Toro, "eavesdropping."

He grasped the man by the shoulder, and lifting him up, showed the face of Silly Webb.

"Lor' me, mister!" said the weakwitted man. "How are you?"

Toro clenched his huge fist menacingly.

"What are you doing there?" demanded Hunston.

"I was picking up this."

"What?" said the fierce giant, giving him a rough shake; "answer quicker."

"Only this."

And Silly Webb popped up a sixshooter under the giant's nose.

Toro stepped back.

"Did you find that?" asked Hunston.

"Yes."

"Where?"

"On the mat."

"Quite right," replied Hunston. "I was wondering where I could have dropped it."

He stepped up, with his hand outstretched to take it; but just as he was close upon it, Silly Webb, the poor, weak-witted fool, presented it, in the stupidest way imaginable, full at Hunston's face.

"Mind what you are at; it may go off."

"Yes," said Webb, grinning in the same meaningless way. "Mind that it don't go off; it might injure you, and I should be so sorry."

"Give it me."

"Oh, no; it feels so nice in my hand."

"But—but," said Hunston, "it is mine."

"Perhaps; now it's mine," said Webb.

Hunston bit his lip till the blood came.

Still the game was to coax the revolver out of the soft-headed fellow's hands.

"Come, come," he said, putting on his most persuasive manner. "You wouldn't keep what don't belong to you?"

"Oh, yes, I would. Besides, I should like to feel it go off."

And the revolver held in Webb's hand seemed to take a direct line first at Hunston's head and then at Toro's.

Silly Webb grinned from ear to ear.

"Findings, keepings," Silly Webb chanted, with an impish stare; "losings, seekings."

Toro's temper rose, and advancing before Hunston, he said, in a voice of thunder—

"Give me that weapon, or this knife shall see the colour of your blood."

At the same moment, he drew a long knife from his coat pocket.

"Please don't," said Webb; "you frighten me, and when I am so put out, I don't know what I do."

"Will you give me that revolver before I strike you?" cried Toro, raising his knife.

"Mind, please, mind your head," cried Webb, looking up at the giant; "I think the revolver is going off. There!"

Bang! A loud report, and Toro's hat went flying off his head.

The next moment Webb went skipping along the corridor, like a schoolboy of six or seven.

"After him," whispered Toro. "I mistrust him."

Without a word, Hunston shot along the thickly-carpeted corridor, clutching his long stiletto.

He gained every step upon the poor idiot.

Did not Silly Webb hear him?

Surely not.

He would certainly have turned round else, in spite of his silliness.

A minute—nay, a moment more, and Hunston, with that slender, snake-like blade uplifted, was upon him, when, in the very nick of time, Silly Webb turned round sharply and faced him.

"Hullo! sir, where are you running to?"

Hunston was transfixed with surprise, and Silly Webb suddenly pushed out his revolver in Hunston's face.

"Mind it don't go off again," he said.

"Put it down," said Hunston.

"What do you want?" asked Silly Webb. "This pistol?"

"Yes."

"Then you can't have it—he, he, he!"

Hunston was furious, yet dared not show it.

"Oh, my!" exclaimed Silly Webb, suddenly; "what a pretty knife."

Hunston tried to conceal it.

"Don't hide it; give it to me."

"I can't—I—I——"

"Oh, do," said Webb.

Then suddenly bringing down his outstretched revolver upon Hunston's knuckles with a hard rap, the stiletto fell to the floor.

At the same moment, he thrust out the revolver as if he meant to fire, and as Hunston stepped back in alarm, he whipped up the stiletto from the floor, and darted off.

"Devil!" cried Hunston. "Give me back my stiletto. Toro, Toro, quick, this way after him. He must not escape us."

The strange man, who had got the best of Hunston, darted along, still grinning, until he ran into the arms of his keeper, Mr. Percival.

"Hullo! Webb, my lad! what's up?"

It was singular then to see how serious and full of earnestness Silly Webb became.

He grasped Percival's hand, and drew him hurriedly into a small room close by, saying—

"Quick! enter here! There is more work, and dangerous work, cut out for us than I expected. Quick, and close the door; we must not be suspected."

* * * * *

A little later in the day Harkaway came after Dick Harvey with an open letter in his hand.

"What now, Jack?" asked Harvey, anxiously.

"Well, old boy, read this."

And he handed him the letter.

Harvey read, and his face grew long and thoughtful.

"Confound it all," he said, "and hang all mysterious correspondents."

"Not all."

"Yes, all."

"But this one appears to be friendly."

Harvey thought awhile, and then he answered, musingly—

"Well, Jack, he may be friendly, or he may not."

And Harvey read once more the letter. It ran thus—

"*Accept my former warning. My worst fears for you are realised. Danger surrounds you. Be on your guard against any artifice. Above all, watch your son day and night—and night more than all.*"

CHAPTER XI.

A VERY BLACK BUSINESS.

NIGHT!

All Boston was buried in sleep.

No, not all.

There were two people moving stealthily about at the hotel in which resided the Harkaway family.

The movements of the two persons in question were of a singular and mysterious nature.

The day had been sultry.

A thick mist hung over the city the whole day long, and the weather-wise had been predicting storms, hurricanes, and other objectionable freaks of the elements.

But the storm had not yet burst forth.

The mist thickened after dark, and now it enveloped the whole city in a fog.

A nasty night to be out.

A night for evil deeds.

What could bring people out from the hotel on such a night as this?

Suddenly two men crept forth from the hotel, cloaked, with mufflers on, too, up to their ears.

Their faces were so carefully hidden that the sleepy negro in the hall, who had to let them out, did not recognise them as inmates of the hotel.

And yet he knew everyone there, for he was a very intelligent negro, and his name, according to his own account, was

Cæsar Augustus Hannibal Constantine Jex.

"It seems bery strange why they go out so dark a night; dis child tink it not correct."

But he could not give himself a satisfactory reply.

So he wisely gave it up for a bad job, and dropping into his chair, fell asleep.

* * * * *

The two mysterious wanderers seemed very anxious not to be seen, for their chief care was to walk on noiselessly in opposite directions, and watch at the corners of the street.

Then, having satisfied themselves on that point, they returned to their starting point.

They looked like spectres gliding along in the fog.

Not the faintest echo did their footfalls wake.

How could this be?

Over their boots they wore large felt slippers, which deadened all sound most effectually.

This was a device well known to all burglars and such midnight marauders.

It looked ugly.

"Where's the lantern?" asked the taller of the two, who towered over his companion.

"Here; but speak lower."

So saying, he threw back his cloak and brought out a bull's-eye lantern, which he turned slowly and flashed upon the basement windows of the hotel.

"Be careful," exclaimed the other. "The night porter is perhaps watching."

"Not he; did you not see that he could hardly stand for drowsiness?"

"No matter; we can't be too careful."

"Get out your bottles."

The other obeyed.

The bottles were made of tin and covered in wickerwork, and from them dangled parchment address labels, upon which was printed a single word in large capitals—

PETROLEUM.

The man with the lantern flashed its rays again upon the iron grating covering in the cellars and basement rooms.

The room immediately beneath where they stood was evidently a carpenter's workshop.

"That's the place to begin on," said the man with the lantern.

"Good."

"Stop; don't break the window. The noise might arouse somebody."

Then stooping, he fastened an india-rubber ring upon the window by means of a species of sucker such as we see used in shop windows as pegs for the display of goods.

He next took a diamond ring off his little finger with his teeth (he was as handy with his teeth as most of us are with our fingers), and taking it in his hand, he proceeded to scratch four lines round the rubber ring, which he had fixed on the glass.

This done, he pocketed the ring and tugged gently at the india-rubber ring, and the pane came out with little or no noise.

"Now for it."

He grew just a little excited and threw back his cloak.

And then you saw why he was so handy with his teeth.

He was a one-armed man.

As soon as the pane of glass was removed, the taller man advanced with his wicker-covered cans or bottles, and emptied the contents of half of one into the workshop.

"The rough wood, shavings, and straw will help us," said the big cloaked figure.

"Now," said the one-armed man, "saturate the cotton wool you have with you thoroughly with petroleum."

Then they threw it down through the window.

"It is done," cried the taller of the two men.

"Now for the window above."

He then took from his companion beneath some balls of cotton wool saturated with petroleum.

These he tossed lightly into the room.

About ten balls he threw in thus.

"Are they out?" whispered the one-armed man.

"No."

"That's good."

"Three have gone out, some are smouldering, and one is already licking the edge of the table cover."

"Good, good!"

The tall man dropped from his perch.

"We must be quick now," he cried.

The one-armed man took a box of matches from his pocket, opened them half way, and ignited the whole box.

This he tossed through the basement window into the shavings bestrewing the carpenter's shop beneath.

They watched eagerly.

The shavings caught fire.

This appeared to be all they required, for as soon as they saw the flames, off they went.

This strange proceeding was repeated in different quarters of the hotel.

Presently the big man gave a cry of alarm.

"What is it?" demanded his companion.

"See there!"

"Where?"

"The room where the shavings are."

He looked round.

The flames had already shot through the basement window, and were licking the grating and wall in front.

"We must be quick," said the one-armed man, in an excited whisper.

"Yes," replied the giant; "this daring work is to my liking."

"Hark! What's that?" said the one-armed man.

"What?"

"Don't you hear?"

"Not I."

"A footstep."

He listened eagerly, and a heavy, measured tread was heard approaching.

"I am well prepared for anyone," said the big man. "I care not."

The one-armed man again spoke in a low tone.

"Silence! it is the police! What's to be done?"

"Leave him to me," said the giant.

There was a fatal significance in the burly fellow's manner as he said this.

They stepped softly over the road, and slunk into the recesses of a deep and dark doorway.

The measured tread came on—nearer—nearer.

"He's turned the corner," said the one-armed man, "and coming this way."

"No, he's gone."

"I hear him, I tell you. Confound it! we were too quick in firing that carpenter's shop; we ought to have left it for the last. It will spoil us yet, if we are not careful."

"Bah!"

"Hush!'

The policeman turned the corner, and came on in the direction of the hotel.

He had not made half a dozen strides when the glare of the fire caught his eye.

With a cry of alarm, he came on at a double.

And then, as soon as he had ascertained that it proceeded from the hotel, he ran off to the front of the house with a view of warning the inmates.

The unfortunate man was never able to carry out his good intention, for a shadowy figure crept up to him, met him crosswise, and cut him off short.

"Stop!"

"There's a fire; the hotel's burning!" said the policeman.

"Yes, and you have done it," said a gruff voice in his ear.

"I? Nonsense! Stand aside; I'm going to give the alarm."

"Take that first."

A terrific blow was dealt at his head, but as the unhappy policeman jerked aside, it glanced off on to his shoulder.

"Murder!" he cried.

And he turned like a brave man to grapple with his assailant.

But courage could not avail him against the brute strength of the giant in whose clutches he was held.

The blow was speedily followed by another, which nearly smashed his head in.

He struggled manfully, and again attempted to beat off his foe, but at that moment a treacherous hand thrust a knife in his back up to the very hilt.

Another crushing blow from the giant's sledgehammer fist stove in the unhappy man's head.

Then, with a dull, hollow groan, he dropped upon the ground, a murdered man.

CHAPTER XII.

NERO AND JEX TO THE RESCUE.

"Come, Toro," said the one-armed man; "be quick now. Look at the blood about your hands and coat."

"I care not for that."

The butchery just perpetrated affected him no more than would the drowning of a kitten.

"We can't leave the body there."

"What, then?"

"Take it up, and throw it somewhere into the flames."

"Good; you are always full of thought and prudence," said the giant.

They dragged it round to the window of the library and reading room.

The giant climbed up, and once in the room, he leant over, and putting forth his great strength, dragged the body of his victim up after him.

"Now, Hunston."

The one-armed man stretched out his hand, and thus clambered and scrambled into the reading room.

It was already ablaze in three different places.

The window curtains had caught, the table was alight, and the flames were creeping up the wainscot and panelling by the fireplace.

The one-armed man looked about him eagerly.

"Where is the dead man?"

"There."

Toro pointed to the body of the policeman, which he had thrown under the table for the flames to devour it speedily, and thus destroy the traces of their crime.

They then made for the door.

It was fast.

"Confusion!" exclaimed Hunston. "It is locked."

"Ha! where is the key?"

"On the other side."

"We must force it."

"Impossible."

"Why?"

"To break it open we shall have to carry away the woodwork."

"Why so?"

"Because it opens inwards," was the reply, "and it would never move unless we could carry away the framework of the doorway."

"We can't stay here to be caught like rats in a trap."

Hunston looked gloomily about him for awhile.

He was calculating the chances.

"There is nothing for it," he said. "We must retreat."

"What?"

"By the window."

"Never!" thundered Toro. "See here; I'll soon make short work of this."

"Stop, fool! you'll alarm the whole house," said Hunston.

"I'll stop for no man, and lose the best prize of the lot," said Toro, indignantly.

"The diamonds?"

"Yes."

"And supposing the diamonds aren't there after all—supposing it is one of those idle exaggerations of the waiters?"

"But I saw them, I tell you, saw them with my own eyes—there, glittering in a desk upon the table. Now, stand aside and let me try my strength on the door, or we shall be baked alive in this flaming den."

Hunston started.

"Are you sure they are diamonds?"

"I swear it!" thundered Toro. "Some of them as big as peas and glittering so that they dazzled your eyes. It is a prize worth a kingdom—an Eldorado!"

"Well," said Hunston, "the boy, young Jack Harkaway, is the prize I care for—even before the diamonds you speak of."

"Bah!" said Toro, contemptuously. "Do you think I'll shirk a little danger for such a prize? Go or come with me, as you please. I'm there. Now clear the way."

So saying, he literally hurled his huge body against the door, and it went in with a crash.

"Come on, or, if you prefer it, seek for the boy first!"

Hunston did not wait now for scruples or prudence, but dashed on after Toro the giant.

All was silent.

The house slept on.

The crackling of the flames and the crash of the reading room door had not yet been heard by the sleeping inmates of the hotel.

They little dreamt of the deadly danger they ran.

"This way," said Toro, when they gained the second floor.

"What number does the old man sleep in?"

"Thirty-three."

"Come on, then; but now for silence."

The door numbered thirty-three stood ajar.

They crept in on tip-toe.

At the end of the room was a four-post bedstead, round which the drapery was closely drawn.

They crept on towards it silently.

It was truly an exciting moment for them.

The time was short, they knew that well enough, for soon the whole house would be aroused.

Their deadly work must be accomplished with expedition.

"Where are the shiners?"

It was Hunston who spoke, and his voice hissed like a serpent when about to dart.

"Try under his pillow."

"Confound it!"

"Hush!"

Toro trod the floor like a fay; a moment more, and he was beside the sleeping man.

Tenderly he slid one hand beneath the pillow, and groped about, while with the other he held aloft a bright and long knife over the sleeper.

Hunston looked anxiously on.

Suddenly a smile of satisfaction illumed the giant's swarthy face.

"I've got it," he whispered.

He drew forth a weighty bag, and jerked it gently, to assure himself and his comrade that the coveted booty was there.

"Open it," said Hunston.

"Why?"

"To make sure."

Toro eagerly tore open the bag, and dropped some of the brilliants into his palm.

They glistened in a way that made their eyes sparkle with maddening delight.

For a moment, they actually forgot the terrible doom of the burning house beneath them.

"I will take care of the bag," said Hunston, making a snatch at it.

Toro turned sharply on him and seized him by the throat.

"No tricks of that kind with me, Hunston," he said, in a deep-toned whisper.

Hunston threw him off.

"You will insist upon taking those liberties with my throat," he said, significantly, "in spite of the warning I gave you to-day, when I had to lance your arm to let out some of your fever. What matters who keeps the shiners—you or I?"

"Just what I think," returned the giant, grimly, "so leave them in my keeping."

During this brief squabble, the owner of the brilliants opened his eyes.

At first he could not understand the meaning of the scene.

His impulse was naturally to cry out.

Luckily for him, he thought better of it, or he might never have called out again.

No; the huge proportions of Toro filled him with awe.

The naked dagger that Hunston carried terrified him.

So he was silent.

He fixed them both beneath his long, shaggy eyebrows, so as to remember them again under more favourable chances, and feigned to sleep.

They stepped out as gently and as quietly as they came.

"Those are nice visitors," said the old gentleman, drily. "Prudence is never thrown away. It was a happy inspiration which led me to hide the real ones and place the dummies in the bag under my pillow while the waiter was in my room. I saw the fellow stare. He's in the pay of these two pretty fellows. But they are deceived; the dummies they have robbed me of are not worth three dollars."

So, chuckling to himself, he turned over on his side.

"Dear me!" he said to himself; "what a smell of smoke!"

He sat up again, and looked about him to see if anything was wrong.

No, nothing.

Yet he sniffed again and again uneasily.

"It must come from outside."

So he rang the bell loudly.

"I pity one of the waiters if those two should meet him on the stairs, and think it prudent to put him out of the way. Well, well, it's only a nigger more or less."

* * * * *

"Now for the boy—young Jack."

This was said by the villain Hunston.

"Which is his room?"

"Next to his father's."

"Be careful, then, Toro, for I would not care to run foul of Harkaway."

Toro sneered.

"Are you afraid of Harkaway?" he said.

"Afraid? No," returned Hunston; "I hate him bitterly. But the man who by his pluck and perseverance destroyed Barboni and his band is not to be despised."

"I know it well," said Toro; "but I fear him not."

"Nor I," returned Hunston, savagely; "only it is not worth while risking all in the moment of success for the sake of showing off our foolhardiness."

Young Jack had locked his door, for he did not want his father to surprise him.

The fact was that, in defiance of his father's orders, he had brought Nero, his big monkey, up to his room.

"There!" said young Jack; "shan't I get a wigging from dad! Here, Nero!"

Young Jack jumped out of bed, and slipped on his trousers and shoes quickly.

Then he popped Nero into the bed and covered him over with the bedclothes.

"Dad'll never go near the bed," said Jack, to himself. "I suppose he has come to wake me, and finding me up, he will go back."

He turned the key gently, and stepped aside, intending to pop out and startle his father.

But what was his surprise and dismay to see two strange men enter?

They brushed by him, and made straight for the bed, and young Jack slipped out into the passage.

Toro and Hunston went straight up to the bed, pulled the clothes back, and—

"The devil !" cried Toro.

Nero did certainly not look unlike his satanic majesty, as he squatted up, grinning at them.

Some curious instinct must have told Nero that they were enemies.

That ordinarily gentle chimpanzee sprang up and bounded on to Toro's shoulders, giving him a playful tug at the hair, and drew out a pawfull of his dyed locks.

"Fiends and furies !" yelled the giant.

Nero leaped off him on to Hunston, and clawed him down the face.

The two of them fought desperately.

But Nero was more than a match for them.

It would have gone hard with them if they had touched him, but they could not get near him.

The monkey was here, there, and everywhere in a twinkling.

Meanwhile young Jack, in his alarm, ran to his parent's room adjoining.

The door was locked.

He knocked hurriedly and called out, but before the door could be opened, the two ruffians were out of the room and after him.

Young Jack only paused for a single moment by the door.

His first impression was that he was more secure near his father than in flight.

But here he made a mistake.

In a case of such danger, prompt action alone can avail one.

That momentary hesitation nearly did for him.

Nimble as young Jack was, the giant Toro's strides were about four of young Jack's, and being in a slight degree taken by surprise, Toro seized him just as he reached the top stair.

"Help !" cried young Jack.

The struggle was very brief—so brief as barely to merit the name of a struggle, and the boy was lifted up under Toro's brawny arm like a baby.

"Fly !" cried Hunston, in an excited whisper. "I can hear doors opening. No time is to be lost."

The alarm was getting general.

Harkaway opened his door, and appeared on the threshold in his dressing gown just as Hunston had got out of sight, and Master Nero was following.

"Confound that monkey !" ejaculated

Harkaway. " Hang me if he isn t up to some mischief. Jack has let him loose, and he's aroused the whole house."

He pushed open the bedroom door and entered.

Empty !

What could it mean?

Was young Jack up to some practical joking again?

Suddenly the recollection of the two anonymous letters flashed across his mind, and his cheek turned pale.

What if any harm had happened to his boy?

The thought was agonising.

In a moment a dismal cry came from below.

Harkaway dashed down the stairs, but at the next landing he was thunderstruck to behold the place filled with thick smoke.

Flames burst through an open door at the further end of the passage.

Harkaway stopped short, utterly dazed.

" I must have slept heavily," he thought. " Jack gave the alarm, but couldn't wake us. Yet surely the boy would never have left us to our fate."

The fire made headway at an awful rate.

The flames crept along the passage, and before long it was very evident that the whole of the great building would be engulfed.

" Emily !" cried Harkaway. " Emily will be lost."

He darted back and dashed up the stairs as the alarm bell rang out, and set the house upon the move, from the cellars to the garrets.

Meanwhile how fared young Jack ?

He fought desperately against Toro; but the giant carried him off as easily as he would a kitten.

Bells were now ringing upstairs and downstairs, and in a minute or two escape would be impossible.

They made for the front door. It was locked, bolted, and barred securely.

" Open it !" exclaimed Toro. " Quick! quick !"

Hunston wanted no urging.

Bars and bolts were withdrawn, but there remained an alarming obstacle.

The door was locked, and the key was not there.

What was to be done?

" Trapped !" cried Toro.

"No !" cried Hunston, "I have it."

" What ?"

" The hall window."

" Quick, then, lead the way."

In less than half the time it has taken to describe it here, they darted out of the passage.

They were at the window—and Hunston had contrived to throw it open.

A moment more, and they would be safe.

" Go first, Hunston," said the giant, " and I will hand you down the brat."

The " brat," as Toro contemptuously styled young Jack, kicked away mercilessly now, and by his struggles very materially impeded their progress.

" Gag him—tie down his arms, strike him !" said Hunston, excitedly.

" I'll kill him at once," said the giant, " if he is not quiet."

They mauled him cruelly, though, happily for poor young Jack, in the excitement prevailing he did not feel the effects of their brutality.

He was rapidly growing exhausted when one of the inmates of the hotel put in a sudden appearance and came to the rescue.

" Leave go your hold of the boy," said a firm voice.

" Stand aside !" cried Hunston, excitedly.

" Not at your bidding. Does the boy want you to drag him about like that ?"

" No, no !" cried young Jack, renewing his struggles; " help, help ! please help me."

" I will, my brave lad; now drop him," said the new comer, resolutely.

He then manfully dashed at them, and it looked as though the giant and his villanous leader were about to be defeated.

It was neck or nothing now for them, and Hunston, never over scrupulous, sheathed a bowie knife in the brave fellow's side, and he dropped to the floor with a hollow groan.

" Now drop the boy through."

Hunston clambered through the window, and Toro handed down young Jack.

Now, just as Toro was preparing to follow, the wounded man rose to his knees, and seeing the giant half through the window, he seized him by the leg, and exerting all his strength, he canted him over into the street.

Toro fell on his head, and lay there as he fell, apparently lifeless.

He was no light weight to fall from such a height.

Then, just as young Jack reached the ground, a dark figure crept up to Hunston, closed upon him, and dealt him a succession of vicious blows upon the head with a bludgeon.

Hunston dropped, felled like an ox, or his head would have been battered in.

And there they lay, the two villanous authors of all this havoc, half dead, insensible to all that was passing around, and in terrible proximity to the mine which their own hands had sprung.

"Yah, yah! come along wid dis infant," said the dusky rescuer to young Jack.

It was the negro whom Harkaway had preserved from the brutality of Toro in the smoking saloon.

"What is the matter? Who are those men? The place is all afire? Where are my father and mother?" asked the bewildered Jack.

"We'll see after dem now, Massa Jack," said the darkey; "I so glad I save you. Yah! yah!"

The brave fellow, who rendered young Jack such service and settled Toro's present devilment so summarily, clutched the window ledge for support with one hand, while with the other he fumbled at his waistcoat pocket for something.

Then he blew shrilly upon a silver call or whistle.

That strange signal brought Silly Webb flying along in the direction, for the wounded man was none other than Percival, the brave and mysterious keeper of the still more mysterious Webb.

Webb gave a cry of alarm as he saw his friend's condition.

"What is it?" he ejaculated, wildly. "Who has done this?"

"The villain Hunston and the brigand fellow," returned Percival, faintly.

"How? When?"

Percival gasped out some hurried words of explanation.

"It was two to one against me, but I heard the brigand fall—a heavy load; he's not got far, I should say."

Webb looked out of the window, and seeing the two scoundrels lying side by side, he gave a cry of exultation.

"Come come, old friend!" he said, turning to Mr. Percival; "lean upon me, and let us be gone. I cannot leave you."

The wounded man made an effort to move, but sank back with a groan, exhausted.

"Let me rest here," he said, faintly; "I cannot stir."

"You must," persisted Webb; "the place is afire—the danger increases every minute! Try, try! Come, old friend, so, so!"

He placed his arm round poor Percival's waist, and exerting all his strength, raised him up.

"Now throw your arm about my neck," he added, coaxingly.

Percival struggled bravely with the deathly weakness which was stealing over him.

But in vain; and after moving on four or five paces, he sank down upon the ground.

He was ghastly pale.

Filled with a nameless horror, Webb dragged open the wounded man's vest, and placed his ear upon the chest.

As he did so, poor Percival opened his eyes, but they slowly closed again, and with a faint sigh he fainted.

"Percival, Percival!" almost shrieked Webb, "look up, old boy. Dear old friend, think of what we have yet to work out; think of our murdered pal, that Emmerson struck down and killed, and whose death we have yet to avenge."

But Percival was for a time past hearing his friend's voice; he lay in Webb's arms like a dead man.

The alarm bell rang out louder and louder.

"Fire! fire! fire!"

The fearful word of warning echoed through the house, too late, alack, in many instances, to save the hapless inmates.

A glance about him showed Webb the extreme danger of his position, so he carried his comrade and friend out through the hall door, which by this time was battered in.

He carefully left his poor friend in charge of some kind people whose attendance he could rely on, and then returned to secure the brigand and Hunston.

But now a fresh surprise awaited him.

When he reached the spot where he

had seen Hunston and Toro senseless upon the ground, they had both disappeared.

Not a trace of them could be discovered.

"Gone!" he cried, in a perfect fury of disappointment. "No matter; hide where they will, let them burrow down into the very bowels of the earth, I'll dig them out."

And Silly Webb, otherwise Daniel Pike, was a man of his word.

* * * * *

The whole of the building now appeared to be one mass of flames.

Retreat by the staircase was hopelessly cut off. In the crowd were young Jack, Mr. Mole, Silly Webb, alias Daniel Pike, and the negro waiter who had so opportunely come to young Jack's rescue.

The whole of them looked helplessly, hopelessly on, while the flames swallowed up the hotel and all their dearest friends.

Poor Mr. Mole was filled with grief and terror.

"My poor, brave Harkaway! A hundred dollars to anyone who will rescue him! Can no one do anything?"

Impossible. There was nothing to be done.

One man in the crowd had brought his patent life-preserving apparatus—a rope ladder, with big hooks or grappling irons fitted on the top.

Just as the inventor and his invention arrived upon the scene, a window was opened, and at it appeared Harkaway and Emily.

Jack was cool and collected enough, but his poor wife could plainly be seen wringing her hands piteously, and her voice could be heard above the roar of the flames, calling upon the people beneath for assistance.

"Have you no ladders?" called out Harkaway.

"No, no."

"Wait, wait," shouted poor old Mole. "For Heaven's sake, wait; we will get some."

And then he turned to the crowd and offered the most extravagant rewards for ladders.

At this moment, a new character appeared at the window.

This was young Jack's monkey, Nero.

Poor Nero began to find it too warm to be pleasant, and so he prepared for a rapid descent by the water-pipe.

It was ludicrous, in the midst of that terrible scene, to see the monkey scramble down and save his skin whole, while the superior animal man was powerless to help himself.

There was a special providence in this, for the incident furnished young Jack with the happiest thought that had ever occurred to him.

Harkaway was evidently preparing for something desperate, for he had begun to throw the bedding and mattresses out of window.

"Stop, stop, father!" shouted young Jack; "we shall save you."

He called out for a rope.

The inventor came forward with his patent ladder.

"If you can get a rope up there," he said, "you can surely get my rope ladder up there."

"Is it light?"

"Very."

"Good," said young Jack, excitedly. "Come here, Nero! good Nero! quick, quick!"

The monkey came up grinning to his young master.

Jack took the ladder and fastened its topmost rung about the monkey's neck.

"Now, Nero," he said, patting the chimpanzee and pointing up to where Harkaway and Emily stood, "I want you to take this to my father, up there. Good Nero! dear Nero!"

And so, partly coaxing, partly commanding, he led Nero to the water-pipe, by which he had first made his descent.

He gave him a hand up, and Nero, who was brimful of intelligence and obedience, scrambled up.

Words cannot describe the excitement of the lookers-on during Nero's desperate climb.

They held the ladder below, so as to lighten its weight as well as they could, and up, up he went.

A few feet more, and the brave monkey would be there.

And now he was but nine or ten feet from the window, he was seen to be in trouble. The weight of the rope ladder was beginning to tell upon him.

Poor Nero struggled on boldly, but it was too much for him.

He paused !

Wavered !

Slid back a foot or two !

An agonised cry burst from below.

Not a word from above.

Harkaway was pale, but patient and resigned.

The last hope was vanishing fast when young Jack burst through the crowd and dashed after Nero.

"Hold him back !" shouted one.

"He will be killed !" cried another.

"It is certain death."

But the bold boy fought them back.

"Keep off from me !" he shouted; "I will save my dear father and mother, or die with them !"

Then, slipping the lower part of the rope ladder over his head, he climbed up the pipe after the gallant Nero.

Somebody cheered him for his brave action, but the cry was soon suppressed.

They feared to startle the two climbers, and make them miss their perilous hold.

The effect of young Jack's action was soon apparent.

It lightened the weight of the ladder to such an extent that Nero scrambled on with a shrill squeak of pleasure—or was it of pain?—for the water-pipe was getting unpleasantly hot.

And now Harkaway could almost reach him.

"Brave Nero," said he, to encourage the monkey. "Bold Nero ! good fellow, come. Come a little further ! Hurrah !" came in clear tones from Harkaway.

"Hurrah ! hurrah !"

Deafening cheers burst from every lip below, for Harkaway held the rope ladder in his grasp. Nero was lifted in.

The ladder was fastened by the iron hooks to the window-sill, and Nero was the first to scramble down it.

He no sooner reached the ground than, much to the surprise of the people, he commenced grinning, squeaking, and turning no end of flip-flaps and hand-springs.

"You next, Emily," said Harkaway. "Come, my dear."

"I dare not go alone."

"You must; it will not support us both together. Come, dear !"

She tried to screw her courage up, but again she faltered.

It was a perilous height.

"My darling !" urged Harkaway, "be brave ; think of our boy. Take heart for my sake. Remember how brave you were in our younger days."

Thus admonished, Emily stepped boldly down, and soon was out of danger.

Then Harkaway slid down the ladder, and caught Emily and young Jack in his arms.

CHAPTER XIII.

EVERYBODY cheered and cheered again for sheer joy when they saw Mrs. Harkaway hugging and kissing her son, young Jack.

And you should have heard them laugh when Nero, seeing that this was the order of the day, leaped on and cuddled Mr. Mole.

"Stop a bit," exclaimed Harkaway, presently. "While we are rejoicing here, we are forgetting Harvey and Hilda and the child, and Monday and Ada—are they safe ?"

Happily, this question was soon settled.

The Harvey family had had a narrow escape by the roof, over dangerous house-tops, and were in perfect safety in an adjoining house.

But the fright had had such a sad effect both upon Hilda and her daughter, little Emily, christened after Jack's wife, that Dick had not been able to leave them at first.

Burning, however, with anxiety to know how his friends had fared, he left Hilda and little Emily in the care of Ada.

Shortly after this, the whole party adjourned to the house which served the Harveys for an asylum.

And then they compared notes for an explanation of the affair.

"Yet," said Harkaway to young Jack, "how came you to leave my bedroom door until I came ?"

"I can answer that," said a deep voice.

They all turned round, and there stood the singular man whom they knew hitherto as Silly Webb.

"What do you know of it, Mr. Webb?" asked Harkaway.

"Everything. I will tell you," said Webb; "but what I have to say had better, perhaps, be confided to yourself and Mr. Harvey in private."

Harvey and Harkaway exchanged significant glances.

These were observed, and their import noted, by the so-called Silly Webb.

"I know," he said, with a sad smile, "you think me silly; but if you will come here, I can soon convince you that I am not quite as mad as you may suppose."

They were struck by his manner, and withdrew to a further corner of the room together.

"Well, for a startler to you," he said; "the cause of the fire is partly through an attempt to carry off your son, Mr. Harkaway."

"Ha!"

"Impossible!" said Harvey; "what grounds have you——"

"Grounds!" interrupted Webb; "no grounds, but positive proof. My poor pal, Nabley (whom you knew as Percival), was knifed—almost killed, in attempting to rescue him from two of your deadly foes."

"What foes have I now following me?" said Jack.

"One," said Webb, "who has followed you with hate from your boyhood."

"Whom can you mean? Speak out, man."

"I will; you must be more on your guard, for it is your enemy, Hunston."

Jack and Harvey started with surprise.

"Will the man never leave me in peace?" cried Jack. "It seems nothing but the grave for one of us, will stop his villany."

"If I meet him," said Harvey, "I will show him no mercy."

"Nor I," replied Jack; "but now let us have the name of our other foe."

"Toro, the brigand," said Webb, slowly.

"Impossible!"

"It is true."

"But how is it that my boy is here safe?" said Harkaway.

"Because poor Nabley stopped and attacked the two of them. When I came up, he was beyond giving me a full explanation, and he is now in great danger of his life."

"Jack."

Young Jack came over to his father.

"How did you escape from the clutches of those men?"

"I hardly know, dad," answered young Jack. "I only remember that Mr. Percival tried to help me, and that he got struck down by the cowardly man with one arm."

"Hunston!" said Harkaway.

"Hunston?" said young Jack, pricking up his ears. "What, Hunston, your old enemy, dad?"

"No matter," returned his father, evasively.

"Well, the one-armed man was just about to lay hold of me, when all of a sudden the giant was thrown out of the window on his head, and lay there. Then, while we were gasping at this, Mr. Jex jumped upon the one-armed man and hammered him with a stick about the head until he dropped."

"Mr. Jex."

"Yes, sar, I am here, sar."

"How did you do it?"

"Do what, sar?" asked the darkey.

"Why, rescue my son."

"Why, sar," responded the nigger, grinning from ear to ear, "I only rubbed the gemman's hair with a little stick backwards and forwards. I gib um toko; him not like it, sar, and then I gib um ' what for, Lady Jane?'"

"Both good," laughed Harvey.

"Yes, sar, but him object to hab any more of Lady Jane; him dropped down. And now me be bery glad to find Massa Jack Harkaway safe. Dis child fight any man any day, sar, to help him."

"Yes," said the mysterious Webb, advancing and taking young Jack's hand, "and I will be near you, my boy, in the hour of danger. We will yet be a match for the villain Hunston and the brigand Toro."

"Thanks, friends," said Jack Harkaway.

Then, turning to young Jack, he said—

"You will have to show your pluck, lad, for you seem to be getting into troubled waters."

"I don't fear, dad," said young Jack. "You have told me a boy of the Saxon race should not know the meaning of the word fear."

Harkaway felt proud of his son, but little knew what fearful dangers young Jack would very shortly have to encounter.

CHAPTER XIV.

"CÆSAR JEX," said Harkaway.

"Beg your pardon, Mister Harkaway, sar, but you am not quite right," said Jex.

"What's the matter, old man?"

"Why, sar, my name is Cæsar Augustus Hannibal Constantine Jex, sar, if you please," answered the nigger.

"Whoo—oo!" said Harkaway.

"Well, then, Cæsar——"

"And the rest of it, Jack," said Dick.

"You are a noble fellow," said Harkaway, "and I shall reward you."

"Dis niggar don't want nuffin," said Jex.

"Something you must have before you go."

"Go," echoed young Jack, dolefully.

"Yes."

"He's not going."

"Not going?" exclaimed his father. "What is Jex going to do, then?"

"To stay with me—are you not, Jex?"

Cæsar Augustus grinned in a way that showed clearly enough he was of young Jack's way of thinking.

"Yah! yah!" he laughed. "You am de rummest chile, Massa Jack, I ebber hear or see. What can them gemmen do wid a poor ole niggar like me?"

Cæsar Augustus was neither old nor useless, but he was a modest nigger, and he put his claims for favour in with diffidence.

"I can tell you," said Dick Harvey; "I shall press Cæsar Hannibal into my service."

"What do you say?" asked young Jack.

The darkey was delighted.

He grinned from ear to ear.

"Dat'll just soot Cæsar Hannibal Constantine——"

"Stop, stop," cried Harvey. "I could never have anything to do with a name like that. You shall be taken, friend Jex, but on condition that you are re-christened forthwith."

"Do what you like, Massa Harvey," replied the nigger, "if you can only keep this poor infant side ob young Massa Jack."

"Very good," said Dick. "What name shall we give our dark friend?"

They all had something to suggest.

"Sambo," said one.

"Snowball."

"Pluto."

"Beauty."

But none of these quite hit their fancy.

Young Jack was seated on the knee of Jex, and seeing a book peeping out of his pocket, said—

"What have you got there, Master Jex?"

"Dat, sar, am a good book, one I read and sing from. It make me feel nice all ober."

"Why, dad," cried young Jack, "it is a hymn book. All right, Jex, I know what your name shall be. Dad's got his Monday for a servant, and as you are a good nigger, we will call you Sunday."

"Dat will do bery well, sar," said Jex; "me like that name. Sunday sound grand."

Sunday, as a name for Mr. Jex, was put to the vote.

"Carried unanimously," cried Dick. "You hear?"

"Yes, sar," said Jex.

"Henceforth you are to be known to fame as Sunday, Jex."

Monday was very pleased to hear this resolution carried, for he could not have endured the presence of a fellow servant known by thirteen or fourteen syllables, while he had to put up with two.

Poor Hilda remained very well.

The doctor attributed it to the scenes of excitement which they had undergone of late, and he prescribed change of air.

Harkaway had taken a house and grounds in an adjoining state, and to it they removed.

Their lives passed on smoothly for a

time, and Hilda, by degrees, recovered her strength.

The tranquility of the place had effect on Mole and the two negroes.

The former, for the want of occupation, dropped into his old vicious courses, and soaked himself in drink.

The darkies had a tussle for supremacy.

Monday felt that his dignity was hurt by being put upon a level with his new-made and newly-christened fellow servant.

Endless were the discussions which they had upon one great topic—the precedence of the two countries—America and England.

Monday was a staunch upholder of the old country.

Sunday contested boldly that the new country could lick creation in a mere canter.

The discussions between the two niggers were renewed daily.

Monday had travelled over Europe, and Sunday had never quitted the state where he was born, or, locally speaking, " raised."

Consequently Monday looked down upon his brother darkey.

He let Sunday see it, too.

Now, the dispute between the two sable disputants grew so warm, that it almost looked as if they were coming to blows, at which point young Jack thought fit to interfere.

" I'll tell you what," said young Jack; " we shall have to hold an official inquiry into this."

" What's that, Massa Jack ?" asked the American nigger, Sunday.

Monday turned up his ebony nose in contempt.

" An officious inquiry, nigger," he said, loftily, " am a speeshy of court partial, dat's what it am."

Sunday looked humiliated.

But he was never hard up for an answer.

" We don't know nuffin about dem sort in dis 'ere free and enlightened country," he said.

" Don't wonder at dat," said Monday.

" Come, come," cried young Jack, " this will never do. You two shall be friends, but we will first have your dispute settled. What do you say, Monday ?"

" Bery well, sar," said Monday. " Appoint a day, and I will come in my new coat and show dis nigger I am a great man in discussion, and will make him say him know nothing."

It was arranged that the party should meet for the settlement of the question the next day.

Monday was resolved to overawe his adversary. So he prepared an elaborate costume of a strange military character.

Hence he would take a rise out of the illiterate nigger, and come off with flying colours.

Young Jack enjoyed the joke.

When the day came, young Jack assumed his sailor dress that he had worn on board of the good ship " Prospero."

Sunday was the first to put in an appearance before the court, which was composed of young Jack, Mr. Mole, and Nero the monkey.

Nero was in high feather.

He capered about in a nightcap that young Jack, his master, had given him, and, secretly prompted by the latter, appeared to take a delight in dodging Mr. Mole to get hold of a bottle containing what Mr. Mole called refreshment.

(N.B.—It bore a suspicious resemblance to rum).

Sunday had not been long present when there arose a great noise from the other end of the plantation. They looked up.

A warrior was approaching.

The coloured labourers of the plantation gathered about the military hero as he marched majestically along, and hailed him with a precious row.

Who could the imposing figure be advancing with such military steps ?

It was Monday.

The Prince of Limbi was gorgeously got up.

His scarlet swallow-tailed coat, his breeches, boots and spurs, all combined to give you the idea of a hero of a hundred fights.

He wore a cocked hat, too, and flowing plume of many colours, that put the finishing stroke to his splendour.

When the comparatively sober Sunday caught sight of his formidable rival, his heart sank for a moment.

" Oh, my, Massa Jack, don't he look grand ?"

*We are giving Cash Prizes to the readers of the " Halfpenny Surprise."
For particulars and names of winners see that splendid Journal.
Published every Friday.*

"MR. MOLE'S GRAND ACROBATIC FEAT."

Poor Sunday was struck with admiration.

It was a sight to see the Limbian prince leaning upon his sword, striking a warlike attitude.

Monday, on facing his adversary, gave him a stiff military salute, which rather puzzled him.

Sunday did not know whether to take it as a compliment, or as a defiance.

So he only grinned.

"Monday," said Mr. Mole, with a hiccup, "where did you get that splendid make-up from ?"

"No matter, Mr. Mole," said Jack; "we must proceed to business."

The parties did not wait to be called, but Monday, in gorgeous array, stepped forward.

"Well, den, Massa Jack," said Monday, "the fact is——"

"Stop, stop !" cried Mr. Mole.

"What am de matter, sar ?"

"You mustn't speak to Master Jack," said Mr. Mole, with a hiccup, "but address yourself to the president of the court."

"That's me," said young Jack, hitching his trowsers and making a bow.

"Well, den, massa—dat is," corrected Monday, "Mr. President of the court ——"

"Of this honourable court," suggested Mr. Mole.

"Horrible court," added Monday, "dat ignorant nigger dere——"

"Stop, stop !"

"What for ?"

"You mustn't abuse the other side," said Mr. Mole.

"I'm not abusing him," said Monday; "I only say that of all de ugly, ignorant niggers——"

"Stop, stop; that's unparliamentary," said Mr. Mole.

Monday paused, then said—

"Oh, you get out, Mr. Mole."

He did not know the meaning of unparliamentary, but continued—

"Sunday pretends dat de ole country is not to be compared wid America."

"Can't hold a candle to it," affirmed Sunday.

"Get along," began Monday, shaking the long sword in the scabbard.

Young Jack interrupted him.

"Stop a bit," he said, with the gravity of a lord chief justice, "let's hear some reasoning ; we don't want a row."

"Hear, hear !" said Mole.

And then he took another suck at his bottle, and leaned against the tree at the back—partly to rest, but chiefly to steady himself.

The disputants began again.

"Stop, stop !" cried Jack ; "you are out of order, gentlemen. Now, Mr. Sunday, just explain your reasons for your patriotic boast."

Nothing loth, Sunday opened fire in this fashion.

"Because, axing your pardon, Mr. President of this horrible court, because de ole country am used up dry, and because dis is a free young land wid go-ahead notions, a free and enlightened constitution. Dere, sar," he added, looking defiantly at Monday, "dat's my platform !"

"Hear, hear !" from Mr. Mole.

"Bravo, Sunday," cried young Jack.

"Go it, Monday, old boy," said Mr. Mole.

"And isn't de ole country's constitution a free and enlightened one ?"

"No, you go along."

"Why, you ignorant nigger," said Monday, with a sneer and a chuckle, "don't you know dat dis here constitution am only a copy of de ole country's ?"

"What of dat, you old nigger ?"

"Don't you know," continued Monday, "dat de sun never sets upon de British empire ? Don't you know, sar, dat dat flag," he added, pointing to the Union Jack, which was planted beside the tree under which the controversy was taking place, "dat flag commands de respect, sar, of de whole world ?"

"And what does dat other flag command ?" demanded Sunday, pointing to the star-spangled banner, which stood beside the British colours.

"Not much," said Monday, with a contemptuous laugh.

Sunday was nettled, so he fired up and rattled away at him.

"Not much ? Don't dey, by golly ! Why, de star-spangled banner could gib all de world a whipping."

Monday contradicted this most vehemently.

"Never, sar ; you could not come near us, could he, Massa Jack ?"

"Not if we had the proper people about us, I suppose."

"That's it," said Mole.

"Yes," said young Jack, "if we only had two or three brave men like Mr. Mole at our head, we could beat every nation."

"Oh, no," said the modest Mole, "perhaps not, although Washington was certainly——"

"Washington!" exclaimed young Jack, "where would Washington have been if you had had the command of the British armies?"

"Where, indeed?"

"No matter what the war might be about, if such a man as Mr. Mole should be there, why——"

"Please draw it mild, Jack," said Mr. Mole.

He was sucking at the bottle, and fast waxing helpless.

"Well, my 'pinion is," said Monday, clenching his fist and shaking it at Sunday, "my 'pinion is dat one Englishman can lick ten Yankees any day."

"And my 'pinion," retorted Sunday, "is dat half a Yankee could eat a village of Britishers."

A loud cry from Mr. Mole interrupted the discussion.

"Hullo! Jack, stop him, stop him, take him off; he's got hold of my bottle."

They turned round, and perceived the cause of the outcry.

Nero the monkey had been intently watching the drunken tutor's movements for some time, and seizing his opportunity, he made a vigorous dash at the rum bottle.

Mole struggled desperately for it.

Over they went, the monkey on the top of Mole.

Then Nero, grinning and showing his teeth, scampered off with his prize, and climbed up into the tree.

Mole jumped up, and staggered in pursuit of Nero.

"Thieves!" he cried; "thieves, give me back my bottle."

Nero, however, was out of reach, and out of danger, grinning every time he took the bottle from his mouth.

At last the contents, being overproof rum, burnt his throat, so he threw it from him, and by chance caught poor Mole in the centre of the back and floored him.

CHAPTER XV.

HARKAWAY and his friends lived on happily.

But one day he received a letter, inviting him to visit New York.

It was from Daniel Pike, alias Silly Webb.

"*To* JOHN HARKAWAY, ESQUIRE.

"DEAR SIR,—*If you like to run over here, I think I can provide you with some amusement. They are here, and, unless I am very much mistaken, I can show them to you.*

"*Yours to command,*

"DANIEL PIKE.

"*P.S.—My poor pal mends slowly. Before we are much older, I shall cry quits with the fellow who has nearly taken the life out of him.*"

Jack Harkaway was like an old war-horse at the smell of fire.

He resolved immediately to be off.

Harvey was not less resolved to go with him.

Young Jack pleaded hard to be one of the party, and, as they had never yet seen New York, Mrs. Harkaway gave her reluctant consent.

The day after their arrival in New York, a Mr. Webb was announced, and the well-known London detective was shown up.

"You see," said Harkaway, "we have accepted your invitation."

"Very glad," said Mr. Pike, shortly.

"I only reached New York last night," said Harkaway.

"I know."

"And had scarcely time to send to you to let you know where we were staying."

"No matter."

"By the way, though, how did you find us out?"

The English detective chuckled quietly.

"It's my business to find people out."

"So I perceive," returned Harkaway, drily.

"I am glad you did not bring Mr. Mole with you."

"Mole?"

"Yes. It was better that only you and Mr. Harvey should have come; but as Master Jack is here, we must look after him."

Harkaway was considerably puzzled at this.

"'Pon my life, Mr. Pike——"

"Webb, if you please," said the detective.

"Well, then, Webb, you appear to know more of my own movements than I do myself."

Webb smiled.

"It is simpler than you may suppose," he said; "but the fact is, that the business upon which I am engaged has become even far more serious than I at first expected."

"How so?"

"By reason of Hunston and that brigand fellow being in league with the murderer I am after."

"Emmerson?"

"Yes."

"They are a dangerous lot," said Harkaway.

"Yes, they will not shrink at robbery or murder."

"No, Hunston would stick at nothing, and as for Toro——"

"The man I most mistrust is Emmerson," said Webb. "He's a cleverer scoundrel than either, and he is really to be approached with the greatest caution when he is in league with two such desperate customers as your friends."

"Friends?" said Jack; "foes, you mean."

"Well, if you should ever come across this Emmerson, be on your guard against him, for he is one of the softest-spoken fellows you ever met, and yet he'd think no more of knifing you than of peeling an apple."

"How romantic," said Harvey, with a smile; "but I and old friend Jack care not for them."

"No," exclaimed Jack; "we have passed through too many dangers together to fear any man, but you excite one's curiosity."

"That you do," added Dick.

"I should vastly like to see this redoubtable Emmerson," said Harkaway.

"You would?"

"Seriously?"

"Of course."

"And so should I," added Harvey.

The detective eyed the two steadfastly for awhile, then said—

"You shall."

"When?"

"To-night."

"To-night?" cried Dick. "Where?"

"At the 'Asteroid,' as is is called," was the reply. "One of the most notorious gambling dens of New York, and to surprise you, it is partly kept by Emmerson, Hunston, and Toro the brigand."

"How strange," said Harkaway.

"A friend of mine—a very brave man in the force here—will get us in quietly. We shall go about eleven. I will fetch you at nine o'clock."

"Nine?"

"Yes."

"Is it so far?"

"No, but we must change our skins."

"Why?"

"Because if Hunston or Toro recognised you, it would spoil all. Emmerson is as keen as a razor, and he has the gift of disguising himself—face, form, walk, voice, all—in a way that is little short of marvellous, so beware of speaking to anyone. There will be great danger."

"Fear not, we will be cautious, and hold our own."

"At nine we will visit Saul Garcia's."

"Is that the theatrical wardrobe man?"

"Yes. He's a regular artist in his way, and will turn you out as President Grant, the Prince of Wales, or Queen Victoria," said the detective.

CHAPTER XVI.

YOUNG Jack felt lonely when he saw his father and Harvey go off, so he strolled out to view the city by night.

"What shall I do?" thought Jack.

Then, after a moment's pause, he suddenly cried—

"I have it. I will go for a walk, and as it is late, Nero shall go with me. Come along, Nero. We will have a ramble together."

And the monkey seemed very glad to go.

"I hope no harm will happen to dad," said young Jack to himself. "However, he and Harvey are together, and it would go hard with any six who ventured to attack them."

Young Jack was like his father; he knew very little what fear meant.

He walked and ran with Nero until he began to think that it was time to turn back, for it was getting late.

But now he could not, for the life of him, recollect the way.

There was no one about to ask the way back to the hotel.

"This is precious awkward," thought Jack. "What a dismal part of the town this is. It reminds one of the catacombs. And hark! What was that?"

A low, dismal groan came along on the breeze.

Young Jack started and turned sharply round.

Young Jack was not a coward.

He stood still and listened.

"This is not pleasant, in the dead of the night," thought young Jack.

The stillness was again broken by a hollow groan.

The next minute young Jack felt ashamed of himself.

So he pulled himself together.

"Was it my fancy?" he asked himself. "I thought I heard something—ha! again that hollow groan!"

Yes, again.

There could be no mistaking it this time.

It was a low, yet long-drawn wail of anguish.

Some poor creature was evidently suffering.

He followed the direction of the sounds, and when next he paused, for fresh indications to guide him, he was so close that he could almost hear the sufferer speak.

"No, no, Noll," said a faint voice, which sounded like a youth's; "keep your jacket on. You'll catch cold."

"No, I shan't, it's quite hot," said a sturdier voice, in remonstrance. "Let me put it round you, Harry?"

"No, no; let me die."

Then followed another moan, which told of keen suffering.

"Come, come, Harry, dear," said the other, in a half-choking voice; "bear up; the night will soon be over, and then ——"

"Yes, then," added the suffering boy, "then we can starve or die by daylight, instead of in this dreadful darkness."

Jack could listen no longer.

The allusions to starvation and death were too much for him.

He turned the corner sharply, still followed by Nero, and the next moment was facing the two boys.

They were lads nearly of his own age.

One was perhaps thirteen; the other about fifteen.

The youngest was pale, thin and wan.

His hollow cheeks and deeply-sunken eyes told a tale of slow starvation.

The other showed it less.

His more robust temperament bore better up against the terrible privations.

Jack faced them unnoticed.

"Can't I help you?"

This was said in a kind voice.

The two boys looked up with a sudden start.

"Do you want anything? I am only a boy like yourselves," said Jack, "but fortune has perhaps been more kind to me than to you."

There was a moment's hesitation.

They saw that they had to do with a lad of their own years, and this gave them courage.

"We do want something," answered the elder of the two.

"What?"

"Bread."

"Have you got no home?"

"No."

"Nor friends?"

"None."

"What!" said Jack, "no father or mother? What do you mean to do?"

And the tears rose in Jack's eyes.

"Starve here, perhaps," replied the younger boy, bitterly; "perhaps jump into the water, if our strength holds out to carry us as far."

Young Jack was greatly shocked at this.

"Commit suicide?" he exclaimed. "Poor boys! how dreadful!"

"Better that than die like a dog here," said the poor boys.

It was very sad to hear a lad of his years speak with such bitterness.

"We haven't a friend or relation in the whole world; we haven't home or shelter; we have not tasted food for two days, and nothing can help us—nothing, nothing!"

And the elder boy threw his arms round the neck of his younger brother, and cried bitterly.

There was a depth of misery in their manner that sent a tingling sensation across young Jack's heart.

"Come with me," he said—"come home with me to the hotel, and you shall have all you want."

The two boys stared as young Jack spoke.

The appearance of this deliverer was so sudden and so unexpected that they looked upon it almost as something more than natural.

"Come," said Jack, placing his hand kindly on the shoulder of the younger boy.

"Is it far to go?"

The boy spoke in a weak and plaintive voice.

"I hardly know."

"Don't know?"

"No, I have lost my way wandering about. You can do me a service by coming with me. You know your way about, I suppose?"

"Every street—every nook and corner."

"Come along, then."

He gave them the name of the hotel, and they both knew it quite well.

But before they had got any distance, the sicklier and younger boy fell so weak that he was forced to give it up.

What was to be done?

"You know the way now?" said the eldest of the two boys to Jack.

"No; but if I did, what of that?" said young Jack. "The agreement was that you were to go with me to the hotel and sup——"

"You are very good; but you had better give it up."

"What for?"

"They wouldn't care," was the bitter reply, "to see you bring two beggar boys into their fine hotel."

"You are no beggars," answered young Jack; "you didn't beg—I invited you."

"But my poor brother Harry can go no farther."

Young Jack was a boy of quick impulse.

He glanced up and down the street; there was no vehicle in sight, so he caught hold of the poor, sickly boy and lifted him to his back, saying—

"Now, my young friend, I'll give you a jolly good ride, and no extra charge."

Then, calling to Nero, young Jack said—

"Now, Nero, do as I do; take one on your back."

Nero, who at all times considered it his duty to imitate his master, had the elder boy on his shoulder in a moment.

"Don't be alarmed," said Jack; "my good old monkey won't hurt you. Now then, Nero, off we go."

But before they had gone far, Jack's sharp young ears detected the sound of footsteps.

"Who can it be coming this way?" thought young Jack.

Then, as the man came reeling round the corner, Jack shouted—

"Mr. Mole, by jingo!"

It was, indeed, the worthy professor, rather unsteady on his legs, and armed with a long pipe and a bottle.

"How came you here?" asked Jack.

"Well, my boy," said Mole, "I have just come over for the night to see you, but must return quickly to take care of your mother."

"Now, Mr. Mole, you have just come up in time to relieve poor Nero of his burden."

"My boy, I must positively decline to make myself a beast of burden."

"You make a beast of yourself another way," muttered young Jack.

"What's that, my dear boy, you say?"

"We must get home," replied young Jack, evasively. "Do you know the way, Mr. Mole?"

"Straight ahead. Forward, my brave Britons! I'll protect you in the rear. Hoorah! Jack, my boy, you are a brave lad."

Luckily the hotel was not far off, and they soon reached it.

*   *   *   *   *

"Mr. Harkaway has not returned, sir," said the waiter to young Jack.

Jack felt just a little bit uneasy at this.

However, he ordered supper for the two poor boys and himself.

When the supper was concluded, young Jack questioned them about their lonely condition.

Their history was full of sadness.

Their mother had been an American woman, their father an Englishman.

The former died about a twelvemonth before, and a change came over their father from that very date.

Drink reduced him in circumstances, and what this began the gaming table completed, until one fatal night a ruined gamester, named John Girdwood, shot himself.

And this John Girdwood was the father of the two poor boys, Oliver and Harry.

CHAPTER XVII.

"Saul Garcia," said Mr. Pike to Harkaway and Dick, "is one of the most extraordinary men you will meet with in his way. This is his shop."

Here he rapped on the glass door, and, as it was opened, Mr. Pike continued—

"Hullo! you are not Garcia."

The man who let them in was a curious-looking Jew, with shaggy, iron-grey eyebrows, and hair to match.

"Where is Garcia?" repeated the detective.

"Come in, gentlemen," said the Jew, who lisped very much. "Mithter Garthia ith out."

"We wanted to see Saul himself. Are you his assistant?" asked the detective.

The Jew nodded.

"I am, thir. I do motht of the work, Thaul getth the credit; but he don't give none, not Thaul. He, he, he! You excuthe my little joke."

Mr. Pike eyed the Jew sharply.

"Well, I want you to rig us out in a complete change from top to toe."

"All three?"

"Yes."

"Take a seat."

At this moment a footstep was heard in the passage without.

But before the door could open, the assistant stepped quickly out into the passage.

Here he was confronted by a man who was the very counterpart of himself.

"Don't go in, Garcia," said the assistant, hurriedly; "there are some people there I am very much interested in. I want to do your work for you; I shall dub up handsomely."

It was strange how very different his voice and manner both were now.

Garcia made some feeble remonstrance, but promises of a heavy bribe induced him to consent at once.

The assistant then returned.

He began by brushing back Mr. Pike's closely-cut locks, and then he fitted him on a wig with a bald crown and scanty light brown hair.

Next he dabbed his cheeks and forehead with ochre, dexterously applied with a hare's foot, and touched up his eyebrows with a soft pencil.

In the space of ten minutes, he was transformed from Daniel Pike into a German professor of mature age.

"Capital," said Harkaway.

"Excellent," added his friend Harvey.

"Now for you, thir," said the Jew assistant.

Harkaway was rigged up in a beard

and curly black hair, and a semi-military dress, which changed him very effectually indeed, and Dick Harvey was so altered that his best friend would not have known him.

"What do you think of that?" demanded the Jew of Dick.

"Very good."

"And yourth, thir?"

"Quite satisfactory," returned Harkaway.

"Glad to hear it," said the Jew; "glad to hear it. Why, you couldn't have a better get-up if you'd been Protean Bob himthelf."

"And who is Protean Bob?" asked Harkaway.

The Jew assistant stared very hard at them.

"You're thtrangerth here?" he said.

"Yes."

"What of that, though?" said Pike.

"Why, don't you know that Protean Bob ith Emmerthon?"

The detective gave a slight start.

"Emmerson?"

"Yeth."

"Do you know him?" asked Pike, eyeing the Jew keenly.

"Of courthe."

"Does he come here?"

"Not while I'm here," replie the Jew, quickly. "No fear of that."

"Well," said Harkaway, "what is there to pay?"

"Twenty dollarth."

Harkaway paid the money, and they left.

As soon as they had gone, the Jew assistant's manner changed.

He stepped up to the door, looked out, and having watched them out of sight to see that there was no chance of their return, he shot the bolts in the door, and drew the curtain to guarantee against observations being taken from without.

"Pike, the English detective!" he said, dropping into a chair. "He has tracked me even here!"

He remained for a few moments lost in troubled thought.

Then, starting up again, he said hurriedly—

"He's after me, and it will be his life or mine."

He walked up and down for a minute or two, muttering to himself.

Then, stopping short, he opened the door leading to the passage, and cried hurriedly—

"Garcia!"

"Yes, Mr. Emmerson."

The sham assistant interrupted him eagerly.

"No names, Garcia. Be very careful now, for I am in danger. I want all your prudence this journey."

"Goodness! You perfectly frighten me."

"Don't be a fool," returned Emmerson, for it was that notorious robber and murderer disguised.

"No, certainly not, Mr. Emmerson."

"Hush!" he cried, half showing a pistol which he clutched in his pocket; "are you mad? Call me by any other name but that."

"What shall I call you, Smith or Davis, or Pike the detective?"

Emmerson turned sharply.

"Garcia, you have been listening."

"Never——"

"You have, and you think to fool me. Now, Garcia, you ought to know better. I am a very good friend, but a devilish ugly enemy. And a Jew more or less in the world is no great matter. Do you understand?" said he, laying his hand firmly on the Jew's arm.

Saul Garcia gave a slight shudder.

Robert Emmerson was a known desperado.

Beneath that soft and simple exterior, he concealed the cunning of the fox, joined to the ferocity of the tiger.

Truly, the wrong sort of man to pick a quarrel with.

"There's no need to threaten me, friend," said Saul Garcia. "I'm no traitor."

"For your own sake, I hope not."

"I will be true."

"Good. Now lend a hand, and I'll put you up to earning a bag of money."

The Jew's eyes glistened while Emmerson was changing his disguise.

CHAPTER XVIII.

THE gaming-house known as the "Asteroid" was a very fine place of its kind.

Upon this particular night there was a pretty fair sprinkling of company present.

Harkaway, Harvey, and the detective looked about, but no signs of Hunston or Toro could be seen.

"Are you sure that they are here?" Jack asked Pike, in an undertone.

"Certain."

"Neither of them is in the room."

"Neither."

The game being played was *rouge et noir*, and in order to keep up appearances, our three visitors joined in for small stakes.

But soon Pike rose from his chair to stroll down the room, followed by Harkaway.

"No signs of them yet."

"None," said the detective.

"Perhaps they are not here to-night."

"They're somewhere about, I should say."

Suddenly Mr. Pike pressed Harkaway's arm.

"Look there," said Pike, in an eager whisper.

"Where?"

"There—that room."

A door on the left stood half open, showing the interior of one of the smaller rooms.

Round a table were four men playing cards.

Two of them were of such unusual height as to merit the description of giants.

One of these two Harkaway thought was Toro.

The second was a stranger.

He stood nearly as high as Toro, yet scarcely so broad.

But there was an angular look about his arms, chest and shoulders, which told of a wiry, muscular form.

The third was a one-armed man, about whom no mystery need be made.

It was Hunston.

The fourth was a dwarf, with the head and shoulders of a colossus.

As Harkaway and Pike paused before the doorway to look in, the dwarf's partner pushed aside his cards.

"I shall not play any more, with your permission, gentlemen."

"Nor I," said the dwarf.

And both rose.

Hunston bit his lip, but was silent.

His companion Toro, however, could not control his disappointment.

"It is generally the custom to give one his revenge when you have been winning," he said.

"Revenge?" replied the tall man, with a light laugh. "I always take my revenge promptly if anything disagrees with me."

Harkaway did not hear the reply, for just then they were pushed aside by one of the attendants, who passed into the room.

He was a Creole, but bore a striking resemblance to a man who left the shop of Saul Garcia within ten or fifteen minutes of their own departure.

This half-caste went up to Hunston, bent over him in an attitude of respect, and whispered something hurriedly to him.

Hunston started slightly.

"Here?"

"Yes," said the Creole; "don't look up, but they are at the door."

"Pike the detective and the others?" whispered Hunston, eagerly.

"Yes."

"Are you sure?"

"Certain; I rigged them up myself."

"I must go, sir," said Hunston, rising and bowing ceremoniously to Toro. "You will please excuse me——"

"You, too?" said Toro, taking the cue with tolerable readiness.

"Yes, sir, I have bad news from home."

"I hope it is nothing serious."

"I trust not, but I must go at once."

"At any rate," said Toro, "your matter is not too urgent for you to join in a bottle of wine before you go."

"If you will let me go then."

"At once."

"And if these two gentlemen will join us."

They demurred at first, but gave way to make themselves agreeable.

"I suppose," said Harkaway, in a whisper, "that, having fleeced their victims, they are going to regale them to make them forget their losses."

Pike looked serious.

"I think they are going to play an uglier sort of game."

"You don't mean that!"

"Indeed I do."

"We must see to this."

"See as much as you like, Mr. Harkaway, but don't be too ready to interfere."

"Trust me."

"I do, sir," replied Mr. Pike, earnestly. "We are in a very rum shop here. I'm no coward, but here we are surrounded by a most desperate set. An imprudent step or hasty word from you would bring us into an awkward mess, and perhaps cost us our lives."

The Creole brushed past them.

Hunston, filling bumpers round, said—

"I drink to our next meeting, gentlemen."

He drained his glass, set it down, and then bowing, left the room.

Passing hurriedly out, he was followed shortly by the coloured attendant who had brought the wine.

Proceeding along the passage, Hunston entered a room of which he possessed the key.

The Creole followed closely at his heels, closed the door after him, and hurriedly brought out of a cupboard a bottle of some effervescing drink.

Hunston drank its contents.

"That Italian fool, Toro," said the dark-complexioned man, who was a croupier, "will spoil all. Did you do anything clumsy?"

"No."

"Why did they want to leave off so soon?"

"I can't say."

"Well, that is of little matter. I tell you there is something up. Pike, the London detective, is here."

"But who for?" said Hunston.

"Perhaps for me, perhaps for you. Perhaps both."

"What do you propose to do, then?"

"I have scarcely thought it over yet. At all events, this is a moment when we want all our wits about us, and not to half fuddle our brains in hocussing a player for the sake of a few hundred dollars."

"True; but now what is to be done?"

The Creole, who was Protean Bob, otherwise the notorious Emmerson himself, looked serious.

"If Pike is here after us, and there can't be much doubt about that, he is of course in league with the police here."

"You think so?"

"I'm sure so."

"Phew! This looks desperate."

"The best course for us would be to clear out, to make a moonlight flitting of it."

"To-night?"

"Yes."

"We have this one great advantage over them, they are not aware that we know them."

"True."

"Shall we consult Toro?"

"Or leave him?"

"I scarcely know; the overgrown fool is more plague than profit. He only shows up to advantage in a free fight. Yes, we had better glide away alone."

*   *   *   *   *

While they were talking there, Toro having drained his glass, begged the two strangers to excuse him for awhile, and stepping hurriedly across the large room, he went straight to the refreshment buffet in the farther corner.

Here he gulped down quickly the contents of two small bottles.

This proceeding was of course watched with considerable interest by Mr. Pike and Harkaway.

"What did I tell you?" said the detective.

"What?"

"Do you see?—seltzer. That is the antidote, I suppose."

Harkaway understood it all now.

All considerations of prudence were forgotten now, and he made a hurried resolve to go and warn the strangers.

"Keep him occupied for a minute or two."

"What for?" asked the detective in some alarm.

"I'll not be a moment."

"For your life's sake, nothing rash."

"Trust me."

" Supposing they are part of the den ?"

This made Harkaway pause, and think seriously for a moment.

" It is not probable. At any rate, I will risk it; go and keep Toro engaged. See, he is returning, I think."

There was no time to remonstrate, for Harkaway had gone off to the ante-room.

So the detective, with the purpose of avoiding an immediate rupture, crossed the saloon and engaged Toro in conversation.

Harkaway slipped into the little room, and seeing one of the gentlemen about to raise his glass to his lips, he hurriedly took it from his hand.

" How now, sir ?" cried the big man, rising with anger.

They were startled at Jack's unceremonious conduct, but Jack said hurriedly—

" Forgive my seeming rudeness. Do not drink; I have reason to fear the wine is drugged. Take no notice; get some seltzer immediately; drink freely of it, but above all, take no notice of what has occurred. I believe our lives may soon be in danger."

And then, before they could offer a word in reply, Harkaway was gone.

The two strangers were taken by surprise at the startling information.

" Is it possible ?" said one.

" True or false," returned the dwarf, sturdily, " it is worth while to take the precaution. The remedy can't hurt."

So they went in search of the seltzer water.

New, just as they had taken it, there was a loud outcry, and in another moment the whole room was thrown into confusion.

A loud voice was heard denouncing the croupier or banker of the table.

The speaker was Harvey.

" It is a swindle !" he cried, jumping up, and seizing the man's hand.

The man struggled to withdraw, but Harvey held him fast.

The croupier dived into his pocket with his disengaged hand, and drew forth a revolver, which he presented at Harvey.

" Leave go your hold, or you are a dead man !" he cried.

Suddenly the hand holding the revolver was stricken up from behind, and down went the revolver, Jack Harkaway almost immediately pouncing upon it.

The croupier flew at Jack, and was met by an ugly blow, like the hit of a steam hammer, straight from the shoulder, and down he fell.

A scene of the wildest confusion ensued, in the midst of which someone put out the lights.

Then there was a general rush for the door.

" Jack !" cried Harvey.

" Hullo !"

" Where are you ?"

" Here, old boy."

The voice sounded near the door.

So Harvey fought his way manfully there, joining Mr. Pike, and presently they found themselves in the street, but no Jack Harkaway with them.

Harkaway was making for the door himself when he heard Dick Harvey's voice.

" Dick's in danger," he thought.

And Harkaway was not the man to desert his friends in danger, let the odds be what they might.

He could have got clear with the rush to the door then had he gone on.

He paused, thinking Dick was not out.

Next moment he heard the banging of heavy, massive doors, and the shooting of bolts.

Then Harkaway heard a rush of feet along the passage.

Suddenly the gas was turned up.

Then a cry of wild exultation burst from a fatally familiar voice, and Jack saw four men facing him.

Four enemies !

Hunston, his enemy from boyhood !

Toro, the brigand !

Emmerson, the murderer !

And the croupier !

Four to one !

All desperate men, who would think no more of taking his life than of rattling a dice box.

Harkaway stared surprised at the odds; then, plucking up his courage, stood bravely at bay.

CHAPTER XIX.

JACK HARKAWAY the elder was left in a very critical position.

In the skirmish at the "Asteroid" gambling house, Harkaway had held back for awhile, fearing that Dick Harvey was still inside, and had thus been surprised and cut off.

And he stood alone, facing four desperate adversaries.

Hunston, the bitter foe of his whole life; Toro, the giant and ex-brigand; Emmerson, the assassin and felon; and their creature, the croupier of the gaming table.

Harkaway was astounded.

It was a fearful predicament.

He knew that but too well.

His thoughts flew back to his dear boy and his Emily, and for one brief second his heart sank.

One brief second, no more.

And then no shade of fear was there for himself.

His heart never quailed in the presence of danger.

Hunston, not thinking that Jack could recollect him, was the first to speak.

"Who are you?"

"I'll tell you that," replied the croupier, promptly; "he is the friend of the thief who kicked up all the row."

"He's no thief," retorted Jack Harkaway, boldly, "but an honester and braver man than anyone here."

"You are evidently just as great a fool as he is," said Emmerson; "as rash with your tongue; so rash, in fact, that I must prescribe a remedy."

"Name it," cried Hunston, eagerly.

"Well," said the English murderer, looking spitefully at Jack, "cut his tongue out."

"Huzzah!" cried Hunston; "a noble fancy."

It was, indeed, the kind of vengeance he would like to take upon his old enemy.

"Brag's a good dog," said Harkaway. "You know the old proverb."

"Holdfast's a better, eh?"

"That's it?"

"Then I'll prove the better dog," cried Hunston, rushing in upon him.

Just as he got within range, Harkaway let fly with his right hand straight from the shoulder spank upon the nose.

Down dropped Hunston, felled like an ox beneath the poleaxe.

The other three closed in upon Harkaway simultaneously.

And now it looked as if the brief fight was over.

Jack Harkaway braced himself up for real hard work.

All his wit, all his activity, all his strength, would be wanted here to give him even a very brief respite.

He gave a sharp glance at the three desperate men advancing upon him, and calculated which was the weakest opening for him to attack.

He had soon decided.

Emmerson, the leader.

Quick to act as to think, Harkaway feinted to rush at Toro, but darting suddenly aside, he threw himself upon Emmerson, and taking him completely by surprise, hurled him to the ground.

Then he dashed to the other end of the room.

They turned round and rushed after him.

Every moment made it more desperate, more fearfully dangerous for Jack Harkaway.

Jack's pluck was good, and his readiness of action was much in his favour, yet a prolonged fight could only end in one way.

He would be at their mercy.

It was but a question of time.

Jack must have known this, yet it did not make him falter for an instant; it did not cause his arm to fall less heavy any time he struck his cowardly foes.

Hunston and Emmerson having both been floored by Jack's strong right arm (the "auctioneer," they used to call it in his fighting days), those two were not so forward in the pursuit of their slippery victim as were Toro and the croupier.

The latter was naturally the more nimble of the two, and so, unfortunately for him, he found himself in at close quarters with Jack before his friends were half across the room.

"This is a regular dinner," said Jack, to himself. "I'll take it out of his ugly mug, whatever I get after."

Quick as lightning, he bored in upon the croupier.

There was no time for the unfortunate man to guard.

Harkaway's fists bored him down like a battering ram, and in that one doughty blow he so decorated his frontispiece that it spoilt his beauty for many a long day.

It was a sight to see our old friend Jack strike out at the cowards, for cowards they were to attack one man.

But soon over and over rolled the croupier like a cricket ball.

As soon as this was done, Jack Harkaway sprang up on the counter.

He was now by the refreshment bar, to which allusion has been made, and seizing one of the nearest bottles, he hurled it at Toro, who was now close in upon him.

It took effect upon Toro's head, and smashing against it, made him howl mightily.

However, it only served to steady him in his rush.

Then on they came in a body to attack.

Now Jack gave a sharp glance about, calculating the chances.

They were pitilessly against him.

However, he kept a good heart—there was, indeed, scarcely time for funking—and boldly faced them, saying—

"Come if you dare; I fear you not. Come one, come all. Jack Harkaway can die, but his enemies shall not live to exult over his death."

"Will you give in?" challenged Hunston.

"No," retorted Harkaway. "Do you think I do not know you, villain? Give in? Ha, ha! You, above all men, should know that giving in is not one of my weaknesses."

"Then in upon him!" shouted Hunston.

Jack snatched up a chair from behind the bar, and driving it down violently, wrenched the back off.

One more snap, and he held one of the legs of the chair; a poor arm wherewith to defend himself against four powerful men.

Now, Hunston's invitation to charge did not meet with a cordial response from his companions, and although they would have liked to have seen him dead at their feet, they could not help fearing him and yet admiring him for his cool pluck.

They had each had a taste of Jack's quality.

Jack Harkaway, perched upon the counter, armed with ever so poor a weapon, was more formidable to look at than Jack Harkaway on their own level, with no better weapons than nature's to help him through.

"Down with him!" cried Hunston, savagely.

"Shall I fetch my barkers and pop him down?" demanded the croupier.

"No."

"Why not?"

"I have my own purpose to fulfil."

"Hang your purpose!" cried Toro, smarting from the blows Jack had given him. "Let us have his blood!"

"So you shall," responded Hunston, with a cruel chuckle, while he fondled his own damaged peeper, "so you shall; plenty of it. But he is to provide us with endless amusement yet, and it would be like the child's trick of cutting open his accordion to look for the music if we were to finish him right off."

Jack returned them a glance of bold defiance.

"Why do you wait?" cried Jack. "I am prepared for you. Shall I commence the attack, as you four seem afraid?"

He knew that if once he fell into their clutches, he must expect scant mercy from them one and all.

Now, while Hunston, Toro, and Emmerson were facing the redoubtable Jack, the croupier disappeared.

Had he funked?

Or had he gone for his "barkers," as he called his pistols?

The men bored in upon Jack, who looked eagerly about, and girded up his loins for the fray.

He did not wait for them to get too near, but seizing a large champagne bottle close to his hand, he grasped it by the neck, and picking out Toro the giant, cried——

"You overgrown beast, take that!"

He swung the bottle round his head, and the next moment Toro fell to the ground.

Then he stood handling his weapon

like a broadsword, and treated them to two of the best-known cuts.

One, two and point.

" One " was Emmerson, and he got it by the side of the head.

" Two " was Hunston, and he caught it full across the face; a precious ugly smack it was, too.

At that moment Toro rose from the ground.

" Point !" cried Jack, and Toro had the nastiest touch of all.

It jobbed two of the giant's teeth down his throat, leaving a gash upon his lip that he kept a mark of to his last hour.

" In on him !" they yelled, now thoroughly roused.

Jack fought like a lion.

He displayed all his old grand form.

But fight like a lion as he did, what could it avail him against such odds?

Jack meant to fall fighting, to fall with his face to the foe.

And he hammered away as merrily as if he had all the chance of gaining the day.

And he decorated the faces and heads generally of his enemies in a way they had by no means reckoned upon.

Suddenly he felt his arms dragged down to his sides with a jerk, and he was held powerless and at the mercy of his bitter assailants.

How was this? Simple enough.

The croupier, who, after Jack's fearful visitation upon his face, had preferred strategy to open fighting, had got a long rope from an inner room, and profiting by his old Mexican hunting experience, lassoed poor Harkaway most dexterously.

Another moment, and Jack Harkaway lay panting upon the floor, pressed down by four cruel, relentless foes, powerless, helpless, and at their mercy.

It looked bad indeed for Harkaway now.

It was indeed a question of minutes.

" We'll have his tongue out at once," said Hunston, feeling for his knife.

Harkaway heard the words and felt uneasy; they were meant for his ear, and Hunston saw Jack Harkaway flinch with feelings akin to delight.

It was a triumph to make his old enemy quail.

But the feeling of fear was only transient, if indeed it ever existed.

And the next moment, Jack raised his head proud and defiant.

" You've not done it yet," he said.

" No, but I will."

" Don't be too sure."

Hunston flourished the knife before his victim's face.

" See that ?" he exclaimed, with a fiend-like grin.

" Pah !" said Jack, with ineffable contempt.

Hunston could dally no longer with his victim.

Revenge was now in his own hands.

" Toro," he cried, " tear open Harkaway's mouth."

But Jack still fought tooth and nail— tooth especially—for he fixed Toro through the hand.

A cry of pain and rage escaped the ruffian.

" Press his throat ! squeeze him !" ejaculated Hunston.

Nothing loth, Emmerson pressed brutally upon Harkaway's windpipe.

A little of this went a very long way.

Harkaway grew purple.

Then his colour deepened; his tongue was at their mercy.

" Now," cried the triumphant Hunston, " for my long-sought revenge."

Jack Harkaway was helpless.

But before Hunston could proceed with his diabolical work, a heavy hand floored him.

Stunned.

Emmerson, with another blow, was sent sprawling in the opposite direction, and Toro was caught by the throat in a grip the like of which he had never felt before.

It was but the work of an instant.

The croupier looked up in amazement.

Two men, whose presence had been utterly unsuspected, had put in an appearance at this most critical time.

These two brave fellows were the two players whom Toro had greedily endeavoured to " hocus," otherwise to drug, and whose schemes had been opportunely frustrated by Harkaway.

The dwarf leapt upon the croupier, and seizing him by both ears, wobbled his head round, until his brain seemed on fire.

This uncomfortable gyration he concluded by a vigorous jerking backward and forward, and then he held his man at his mercy.

The dwarf still held on at the wretched croupier's ears, and bumped his head on the floor, by way of varying the performance.

A curious instrument for knocking nails in, surely.

The croupier was not able to say a word.

Crack, crack, crack, went his unfortunate nob, and now a little one in, and he was thoroughly disposed of for a time.

Now Toro, finding himself attacked thus in the rear, struggled desperately to get to his feet, and then, with a mighty jerk shaking himself free, he turned to face his assailant.

The latter was a long Kentuckian, standing fully as tall as Toro himself.

The Italian had the advantage in weight, and he had never yet met the man who could cope with him for sheer brute strength.

So he closed upon him.

The American, nothing loth, fastened his arms around Toro's huge carcase.

It was a fearful sight to see these two giants locked in each other's embrace, swaying to and fro.

But Toro had strength alone on his side, while the American had both strength and skill.

"I have you now, villain!" came in deep tones from the brave American.

What, then, was the brute Toro's amazement, when he found himself lifted off his feet, and hurled fairly over his adversary's head?

He fell no light weight.

And where he fell he lay still, or nearly still, a slight quiver of his huge carcase, and an occasional dull groan, alone telling that he still lived.

"Jeff, Jeff!" cried the dwarf, at this precise moment.

The other turned, and finding his little friend hard pressed, while protecting the poor Harkaway, by Hunston and Emmerson, he turned sharply round to lend a hand.

"I am with you, lad," he shouted.

Then, catching Hunston by the collar and the waistband, he lifted him up by sheer strength, and with a mighty jerk, hurled him a dozen paces off.

Then he planted his fist heavily in the back of Emmerson's neck, and the ruffian dropped without a murmur.

"Now," said he, coolly, turning to the dwarf. "Now for the door. I'll carry this poor fellow."

And he picked up Harkaway as easily as he would a baby, and bore him to the door.

The enemy tried to arouse and intercept their escape.

But that long, raw-boned Jeff, the American, inspired them all with a wholesome respect.

A moment more, and they were fairly in the street.

Once more was Jack Harkaway out of the toils.

CHAPTER XX.

Mr. Mole started from the hotel early in the morning, and returned to take charge of Emily, Hilda, and her little daughter.

He was not exactly the sort of person to leave in charge of a family, for no sooner had Jack Harkaway and Dick Harvey left, than he gave way to his well-known weakness for stimulants.

The ruby hue of his nose deepened, and it spread like a rich sunset across his cheeks.

His latest fancy was, that it was incumbent upon him to marshal the negro servants upon the plantation and estate generally, in the regular old nigger driver fashion.

The only effect which Mr. Mole's maudlin severity had upon the coloured dependants was to make them laugh a good deal at his expense.

However, his latest illusion was not attended with any baneful results.

The worst was only the purchase of a Legree hat and whip, and an attempt to grow an imperial or fringe on his chin, which was probably the portrait of Legree, which Mr. Mole had seen in some illustrated edition of "Uncle Tom's Cabin."

"HARRY SEIZED THE GIANT'S WRIST WITH HIS TEETH."

His pleasantries went all very well with most of the negro servants; but when he tried it on with Monday, our old friend's dignity was touched.

The worthy black considered himself quite upon a footing with the tutor.

They were in fact both retainers, with this trifling difference, that Monday rendered some really efficient service for what he got from the family.

Mr. Mole called a general meeting of the servants the second day after Harkaway's departure.

This was the occasion for high fun amongst the darkies.

Mr. Mole paraded them all, men, women and children, calling over a muster-roll, to the infinite amusement of them all.

"When I was colonel of the Horse Guards Blue, in Old England," said the truthful Mr. Mole, "we were in the saddle at five a.m., winter and summer."

"Be golly, Massa Mole," said Sunday, chuckling, "you bery fierce orsifer."

"Stern, Sunday, not fierce—I was a disciplinarian."

"Oh!"

"When one has once contracted habits of discipline," said Mr. Mole, "it becomes a sort of second nature to command— some of us are born to command, some to obey. Now, I was born to command."

"Of course, Massa Mole, you look so beautiful and grand."

"Thank you," said Mole, "but, in point of fact, there is a species of military instinct in some of us, which——"

"Massa Mole speaks like a book," said Sunday, producing a bottle of rum from his capacious pocket, and looking slyly round.

As soon as Mr. Mole dropped his eye upon the bottle, he was a lost man.

"Dear me," he said, "I think it is a very warm day, and I really feel terribly thirsty."

He grew thirsty at once on seeing the bottle.

Sunday knew his weakness.

"There's nothing like discipline," said Mr. Mole, rearing himself up so as to lose none of his height. "Nothing like discipline for niggers.

"Sunday," he said, "how dare you have that bottle of rum with you? Bring it here, sir, and place it by my side."

"Quite right, Massa Mole," said Sunday, with gravity.

"If we had had lots of discipline, we should never have had any mutiny, never any rebellion in India."

"You think so?"

"I'm sure so."

"Ah, Massa Mole, you much wanted here."

"What for?"

"To keep de folks in order."

Mr. Mole smiled.

"There's not much fear of mutiny here, Sunday," said he, with a patronising air.

"Dere is just dat, Massa Mole," said Sunday, seriously.

"What?"

"Mutiny."

Mole opened his eyes.

"Impossible."

"No, Massa Mole," returned the negro, shaking his woolly head. "Not impossible. It am a fack."

"You don't really mean——"

"I mean," said Sunday, "dat dem dam niggers is bery pecooliar, and dey'd tink no more ob eating you, Massa Mole, and picking your bones, dan of chivying a 'possum out of a gum tree."

Mr. Mole began to feel, he scarcely knew why, just the least bit uneasy.

"What have they been doing?"

"Nuffin'," answered Sunday. "Dat's jest it, sar. Dey won't do nuffin, wus luck, and when we tries to put 'em to it, dey kicks up most awful rumpagious."

Mr. Mole pulled a long face.

"This is very serious."

"Bery serious, for I heard dem whisper dat you would boil down well."

"Boil down? Dear me; we ought to get assistance immediately."

"Don't want no 'sistance, Massa Mole," said Sunday. "Habits of discipline, you know, Massa Mole—habits of discipline'll make it all right; only wants you to face 'em."

"Ahem!" said Mr. Mole, flattered, yet inwardly uneasy.

"Dey'll never dare to disobey a great man like you, Massa Mole."

"No, Sunday."

"And if they dare——"

"We'll show them the meaning of the word discipline," said Mr. Mole, strutting about.

Sunday went off to summon the black servants, men, women, and children, into the presence of the august Mole.

The latter was deeply interested in a book, when he heard a loud " Yah, yah !" and the whole tribe came clattering down about him.

For a dissatisfied and disaffected people they looked uncommonly merry.

Not one of them wore a serious face.

Indeed, every man Jack appeared to be labouring under a desire to suppress a smile.

" Oh, there you are," said Mr. Mole, looking up at the mob surrounding him. " Now, I want to talk to you."

" Don't talk, Massa Mole," interrupted one of the darkies. " Gib us a song, old nigger Mole."

" What !" ejaculated Mr. Mole, aghast.

" A song."

" What, you wretched creature ?" cried Mole. " I sing a song ! Never. But I demand you to be serious."

" But we don't ; dat's whar it is, Massa Mole, we don't please. So here goes, Massa Mole ; you jine in de chorus."

And a nigger at once began in a loud voice—

> " Old King Mole
>   Was a swipey ole soul,
>   And a swipey ole soul was he ;
>   And he called for his prog,
>   And he called for his grog,
>   But he never cared nuffin' for tea."

" Yah ! yah ! Now, den, you dark angels, all togeder—

> " And he called for his prog,
>   And he called for his grog,
>   But he never cared nuffin' for tea."

Mr. Mole jumped up, and made a rush at the audacious singer, intending to wreak condign vengeance upon him, when a juvenile nigger, who had been distinguishing himself by the boisterousness of his mirth, somehow got between the worthy tutor's legs, and tripped him up.

Poor old Mole went sprawling on the ground.

Thereupon a wild scene occurred.

The niggers, young and old, joined hands in a savage dance around him to the chorus of—

> " And he called for his prog,
>   And he called for his grog,
>   But he never cared nuffin' for tea."

" You scoundrels !" shouted Mr. Mole, shaking his umbrella. " I'll flay you alive—you—you——"

" Once more—chorus !" yelled the lively nigger, whose name was Diogenes Brown.

Round they went again to the same chorus, keeping the circle fast, and defying Mr. Mole's most desperate efforts to get out.

At length Mr. Mole grew furious.

One wild rush, a lunge with his umbrella, and Diogenes Brown was prodded violently in the wind.

Momentarily doubled up, Diogenes Brown howled vociferously.

Then recovering himself, he ducked his head, and butted at Mr. Mole, who jumped on one side, allowing poor Diogenes to career madly past.

Now Diogenes pulled himself up short and turned round.

The laugh had gone against this mirthful nigger.

So he made up his mind to take his turn now.

" You shall repent this," said Mr. Mole, wrathfully. " You think to frighten me, but you shall repent of your audacity, mark my words, for my name is Mole, do you hear ?—Mole !"

" You hear what he says," observed the nigger.

" Yah, yah !" responded the crowd, generally.

" And what ought to be done wid Mole ?"

" Killed !" suggested a voice in the background.

" Drownded !" added another, immediately.

" Hung !"

" Him be nice biled down !" suggested a boy, popping forward saucily.

" What for ?"

" Candles."

" No," said Diogenes, as if considering all the various suggestions, very gravely, " he's not fat enough."

" Roast him over a slow fire," suggested a more inventive nigger. " Make him crackle."

" Good again !" cried Diogenes, who enjoyed Mole's look of blank dismay as these atrocities were coolly suggested.

" Shall I make a fire ?" asked one of the boys.

Mole groaned.

"Have you all gone stark staring mad?" he exclaimed.

They took no notice of his protests of indignation.

"I think we had better not roast him," said Diogenes; "it would make such an infernal smell, as he has no fat on his bones; he'd only frizzle, being such an old bag of bones."

This caused a regular storm of laughter and applause.

Yet Mr. Mole could see nothing in it so very laughable.

Mr. Mole, however, was no particular judge of a joke.

"Yah! yah! I have got an idea," said Diogenes Brown; "he must be either tarred and feathered immediately, or else he must sing 'Old King Mole' upside down."

"Hurrah!" yelled the niggers, with one voice. "'Old King Mole,' upside down."

"Now, then, Massa Mole," said Diogenes, with a grin. "What'll you have?"

"A little warm——"

"No grog, no grog," interrupted Diogenes. "Song first."

"Oh, I thought that it was an invitation," said the unfortunate Mole, "to take a little warm rum."

"Now, then, Massa Mole, you're wasting de time of dis honourable company. Which am it to be? Tarring and feathering—or will you stand on your coker nut and chant?"

"Neither, sir," said Mole.

"You must hab one or de oder."

"Never!"

The niggers then kicked up a fearful row, dancing about Mole, and uttering the wildest yells, until the martial spirit of the disciplinarian Mole was momentarily cowed.

It was really an alarming effect to see a mob of twenty or thirty negroes, kicking up their pick-axe feet at once, and yelling as though they were undergoing the most hideous tortures. Mole shrank affrightedly before them.

"Bring out de tar," commanded Diogenes Brown, "and let it be hot and thick."

"No, no!" shrieked Mole.

"Will you stand on your coker nut?"

"Stand a coker nut?" repeated Mr. Mole. "I'll stand a hundredweight,

my good friends, if you like that refreshment."

"We don't want you to stand no coker nuts," replied Diogenes, "but to get up on your own, and chant, and if you don't double-quick, we mean to tar and feather you. So dere now; dat's our law."

"I'll never do it," cried Mr. Mole. "I'll have you all imprisoned for this—I'll——"

"Will you hab de hot tar?"

"No!" thundered the unhappy Mole. "I don't want it; give it to somebody else."

"No, it is for you. Now up you go."

"Never!"

"Bring out de tar, Pompey," said Diogenes to an ebony urchin, who then started off with a laugh that sounded like a cracker exploding.

"Beware!" cried Mr. Mole. "I'd have you beware."

"Bring out de hot tar."

The little nigger came back struggling under the weight of a huge jar, supposed to contain the tar.

It was the best substitute they could find; and after all, whether you are covered with molasses or tar matters little, so long as it affords a good hold for the feathers.

Mole gave way at the sight.

It was no use holding out further.

Fearful images rose up in his mind of the atrocities of the Indians in our Eastern Empire; of the Africans in their never-ending feuds, and of the horrors perpetrated (according to Fenimore Cooper) by "the noble savage" of North America, and his big heart sank.

Humble pie is not the most digestible of dishes, but Mr. Mole had partaken of it upon previous occasions, and yet contrived to keep up what he thought to be a dignified appearance.

"Oh, dear me, dear me!" he whined. "I shall never be able to do it."

"Well, den, have de tar."

"Stop—here I go."

And Mole tucked in his "tuppenny," and made a first trial.

"One, two, three, and up——"

"Bravo, Massa Mole!" yelled the juvenile niggers, with enthusiasm.

"Higher, higher!" ejaculated Diogenes.

Thus urged, Mr. Mole jerked up violently, and came down a cropper, like " vaulting ambition that o'erleaps itself."

" Oh !" cried he, rubbing himself on the part hurt, " this is more than I expected."

And then you should have heard the niggers laugh when Mr. Mole tried again and found himself suddenly the other way up !

There was one little rascal, for all the world like one of those black rubber babies you have met in the Lowther Arcade, who went frantic with delight.

" Up again, old man !" cried Diogenes.

Mole showed signs of sullen resistance.

" Hot tar !" shouted a nigger.

Up went Mole again.

Now much can be accomplished under the influence of fear, and this time he was within an ace of accomplishing it.

But he swerved a little, and down he came, whack ! cricking his neck a little.

His third essay was made promptly upon the other.

He had actually become ambitious by this time of distinguishing himself, and in his eagerness he contrived to hoist his body like a badly-used corkscrew.

The niggers absolutely yelled with delight.

" Rayther on de off skew whif," said the critical Diogenes. " Once more, Massa Mole. Now, den, sare ; one—two !"

The little India rubber nigger, aided by another, here showed the luckless tutor how it could be done. But the little nigger was held up by the ankles.

" If Massa Mole don't do it dis time," said Diogenes Brown, in an awesome voice, " bring out de tar."

Mole made a frantic attempt, and then rose on his head, with his legs wide apart, and with some little manœuvring managed to find the centre of gravity.

Up he stuck somehow.

A shriek of delight came from the grinning niggers.

But even then Diogenes was not satisfied.

" Now, Massa Mole," he exclaimed, " keep up, and sing away ' Ole King Mole.' "

" Never !" gasped Mole, nearly choking.

" De tar ! de tar ! we will wait no longer," cried Diogenes.

Mr. Mole was helpless in their hands,

so he chanted up this slightly-altered version—

" Good Mister Mole
Was a sober soul,
And a sober soul was he ;
Abjuring grog,
Not caring for prog,
And he stood on his head for a spree."

" No, no !" they shouted, for they would not be put off their own version, which was the composition of young Jack, and had been taught them by him on the sly.

They cried loudly for the original version, and, by dint of threats, were about to prevail, when Sunday and Monday put in an appearance from opposite quarters, both armed.

Thereupon, the niggers scampered off in all directions.

This had been agreed upon between them ; for, of course, although secretly of their own prompting, they could not be supposed to countenance any such indignity being offered to Mr. Mole.

" Well, Massa Mole," said Monday, " they're all gone ; don't be afraid now."

" What ?" ejaculated Mr. Mole ; " afraid ? Who's afraid ?"

" We thought you were, Massa Mole."

" Never !"

" What was dey doing ?" asked Sunday, with an assumption of surprise.

" They ?—nothing," replied the unblushing Mole. " I was merely endeavouring to amuse and instruct them at the same time ; a lesson on the laws of gravity, with practical illustrations. You see, I rather like standing on my head."

" Bery good, Massa Mole," said Sunday, seriously ; " but my opinion is, dat dey'll make short work ob you if dey get a chance—dey're desperate."

" Gracious me ! you cannot mean it."

" Yes, sare ; you'll hab to run for it."

" Where to ?"

" Anywhere—to New York, to Massa Harkaway and de young gentleman."

" What, for assistance ?"

" Yes, sare."

Mr. Mole thought that this was really worth considering.

They did not leave him after that. But they so worked upon his fears, that he resolved to get off that very night.

But what befell our old friend Mole, and how his future life was altered, must be reserved for another chapter.

CHAPTER XXI.

It was a mercy for Jack Harkaway that his preservers had put in an appearance so opportunely, for never in the whole course of his life had he had a narrower squeak.

They had not got a great distance from the gaming house, when two men came up to them at a sharp trot.

"There he is," said one of them.

"No," said the other. "And yet—surely it is."

"Keep clear," replied the Kentuckian, half taking off his coat to prepare for another struggle, "or look out for broken nobs."

"Let me get in front," said the dwarf, springing forward. "Now then, try it on if you dare."

It was rather a comical thing to see this little pigmy protecting his huge companion and the as yet helpless Harkaway.

"You have nothing to fear from us," began one of the men.

"Fear? We don't," retorted the dwarf; "not exactly."

"It is our own friend," said the former speaker, who was none other than Harvey.

"I remember you now," said Harvey's companion to the American. "You were playing in one of the side rooms with two of the thieves."

"Yes."

"And he whom you have there warned you."

"He! Who?" exclaimed the Kentuckian, quickly.

"Why, our poor friend, Harkaway, whom you are carrying."

"Well," cried the big man, in surprise, "blame me if I recognised him."

Jack had by this time revived enough to help himself over the ground, and to thank his two preservers for their timely aid.

"These are friends," he said, smiling faintly.

"Perhaps," responded the big American; "but you don't owe much to their friendship."

This speech cut Dick Harvey to the quick.

"It was no fault of mine, Jack, old boy," he said.

"We thought you had fought out of the place," added Pike.

"Of course you did," returned Harkaway, with warmth; "I know that well; but, as it is, I owe my life to these good gentlemen, for without their help it was all over."

And Jack Harkaway took the hands of the two Americans in his, saying—

"You represent your nation well, for you are both noble fellows, and I thank you.

"I did my best," said Jack, "but four to one were long odds."

"You made a pretty good fight of it alone," said the dwarf. "I saw you playing with them before we came in to help."

They all went off together to the hotel where Harkaway and Dick Harvey were staying.

And as they went along, they each explained the part they had taken in the eventful hour of the past.

It was the following.

Dick Harvey and Pike the detective, when they got into the street, found themselves together, and their first inquiries were for Harkaway.

Not seeing him there, they could only suppose that he had got clear of the house.

But as they went on, they grew a little uneasy, and returned to the scene of the fray, with the intention, in case of need, to force their way into the gaming house.

When Jack's preservers were asked how they came to be lingering in the gaming house after the row, it transpired that they were still suffering from the effects of the drug which had been administered to them.

Suffering is, perhaps, an exaggerated expression for what they felt.

It troubled their heads a bit—just enough to make the little man feel vicious, and resolve to take it out of the scamps who had tried it on.

He took a prime vengeance, as you have seen.

Just as they were thinking of leaving, the row began in the great saloon.

Then followed a smashing of mirrors and lustres, cries, blows, and the lights turned down.

"Let's keep snug," said Mr. Jefferson to his companion, "and watch what is going forward."

"And collect evidence to make sure of them," chuckled the dwarf.

"Evidence is not much good," replied Mr. Jefferson. "Let us take it out of their carcases first."

And so it fell out that, when the desperate skirmish began between Jack Harkaway and the four desperadoes, the giant American and the dwarf were still in the gaming house.

They had a dim sort of idea that a cowardly and treacherous business was proceeding, yet who were the actors in it they would have been puzzled to explain.

But the cries and taunts that the combatants were exchanging roused the listeners.

There is nothing like a strong excitement to chase away the lingering effects of an opiate, and it braced them up for the part they had to play.

To see four men attacking one, was a scene calculated to enlist all their sympathies at once.

But they little thought that they were engaged upon the rescue of the very man who had rendered them such signal service.

*   *   *   *   *

They all went off to Harkaway's hotel together, and wound up the night's excitement in a gathering and general merry-making.

"Tell us all about it, Jack," said his friend Harvey.

"I will," said Harkaway; "but it's thanks to Mr. Jefferson and to Mr. Brand that I have the power of speech left."

"What do you mean by that?" asked Harvey.

"Why, Hunston's avowed purpose was to cut my tongue out."

A groan of horror greeted this.

"The villain!"

"Villain, indeed! He very nearly managed it, too. I can feel the effects of their brutal fingers upon my throat yet."

And, in point of fact, there was pretty good evidence of the severity of the handling Jack Harkaway had suffered.

Around his throat was a deep black ring of bruises where the brutal hands of the would-be assassins had pressed.

While the conversation was proceeding with great animation on all hands, Daniel Pike the detective was observed to be keeping a dead silence.

He was thinking.

There were certain incidents in the late stirring adventures which bore a deeper significance to him than to the rest of the persons engaged in the business.

"It is evident to me," he said, presently, "that we were known by Emmerson and his fellow scoundrels."

"What!" said Harvey. "In spite of our wonderful disguises?"

"Yes."

"I should scarcely believe that possible."

"It is more than possible," returned the detective; "it is a certainty."

"That would make us doubt Saul Garcia's skill."

"Or rather that of his assistant," put in the detective.

"Scarcely."

"How, then, could it be?"

The detective had thought the matter over shrewdly before he pronounced himself, this was evident.

"Do you remember the words of that Jew fellow just before we left?"

"What words?"

"He compared our disguises to Protean Bob's."

"True," returned Harkaway and Harvey, in a breath.

"Which proves that if he was not Emmerson himself, he knew him well."

"Yes, yes."

"And that Emmerson is in the habit of patronising them."

"He almost admitted as much," said Harvey.

"What if Garcia should be in league with him?"

"Do you believe that to be possible?"

"Everything is possible," replied the detective. "But to-morrow morning I'll make it my business to sift the matter thoroughly. I wish my old pal was well, for I miss him much."

*   *   *   *   *

Daniel Pike was not a man to be put easily off his purpose, once resolved on.

Early upon the following morning he went, in company with a well-known officer of the New York secret police, to the shop of Saul Garcia, the Jew wardrobe man and barber.

As luck would have it, they found the worthy Israelite standing upon his own threshold.

He recognised Pike's companion at once, as the quick-sighted officers saw.

Yet the way in which he was upon his guard in a moment was worthy of admiration.

"Good morning, Saul," said the American officer.

The Israelite made a profound obeisance.

"Well, gentlemen. Anything I can do for you?'

He wanted to talk to them in the passage, but the American detective, placing a hand on his shoulder, pushed him gently before them into the shop.

"Forward, Garcia; I want a word or two with you in private," he said.

"Private, sir?" said the Jew; "goodness gracious!"

"There's nothing to alarm you in that, Mr. Garcia."

"Oh, dear no," replied Garcia. "I'm not alarmed at all."

The American detective looked about the place, went to both doors, and having ascertained that there was no fear of immediate interruption, he drew up a chair for himself, at the same time bidding the Jew to be seated.

"I want to ask you a few words concerning a friend and customer of yours," said the American detective.

"Who?"

"One you know well."

"His name?"

"Robert Emmerson," replied the detective.

Saul Garcia never moved a muscle.

He put on a look of well-affected ignorance.

"Don't know him."

The detective looked Saul Garcia fairly into the eyes, as he replied, slowly—

"That's a lie."

The Jew jumped up with an ejaculation of offended dignity, but the officer pushed him back in his chair.

"See here, now, Garcia, don't you try it on. Don't fool away your own time and mine too, or look out for squalls," said he.

"Really, sir, I don't understand you."

"Don't you?" said the American detective, sharply; "then hang me if you precious soon shan't! Now pay attention; Robert Emmerson's wanted. With your help or without your help, we shall have him. If with it, so much the better for you, if without your aid——"

"Well, sir?" said the Jew.

"Why, my honest friend, you will find English and American detectives will be down upon you like death."

"I'm an honest, hard-working man," retorted the Israelite, "and I fear no man, d'ye hear that—d'ye hear that?"

The American detective smiled, and said, softly—

"Oh, yes, I hear it."

"Well, then?"

"But I don't believe it."

"What do you mean?"

"Why, that you are champion liar, Saul Garcia, and that the day that we take Bob Emmerson, without owing anything to your information, you will find a search warrant brought in; you will find a regular rout will be made over your place, for that portable furnace and melting pot, eh, my honest friend?"

The Jew changed colour.

"I don't know what you mean," he faltered.

"Don't you? Then you're a fool. Well, do you know what Emmerson is wanted for?"

"No," said the Jew. "What for?"

"Murder!" cried the detective, placing his mouth close to the Jew's ear.

"Murder! Whose murder?"

And the Jew gave a frightened start backwards, while the American detective's eyes were fixed on his.

"Now you have heard me," said the American, "no humbug; what of Robert Emmerson?"

"I really—I——"

"I shall ask no more. Look to yourself, for you may be wanted."

He turned again towards the door.

"Well, yes, I confess then—that is, I do know Mr. Emmerson. He has been here."

"I thought so."

"But it is very little I know concerning him."

"Tell that little at once," said the detective, "or else I'm off."

"Dear me! dear me!" groaned the Jew; "Mr. Emmerson is a very dangerous man, and very violent."

"Yes."

"And if I should interfere in his business, my life will be in danger."

"You needn't fear," said the American detective, "for when he's bagged, he will never trouble you again."

The Jew looked eagerly at his questioner.

"Do you think that true?"

"I do."

"He's a dangerous man. He wouldn't mind doing anything desperate, and I don't want to be killed; he's such a devil-may-care rascal."

"You need fear nothing. In the first place he will be, as I tell you, very carefully looked after, and in the next place he will never hear from anybody where we got our information. Now listen to me, Saul Garcia."

"I am all ears," said the Jew.

"As the donkey said," muttered Pike.

"With your help, Robert Emmerson will be lodged in limbo. Mark my words; once there, he will be dead to the world."

The Jew's eyes glistened.

He lived in constant fear of Emmerson's violence, and lately had had a series of very ugly dreams about him.

However, once resolved, he made a clean breast of it.

"Emmerson was here last night," he said.

"I thought as much," interrupted Pike.

"He had been trying to make himself up as my assistant, what for I can't say, for he's mighty close, is Bob Emmerson. When some customers came in——"

"Three men?" interrupted Pike, eagerly.

"Yes, sir, and he insisted upon serving them. Do you know that Emmerson is so very violent that I didn't dare to interfere? I had to wait outside——"

"In the passage."

"Yes."

"I see it all now," said Pike, eagerly; "you waited outside, and he took your place."

"Yes."

"And he persuaded the three customers that he was your head man."

"He did—he did."

"And then he changed his dress again, as soon as they were gone."

"Yes."

"For what dress?"

"That of a dark-coloured waiter."

Pike could not repress an exclamation.

"I see it as clear as daylight. What an arrant ass I've been! What a laugh the villain has had at me! But I'll have him yet, as sure as my name's Daniel Pike."

"Daniel Pike! Are you Daniel Pike, the English detective?" cried Saul, in surprise.

"Yes."

Saul Garcia was silent, for he had heard of the great English detective.

"Where is Emmerson now?" said the American.

"Really you mustn't press me for that," whined the Jew; "you mustn't indeed, Mr. Silkey."

"Hullo!" exclaimed the American detective. "I thought that you didn't know my name."

The Jew smiled at his involuntary admission.

"Who doesn't know the clever Mr. Silkey?" he exclaimed. "Who doesn't know President Grant?"

Mr. Silkey was less harsh in his tone when next he spoke.

Yet he pressed his point just as firmly as ever.

"Now, look you here, Saul Garcia," he said. "You know that Emmerson is wanted for murder?"

"So you say, sir."

"Yes, murder of a brutal kind," said Pike; "but Silkey will explain."

"I will," replied the American detective.

Then, turning to the Jew, he said—

"It's the murder of one of your people. A Jew, who was a pal of his, rendered Emmerson all kinds of services, and in return Emmerson struck him to the heart with a knife, and followed it up by striking to death an English detective—a pal of Pike's, and his poor friend Percival's brother."

"Now," said Mr. Silkey, "the man whom Emmerson killed could have sold him for a large sum. Think of that; but being bound together by a sort of old friendship, the Jew wouldn't hear of selling him."

"He wouldn't," exclaimed the Jew, much struck by the recital; "and Bob Emmerson killed him; then I'll do for him."

"Quite proper," said Mr. Silkey.

"I will," said Saul Garcia, excitedly. "Can I rely upon you?"

"Keeping dark?"

"Yes."

"Mum's the word," said Mr. Silkey. "I know the man well."

"Of course you do. And he killed one of my people, did he?"

The Jew ran to the door, and peered eagerly out right and left.

Then he came back, and whispered to Silkey—

"What about your friend? Is he true to our cause?"

"Oh, he's right enough."

"He may be; but I don't mean to speak before any strangers."

"Don't fear," retorted Mr. Silkey. "My friend here has travelled all these thousands of miles to take Bob Emmerson, and take him he must, or be disgraced for ever."

"Very well," said the Jew, evidently now resolved. "I will help your friend."

Then, after a moment's pause, the Jew said—

"Come here close and be cautious. Emmerson is to be found not twenty yards from here, waiting and watching for a favourable opportunity to sneak off."

"Where to?"

"New Orleans."

"Good," said Daniel Pike, smiling at the American detective. "Emmerson's game is over; he's as good as ours."

Was he?

We shall see further on.

CHAPTER XXII.

ISAAC MOLE APPEARS ON THE SCENE AGAIN.

"MR. HARKAWAY?"

"Yes, sir."

"What's his number?"

"We'll send up your name, if you please, sir."

"Well, then, young man, I don't please."

"Very well, sir."

"Very well, sir! Do you know to whom you have the honour of speaking?"

"No, sir."

"Then I'll tell you, and you may convey the news to Mr. Harkaway, if you think fit. Isaac Mole, Esquire, B.A., LL.D."

"And A.S.S.," said the waiter.

"No."

"I should have thought so, sir."

"Tell Mr. Harkaway that Mr. Mole will be very glad to meet him at breakfast."

"Yes, sir."

"And—stop, where is Master Jack—I mean, Master John—'situated?'"

"In the next room to Mr. Harkaway, sir."

"I presume that I may go up to the young gentleman?"

"Really, sir, it is quite against the rules. We should prefer to announce you."

"Very good," said Mr. Mole, with dignity. "I am his tutor and have the total charge of him, but as you please."

"No offence, sir."

"None whatever," returned Mr. Mole. "I shall let the authorities here know that you appeared doubtful as to whether I was not about to clear out the hats and coats in the hall."

"Very good, sir," replied the man, bowing. "I shall know what answer to make to that."

The fact was, that Mr. Mole had only just arrived, and having beguiled the tedium of his journey with rather copious libations, he did not present a very decorous appearance, considering the very early hour.

The man, after some hesitation, asked Mr. Mole to step up to young Jack's room.

Up he went with sundry misgivings.

What should he say for leaving the ladies once more unprotected?

On mature consideration, he would not mention how he had been forced to stand upon his venerable head.

"No—mum about the negro revolt," thought Mr. Mole.

He knocked at young Jack's door.

"Who's there?"

"Me."

"Me—who's me? It sounds like Mr. Mole."

"And so it is Mr. Mole," replied that worthy gentleman. "Mr. Isaac Mole, at your service."

"Mr. Mole!" exclaimed young Jack. "Wait a bit; I'll let you in."

He jumped out of bed as he spoke, and began to slip on some clothes.

Now, Nero slept in a kind of cupboard, situated in a small passage, connecting young Jack's room with the one in which the two poor fatherless lads had been quartered; and no sooner did the monkey hear his young master stirring, than he capered out of bed to shake hands with young Jack.

"Good morning, sir," said young Jack, making him an elegant bow.

Nero grinned, and replied by a bow, rather more formal and stately, if possible.

This tickled young Jack mightily, and he roared again.

Thereupon Nero, who knew that his young master was ripe for fun, capered about the room, kicking up all kinds of antics.

He began by darting off with young Jack's trousers, just as he was about to put them on.

Nero got into them in half a crack.

"Come here," cried young Jack, bolting after him.

Nero waited until Jack was all but on him, and then bolted off, grinning defiance.

Jack, in his shirt, laughing until he was powerless to do any good towards recovering his continuations, made another dash and a grab at Nero.

But the latter kept up the same tactics.

Just as young Jack thought he had got hold of him, off he flew.

And then, when the chase got very hot, Nero flew up the bed furniture, and sat looking down upon young Jack from aloft.

"You rascal!" said his young master, shaking his fist at Nero, and trying to look stern. "I believe you could walk on the ceiling like a fly if you only tried. Come down."

Nero's sole reply was to grin, and begin an active hunt for a flea.

In the midst of this there came another knock at the door.

"Are you forgetting me, Master Jack?" said Mr. Mole.

"No, sir."

"You are rather a long while."

"I have just lost my trousers," replied his pupil.

"What?" ejaculated the astonished pedagogue.

Young Jack, ever alive for fun, had a happy thought.

"Nero shall go and greet him for me, since Nero has bagged my bags."

So he beckoned the monkey, who immediately came down from his perch, and hurriedly finished dressing him.

"Here, Nero," said Jack, "take this towel; hold it over your head this way, and he'll think you are drying your face. You understand?"

Of course he did.

There was precious little that this monkey did not understand.

Jack led him up to the door, and placing Nero in position, with the towel about his head, he opened the door and stood behind it himself.

Mr. Mole rushed in, saying—

"My dear boy!" and commenced hugging Nero.

Nero responded most affectionately.

Dropping his towel, he cuddled Mr. Mole right vigorously.

"Ugh!" shouted the tutor. "Who is it? Oh, hang the monkey! confound the monkey! Here, my boy—come and help me, Jack!"

Mole endeavoured to shake himself free, but Nero would not be denied.

He hung on, caressing Mr. Mole affectionately.

Mole roared and rolled all over the room.

And the more he roared with fright, the more young Jack laughed with glee.

"Come here, Nero," he said. "Come here, sir."

But Nero would not; he still clung close to Mole, rubbing up his hair, and pulling his ears.

"If you don't get off my back," said Mr. Mole, panting with his exertions, "I shall do you a mischief."

Nero's sole response was to transfer Mr. Mole's hat to his own head.

Mole wriggled all over the room, but Nero was like the little old man of the sea in "Sinbad the Sailor."

Nothing could displace him.

"Do you mean to take him off, Jack?" ejaculated the tutor, now goaded to fury; "or shall I slay him?"

"Sorry I can't get him away, Mr. Mole," said young Jack, half convulsed with laughter. "I hope he won't hurt you."

"Hurt me!" said Mr. Mole, indignantly. "He'll kill me."

"I hope not, sir, but he has been showing a craving for human flesh of late."

"Oh! you don't mean he has been eating human flesh."

"I am sorry to say he has," cried Jack.

This was too much for Mole.

Down he flopped on to the ground, and rolled over and over, Nero dancing about him as gracefully as the Highlander doing a caper among the crossed claymores.

"Murder!" yelled Mole, now forgetting his dignity in his fright. "I shall be killed. Somebody come and take him off."

In the midst of this diverting scene, Jack Harkaway the elder appeared at the doorway.

CHAPTER XXIII.

EMILY'S LETTER.

"MR. MOLE!"

"Good gracious me!" said Mr. Mole, jumping up, while his late tormentor bolted away at the sight of Harkaway senior armed with a stick.

"Why, wherever did you come from, Mr. Mole?" asked Harkaway.

"I have only just reached New York," replied Mr. Mole, panting for breath.

"And your reason for coming?"

"Well, nothing in particular," replied Mr. Mole, smoothing his chin. "The fact is, I—I was taking a little exercise, and I—I stepped over."

"Stepped over!" exclaimed Harkaway, in amazement.

It was rather a long step, you will admit.

But Mr. Mole was not a man to stick at trifles, and he fancied that it gave him a rather grand appearance to speak of the journey from Boston to New York as a mere step.

Harkaway's first feeling was of anxiety respecting his wife.

Was she ill? And his noble heart sank within him at the thought.

"I hope that all is well yonder," he said.

"Yes," returned Mr. Mole. "I am the bearer of a letter for you."

"Where is it?"

"That's just what I was asking myself," replied Mr. Mole, who was feeling in his pockets with great energy.

At length he routed it out, and handed it to Harkaway.

He would not have done it had he known its contents, for it was from Emily, and enlightened her husband as to the cause of Mr. Mole's sudden flight.

This is how it ran:—

"My DEAR JACK,—Poor Mr. Mole has been frightened out of his wits. Sunday and Monday have got up a conspiracy and a mock rebellion, and they have played off all kinds of extravagant pranks upon him. The end of it is that he is off in very undignified haste, never suspecting that I know why he was so anxious to get away. I am not sorry to be rid of his presence for awhile, and I shall join you soon unless I hear from you that you are about to return to us. Write to me by next post, that I may hear if you and our dear boy are well.

"EMILY."

"So," said Harkaway, "everyone is well, I hear."

"Oh, yes."

"Nothing wrong at home?"

"No; the real fact is, that there are several reasons for my presence here."

"Indeed!"

"Yes. In the first place, I was getting very anxious about my young pupil."

"Young Jack?"

"Yes."

"Why anxious?"

"I feared that his education might be getting neglected. These are precious moments that he is losing."

"All right," interrupted Harkaway, shortly. "What was the other reason?"

"What is the—oh, I know. My other reason was that I have a friend staying in Fifth Avenue here."

"Indeed."

"Yes, a relation, in fact; and as I have some expectations from him, I could not afford to neglect him."

"How very singular," said Harkaway, apparently taking it all as gospel. "Now I always understood from you that you hadn't a living relative."

"Quite a mistake," said Mr. Mole. "However, there is no particular urgency in all that. How are you getting along here, eh!"

"Moving, Mr. Mole, moving. Hunston is here, and so is his creature, the brigand Toro."

And then he told Mr. Mole all about their old enemies, and the exciting adventures of the previous night at the "Asteroid."

* * * * *

"The worst part of Harkaway," said Mr. Mole, subsequently, "is that he will insist upon rushing into all sorts of dangers. It is no doubt very amusing from his point of view, but I look upon it as an acquired taste; and I shouldn't object to a little peace and quiet."

Poor Mr. Mole!

He little dreamt then that in quitting the country for New York he had popped, in a manner of speaking, out of the frying-pan into the fire.

If he could but have foreseen how unfortunately some of the adventures were to turn out for himself, he would certainly never have left the rebellious negroes even at the risk of being forced into standing upon his head thrice a day.

He naturally preferred standing upon his feet.

Yet he little dreamt that before long he would stand upon his feet for the last time.

This perhaps sounds like a riddle.

Alas! it proved no riddle to him, but a sad reality.

CHAPTER XXIV.

A YOUNG LIFE FADING AWAY.

YOUNG JACK was pleased to get his father in a good humour, for he had a favour to ask him.

It related to the two unfortunate orphan boys.

He was anxious to keep them with him.

Short as the time was that they had been together, a strong affection had already sprung up between them.

Jack had saved their lives.

Of this there could be no doubt, for if they had not succumbed upon that dreadful night to the bitter pangs of hunger, they would have crawled to the river, and with one desperate plunge, have buried their sorrows for evermore beneath the dark waters of the Hudson.

Can you wonder, then, that they should feel a deep and earnest affection for their generous young preserver?

It is natural, too, to love those whom you have served, and young Jack warmly reciprocated the tenderness which the two orphan lads bore him.

Jack could not bear the thought of losing them, so he asked his father to adopt the two boys.

He chose his moment well, and pressing his suit hard, carried his point.

"You have been too good to us," Harry Girdwood would say to young Jack, "and I only hope that we may be able to repay you for all your kindness."

"I am repaid," young Jack would reply, "by the pleasure it gives me to see you getting better."

The younger of the two brothers, poor

boy, had a transparent, waxlike complexion, a dry, hacking cough, and two bright red spots upon his cheeks, which told a sad tale.

Originally a delicate lad, want and privation had undermined his frail constitution and sown in him the seeds of that most fatal of all diseases, consumption.

Harkaway's first care was to have the best medical advice for him that could be got for money.

One of the first physicians of New York saw him, and speedily pronounced his doom.

"Is there any hope for him?" asked Harkaway.

"None."

"Would not a change of climate preserve the poor boy's life?"

The doctor shook his head.

"Nothing could. Care and attention may prolong his life for a month or so, but he is already too far gone. Nothing can save that boy."

"Poor lad," said Harkaway. "Poor boy, it is very dreadful to be doomed so young. His death will lie at Hunston's door—at his and that of his companions in villany, for the boy's father shot himself after they had ruined him at their gambling house."

* * * * *

Now the hunt after Emmerson grew hotter than ever.

But Emmerson was not easily caught.

His cunning, and his remarkable cleverness in the art of disguise, served him in good stead, and he contrived to baffle the vigilance of the officers, Daniel Pike and Silkey, for a considerable time.

On the very day that they had their information from Saul Garcia, the villain Emmerson had shifted his quarters, and without suspecting the Jew of treachery, thought it prudent to avoid his old haunts.

The three confederates, Hunston, Toro, and Emmerson, for the same reason kept apart for awhile, only meeting in secret places.

But the hunt of the detectives grew hotter and hotter.

Now while they had such difficulty in getting upon the scent, Emmerson had contrived to post himself up in the movements of Harkaway and his friends.

And Emmerson swore that he would help Hunston to hunt down Harkaway and his friends for their share in his discomfiture.

"He's a difficult customer to tackle," said Hunston.

"He is, and I almost begin to think with Toro," said Emmerson.

"What?"

"That there is a charm over Jack Harkaway's life."

"Perhaps so; but there cannot be a charm over his boy's life—that we will have," said Hunston.

"We have tried that on before," said Toro.

"Yes," returned Hunston, uncomfortably, "we have, worse luck. But they can't always be so fortunate."

"It looks like it."

"It does indeed," said Emmerson grimly. "But the luck can't always favour them so, and I may as well tell you that I have got a scheme for settling it with this boy—this young Jack."

"What is it?"

"You shall see."

"When?"

"To-night."

"Where?"

"Not a thousand miles from Fifth Avenue," returned Emmerson, significantly. "Come with me, and I promise you a glorious revenge. Such vengeance as you poor haters never dream of."

And then he briefly unfolded to them his diabolical schemes for the destruction of young Jack.

CHAPTER XXV.

THAT same evening, as Harkaway and Dick Harvey were leaving the hotel, an Irishman came up to them with a note.

"Are you Mr. Harkaway, sir?" he asked.

"Yes."

"From Mr. Pike," said the man, presenting his note.

"From Pike?" said Harkaway to himself.

He scanned the note half through, and passed it on to Harvey.

"Shall we go?"

"If you like."

It was not a very inviting place that Pike had appointed for the rendezvous.

The Bowery is not the most refined quarter of New York, and the drinking bar to which Mr. Pike invited them was far frcm being a safe place of resort.

They thought twice, therefore, before setting out.

"Decide," said Harkaway. "Go or stay?"

"Go," said Harvey; "we want to see a little of all sorts while we're here, and I don't know that we could do better than this."

The Irish messenger touched his cap.

"What'll I say, jintlemen?"

"We will go."

"Very good, sirr. Can I drink your honour's health?" returned the man, touching his cap respectfully.

"Yes, but stop. Where are you going?"

"Back to Mr. Pike, your honour."

"Direct?"

"Sure I am that same, sirr."

"Then you can show us the way, as we don't know the ground too well."

The Irishman was taken aback at this.

"I have to be back, sirr, in double quick time," he said.

"So you shall," answered Harkaway; "we are going at once; and, understand, you go with us."

The man was in the act of starting off, but, pulling up short, altered his mind.

"No, I had better go with them," he said to himself; "they might not keep the appointment, they are so very downy."

As he said this, he gave a very significant leer.

They might not have felt so much inclined to keep Mr. Pike's appointment had they noticed the singular behaviour of the Irish messenger.

Suddenly the Irish messenger somehow or other got separated from the two gentlemen when near the appointed place.

And, as they could not find him, they inquired for the address given in the letter sent by Mr. Pike.

But, strangely enough, when they routed out the place, there was no Daniel Pike present.

Nor indeed was the detective known there by either of his names—Pike or Webb.

"We have made a mistake, I think," suggested Harvey.

Harkaway had begun to look very grave by now.

"Either a mistake, or there is something up."

"What do you mean?"

"Can't you guess?"

"Not I."

"What if it is a forgery?"

"The letter?"

"Yes."

Harvey looked blank.

"Is it likely we are sold, Jack?"

"I fear it is," said Harkaway.

They exchanged glances, and although they said nothing, they came to a silent understanding.

They knew each other's thoughts well enough upon the subject.

If the cheat had been practised upon them, the authors of it could only be their old enemies.

What would they have thought had they seen the Irish messenger enter a low drinking bar, and presently emerge therefrom in a fresh rig-out from top to toe?

It was Robert Emmerson, the English murderer.

Soon after this a man presented himself at Harkaway's hotel, asking for Master Harkaway.

Young Jack was with his two new friends and companions, and they had just returned from a stroll with Mr. Mole about the town, when a negro waiter brought them the following message from some strange man who had called.

"A big monkey has been found, sir, and they think it is your Nero."

"Where?"

"Close by."

"Have they given the address?"

"No, sir; the man is waiting to take you there if you will go with him."

"Very well."

This was just after the departure of his father and Dick Harvey for the Bowery.

Young Jack had hardly noticed Nero's absence before the message was brought.

"I will go and get him back," he said. "Will you come with me?"

"You had better not go," said young Girdwood.

"AS YOUNG JACK ENTERED WITH MOLE THERE WAS A SHOUT OF LAUGHTER."

"Why not?"

"I don't know why," replied the boy, "but I think you had better not."

"But I can't leave Nero."

"Send for him."

"I must go myself. He would never go with anybody but me."

"I'm sorry for that," said Harry Girdwood, with a sigh.

"I shall not be long."

"It is not that," answered the sick boy, nervously, "only I wish you wouldn't go at all."

The two others looked at him earnestly.

"Have you any reason, Hal?" asked his brother Oliver.

"I can't say I have," was the reply, "only I feel low-spirited. I feel as if something very unpleasant was going to happen."

"To whom?"

"To Jack and to me, too," added the boy, seriously.

His brother Oliver looked grave at this.

"Hal's down upon his luck to-day," he said, trying to raise a laugh. "Well, and suppose we don't go?"

"Ah, I wish you wouldn't," said Harry Girdwood, eagerly.

His brother made signs to Jack to follow him out of the room.

"Don't you think that someone could go instead of you, Master Jack?" he asked.

"In the first place," was our young hero's reply, "don't call me Master Jack."

"What then?"

"Jack."

"Well, then, Jack."

"Why shouldn't we go?"

"Because Hal says not. He's full of fancies, and he fears that something wrong will happen."

"That," replied young Jack, "is because he is weak and ill; but of course, I don't want him to go if he's afraid."

Oliver Girdwood took him up sharply at this.

"Hal is no coward," he said. "He is no more frightened for himself than I am. He is afraid upon your account, not upon his own."

"No offence, Noll," said young Jack, taking him by the hand. "I did not say that to hurt your feelings."

Oliver Girdwood melted at his young benefactor's generosity.

"I know that well. You are too good, too kind, to mean to hurt our feelings."

Now Mr. Mole had been prowling about until he had got tired, and he made up his mind to have a good long rest, and a snooze over his paper and grog, with his boots off.

Great, then, was his discomfort when he heard the subject mooted.

"Go out at this time of night?" he said.

"I shan't be long," said young Jack.

"You must not go without me," said his tutor.

"Why not?"

"Your father's orders," said Mr. Mole.

"Dad's afraid of everything about me," replied young Jack. "Anyone would think I was sugar and in danger of melting.

"Besides, you needn't get so fierce, Mr. Mole. I don't want to disobey the governor's orders; everybody seems very sore about stepping out, and I believe that everybody would only be glad if anything would happen to my poor Nero; and he's the only friend I've got to care for me."

"Hush, Jack," said Mr. Mole, reprovingly. "Don't I care for you?"

"Well, yes."

"And our young friends here?"

"Yes."

"Then, what do you mean by saying that Nero—that monkey thing—is the only friend you have got?"

"I only mean, Mr. Mole, that I want to go after Nero."

Now Mr. Mole, with all his drawbacks, was really very much attached to his wilful young pupil.

So he gave way and agreed to go in search of the wanderer Nero.

The sick boy made a last effort to dissuade young Jack from going out.

But in vain.

So, finding him determined, he insisted upon accompanying them.

Now, the place to which the man who had come for them was leading them was close by, in fact, so close as to make a guide quite unnecessary.

"You are afraid of the monkey?" he said to young Jack.

"Afraid? No."

"You seem to want a lot of you, sir, to catch him, though."

"No," answered young Jack; "only they will come with me."

"I wouldn't have them," answered the man, sullenly.

"Why not?" asked young Jack, turning sharply upon him. "Why not? And whatever can it be to you whether I go alone, or whether forty people go with me?"

"Me—oh, nothing," was the reply; "I only spoke. It looks as though you were afraid to go alone."

"Don't talk stuff," replied young Jack. "You'll get paid for your trouble, whoever goes. It will make no difference to you."

The man grumbled surlily something indistinct, and led on.

He came to a halt in front of an empty house, at which he pointed.

"There," said he, "that's where he ran in. I tried to get him out, but hang me if I could make him move."

"Because he doesn't know you," suggested Mr. Mole.

"Does he know you?" retorted the man, sharply.

"Yes. That is——"

"Very good. If he does, you'd better go in and look him up. I don't care for the job myself."

"Ahem!"

"Will you go?"

"Why, you see," said Mr. Mole, "I have no fear of the poor monkey, none in the least, but his affection for me is rather too much, and——"

"Of course he does like you," laughed young Jack.

"But I am not the best person to go on a monkey hunt. I might hurt the poor animal, and I would not for worlds."

The man interrupted Mr. Mole with a laugh of derision.

"All right, governor," he said, sneeringly, "you stop here, and I'll go and lock up Jacko, and when I chivy him out, you catch him tight and hold him."

"I will," said Mr. Mole, who could not resist the opening for a bit of brag. "If there is one person more calculated than another to hold Nero, or even a wild tiger, it is myself."

Young Jack could not help laughing at this.

He knew that Mr. Mole was in a mortal fright if Nero ever got near him.

The man entered the house, and shortly afterwards a whistle was heard, and a voice cried—

"Now, young master."

"What's that?"

"For me," said young Jack.

He was about to dart forward into the house, when the younger of the Girdwoods stopped him.

"Don't go in there; pray don't."

"Why not?" said Jack. "You can't think the man means me any harm?"

"I fear he means to murder you."

"But how about you three here?"

"How could we prevent harm here if anything happened to you in the house?"

Again the whistle was heard, and the voice of the man crying out—

"Are you coming, young sir, or shall the monkey escape?"

"No fear. They would never try it on while you were all about here."

While they were speaking, Mr. Mole advanced to the door of the empty house, and peered in.

Then, as there were no signs of anybody, he ventured up a few stairs.

Poor Mole soon got more than he expected.

On ordinary occasions he smelt danger half way, and rather more.

Now that there was real peril before him, he actually put his head into the lion's jaws.

There was a sudden rush, a low but fiercely muttered oath, and Mr. Mole was dashed in the face and sent flying backwards.

So sudden was the assault, and so ferocious, that it sent the luckless tutor over and over, until he lay upon the path, maimed, stunned and senseless.

The three boys were momentarily paralysed with fright.

And before they could regain their presence of mind sufficiently to see after poor Mr. Mole, the attack was followed up from the house.

Two men darted out and made a rush at Jack, clutching him savagely by each arm.

"Hullo!" cried the startled boy. "What's this? Let go your hold."

"Let go," said the elder Girdwood, stepping bravely forward.

But the two men proceeded to drag young Jack off.

One of the men was a perfect giant—

one who could never disguise himself effectually on account of his huge bulk, the villain Toro—and young Jack was like a baby in his grasp.

The other—Hunston—held Jack's left arm powerless.

And together, it was clear, they meant dragging him into the half-finished house.

Young Jack fought hard, and the two Girdwoods fell upon the giant Toro, and fought bravely for Jack.

But struggle as they would, what could they do against such brute strength?

Toro turned savagely upon Noll Girdwood, and drove fiercely at him with his fist, hurling the brave boy senseless and bleeding to the ground.

Young Jack and poor Harry Girdwood alone were left to fight against two such powerful men.

" Ruffians," cried young Jack, " would you murder me ?"

Suddenly a diversion was created in their favour in a way they little expected.

The innocent cause of all these disasters, Nero, at that moment came dashing along from the hotel, and with a single leap bounded upon Toro's shoulders.

Perched up there, he took out a few handfuls of the giant's curly locks.

Then, before Toro could retaliate, he transferred his favours to Hunston, whom he clawed down the face.

Hunston fought like a madman.

But Nero was too much for him.

The sagacious monkey knew that these were the enemies of those who were kindest to him, and so he gratefully threw in his help where it was most needed.

But Toro, intent only upon dragging young Jack into the empty house, had got him off, and was nearly accomplishing his purpose, when young Harry Girdwood sprang upon him and fought desperately.

" You shall not injure Master Jack !" he cried; " I will kill you first, you monster, or die for good Master Jack."

But his feeble strength could not aid him much.

Yet he threatened, by his great activity, to trip the giant up.

So, with a muttered curse upon his lips, Toro pinned young Jack to the wall, and held him powerless, squeezing the very life slowly out of the hapless boy.

With the other he tried to fix upon Harry Girdwood in the same way.

But tried in vain.

The boy was slippery as an eel, and when Toro was nearly fixing him, poor Harry seized the giant's wrist in his teeth, and bit it through.

Toro jerked the poor lad backwards and forwards to free his hand from the teeth of Harry, and then at last threw him heavily to the ground.

Then, seizing his ever ready knife, he struck savagely twice at the boy, and he fell, bathed in blood.

" Help, help !" he murmured, faintly ; " help for Master Jack !"

Then his senses fled.

" Now you're mine," said Toro, with a savage laugh of triumph, and he dragged off Jack into the house.

This probably saved Hunston's eyesight.

Nero's purpose was clearly enough to tear out his enemy's eyes, and Hunston's one arm was scarcely able to guard them from the nimble foe.

Nero no sooner saw his young master going off, than, giving Hunston one more scratch, he jumped after them into the house.

" Hunston—Hunston, this way !" called the giant.

" I'm here," cried his comrade in villany from the foot of the stairs.

" Shut the door."

" I'll see to that."

He bolted it, too, to guard against interruption.

Poor Jack ! it would go very hard with him now.

" What do you want with me ?" asked young Jack, boldly.

The giant replied by knocking him down with his fist.

" What do we want? Why, we're going to kill you," he said, deliberately ; " to kill you slowly, and to let your father know it, so that he may suffer as much in mind as you shall in body."

The boy stood up again defiantly before his captors.

" You may kill me," he said, " because you are stronger, but keep out of my father's way henceforth, for no death that he could invent would be horrible enough for you."

" Silence, cub !"

And the brutal Toro dashed his fist into the bold boy's face again, hurling him to the ground.

CHAPTER XXVI.

Two gentlemen were walking along in the vicinity of Fifth Avenue, when they heard loud cries proceeding from close at hand.

"There's someone in danger, I think," said one of them.

"I heard a cry."

"Which way did it sound?"

"It sounded here to the right."

"Let us listen again."

"Hark!"

"Come along, Jeff, this way," said the dwarf, for it was indeed those two adventurous gentlemen.

They hurried along, guided by the cries of the poor, wounded people, and in two or three minutes came upon the fatal scene.

There lay poor Mole, writhing on the ground in the most horrible suffering.

The boy Oliver Girdwood was still insensible.

But alas for poor Harry Girdwood!

His life blood was ebbing fast from two ghastly wounds in the chest and side.

"Poor boy," said the big Kentuckian, kneeling over the young sufferer. "Poor little fellow."

Harry Girdwood opened his eyes and moaned faintly.

"Poor lad," groaned the Kentuckian, who was a very glutton at taking punishment himself, and yet was ready to show his heart by weeping over the poor little fellow's sufferings. "Who has done this?"

Harry Girdwood struggled vainly to speak at first.

Then, after a moment's pause, he gasped—

"I think it must be some of Emmerson's men——"

"Emmerson's men?"

"Yes."

And the poor boy lay heavy in the big man's arms.

They could scarcely believe that they heard right.

"They rushed out on us and tore Jack Harkaway away," continued Harry.

"Who?—what? Jack Harkaway, did you say?"

"Yes, sir."

"The elder?"

"No, the son."

"Where to? Tell me — tell me. quick, my poor, poor boy!"

"In that empty house."

And then again, overcome by weakness, the unfortunate boy fainted.

"What shall we do with this poor child and the others?" exclaimed Jefferson, looking about him in sore perplexity.

"Leave us here," groaned poor Mr. Mole. "See after my boy—my Jack."

They turned eagerly to Mole for information.

"He's in the house?"

"Yes."

Mr. Jefferson, the brave American, waited for no more, but made a dash at the door.

It was fast.

So fast, in fact, that it would require something more than mere strength to move.

"Darn you, go open!" ejaculated Jefferson.

He literally hurled himself against it.

But although the shock shook the whole house, the door stood firm.

"Try, try, once again," urged Mole, between his groans. "I shall never dare face his mother. Oh, try to save young Jack!"

The doughty Kentuckian needed no urging.

He was performing prodigies as it was.

But that kind-hearted giant, who was ready to cry over the wounded boy, was an ugly customer when he lost his temper.

He had lost it.

Woe be to Hunston if he should get at him now!

Woe be to Toro if they should meet while this rage was on him!

The baffled Kentuckian, in sheer vexation, dashed at the upper panel of the door, and actually splintered it with one blow of his fist.

"Stand out of the way, Jefferson," said his little friend.

"Why?"

"I can do it."

"You?"

"Yes; see here."

He produced a six-shooter from his pocket.

It had been his constant companion since the battle at the "Asteroid."

"It is not bolted, I can see; it is only the lock."

Saying which, he inserted the muzzle of the pistol in the keyhole, and drew the trigger.

A loud explosion followed, and the door flew open.

"Well done. This way!" cried Jefferson, dashing before him.

Up the stairs he flew, followed by the dwarf, and dashed open the first door he came to.

No signs of Jack or of Nero.

"Not here."

"Stop a bit," said the dwarf, rushing in; "I can hear a noise upstairs. They're trying the roof."

* * * * *

Poor young Jack had suffered severely in the meanwhile.

All kinds of small torture which the invention of the cowardly ruffians could suggest were gone into with the cruellest deliberation.

But they had not time to accomplish their diabolical designs, happily for young Jack.

When matters were growing desperate, a pistol-shot was heard below.

It sounded in the house.

Of this there could be no doubt.

"What was that?" said Hunston.

"It was plain enough," replied Toro; "someone firing below."

"They have got in the house."

"What then?"

"It is time for us to get out of the house."

"Bah!"

"Come," said Hunston, seriously, "no foolhardiness, Toro, if you please; there is no use in that."

"Go, and save your own skin, if you like," said Toro, with a sneer; "no one prevents you—only leave me to do as I like; and I like to stop here and face the man that dares to meet me."

Steps were heard upon the stairs.

The moments grew precious now, for in two minutes more it would be too late.

"Do you know what vengeance is?" asked Hunston.

The ex-brigand replied by a fierce oath.

"Do I know what vengeance is?" he ejaculated. "I have tasted its sweets, and I live only to taste them again. I'll have an eye for an eye, a tooth for a tooth, from this hated Harkaway crew —one and all! and I'll begin with——"

"Hark!"

A crash at the adjoining room door.

"It will be too late presently," whispered Hunston, hoarsely.

"Go, then, and leave me," said the brigand.

Just then they could hear the splintering of wood and a heavy tramping of feet to and fro, and a burly voice crying out in angry tones—

"Not here! I'll have the floor up and the walls down brick by brick, but what I'll find him."

Hunston and Toro once more exchanged glances. The latter changed colour.

The giant brigand recognised Jefferson's voice.

Once only in the whole course of his life had he found a man with whom, on the score of sheer brute strength alone, he feared to cope.

This was Jefferson, the American.

And there he was in the house—on the track—in hot pursuit.

Hunston noticed the change in Toro at once.

Passing their lives together, they became so accustomed to each other, that they understood what was passing in each other's mind without a word being spoken to put them upon the scent.

"Come, Toro," he said, "there is yet time to escape."

The giant appeared to be convinced by the arguments of his companion.

"I'll go," he said, "but only on your promise of early vengeance."

"Count upon it."

"I do."

"This way, then. Quick!"

And then, having bound and gagged young Jack, they flew out by a further door, and made for the roof.

At that very moment, Jefferson and the dwarf burst into the room.

The dwarf bounded up to young Jack,

and with a single stroke of a knife, severed the rope which bound him.

Then the gag was hastily removed from the poor boy's mouth.

"Where have they gone?" were Jefferson's first words.

"That way," gasped young Jack, who was well-nigh exhausted, pointing to the door by which they had escaped.

"They shall not escape!" cried Jefferson, darting off.

The dwarf would have followed, but his friend persuaded him to remain.

"Stay and look after young Jack," he said; "they might return. Be prepared."

"Woe betide them if they do," said the dwarf, reproducing his revolver, which had already rendered them such signal service.

Jefferson rushed off in pursuit, but ere he had got far, stopped short.

He heard footsteps on the stairs below.

They had contrived to conceal themselves, perhaps, and doubled on their pursuers.

No sooner had this thought crossed Jefferson, than back he rushed and made for the stairs, but before he could even reach the door, it was dashed open, and Harkaway appeared.

"Mr. Jefferson!" ejaculated Harkaway.

"All right!" cried the Kentuckian, seizing Harkaway's hand and giving it a hurried shake. "I am glad to see you here."

Harkaway was closely followed by Dick Harvey and a whole mob of policemen and volunteers.

By this time a great crowd had been drawn to the spot, partly attracted thither by the cries of the poor unfortunates below, but more especially by the alarming pistol shot by which the lock had been blown off.

"Are they being cared for below?" demanded the big American.

"Yes, our servants are with them."

"Then let the house be surrounded. Let every outlet be guarded," cried Jefferson, excitedly; "for I'd rather lose a thousand dollars than fail to bag those murdering ruffians. Would I had once more that giant brigand in my grip!"

CHAPTER XXVII.

HUNSTON and Toro were too cunning for their pursuers.

The house was ransacked, and every visible outlet guarded. But all in vain.

They could get no trace of them.

How the ruffians had escaped the vigilance of such eager pursuers was no easy matter to guess.

They must surely have possessed some hiding place which baffled the scrutiny of the searchers.

In this way alone could they account for their mysterious disappearance.

When Harkaway and his party returned with the happily-rescued young Jack, the maimed tutor and the two Girdwood boys were already being tended.

And by whom?

Who but the brace of faithful darkies —Messieurs Sunday and Monday?

The protracted stay of Jack Harkaway senior and junior and Dick Harvey had induced the whole family to migrate suddenly, and without previously writing to New York.

They reached here at a very sad time.

It might have been much worse, it is true, but for the proverbial good luck of the Harkaways, which had once more stood the son and heir of the house in good stead.

For the other members of the party it was bad indeed, as you will see.

Oliver Girdwood had come to no particular harm.

A few bruises and a severe shaking, but no bones broken.

With his young brother Harry matters were worse.

A litter was procured, and he was borne tenderly and carefully to the hotel.

But alas! all the tenderness they could bestow, all the care they could give him, could avail him nothing.

The poor boy's hours in this world were numbered.

This was so apparent that they scarcely needed the doctor's confirmation of their fears.

As for poor Mr. Mole, his groans were heartrending when they attempted to move him, and it was evident that he had sustained some very serious hurt.

The fact was that, knowing the worthy tutor to be possessed of no very great courage, they were not inclined to believe him to be as gravely injured as he was, and they were one and all inexpressibly shocked to learn that one of his legs was so cruelly maimed as to render amputation necessary.

The last moments of Harry Girdwood, the poor little orphan boy, were at hand.

His new-found friends were gathered around the poor boy's bed—new-found friends so soon to be lost—in silent sorrow.

Grief was in every face.

His brother and young Jack stood upon either side of his bed, each tenderly clasping a hand, as though they thought thus to hold him back from the grave which was so soon to claim him.

"Don't fret after me, Noll," said the poor boy, with a faint smile at his brother.

The latter could not reply.

He essayed to speak.

But in vain.

The huge lump rose higher and higher in his throat, and threatened to choke him.

Harry gazed sadly at his grief-stricken brother for a moment, and then he turned to young Jack.

"You'll be his brother," he said, "now that I am going—won't you, dear Jack?"

"I will, I will," answered Jack, gulping down a sob that he could not repress.

"And you, Mr. Harkaway," added the dying boy, appealing to Jack's father, who was sorrowfully gazing down upon him.

"What, my child?" said Harkaway, tenderly.

"You'll not forget poor Noll?"

"Never."

"You'll not forget that his brother died in trying to save dear Jack?"

"Forget?" murmured Harkaway, covering his face with his hands. "Can I ever forget? Heaven help you, poor boy!"

It needed not the dying boy's appeal to remind him all this trouble had been brought about by his enemies in their hunger for vengeance upon him.

"There, Noll," said the sufferer, pressing his brother's hand gently, "there, you see it's an ill wind that blows nobody good."

He smiled faintly as he said this.

But the elder Girdwood could not catch his meaning, and some suspicion crossed him that his brother was wandering a little in his mind.

"What do you say, Harry dear?" he asked, gently.

"I say it is an ill wind that blows nobody good. I am carried off, a useless, sickly fellow, no good to anybody."

"Oh, Harry!"

"It's true, and you get young Jack for a brother. You profit by the exchange, Noll, and Jack gets a brother like few fellows have, and—and—I'm quite content to leave this world."

His concluding words were full of meaning.

He was quite resigned to his fate.

He was quite content to die—nay, he was more than content; the prospect of death to him was as welcome as sleep after a laborious day.

His life had known more sorrows than sweets, more tears than smiles, and he looked forward to his rest with feelings akin to pleasure.

The one great sorrow was the separation from his brother.

The severe struggles for bread, the hardships they had undergone together, endeared them to each other with more than an ordinary brotherly affection.

"It might have been worse," pursued the poor boy, looking up at Harkaway; "if I had not been sacrificed, they might have done as much for young Jack. He has a bright future before him, whereas I might have dragged on miserably for some time, and died in great suffering."

"Do you feel any pain now?"

"None."

He closed his eyes as he said this, overcome with weakness.

His strength was ebbing fast now, and this exertion of sustaining a conversation was almost too much for him.

As he lay there, with closed eyes, he sighed and murmured the name of

"Mother" gently, and then lay so still that they thought the end was coming.

So calm, so placid he looked, that even the doctor thought so too, and, with his finger on his lips, he motioned them to silence.

In that dread moment the spectators of this harrowing scene held their breaths, fearful of disturbing the last moments of the fast dying boy, and in the awesome silence the ticking of the clock on the chimney-piece sounded louder and louder.

The two boys, still holding his hands, ever afterwards remembered this dread hour, and never heard the ticking of a clock, but they likened it in their fancy to poor Harry Girdwood's death knell.

And while they were watching thus in sad expectation, the door was gently opened, and two men stepped noiselessly into the room.

One was Daniel Pike.

The other was his comrade Nabley, or Percival, just recovered.

Oliver Girdwood looked up and gave them a nod of recognition.

"Come here, Mr. Nabley," he said, in a whisper.

The detective stepped reverently to the boy's side.

"You have known what it is to lose a brother," said Oliver Girdwood.

"I have," replied the detective, with a sigh; "a murdered brother."

"Remember this scene, then," he added, in low but impressive tones, "and help me in what it must be the purpose of my life to accomplish."

"I will."

The dying boy opened his eyes.

"Let vengeance alone, Noll," he said, gently but earnestly; "leave it to justice, and surer hands than yours or any mortal's. 'Vengeance is mine,' saith the Lord."

Oliver Girdwood hung his head before his dying brother's rebuke.

A change came over the boy's face, and his voice grew weaker and weaker.

"Kiss me, Noll," he said, faintly, "kiss me. I fancy, Noll dear, I can hear our dear mother's voice calling me. Good bye; good bye, Jack dear. God bless you all!"

His lips moved slightly after this, and seemed to form the word "Mother" but no sound came.

A gentle sigh, and all was over.

Poor Harry Girdwood's troubles were ended.

CHAPTER XXVIII.

THE murdered boy was scarcely in his grave before the thirst for vengeance came back in full force upon Noll.

He could not forget how his poor, weak brother had been struck cruelly down by the brigand Toro.

Day and night it was in the boy's thoughts.

Sometimes he would struggle against it.

But all in vain.

The thought of his poor brother's cruel murder goaded him to fury, and he made a deep vow of vengeance.

Once the oath taken, he regarded it as his duty to devote his whole life to the task.

"Yes," he said, and the big tears rolled down his face; "I will track the murderer of my poor brother, even if it costs me my own life!"

How he fulfilled that vow you will learn as you read on.

* * * * *

But now we must return to the worthy Isaac Mole.

His leg was broken in the fall—nothing could save it.

All that skill could do was done, every care and attention that money could procure were of course seen to by his friends.

All to no use.

To do Mr. Mole full justice, he learnt the unpleasant truth with far more self-possession than you would have anticipated.

During his illness, he was nursed with untiring care by a young negress, to whom the patient grew greatly attached.

And after the painful operation of having his broken leg taken off, he could not resist the opportunity of throwing the hatchet, even when down on his back on a bed of sickness, and the young negress believed implicitly in his romancing.

The consequence was that she regarded Mr. Mole as an Admirable Crichton.

Mole, upon his side, looked upon his nurse as a ministering angel, and he did not scruple to tell her as much.

"When I am back in my country, Chloe," said the tutor, "I shall give you some solid proof of my gratitude."

"Oh, sar," the dark Venus would exclaim, quite overwhelmed with his magnanimity; "you bery much too good to poor black gal."

"Not a bit, Chloe," said the patient, with fervour, "for you are an angel."

"Massa Mole, Massa Mole!" exclaimed the nurse, laughing, "why, angels are all bery lilly snow white. I seen lots of pictures of dem beautiful gals, and dem little boys' heads, dat look as if de wings had carried 'em off de little fellars' bodies cause dey too heavy."

"No, Chloe," said Mr. Mole. "No, when I call you an angel, that is a mere figure."

"What dat, Massa Mole?"

"A figure? A figure of speech, you understand."

But it was very evident that she did not understand.

"My figger?" she said, with a half puzzled air. "How you poke fun at a poor gal ob colour, Massa Mole."

At this the invalid made a very vigorous protest.

"Never, Chloe, never; I swear it. I should be the most ungrateful villain alive. Why, you have saved my life by your careful nursing, bless you, Chloe!"

This made the sensitive negress weep.

"Come, come, Chloe, my girl," said Mr. Mole, in great distress, "I don't mean to hurt your feelings; I want, on the contrary, to express my gratitude."

"Oh, sar."

"In fact, Chloe, I intend doing something very handsome indeed for you. I may tell you that, in my own country, I am certainly not King of England, but I am a man of consideration."

"A bery great grand gentleman, I s'pose," said the girl.

"Yes, I am so; in fact, very little is done in my country without my consent," returned the invalid, modestly; "but I leave people to say what they like of me."

"You bery fine handsome man, Massa Mole," said the girl.

"You are a young woman of undoubted taste," said the tutor.

"Glad you tink so, Massa Mole."

"I know so," rejoined Mr. Mole, emphatically; "and let me tell you, Chloe, that at any time you express a wish or ask me a favour, it shall be law."

"You bery much too good, sar, to poor nigger gal."

"Not a bit. Once let me move about the world again, even though on a wooden leg instead of flesh and bone, and you shall see. Come when you will, Chloe," he said, with an air of solemn majesty, which inspired the nurse with awe, "come when you will—ask what you will; if in my power it shall be granted. You hear me, for I have given my kingly word?"

"Yes, sar."

"And you thoroughly understand me?"

"Yes, sar."

"Then bear in mind, any favour you ask shall be granted."

The dusky nurse sat upon the foot of the bed, surveying her patient with undisguised admiration.

"Massa Mole," she said presently, in a tender voice.

"Yes."

"I have something to show you."

"Have you, my good nurse? What is it?"

"Would you like to see the new one now?"

"What new one, Chloe?" asked Mr. Mole, innocently.

"Got something bery handsome."

"What is it?"

"It am like a beautiful leg of a table."

"A leg of a table!" said Mole, looking hard at Chloe.

"Yes; de new leg dey bring you, Massa Mole."

He made a wry face at this.

It was a sad reminder for poor Mole.

"I suppose I must make up my mind to like it. Bring in my timber—ugh!"

According to Chloe's notions, it was rather an ornament to the human form, so she had had it gaudily coloured, with bright green and white in stripes, until it reminded you of one of those rods which land surveyors put to some mysterious use.

"Everyone take you for a great warrior, sar. Dey tink you lose your leg in battle."

"They'll know one thing, Chloe," said Mr. Mole, with a grim smile.

"What dat, Massa Mole?"

"Why, that while I've got that leg to stand upon, I shall never desert my colours."

"Course not."

She looked quite seriously.

"Colours, don't you see, Chloe," said he. "Colours—eh?"

"Yes, sar."

"A joke, Chloe."

But she could not see any joke in this, so the waggish invalid was forced to abandon the attempt.

At length Mr. Mole was sufficiently strong to venture out in all the glory of a spick and span new wooden leg.

His nurse regarded the painted wooden lump with a certain pride.

Consequently she was not a little disappointed when her patient showed a desire to cover it up with the trousers leg.

So she exerted her eloquence to dissuade him, and used as her chief argument the probability of his being looked upon as a veteran warrior.

"They would not be far out, my good Chloe," said Mr. Mole, with a touch of pride, "if they did take me for a warrior."

"Of course not, Massa Mole."

"I have done my share of fighting, I can tell you."

Chloe opened her mouth—it was a good size—to its fullest extent.

"You fight, sar?"

"Yes, Chloe."

"You eber a sojer, sar?"

"Well," said Mr. Mole, "not to say a downright soldier, Chloe, because a soldier might be a mere private. No, I have led brave men to battle, Chloe; I have had kings for my companions, and I have fought and bled with them for days together."

He drew himself up to his full height as he said this.

At first our poor friend Mole made but slow progress upon his new leg.

"It is for all the world like walking upon stilts," said Mr. Mole, "and if any young lady was to ask me to waltz, I really think I should decline that pleasure, for fear of treading on her toes."

However, he soon found that it was not necessary to be born an acrobat to preserve his equilibrium upon a wooden leg.

Chloe accompanied him in his walks abroad at first, until he grew strong and confident in himself; and during those walks Mr. Mole told such wonders, related such astounding scenes of which he was the hero, that she would have thought him a combination of Cæsar, Mungo Park, Hannibal, Robinson Crusoe, and the late Wizard of the North.

And so, in Yankee phraseology, he "piled it on thick," and, what's more, he believed it all himself.

"Do you know, Chloe," he said one day, "you are a very remarkably shrewd girl, and—and it's a pity you are so dark in your complexion."

"Poor nigger," sighed the young nurse.

"Nigger or no nigger," said the tutor, magnanimously, "your heart is whiter than the fairest lady's in the land."

"Lawks! Massa Mole."

"And I shall have to do something very handsome for you."

"I don't want nuffin'."

"I suppose not," said Mr. Mole, "but you will have to be rewarded for your goodness, and you must think it over. A man with all the cares and troubles on his mind that I have, can't always think even. And mark my words, Chloe —are you listening?"

"Yes, sar."

"You must think for yourself what form the reward shall take. Whatever it is, it shall be granted; you have the word of the great Isaac Mole."

The negress stared again and grinned with pleasure.

Meanwhile the kingly promise of the worthy tutor sank deeply into the coloured girl's mind.

She obeyed her patient.

She did think it over.

And when she claimed her reward, the fulfilment of his promise caused Mr. Mole very considerable embarrassment.

What she claimed, you will see all in good time.

CHAPTER XXIX.

Mr. Mole was getting very white about the hair for a long while past, and since he had been in America he had lost his leaden comb with which he was wont to tiddivate his whiskers.

"Ha!" said Mr. Mole, "I am losing my youthful looks. I am afraid I am getting very grey. What shall I do with my whiskers? I certainly must improve them."

"I could dye them for you," said a voice behind Mole.

"You could, Jack?"

"Beautifully."

"Are you sure?"

"Of course," replied his pupil. "Do you want to see a specimen?"

"Well, Jack," answered the tutor, "I certainly should—not that I doubt your skill, but——"

He paused.

"But what, sir?"

"You are, I fear, rather given to practical joking."

"Me, sir?" said innocent Jack, looking demure.

"Yes, Jack, you have inherited that reprehensible weakness, I fear, from your father. But could you really improve my appearance?"

"It would give me great pleasure, sir."

"You really think that you could do it for me, Jack?"

Jack smiled.

"Do it, Mr. Mole? Why, of course I can."

"Well, you shall try."

Mr. Mole sat himself down in a chair as he spoke.

"But have you got the dye handy, Jack?"

"Oh, yes, sir; in one moment."

Young Jack soon got his dye and appliances ready, and he set to work.

"I think a good chestnut brown, Mr. Mole, is as good a colour as a young man of your age could choose. What do you say, sir?"

"Brown is a good colour," said Mole.

"Yes."

"What do you think of black—a raven black?"

"It has got such a 'dyed' look, sir."

"Do you think so?"

"Yes. You look at those old beaux who want to make themselves look juvenile by dyeing; they always choose raven black, as you call it, and what do they look like?"

"Can't say."

"Can't you?" said young Jack. "Then I can. They look for all the world like barber's dummies."

"Then you say brown?"

"Yes."

"My dear Jack, turn my hair a brown colour, but let it be rich and glossy."

"Very well, Mr. Mole. Brown be it."

Jack set to work, and in a remarkably brief space of time, one whisker was completed.

"That's done, sir."

"Let me see it."

Jack rang for a hand glass, and Sunday appeared with it.

"Oh, Massa Mole," said Sunday, "dat one whisker look magnificent."

Mole frowned.

"Sunday," he said, with dignity, "I don't want your criticism upon my personal appearance."

"Why not, sar?"

"Because I can dispense with your taste, or that of any nigger."

Sunday drew himself up and expanded his chest.

"Niggar, Massa Mole?"

"Yes, nigger."

"Am not a niggar a man and a brudder?"

"In a certain—only a certain sense—a very limited sense."

Sunday scratched his wool at this.

"Am dis child in de limited sense, Massa Mole?" he asked. "Am not dis chile de brudder ob Massa Mole?"

The latter made a grimace.

"Not exactly," he said.

"Why not, sar?"

"Because you are an ignorant nigger, a black doll, such as they hang outside the ragshops in my country, and because I am a gentleman, you ebony effigy."

"Don't call names, Massa Mole," said Sunday. "You one day glad to call me brudder, perhaps."

"What?"

"Jes' you tink of what dis niggar tell you, Massa Mole."

"You are cracked, you Snowball," said the tutor, who was in high spirits to-day. "Get out," and Mole took up a boot, and threw it at the head of Sunday, who popped out just in time to save himself.

Soon after, Sunday again came in, saying—

"All right, Massa Mole, all right. I got to take de glass away, Massa Jack."

He grinned at young Jack behind the tutor, and the mischievous Jack nodded in a way to show that he quite understood it all.

There was something wrong in all this.

What could it be?

"Get out, you imp of darkness," said Mr. Mole, getting gayer and younger with the thoughts of banishing his grey hairs.

"You a imp yourself, Massa Mole," said the indignant Sunday.

And he left the room singing.

Mr. Mole heard it, but at first he did not pay any attention to the strain.

He caught a few of the words the next minute, and then he remembered it but too well.

These were the words—

"Mister Mole
    Was a swipey soul,
        And a swipey soul was he,
    Never caring for prog,
    He called for his grog,
        And he never care nuffin' for tea."

"Get out, you scoundrel!" cried Mr. Mole.

He stumped after Sunday's retreating figure to the door, but the negro was out of reach, and laughing derisively at poor Mole.

He turned to young Jack, who was laughing heartily.

"He's a most insolent nigger, Jack," said Mole.

"Yes, sir."

Jack thought it best to agree with his tutor upon this point.

"Ignorant as he is ugly," added Mr. Mole.

"Yes."

"Wanting in respect to his superiors"

"He is, he is," said Jack; "badly wan ing in respect."

"Not but what we are all weak ar frail," said Mr. Mole.

"Not all," said Jack.

"Yea, all," said Mr. Mole; "I affir all. We are but poor worms——"

"Worms!" exclaimed young Jac "How nasty."

"All mere bipeds," groaned Mr. Mol working himself up into a fit of religiou fervour, in his anxiety to do justice to h pupil.

"Not all."

"Yea, all."

"Not all, I say. What is the definitic of biped?"

"Biped is a two-legged animal," r plied Mr. Mole.

"Then you are not a biped," said your Jack, pointing to Mr. Mole's timber toe

"Ahem!" coughed the tutor; "procee from where we were interrupted by th ignorant nigger."

Mr. Mole was so thoroughly satisfie with his first whisker which had bee dyed, and he had seen in the hand glas that he trusted himself implicitly now the hands of his pupil for the rest.

Alas for Mr. Mole! young Jack mea mischief, and he artfully changed the dy pots when the tutor's back was turne and set to work vigorously upon the othe whisker and his scant grey hairs.

A few moments after, Mr. Mole looke rather a singular sight for a dinner part

One whisker was a glossy brown.

The other was a bright blue.

And his grey hair was dyed a fier red.

"Is it done? Have you quite finishe my dear Jack?"

"Yes, sir," said his pupil, hardly ab to contain himself.

"And it looks well?"

"Beautiful."

"Where is the looking glass, Jack?"

"Sunday has taken it away."

"Ring for it."

Jack obeyed, but when Sunday ap peared, it was only to say that he had re turned the glass to its owner, and tha there was not another hand glass disen gaged in the house.

Just then a servant came to tell the that the assembled company was callin for Mr. Mole, and anxious to begin the banquet.

"No matter, I look well and young, I hope," said Mr. Mole; " it is of no consequence. Come, Jack."

"Yes, sir."

So Mr. Mole, conscious of his own commanding figure and personal attractions, strode majestically on.

His step, now more than ever, reminded Jack of his early lessons in arithmetic, and as the door was thrown open by one of the negroes, young Jack announced him from the rear.

"Dot and carry one."

Nero was in the room, and as soon as he heard the voice of his young master, he walked on before Mr. Mole on his hands.

But the only thing which disturbed the majestic movements of the procession was the titillation which Nero's tail occasioned when coming in contact with Mole's rubicund nose.

As they entered, there was a start, a stare of wonder and amazement.

For Mr. Mole, with one whisker dyed brown, the other sky blue, and his bright red head of hair, looked a very comic figure.

The next moment the company generally burst into a loud laughter

CHAPTER XXX.

WE must wander from the fashionable precincts of Fifth Avenue to the less salubrious quarter of New York called The Bowery.

In a dark and ugly back slum there were a number of men assembled, men as dark and ugly as the slum itself.

With these men we have to deal.

Their meeting house was a cellar that somehow or other escaped the vigilance of the police.

The master spirit of these scamps was an Englishman, known as Protean Bob.

These men who now skulked in a cellar, and dared not show up above the surface of the earth in daylight, had not long before been proprietors of a magnificent swindle.

But that one dark night's work at the "Asteroid" had made them marked men.

The police were on their track.

It was only a question of time, when and where they were to be taken.

Their money and present resources were nearly exhausted, and it was very sure that in a very little time indeed they would feel the pangs of hunger.

They endeavoured to keep up their spirits, however, by sundry devices, gambling being their chief occupation as a rule.

The gang at this time had begun to feel the unpleasantness of their position, and they had grown desperate.

"Have a little patience," said Emmerson; "there's no object in going out yet.

Let a few days go by; let the excitement soften down. There is nothing dies away so soon as the ardour of the police."

"But these are not ordinary police," said Hunston. "They have a private grudge against us, as well, to help them to keep to their purpose."

"Curse them!"

"And as for the Harkaway crew, it is not likely that they will forget; they haunt us like our shadows."

"I tell you what," said Toro, savagely, "if I stay here much longer, I shall go mad; I can't endure confinement."

"Stuff!"

"I tell you I would sooner be dead, hung, shot—anything, sooner than be stived up here."

"There's a good chance of that," said Emmerson, significantly.

"Of what?"

"Hanging."

The burly brigand changed colour.

In spite of his boast, the thought of hanging made him quail.

It was not death, for he had faced death in many ways, and with all his infamous qualities he was a brave man.

It was only the manner of the death that filled him with fear.

"I'll thank you, Emmerson," he said, sternly, "not to joke with me."

"I don't joke."

"What do you mean then? There's no such thing as hanging for gambling, or anything short of—of——"

"Murder ?"

"Yes."

"Of course not."

"Well, then ?"

"Well, then, what if I told you that the boy Girdwood is dead, that warrants are out, and a heavy reward offered by Harkaway; so large a reward that the whole of the New York force is on its mettle ?"

"Ugh !"

"The halter is as good as round your neck; it is only a question of days. Follow my advice, and I may yet save you."

"I will."

"Lie snug here, let the noise blow over a bit, and—who knows ?—they may begin to think that we had got away before the hue and cry was raised, and are now at San Francisco, or New Orleans, or goodness knows where."

"But, in the meantime, what are we to do ?"

"For what ?"

"Food."

"Leave it to me."

He had a scheme of his own in his head, but wanted to put its efficacy to a great test, as you will see.

Later in the day there was a knock at the door, that threw them all into a momentary excitement.

"The guilty thief doth fear each bush an officer."

Hunston ran up the stone steps, opened the wooden trap a little way, and peered through the iron grating.

"Who's there ?"

"A poor old man who wants relief."

"Be off."

And he abruptly terminated the interview by banging to the trap.

But the man was not to be got rid of. He rapped again.

"Let me in; I am a friend."

Hunston paused at the words.

"What do you want ?"

"I bring a message."

"Who from ?"

"I'll give no answer from the street here. Let me in, or I'll go back to him; just as you please."

Hunston turned to his companions.

"Shall I let him in ?"

"Yes."

"Is it prudent ?"

"There can be no harm; such a poor old worm."

The door was unbarred, and opened just sufficiently wide to let the old man squeeze in.

Then it was immediately shut and carefully barred.

The old man was white-haired, and bent nearly double with age and infirmity.

"Now, then," said Hunston, "what is your message ?"

"Wait a bit, young man, until I've got my wind."

"Hang your wind; say what you've got to say and get off, will you ?"

But never was there a more aggravating old man.

He puffed and blowed, and blowed and puffed, and grunted with rheumatic pains until they were, one and all of them, goaded to fury.

"Who is your message from ?" demanded Toro.

"From Mr.—but there's no one here you mind me speaking before ?" he asked, looking about him suspiciously.

"No, no."

"All friends here ?"

"Yes."

"Then I am sent here by Mr. Emmerson."

"Emmerson ! Why, he is here."

"It's odd to me if he is," returned the old man. "Ugh, my back !"

They looked about for Emmerson.

But surely enough he was absent.

This astonished them all the more inasmuch as their present hiding-place was anything but spacious.

How Emmerson had contrived to slip out unobserved, was rather a puzzle.

"I left him at the corner of the street yonder," said the old man.

"Why didn't he come himself ?" asked Hunston, suspiciously.

"Because he was watched by two men."

"Did he say who the two men were ?"

"Pike and Nabley, the English detectives."

"Confusion !"

"It is all up with us."

"Curse his venturesome spirit !" said Hunston. "Emmerson has ruined us. It strikes me we're caged here."

"Like so many rats in a trap," said the giant Toro, with an oath.

"Softly, softly," said the old man; "while you are blaming him for imprudence, think of your own conduct."

JACK HARKAWAY AND HIS SON'S ADVENTURES.

"YOUNG JACK AND MR. MOLE THINK THEMSELVES GOOD PORTRAIT PAINTERS."

"What do you mean?"

"Why, in the first place, in letting me in."

"You brought a message from Emmerson."

"You've only my word for it," said the old man, sharply.

"But you don't mean to tell us——"

"That it is false—yes, I do—and what if I told you that, instead of being the old man I appear to be, I am Daniel Pike, the detective?"

Saying which, he jumped back, tossed off his broad-brimmed hat and snowy locks, and presented two pistols at the astounded men.

CHAPTER XXXI.

"Pike!" The gang was taken by surprise. So judiciously was his place taken, that the sham old man covered all with his pistols.

"Ha, ha, ha!" he laughed; "you are a pretty set of fellows, 'pon my life, all of you taken by surprise by a feeble old man. Now, I'll show you that I'm more than a match for you, even without my barkers."

Saying which, he threw down his pistols and folded his arms.

This looked like a very imprudent move, indeed.

In a moment they ran in upon him, and held him powerless.

Instead of fighting for freedom, nay, instead of manifesting the least alarm at what had taken place, the sham old man burst into a boisterous fit of laughter.

"You shall suffer for this, my friend," said Hunston.

"Shall I?"

"Indeed, you shall."

"And who will—stop," he added, pulling himself up short; "I'll wager you ten dollars that I get out of this with a whole skin, and make you all heartily ashamed that I have had all the laugh to myself, in spite of you."

Suddenly he jerked himself free of his captors, and whipped ten dollars in silver from his pocket.

"There's my money down," he said. "Are you afraid to bet me, all of you? What, the intrepid Toro, the daring Toro, afraid to bet ten dollars, when the odds are ten to one in his favour, and I offer to bet level? The brave Toro. Oh, oh, oh!"

Now, the ex-brigand was so much surprised by the fellow's audacious taunts, that he blurted out his acceptance of the challenge to bet.

"You do? Very good, then; see here," said the sham old man.

And at this he took off his mutton-chop whiskers and horsey cravat, with which he had contrived to disguise himself as Daniel Pike.

And then, this very slight change effected, he stood before them, as large as life, as Protean Bob.

Yes, it was indeed so, the notorious Robert Emmerson himself.

They stared at him in a half frightened way, silent, stupid, gaping.

Wonder, amazement, fear, curiosity, were all blended in their faces.

"Emmerson!" ejaculated one, whose amazement overcame him. "Is it possible?"

"Yes, it is."

"Hang it all, he has won," cried Hunston.

"Where are your ten dollars, Toro?" asked Emmerson.

Toro growled out something in a very ungracious spirit, something to the effect that he did not care to be made a fool of.

"It would take a cleverer man than Robert Emmerson," said Protean Bob, with a laugh, "to make a fool of you, Toro; you're such a precious blockhead already."

At this they laughed so boisterously that the peppery Italian was goaded to boiling heat.

But they all felt anxious to know how Emmerson had got out unobserved.

"You were nearly all asleep," said Emmerson.

"Yes, granted," said Hunston; "but I don't quite see how you got hold of your rig-out."

"Easily enough. I have plenty of friends."

"But was it not dangerous to let them know where you were?"

"I did not tell them where I was hiding."

"That's right."

"I'm not quite a fool."

"But you haven't told us," said Hunston, "where and how you got hold of your togs."

"Easily enough. You know Saul?"

"Isn't it precious dangerous to go there?"

"Deuce a bit."

"I wouldn't trust Saul Garcia, nor any man."

Emmerson laughed at their fears.

"I'd sooner trust Garcia than any man I know," he said; "Garcia is bound to me by something stronger than love or self-interest."

"What is that?"

"Fear."

"Do you think so?"

"I know so," responded Emmerson, emphatically. "Saul Garcia daren't betray me if he could."

"Why not?"

"Because he knows I'd have his life for it. No, no, there's no fear of his trying on his tricks with Robert Emmerson."

How differently would he have thought, could he have looked into Saul Garcia's private room at that precise moment.

Little did he dream that, while he had been there effecting his metamorphosis under the Jew's cunning touch, a message had been sent to scour the town for Daniel Pike and Nabley—otherwise Percival.

"You think I can venture forth in safety now?" asked Emmerson.

"I should think you could," said Hunston. "I am not given to complimenting, but in your rig-up you might deceive the mother that bore you."

It was true.

Had Robert Emmerson been a different man, he would have made an actor of the first rank, for he executed each part with a finish which a veteran actor might have been proud of after a hundred representations.

"Now," said he to his comrades, when they had recovered from their surprise, "I'll tell you what my plans are."

And then he gave them a sketch of his purpose, which was to put Pike and Nabley off the scent by having forged letters written, purporting to come from the very opposite direction to that in which this exciting scene had taken place.

But he had not taken one contingency into his calculations.

This was the treachery of Saul Garcia, his masquerading friend.

He would have felt less easy had he seen Garcia send a fleet-footed messenger out by the side door while he (Emmerson) was there changing his dress.

Robert Emmerson little dreamt what a narrow escape he had.

By some strange accident Oliver Girdwood, who received the Jew's message, did not know where to put his hand upon Daniel Pike.

However, he was ready himself.

A dress had been provided for him by the far-seeing Pike, and within a few minutes after an old woman left the hotel, and hurried to the house of Saul Garcia, where she crept into a doorway nearly opposite, and watched and waited with patience.

She knew well that it was a dangerous business that they had engaged in, and that haste or rashness might mar all.

And when Robert Emmerson, disguised in his broad-brimmed hat and long, lank white hair, hobbled and tottered along on a stick Bowerywards, the old woman followed like his shadow until she had seen him housed.

Then, shaking her fist at the door, she exclaimed to herself—

"At length I have trapped you."

Hurrying along, she was nearing the hotel when she plumped into the arms of Daniel Pike.

"Hullo, madam!" exclaimed the detective.

"Mr. Pike."

"That's me."

The old woman lifted her veil, and disclosed the features of the boy Oliver Girdwood.

"You!" ejaculated Pike. "What—what's up, lad?"

"I've found them."

"Who?"

"The gang."

"Are you sure?" said the detective, subduing his voice and growing wonderfully interested.

"I am, and can lead you to them when you please."

"Then they are caged before many hours are over," said Daniel Pike, em-phatically. "Nothing shall save them. Once let Nabley's and my grip be upon them, and the villains are all doomed men."

CHAPTER XXXII.

MR. MOLE'S MATRIMONIAL VIEWS.

"MR. MOLE."

"Jack."

"Good gracious !"

"What can have happened ?"

"Something surely is wrong."

Then another burst of laughter.

Such was Mr. Mole's greeting as he entered the room.

Mr. Mole smiled benignly upon the company.

He took the sensation which his appearance caused as a compliment to his personal appearance.

He did not catch their various exclamations, but could only judge from their manners that his entrance was a success.

It was certainly unfortunate that Nero should flourish the tip of his tail in Mr. Mole's face, for as it tickled his nose, it detracted in some slight degree from his dignity.

Young Jack had hold of his tutor's arm, and he kept a little behind him, as he had great difficulty in repressing his laughter.

At the end of the room stood Mr. Mole's faithful nurse Chloe, and she was grinning from ear to ear at the quaint figure her late patient presented.

Beside Harvey sat Hilda, who was very considerably amused at the sight of Mr. Mole.

Close by the door sat Jack Harkaway himself, and leaning over his chair was Emily, who, albeit amused at the scene, did not think that she ought to laugh in the presence of the culprit, her beloved boy Jack.

As for Harkaway senior, he wore a mingled expression of amusement and anger.

Still, they did not like to tell Mr. Mole how brilliant his hirsute adornments had become.

Indeed, Mr. Mole's eccentricities took such extravagant flights, that they scarcely knew what to think.

Had he dyed himself in this gaudy manner purposely ?

Was it his idea that he was beautified by this parti-coloured figurehead ?

Mr. Mole took his seat at the head of the table, in the place reserved for him.

"I am very glad to see you among us again, Mr. Mole," said Harkaway.

"And I, too," said Dick.

"And so am I," said Emily.

"And I."

"And all of us."

And they were, too.

With all his weaknesses, they were really very fond of Mr. Mole; and he, on his part, bore them one and all great affection.

"I am very glad indeed," said the gratified Mole, "very. It gladdens the heart to be once more with you, to look around and see all the kindly faces I have learnt to love and esteem so many years."

The old gentleman's eyes were moist when he spoke, moist with genuine emotion; and when young Jack saw his quivering lip, and heard his faltering voice, his heart smote him, and he began to look upon himself as a hardened young villain.

"I ought to have a good beating for that," he thought.

"Mr. Mole," said Harvey, presently, "fill your glass, and, company all, bumpers round."

"Hear, hear !"

"I want to give you a toast."

All the glasses were fully charged.

"Ladies and gentlemen," said Dick, "I may say ladies especially, for the object of this toast is a favourite with the sex, an unusual favourite, I may say."

He fixed his eyes upon the blushing Mole.

"Come, now," he murmured, in gentle remonstrance, "I say, Harvey."

"I repeat, an unusual favourite. I have to propose a toast which will, I am sure, be drunk with the greatest enthusiasm and sincerity. I need not beat about the bush at all, ladies and gentlemen; I give you the long life and happiness of Mr. Isaac Mole, and may his shadow never grow less, may his whiskers never be less brilliant."

A roar of laughter greeted this, then a volley of cheers, and when the enthusiasm had somewhat subsided, Mr. Mole got on his legs—we beg pardon, his leg, and made a suitable acknowledgment.

These were his words—

"Ladies and gentlemen, and good, kind friends all, accept, in as few words as possible, my warmest thanks. You are too good to me."

"No, no," from Harvey.

"You are indeed."

"Not a bit."

"I maintain that you are far too good. I hope I am duly sensible of your kindness, although I can never repay it; I say I hope I am. I have had the honour of being tutor to our good friend on my right; I have the honour of officiating in a like capacity to his son, a good and warm-hearted boy as ever breathed."

Young Jack thought himself a greater villain than ever when his tutor began to sound his praises.

"And," added Mr. Mole, impressively, "I may live to grow grey in the service, as who may not, for grey hairs bring no dishonour; grey hairs, I say."

"Nor blue ones either," murmured Dick Harvey.

"I beg pardon, Mr. Harvey," said the tutor.

"Pray don't."

"Oh! Well, as I was saying, when I grow old and grey in the service, the recollection of this day will be one of the proudest and happiest reminiscences in my chequered career. And now, in returning thanks to you, let me couple with my acknowledgments the name of my good nurse, who has helped very materially to procure me the indescribable happiness of meeting you here."

"Hear, hear!"

"I allude to the worthy Chloe."

"Let's give her a cheer," said Dick.

"Yes, yes," said young Jack.

"Now then; hip, hip——"

"Stop a bit," said young Jack; "let me give the time, for this must be a royal one. Here's the health of Coaley."

"Chloe!" ejaculated Mr. Mole. "Come, come, Master Jack!"

"I mean Chloe; a slip of the tongue."

"I hope, Jack," Mole said, seriously, "that it was no reflection upon my nurse's colour."

"I don't see it," said young Jack.

"Chloe—Coaley," explained Mr. Mole; "black face."

"Oh-h-h, dear!" ejaculated the boy, as if he had just lighted upon some wonderful discovery; "Coaley—I couldn't think of that. She doesn't wear a fantail."

"A what?" ejaculated the preceptor, aghast.

"A fantail hat."

Mr. Mole groaned.

"Besides," continued the irrepressible Jack, looking around and seeing everyone laughing at him, "I shouldn't have gone so far as Coaley if I had wanted to use an expressive name."

"I thought not."

"No, sir," said his pupil, demurely; "the line must be drawn somewhere."

Mr. Mole nodded, and smiled approvingly.

"No, sir," concluded young Jack; "I should have drawn the line at Chummy."

"Chummy!"

"Yes, sir."

And then, before the amazed tutor could offer a word of remonstrance, young Jack led off the cheering.

"Nine times nine," cried the boy, "and a little one in."

Chloe stood by with a beaming countenance.

"I have told my good, kind nurse, Chloe," said Mr. Mole, with his old touch of grandeur, as he returned to the subject, "that she has only to ask to have; that any gift she may claim of me, if in my power, shall be granted."

"Yes, sar," said Chloe.

"I wish it to be some lasting token of my esteem and gratitude. I think, perhaps," he added, looking around him, "that there is no time like the present."

"The present you mean to make Chloe?" asked young Jack.

"Present?—oh, I see. No, no; present

time. So, Chloe, my kind nurse, make your claim now."

The black nurse smiled, and showed the finest set of teeth in the company.

She wriggled about, and then gnawed at her coloured cotton handkerchief.

Then she burst out into a loud laugh.

It was a laugh that told of a long-suppressed mirth, and it caught the company one and all.

In a moment they were laughing one and all, in the noisiest manner possible.

And all about what?

Nobody knew.

Chloe did probably, but the notion that so caught hold of her risible faculties was anything but a joke.

It was, in fact, a very serious matter, which she thought of very seriously.

"Have you anything to claim now you have done laughing?" demanded Mr. Mole, grandly.

Off she started again; and when she could speak she said—

"Must I ask here, sar?"

"Of course."

"Before Massa Jack?"

"Yes, certainly."

"And Massa Harvey too?"

"Dear, dear me," exclaimed the tutor, irritably; "of course, Chloe. Why not?"

"Because dey laugh," said Chloe, simpering.

This, as you may suppose, set them off again.

"Well, Chloe, what can I do for you? What boon have you to claim at my hands?"

"You won't refuse?"

"Is not my word plighted?" demanded Mr. Mole, loftily.

"Den, Massa Mole," said Chloe, hiding her face in her handkerchief for very shame, "den, sar, I ask you to be my husband."

Had a thunderbolt fallen in their midst, the effect could not have been more stunning.

Mr. Mole gasped—

"Husband!"

The company looked from one to the other, and then every eye was fixed upon young Jack.

They thought this was his work.

"Your what, my good girl?" demanded Mr. Mole, gasping for breath.

"My husband, sar," repeated Chloe. "My beautiful husband, with um wooden leg."

A long silence took place, Mr. Mole looking the picture of astonishment, glaring at Chloe with his mouth wide open.

At last he said—

"Are you dreaming, Chloe?"

"No, sar, I'se wide awake."

"And you mean——"

"Yes, sar. Dere, now, you gwine to refuse me; I thought so. You laugh at me, sar, 'cause I'se a poor nigger."

And then she set up a howl, and buried her face in her handkerchief.

Poor Mr. Mole looked about him in distress.

"Don't cry, Chloe," he said; "I don't wish to repay your kindness in that way. Just think of something else. It will oblige me."

"Don't want nuffin' else," sobbed the nurse; "I want only you."

And she turned to the door, hanging her head, really overcome with grief and shame.

Then Mr. Mole's good part showed uppermost.

"Stop a bit, Chloe, my good girl, stop," he cried. "It is very distressing; but do you really mean it?"

She nodded.

She was too grief-stricken to speak.

"Then," said he, looking around him with an air of determination, "Isaac Mole is a man of his word. I'll keep my promise."

"You'll marry me, sar?"

"Yes."

Silent amazement was upon the face of everyone.

In a minute it was broken by young Jack.

"Here's three cheers for Mr. Mole. Hip!—hip!—hip!—hurrah!"

And the company responded with a will.

"Now one more for Mrs. Mole that is to be."

CHAPTER XXXIII.

YOUNG JACK LETS MR. MOLE INTO A SECRET.

SOME time had elapsed since the performance of the little trick which produced such a startling transmogrification in Mr. Mole's hair and whiskers.

The effects of the hair dye had not disappeared, and the irritating recollection of the practical joke still floated unpleasantly in the mind of the tutor.

One morning, after breakfast, he was moodily taking stock of himself in the mirror.

The result of his personal inspection was anything but satisfactory, and at length, addressing himself to his own reflection in the glass, he exclaimed, in a fretful tone of reproof—

"Mole, Mole, your personal appearance is getting very mouldy."

"What's getting very mouldy?" inquired a light voice behind him.

Turning sharply round, the tutor beheld at his elbow his hopeful pupil, young Jack Harkaway.

The sight of the latter brought his wrongs vividly before him in an instant, and he answered, snappishly—

"You ought to know, sir, why I look so mouldy."

Young Jack shook his curly head in the most innocently unconscious manner.

"No, I don't, indeed," he replied.

"Look at my hair, sir," said his tutor, imperatively ; "look attentively."

Jack looked attentively with both his eyes.

"Now, then," continued Mr. Mole, "have the goodness to tell me what my head of hair and whiskers look like."

"It all looks as if it had been well peppered, or struck by all the colours of the rainbow," returned Jack, throwing a scrutinizing look into his features.

"Well peppered, sir, and the colours of the rainbow?" echoed Mr. Mole, aghast.

"With white pepper and a little nutmeg, helped with the beautiful colours of brown, blue and red," added young Jack, coolly.

"Jack, Jack," cried his angry tutor, " I'm surprised at the levity of your remarks. When you look at me, don't you feel the stings of remorse very acutely, eh, sir ?"

"Not very, sir," returned our hero, with refreshing candour, feeling strongly inclined to laugh.

"What, not after the abominable trick you played me ?" cried Mr. Mole.

"Trick, sir ! I didn't play you any trick, sir."

"Jack, you are worse than your father was at your age," exclaimed the tutor, who was rapidly working himself up into a great passion. "If it hadn't been for that infernal stuff you applied to my hair, and——"

"Oh, Mr. Mole," interrupted our hero, vehemently, "I hope you don't believe that was my doing."

"But I tell you I do believe it," returned Mr. Mole, emphatically.

"Then I am very sorry, for you're quite mistaken, I assure you."

"Mistaken ?"

"Yes, sir."

"Impossible !" angrily exclaimed Mr. Mole. "Didn't I confide to you the secret that I was getting mouldy and wished to dye—a—that is, I mean, restore the natural colour of my once beautiful hair ?"

"You did, sir."

"Didn't you procure me a bottle of liquid hair restorer ?"

"Quite true."

"And didn't you, instead, bring me some vile concoction ?"

"No, sir," interrupted young Jack, with all the boldness of unimpeachable innocence. "The vile ' concoction' was not my fault."

"The deuce it wasn't !" exclaimed Mr. Mole. "Whose fault was it, then ?"

Jack was silent.

"Tell me, my dear Jack. I'm sure you know, and I will have revenge ; yes, Jack, revenge."

"Well, sir," resumed our hero at length, with well-feigned hesitation, "I don't like the idea of splitting upon others ; still, I must say I think such a disgraceful trick as this deserves to be exposed."

"Undoubtedly it does, my dear boy; you are quite right. I honour your sentiments; go on, pray."

"I hope you won't say I told you," said Jack.

"Not a word, not a word," protested Mole, eagerly.

"Well, then," continued his pupil, "I entrusted the purchasing of the hair dye to Sunday."

"Did you, indeed—to that rascally nigger?" ejaculated the tutor, in a tone of dismay.

"Yes, and he promised to get me some of a lovely chestnut brown."

"Chestnut brown, ha, ha!" laughed Mr. Mole, hysterically, at the horrible absurdity of the idea. Ha, ha! sky blue and red."

"Well?"

"Well, it seems Sunday took Monday——"

"Another rascally nigger," growled Mr. Mole.

"Yes—into his confidence, and they must have made up their minds to play this trick upon you, for they bought the dye together."

"Yes, yes; I see it all now clearly enough; two rascally niggers in the plot," almost gasped Mr. Mole. "Bless my soul! it's a wonder I wasn't dyed the colours of the rainbow all over."

"It was a cruel joke on their parts, very cruel," remarked Jack, shaking his head reprovingly; "and on the very night, too, that the lovely Chloe asked you to make her happy."

"Cruel!" echoed his tutor, savagely; "it was diabolical. And you gave these sooty vagabonds the money to purchase the—the—hair restorer, and they——"

"Brought me three bottles, which I used as the labels directed," affirmed Jack.

"Oh, they were labelled, were they?"

"Yes, sir. No 1. Right whisker; 2. Left whisker; 3. For his nob, to be well rubbed in."

Mr. Mole stamped his foot, and rubbed his head fiercely.

"I'll give them something for their nobs for this," he growled, through his clenched teeth. "I will, the ugly black beggars! Ugh! how I hate black niggers!"

"I wonder, for my part," said young Jack, who was trying to draw out his preceptor, "why 'black niggers' were ever allowed to come into the world at all."

Just at this moment, a peculiar sound became audible from without.

Like one or more persons endeavouring to smother a laugh.

The voices, too, had a remarkable resemblance to the voices of the two niggers Sunday and Monday.

But Mr. Mole, in his angry excitement, was striding up and down the room, and did not hear them.

Our hero did, but took no notice, being more profitably employed.

Like a true scion of the Harkaways, he never lost a chance of a bit of practical fun, and had taken advantage of his tutor's absorption to fix a pin in the seat of his armchair.

It was a very nice sharp one, and of course the point was uppermost.

This being comfortably arranged, Jack went up to Mr. Mole, and laid his hand gently on his arm.

"I hope, sir," he said, entreatingly, "you'll forgive poor Sunday and Monday."

"Forgive them?" growled the preceptor, catching sight of himself in the glass. "Ugh! I should like to smash the pair of them."

"But they don't know any better, sir," continued our hero, pleadingly. "They're not possessed of your nobility of disposition."

"That's true, my young friend, very true," said Mr. Mole, as he took out his toothpick and began picking his teeth; "and——"

"You're of such a forgiving spirit,' interrupted his petitioner.

"Yes, of course," continued Mr. Mole, "it's our duty, as Christians, to return good for evil, and cultivate feelings of love and charity towards—oh, dash it!—d—n it!" he shrieked, suddenly, as his youthful pupil, either accidentally, or in a fit of boyish exuberance, lurched forward and playfully knocked up his arm.

It happened, too, singularly enough, to be the toothpick arm, and the jerk had caused Mr. Mole to stick the point of the useful little instrument he was using into the nerve of his hollow tooth.

"Oh—oh—ugh!" groaned the preceptor, as he clenched his hands, and performed a sort of agonized Highland fling on the hearthrug. " O—h !"

" What's the matter, sir ?" inquired his practical pupil.

" You've driven me mad," gasped the distracted tutor.

" It's that poor tooth again," said the hopeful, in a well-assumed tone of pity ; "hold your jaw, sir," he exclaimed, earnestly.

" Hold yours," shouted Mr. Mole, in a fury.

" With both hands, sir ; it will relieve the pain," continued the imperturbable Jack.

Up went the hands of the agonised preceptor to his chin.

He was desperately holding his jaw as directed, with all his might.

" Is it better ?" asked his pupil presently, in a tone of much concern.

" Much better, much," answered Mr. Mole, complacently, as the anguish of the irritated nerve subsided.

" And you'll forgive poor Sunday and Monday, won't you, Mr. Mole ?"

" The infernal rascals !" again burst out the tutor ; " I should like to——"

" But as a Christian," interposed our hero, suggestively.

" Ah, yes—true, I forgot," admitted Mr. Mole, calming down ; " well, as a Christian, I suppose I must forgive the black vaga—I mean the ignorant darkies; but I must teach them a lesson."

" Suppose you sit down, sir, and think the matter over ?" said Jack, suggestively.

" That's the very thing I'm going to do," replied Mr. Mole, as he walked to his armchair and dropped into it.

The pin took immediate effect, and he started up like a Jack-in-the-box, with a loud yell.

" Ugh, murder ! I'm impaled !" he shrieked, as he clapped his hands behind him, and rubbed away vigorously.

Whilst at the same moment the door flew open with a loud bang, admitting, with startling abruptness, Messrs. Sunday and Monday, who had, for some time past, had their ears to the keyhole, and who now fell sprawling into the room upon their hands and knees.

Forming what is called upon the stage a picture of astonishment.

Mr. Mole, who had, in his anger and surprise, entirely forgotten all his sublime sentiments of love and charity, glared down at the two darkies like a grey-headed fiend.

They in their turns glared up at him.

Jack took advantage of the momentary tableau to possess himself of his pin.

The tutor was the first to speak.

" What do you mean by bursting in upon my privacy in this manner, you two black fellows, eh ?" he demanded, fiercely.

" Golly, Massa Mole," returned Sunday, whose eyes were open as wide as saucers, " him beg um pardon."

" Beg my pardon—be hanged, sirrah ! Stand up, both of you, and let me know the meaning of this conduct."

The two niggers scrambled up from their knees, writhing their features into strange contortions, as though something tickled them, and they were trying not to laugh.

" Now, then, explain," said Mr. Mole, wrathfully.

" Well, den," they commenced, " we was coming up de stairs to speak to you, massa."

" Both togeder, arm in arm."

" One arter de oder."

" How could that be ?" roared the tutor. " How could you be together, arm in arm, if you came one after the other ?"

" We come up sideways, Massa Mole," explained Monday, with a grin.

" Well, and you were coming to speak to me, eh ?" said Mr. Mole, viciously.

" Yes, massa ; well, when we got to de door, I felt drefful tired."

" Golly, so did I," joined in Sunday ; " and say to my brudder here, ' Let's hab a rest on de mat afore going in to speak to de grand Mole.' "

" Dat quite true, s'elp me golly !" affirmed Monday ; " so we stop on de mat."

" And lean against de door to get our breaf."

" Or to peep through the keyhole— which ?" asked Mr. Mole, suspiciously.

" No ! 'pon him honour, massa, him wouldn't do sich a ting !" protested Monday, placing his hand on his heart with much dignity.

" Him rather tink not," exclaimed his companion.

" What made the door fly open then so abruptly ?" demanded the tutor.

" Well, it war jiss this way," replied Monday ; " while we was leaning our backs agin de door, Brudder Sunday war took wid a drefful sneezing fit."

" Dat's a fact," admitted the African.

" And all of a sudden he let off one of dem big sneeze like de report ob a cannon, an' dat blowed de door open, and shot us both into de room."

" Yes, massa ; dat's 'xac'ly how it war," corroborated Sunday.

" Oh, was it ?" returned Mr. Mole, in a quietly sarcastic tone, that proved he had considerable doubts of the veracity of the speakers ; " then answer me one question."

" Yes, massa."

" If you were standing, as you say you were, with your backs to the door, how is it, when the door opened, you fell in with your faces foremost ?"

The two darkies were rather puzzled to account for this phenomenon without betraying themselves.

So, after scratching their heads in a perplexed manner for several seconds, Monday replied—

" Dat's jiss what boders us, Massa Mole. Dere's some tings in dis world partic'lar bodering."

The tutor laughed sarcastically.

" It doesn't bother me at all, you pair of vagabonds," he said, sternly; " you were listening at the keyhole."

The darkies turned almost whitey-brown with indignation at the charge.

Young Jack Harkaway came to their assistance with a brilliant suggestion.

" Perhaps the violent shock of the sneeze caused them to turn over, Mr. Mole," he said.

" Dat was it, Massa Jack," exclaimed the niggers, pouncing upon the idea like a couple of crows on a slug.

" De shock turn us de wrong way up'ards."

Mr. Mole seemed to retain his own opinion on the subject.

But he said at length, after a pause—

" Well, and what was it you had to say to me?"

" Um wanted to tell you sometink bery partic'lar, sar," replied Sunday, with an important wink.

" What ?"

" Dis child wanted to tell you dat to-day war him birthday."

" Ugh !" grunted Mr. Mole, in profound disgust.

" Yes, massa, dis bery day twenty-eight years ago, I come for de fust time into dis wicked world."

Sunday grinned at this, as though it was a great national benefit.

But the tutor checked him by remarking—

" Then I think the sooner you're out of it the better. Of what use are you, and what has your birthday to do with me ?"

" Him thought p'r'aps—you sech kind-hearted man—you might like to drink our health, Massa Mole," said Monday, insinuatingly.

" Or gib him lilly drop ob someting to drink him own health," suggested his companion, modestly.

" I should like to give you both a good dose of arsenic, you two smutty-faced villains," muttered the tutor to himself, between his teeth.

At this juncture, young Jack pulled his coat tail slightly to attract his attention.

" Massa Jack's speaking for us," whispered Sunday, with a chuckle to his comrade ; " we get sometink, you see— drop of Mole's rum, perhaps."

Whatever it was that our hero said to Mole, it was evidently satisfactory.

A smile, of rather a grim quality, however, overspread his features, and turning, he left the room.

He soon returned with a benevolent smile on his face, and a bottle in each hand.

" I have something here," he said, " that will do you good. I will take a glass of it with you, and wish you better manners."

" Hair, hair, hair !—I mean hear, hear, hear !" shouted young Jack, vociferously.

The negroes brightened up immensely at the words.

" Him bery much obligated to you, Massa Mole," exclaimed Sunday.

" We both bery much obligated, Massa Mole," said his equally rejoicing companion.

" Don't mention it, you pair of ug—I mean my excellent, worthy—a—friends," returned the courteous preceptor, as he filled two glasses for his guests out of one bottle, and one for himself out of another.

" I know you like good old Jamaica,"

he continued; "try that. I prefer a lighter beverage. Your very good healths! My dear friend, Sunday, I wish you many happy returns of this day."

"I wish the same to both of you," joined in young Jack.

"And dis child wish de same to both ob you, s'elp my golly he do!" exclaimed Sunday, as he took the glass, and smacked his thick lips eagerly.

The glasses were emptied in a twinkling.

"Is it good?" asked Mr. Mole, with a grin worthy of Mephistopheles.

"Him fust rate; reg'lar golopshus," replied Monday, glowingly.

"It de most scrumptious drop ob rum him eber taste," exclaimed his companion.

"Try another," said the tutor, as he replenished the glasses.

They were emptied as quickly as before, and as quickly refilled.

This process was repeated several times.

The darkies began to stagger.

Their eyes rolled in their heads.

The rum, or something else, was rapidly taking effect upon them.

"I say, brudder, how you—hic—feel, eh?" hiccoughed Monday at length to his comrade.

"Him feel jess like—hic—bery queer?"

returned Sunday, drowsily, as he staggered and leant against Monday.

"Dat's jess how dis chile feel himself," murmured the Limbian, as he tried to steady himself against his companion.

After standing in this helpless position for a few seconds, Monday exclaimed, in an imbecile manner—

"It time—hic—go home—hic—dinner."

The two darkies gradually grew more and more incoherent, and more incapable of supporting themselves.

And Mr. Mole and his pupil, having placed a couple of chairs for their accommodation, kindly gave them a final push, and they dropped into them.

There they lay with their eyes shut and their capacious mouths wide open, snoring like a couple of grampuses, utterly unconscious.

"Bravo, morphia!" exclaimed Mr. Mole, triumphantly.

"Did you put anything in the rum?" asked Jack.

"Yes, I drugged it!" replied his amiable preceptor, with an intense chuckle, as he rubbed his hands together joyously; "and now they're quite at my mercy—now it's my turn. Ha, ha! my turn, Jack, my boy."

CHAPTER XXXIV.

A PLAN OF RETALIATION, ON MOLE'S PRINCIPLES OF LOVE AND CHARITY.

FOR full five minutes did Isaac Mole gloat like a vampire over his sable victims.

"Don't they look ugly?" he exclaimed at length.

"They don't look very pretty, certainly," admitted his pupil.

"Pretty! They're frightful! Ugh! the brutes! They're hideous!"

Here Mr. Mole became so virtuously shocked at their physical imperfections that he boxed their ears and was about to administer sundry punches in the region of their ribs. But Jack stopped him.

"You should not hit a man when he's down, Mr. Mole," he said, quietly; "it's cowardly."

"Psha!" returned the enthusiast; "these things are not men."

"What are they, then?" asked his pupil.

"Pigs! Black puddings!" answered Mr. Mole, indignantly; "anything but men. Did they not cause my hair to turn brown, red and blue?"

"Yes, and now what are you going to do with them?" asked Jack.

"I'm thinking. We can't shoot them, or smother them, or boil them," he remarked, in a reflective tone.

"Not very well," said young Jack, "and I don't think they quite deserve that, even if we could."

"I do," returned the ferocious Mole, quickly. "I think they deserve the worst at my hands. Look at me, and see the painful remains of red, brown and blue, the wretches!"

"Yes, but they didn't shoot you, or smother you, or boil you," argued Jack.

"Hang me if I know what to do with them," confessed the tutor at length, in a perplexed tone.

"We can't dye them, can we?" said Jack, after a moment.

"Dye them—no!" exclaimed his preceptor, viciously; "they're past dyeing. We might whitewash them, though, perhaps, eh—eh?" he asked, eagerly.

Mr. Mole chuckled and rubbed his hands in a particularly energetic manner at this idea.

"I think whitewashing would do well," he continued, cheerfully; "excellently well."

"It wouldn't be bad," laughed Jack. "You'd lay it on pretty thick, I suppose, wouldn't you?"

"I believe you, my boy! I would spare no expense. They should have three coats apiece—nothing less. I'll plaster them inside and out, the dirty beggars! Yes, they shall be whitewashed."

Mr. Mole became so ecstatic at the prospect that he stumped up and down the room like an elderly harlequin.

Suddenly he stopped, and exclaimed, as though the thought had just occurred to him—

"Where's the whitewash?"

"In a shop close by," returned his young companion.

"Will you run at once, my dear boy," continued the tutor, excitedly, "and order a—a—let me see; how much whiting shall we want?"

"Well, I should think two hundredweight would be sufficient," returned young Jack, stolidly.

"I should think so too, but by all means let's have enough while we're about it."

"That will be plenty."

"Well, then, we shall want a tub of size?"

"Yes."

"And a plasterer's brush, a good, big, flapping one, that will wind about the rascals' ugly ears, and tickle their flat noses."

"And fill their mouths, eh, Mr. Mole?" grinned Jack.

"I'll fill 'em, trust me," grinned the tutor, in an ogreish manner, in reply.

"And now go; don't lose a moment; run all the way.

"Stop!" cried Mole; "as you go down, tell them to bring up two of the largest pails they have in the house."

"All right!" cried our hero.

"And here, stay!" shrieked the excited Mr. Mole. "I must also have one of the biggest soup kettles immediately."

"I'll tell 'em to send up the kitchen boiler."

Mr. Mole, left alone with his prey, first performed a kind of triumphant war dance all to himself.

"Ugh, you sleeping beauties!" he exclaimed; "there's a pair of noses. What do they mean by spreading out all over their faces, eh? They must be compressed, squeezed, ha, ha! So they shall be; where's the tongs?"

Mole hopped to the fireplace like a nimble old jackdaw, and seized the steel implements alluded to.

"Now for it," he cried.

But just at the interesting crisis, a voice behind him cried—

"Come, drop the tongs."

The startled tutor did as he was ordered, and dropped the tongs with a crash.

"What, got back already?" exclaimed Mole, in surprise; "why, you must have flown."

"No, I haven't started yet," returned Jack.

"Not started! Am I to lose my revenge?"

"No; but I've got a better idea."

"Better?"

"Ever so much."

"What? Let me hear. Quick, dear boy."

"Well, then, I was thinking, instead of whitewashing these darkies, suppose we were to perform another operation?"

"What, what?" asked Mr. Mole.

"Paint them," grinned Jack.

"Paint them?" echoed his master.

"Yes, with oil colours."

"Oil colours?" repeated Mole.

"Don't you see the advantage?" continued the youthful lover of mischief.

"Not very clearly," replied his tutor.

"I'll explain, then. Whitewash can be easily got off by washing; oil colours, when dry, can't."

"True, true," cried Mole, admiringly. "Clever boy; we'll have oil colours, by all means. I'll leave it to you, only be quick."

"May I choose the colours?" asked Jack, as he approached the door.

"Choose what you like, but be sure and bring plenty of dryers," replied Mole.

"I will. A little glue wouldn't be a bad thing to rub in their hair, would it?" suggested the youth, playfully.

"No, capital, dear boy; bring lots of glue and brushes."

"I'll bring all they've got in the shop," cried Jack, as he once more rushed from the apartment.

"Don't forget the oil and turps," shrieked the enthusiastic Mole after him, in a fever of excitement.

Jack soon reappeared, bristling with bristles in the shape of paint brushes from head to foot, and with a bright smudge of emerald green on the tip of his youthful nose, closely followed by two porters, who carried the rest of the materials, including an immense variety of paintpots of all sizes.

"Are you sure you've got everything, my darling boy?" eagerly inquired Mr. Mole.

"Quite sure."

"What colours have you brought?"

"White for the groundwork."

"Good."

"Red for the complexion."

"Red, ah! I had it in my hair," remarked Mole; "and what are you going to use for those rascals' wool?" he asked.

"Glue as a preparatory coating, and emerald green to finish their noble heads of hair."

"Emerald green for their wool," roared the exulting preceptor, "emerald green hair. Ha, ha! excellent. One of my whiskers was blue, I remember."

"Yes, and theirs will be green. There was no green about you, though, was there?"

"No, no, no green," chuckled Mole,

"no green; but where's the glue, dear boy?"

"Here, sir," answered Jack, holding up a bag containing about six pounds.

"Right," returned his tutor; "now the size?"

"Here, sir, in this tub. It's quite full."

"Good. And this can?"

"Contains linseed oil."

"And this?"

"Turps."

"Bravo!"

"And here's the white lead."

"Excellent youth, boy of my heart," murmured Mole; "come to my arms."

Mr. Mole embraced his clever pupil warmly.

"Oh!" he exclaimed, stopping in the midst of his caress, "the dryers! I don't see the dryers, that most important ingredient of——"

"Here they are, sir," said Jack, as he shied the packet at his respected tutor and caught him on his nose; "nothing, you see, is wanting."

"Jack," said Mole, "I was not wanting that hard packet on my nose, and understand, if I should ask you for a paint pot, please place it in my hand and not throw it in my face. The feeling is most unpleasant."

"Quite an accident, sir," said young Jack.

"Well, then, my dear boy, now for my sweet revenge!" exclaimed Mole, as he recovered himself.

"All right," returned Jack, with much animation; "and, first of all, we'll put on some glue in a pipkin to melt, while we're getting the paint ready."

"Quite right; thoughtful boy, quite right," assented Mr. Mole, admiringly.

The earthen vessel, containing the glutinous material, was then placed upon the fire.

And our hero hauled forward a large paint pot.

CHAPTER XXXV.

SUNDAY AND MONDAY ARE OPERATED ON ARTISTICALLY IN THEIR SLEEP.

"WE'LL mix the white ground colour, to commence with," said young Jack.

"Ah, yes—white. And which of the ingredients do you put in first?" asked

Mr. Mole, whose ideas on the subject of paint mixing were indefinite.

"I don't think it matters much," returned our hero.

"We may as well be right if we can," remarked Mole. "I wonder which ought to go in first," he continued, thoughtfully; "the turps, or the oil, or the white lead, or——"

"Suppose we put 'em all in together?" suggested Jack, who began to find the mixing process progressing a trifle too slowly; "all we want is to get it nice and thick."

"Ah, yes, nice and thick," eagerly echoed Mr. Mole, rubbing his hands gloatingly; "that's the principal, nice and thick, my dear Jack, so that they cannot get it off for a twelvemonth."

"Here goes, then," cried Jack, as he emptied a quantity of white lead into the pot.

"Now a little oil, sir, if you please."

Mr. Mole poured in some from the tin can.

"That will do," said our hero, as he stirred it round with a brush; "now a little turps."

The turps was added.

Jack stirred away manfully.

"Now you have a turn," he said to his tutor, when his arm got tired.

"Certainly, my boy, that's only fair," said Mr. Mole, readily, as he stirred away vigorously.

"Capital exercise for the muscles, isn't it, sir?" asked Jack, presently, with a quiet grin.

"Capital," returned the tutor, who was almost black in the face with his exertions.

"Lovely smell, turps," remarked our hero, presently; "don't you think so, Mr. Mole?"

"Delicious! there's something very wholesome about the odour of turpentine," gasped the tutor, as he stirred the compound, "but rather pungent to the (atishoo! atishoo! atishoo! he sneezed suddenly) nostrils."

Mole's eyes were watering from the effects of the turps.

"Pray don't forget the dryers," exclaimed Mr. Mole, anxiously.

"I'm not forgetting," returned Jack; "I thing you may add some now."

"That's capital," exclaimed our hero, as he worked the brush round and round. "There, the ground colour's ready; and now for the vermilion and the emerald green."

"Ah! yes, yes," returned Mr. Mole, looking as eager as though the happiness of the whole human race depended on the proper preparation of these colours.

Our hero went to work again.

"Put in plenty, Jack, put in plenty," urged Mole; "don't spare the colour."

"I don't intend to," grinned our hero.

"And lots of dryers; pray put in lots of dryers," Mole entreated.

"I have put in lots," said Jack, assuringly.

"Oh, how I long to begin my work on the two wretches! I shall never forget my sky-blue whisker and red hair they treated me to, Jack," said Mole.

At length all the paint was mixed.

By this time the glue on the fire was melted.

All was ready for the operation.

Mr. Mole hopped up to the sleepers with a nimbleness which can only be accounted for by the intenseness of the gratification he felt, and glared at them with the hungry ferocity of a gigantic vampire bat.

The two darkies had not stirred a peg.

There they sat in their chairs, with their legs stretched out, and their arms dangling at their sides, their heads thrown back, their eyes shut, and their mouths open; playing a powerful but not very harmonious instrumental duet on their noses.

"Now then, Jack! Now then, my beloved pupil!" exclaimed Mole, in a mingled tone of affection and nervous excitement, "how shall we begin our painting lesson?"

Our hero considered a moment, and then replied—

"I think we'll begin with the glue, sir."

"Ah, yes. And what's to be done with the glue?" asked Mr. Mole.

"It must be rubbed well into their hair," Jack explained, as he took the bubbling pipkin from the fire and placed it on a stool.

"I see," returned his tutor. "And who is to do the rubbing in, you or I? Perhaps you had——"

"No, sir," interrupted Jack, blandly, "that's too difficult an operation for me. It requires your skill, Mr. Mole. I think you'd better rub in the glue."

"Um—ah!" returned the tutor, looking down rather doubtfully into the pot, and scratching his nose in a reflective manner, "perhaps I had."

Mr. Mole having come to this conclusion, took off his coat and tucked up his shirt sleeves.

In the meantime, our hero had poured some of the hot glue into another pipkin to cool.

"There," he said as he pointed to the latter; "it's in capital condition to use, sir."

"It was awfully hot a minute ago," remarked his worthy preceptor.

"Oh," returned Jack, "it's only pleasantly warm now."

Mr. Mole, in the extent of his confidence, plunged his hands into the pleasantly warm material.

A prolonged howl was the result.

"Oh, murder!—fire!" he shrieked, stumping about on his wooden leg, and wringing his hands in his agony. "It's boiling."

"Suck your fingers, sir, suck your fingers," cried Jack; "it's a certain cure."

"Suck the devil!" raved Mr. Mole, angrily; "get me some cold water."

Our hero ran for a basin of cold water, in which the preceptor immersed his hands.

The water having allayed the pain, he became once more anxious to commence operations.

The glue being now cool for his purpose, he scooped up some in the palms of his hands, and rubbed it thoroughly into the woolly heads of the negroes.

After this operation, young Jack painted their heads with emerald green, the glue causing them to take the colour readily.

"Doesn't it look capital?" said our hero, admiringly, as he completed his task.

"Excellent; admirable," grinned Mr. Mole. "Ha, ha! black faces, and emerald green hair; exquisitely ludicrous. What next?" he asked.

"Now we must paint their faces with white," said Jack.

"My dear Jack, let that be my task," said Mole. "I will lay it on thick for them."

"Suppose you paint them half white, and leave half black; that would have a good effect," suggested our hero, eagerly.

"Oh, yes, so it would," assented Mole.

"I will do so. Bring the white paint here, and plenty of it."

Jack brought the paint pot, and Mole gave it a good stir-up.

"It's jolly thick, isn't it, sir?" remarked his pupil.

"All the better, my dear boy," said Mr. Mole, as he raised the brush full of colour.

"You'd better draw a line right down from the top of their foreheads to the bottom of their chins," counselled Jack; "that will be a guide for you."

"So it will," returned Mr. Mole.

The two lines were instantly drawn according to order.

"Now, then, fill in the right half of Monday's face with white paint," Jack continued.

Mr. Mole took a good dab of paint on his brush, and "filled in" vigorously.

"There," said Mole, "I think they have it thick enough to last some time. Take that, you brute," he continued, thrusting the brush, loaded with paint, up one side of Monday's nose; "that will stop you snoring in such a horrid way."

"Very good!" remarked our hero, in an encouraging tone. "Now, then, fill in the left half of Sunday's handsome face in the same manner."

"Ha, ha! Jack, this is splendid work," and Mole's brush went to work again.

"Capital!" cried Jack. "And now, then, I'll rub in a little red on their cheeks, and give them an eyebrow apiece; shall I?"

"Yes, yes, do, my dear boy," grinned his delighted tutor.

In an instant this also was done.

The right and left cheeks of the two darkies, under the artistic touch of young Jack's brush, bloomed with a glowing hue.

Whilst, by scraping away a little of the white groundwork, he delineated a very effective, handsome arched eyebrow.

The work was accomplished.

Our hero was as much amused by the vagaries of his tutor as at the comic appearance of the victims.

But gradually the effects of the drug began to wear off.

The sleepers gave signs of returning consciousness.

Monday woke first, and with a sudden start sat up in his chair.

"'PULL, BAKER! PULL NIGGERS!' EXCLAIMED MONDAY."

CHAPTER XXXVI.

THE SLEEPERS AWAKENED.

THE first thing Monday did was to attempt to scratch his head.

It was but an attempt, however.

The glue had dried so hard that his head scratched him instead.

Something then seemed to tickle his right nostril.

He sneezed violently, and out flew a plug of white paint, with a report like a pop-gun.

This seemed to relieve the darkey, who, after making a variety of extraordinary grimaces, at length succeeded in opening his eyes and sitting up.

"Golly! Whar am I?"

He turned his head, and caught sight of the half of his slumbering comrade's face.

"Oh, Jerusalem!" he exclaimed, in a tone of intense astonishment. "Who the debbil dis?—dis not Sunday."

He turned himself in his chair, and contemplated the African intently.

"Him certainly like Sunday," he soliloquised; "bery like, all except de top ob him. Dat not a bit like. Him head green, and him complexion white. What de matter wid him? Am he ill, am he dead, or am he——"

He was about to rise for a closer examination, when young Jack pulled him by the sleeve.

"Ah, Massa Jack, am dat you?" he asked, as he turned and recognised his master's son.

"Yes, it's me," returned the youth, unable to restrain a grin at the comical appearance of the black.

Monday observed these signs, and gradually a smile began to glimmer on his own features.

"Anything up wid dat nigger, Massa Jack?" he asked, in an under tone.

"Rather," returned our hero, confidentially. "Hush, listen here."

Monday put down his ear.

"Mole's been having a lark with Sunday," whispered Jack.

"Hab he, though?"

"Yes; he's given him a coat."

"A coat?"

"Yes, of paint, while he was asleep. Don't say a word."

"No, sar, so help him golly he won't," chuckled Monday, who was immensely tickled at the idea, little suspecting he had been operated on himself.

"Oh, what a guy him look!" he continued. "Yah—y——"

He was about to laugh, but stopped short all of a sudden, and clapped his hand to his cheek.

"Golly, what dis?" he exclaimed, as, with a terrific grimace, he came in contact with the coating of paint, which, thanks to the dryers, was now as hard as enamel.

This unusual pecularity caused him unbounded astonishment, and turning round to our hero, he asked, in no little perturbation—

"Anything de matter, Massa Jack, wid my face?"

"Anything the matter?" returned Jack. "No. What should there be?"

"Golly, dis chile feel as though him got a big gum bile all over him cheek."

"You've been sitting in a draught and caught cold, that's what it is," said our hero. "Never mind that, it's nothing. Keep quiet; see, Sunday's waking, and mind, Monday, you must keep the secret."

"All right, Massa Jack, me neber tell him," returned the Limbian, as he threw himself back in his chair and pretended to be asleep; "him quiet as a mouse."

When Sunday came to consciousness, his proceedings were very much like those of his comrade.

Like him, he tried to scratch his head, but failed.

Like him, his nose tickled him, and he sneezed, and fired off his plug of white paint.

Lastly he opened his eyes.

"Whar de dinner?" was the first remark he made.

"Whar ole Monday got to, I wonder?" was the second.

As he said this, he turned his eyes to the left.

There was Monday, lying perfectly motionless in his chair, and looking altogether so entirely unlike himself that his comrade began to think something very serious was the matter.

"Gorra," he murmured, to himself, apprehensively, "what de matter wid him? Monday!" he called, softly.

There was no answer.

"Monday, anytink de matter wid you?"

But still no answer came from Monday.

"Gorra, mussy!" murmured Sunday, his fears increasing, "something drefful's come to him. Him hair have turn green, him old mug turn white. I think him kick the bucket in him sleep, and dis de fust stage ob fortification."

Sunday meant to say mortification.

Finding that no notice was taken of his appeals, he was about to start up and try to bring his friend to life by shaking him, when suddenly young Jack, who had slipped round to his side, plucked him by the sleeve.

"Hush, Sunday," he said, in a low, hasty tone. "Don't say a word; it's only a bit of fun."

"What, dat dere fun?" asked Sunday, glancing at his companion's profile.

"Yes," whispered our hero. "It's only a little trick Mole's played him."

"What, de green an' white?"

"Yes, paint. Mole's made him beautiful for ever. Keep quiet; don't tell him what we have done, and see what he does when he wakes."

"What a ugly nigger him look, Massa Jack," exclaimed Sunday, making a desperate effort not to laugh, but opening his mouth suddenly, and shutting it up again as quickly as his comrade had done before him.

"Oh, gorra!" he exclaimed, "what am de matter wid dis infant? Him feel as though he got de tic toddle doo in him jaw!"

"Never mind your jaw. Hold it," enjoined Jack.

"Him will, sar; but him feel bery funny 'bout de jaw."

And Sunday fell back in his chair, and was silent.

It was immensely comic to watch the two darkies as they sat there, both pretending to be asleep, but each watching the other out of the corner of his eye.

Mr. Mole and Jack stood a short distance aloof enjoying the fun.

At length Jack thought it was time to have a little more fun out of them, so he cried suddenly, in a loud voice—

"Hullo, you two, Sunday and Monday, isn't it time for dinner?"

The two niggers sprang to their feet, glanced at each other slyly, and turning away, went into such a paroxysm of subdued laughter as almost to produce suffocation.

"Massa Jack, Massa Jack," gasped Monday at length, to our hero, with the tears running down his cheeks, as he pointed his thumb over his shoulder at his comrade, "look at dat nigger dere, only do look at him! Ain't him darned ugly? Oh, oh! Yah, yah!"

Sunday the meanwhile had got hold of the tutor.

"Massa Mole, Massa Mole!" he gurgled, his mouth extending almost from ear to ear with delight, as he pointed his thumb in his turn, "did you ever see sich frightful-looking, ugly fellah as dat nigger? Yah, yah, yah!"

"Never," shrieked Mr. Mole, holding his sides. "Ho, ho, ho!"

The mirth grew quite infectious.

At length Monday, looking round, and presenting his white side to his comrade, said—

"What for you laugh, brudder?—yah, yah, yah!"

"Him larf cos you larf, brudder—yah, yah, yah!" returned Sunday, showing his white half in return.

They were both convulsed with laughter at the sight of each other, and Sunday rushed from the room and downstairs to roar himself out in the street.

Monday, after his comrade disappeared, calmed down rather abruptly, and dropping into a chair, began to rub his plastered cheek, and to look exceedingly doleful.

"What's the matter?" asked young Jack.

"Him got drefful toothache come on all of a sudden on de top of him gum biles," replied Monday, as he rocked himself in his chair.

"You'd better tie up your face and get home to your wife, then, as soon as possible," said Mr. Mole.

In a minute Jack had got a dark-coloured wrapper, and tied it over the black half of Monday's face.

"Dat's not right side," groaned Monday.

"I tell you it is," insisted Jack.

"But de big gum bile on de oder side," protested the nigger.

"No matter," returned our hero; "you keep the wrapper as I've tied it, and you'll find it will very soon draw out the pain."

Jack then made his victim put on Mr. Mole's dark cloth cape, and showing him politely to the door, wished him a good appetite, and showed him out.

Monday, with his teeth aching furiously, hurried along the streets, utterly unconscious of the mirth his singular appearance created.

Before he reached home, however, he began to think as to the reception he might receive from his wife, he being three hours behind his time.

"Neber mind," he argued; "I must tell Ada Massa Mole keep me. Dat'll do nicely."

But it didn't do nicely, for when his wife opened the door and he was about to step in, Ada gave a cry of surprise.

He was rather taken aback by this unusual treatment, and he said, rather ruefully—

"What am de matter, Ada? Let me come in and lub you."

"No, you won't, you villain!" exclaimed Ada, flourishing a broom handle in the doorway defiantly, and not allowing him to pass.

"Well, but won't you let your dear husband hab him dinner?" he asked.

"You're not my husband, sir."

The hapless Monday's eyes rolled in his head with dismay at the assertion.

"If dis chile not your husband, who am den?" he gasped.

"Not you," replied the indignant female; "my husband's a handsome coloured gentleman—you're a horrid guy."

"Me, Ada—me horrid guy!" faltered Monday, feeling as though the world was coming to an end.

"Yes," Ada vociferated, "though you do try to imitate my husband's voice to get in and rob the house; but you're no more like my Monday than black's like white. You're an impostor. Go away."

"But him want him dinner," wailed the hopeless victim.

"There is none for you."

"No dinner, my lub?"

"Go and get it elsewhere."

"But I tell you I'm——"

Down came the broom handle on Monday's devoted head.

The door was slammed violently to, and he found himself outside, hanging on to the knocker, the cause of all being the simple fact that, from his extraordinary disguise and the paint on his face, his wife did not recognise him.

But Monday did not feel disposed to be thus expelled from his own home, and, having the knocker ready to his hand, he hammered away at it with all his might.

Presently the window opened above, and his wife looked out.

"Open de door, my lub!" he exclaimed, desperately. "Him got de tooth aching and de collywobbles for want of something to eat."

"Ugh! you noisy wretch," exclaimed Ada, and immediately disappearing, but returning very shortly with something in her hand.

"If you won't let um in, my lub, den gib him sometink to eat out ob de winder," he pleaded.

"There's something to drink, and I hope you'll like it," cried his wife, passionately.

This was the contents of the water jug, and the handle breaking, the jug came too, and sent the innocent applicant rolling to the bottom of his own door steps.

"Oh, golly! him be drowned," he groaned.

Just at this moment loud shouts and peals of laughter were heard, and Sunday, with his emerald green head and whitey-black face, came bolting up to the spot, pursued by a crowd of his sable brethren.

The African had, in a spirit of fun, hurried away to collect his acquaintance, to join him in ridiculing his comrade.

But the absurdity of his own appearance turned the tables upon himself, and they ridiculed him instead.

"What am de matter wid you niggers?" said Sunday, not knowing that he had been painted half white.

"Oh, there's a guy!" shouted the niggers.

In vain he tried to escape. They followed him.

As a last resource he bent his steps to Monday's house, where he arrived just in time to pitch head foremost over his prostrate friend.

The yells were redoubled when, on Monday being hoisted on to his feet, he was found to be in a similar state of white and green.

The darkies could hardly believe they were looking at one of their own race.

In an instant Monday was lugged out of Mr. Mole's black cape, the wrapper was torn from his face, and the veritable Monday stood revealed.

At this juncture his wife, naturally curious to ascertain the effect the water jug had taken, peeped from the window.

The black half of her spouse's face was now turned towards her.

She recognised him at once.

"Monday, Monday!" she cried, excitedly, as she flew downstairs and out at the door, amongst the crowd, to reach her husband. "Monday, my dear, what's the——"

She stopped short, and uttered a cry of dismay at the sight presented.

"Whatever has happened?" she asked.

Sunday and Monday were both too much engaged in their struggle with the crowd to answer Ada.

"Pull, baker! pull, niggers!" exclaimed the Limbian, as Sunday caught him by the arm, for Sunday had been seized by a tribe of the small black fry, who were pulling back with all their force.

"Here we is!" shouted Sunday, as with his friend he made a final rush, which carried them inside the house.

Then they shut the door to keep out the yelling crowd.

Mr. Mole, late in the afternoon, sent for his cape and wrapper, and forwarded per messenger a large iron currycomb, to comb their hair with, and a couple of bottles of old Jamaica, to drink his health.

CHAPTER XXXVII.

THE RIVAL NIGGERS, OR SUNDAY VERSUS MONDAY.

YOUNG Jack Harkaway looked upon Sunday with as much affection as his father regarded Monday.

Sunday had saved the boy's life by his bravery, and thought it a very fine thing to have him for his young master.

Neither he nor Monday had much work to do.

There was plenty of time hanging on their hands.

The consequence was, that they were perpetually quarrelling.

Very naturally, Monday looking back on his past services to Jack Harkaway, and the length of time he had been in the family, considered Sunday an intruder.

It was hard lines, he thought, for him to have to give in to an ordinary American negro.

His hair, though dark, was straight, and he was a prince in Limbi.

The other one had woolly hair, and was the son of nobody knew who.

Feeling that he wanted a brief change, Harkaway left New York, after the laughable events at the hotel, and went a little way into the country.

It was in one of the suburbs of New York—Long Island, as it is called—that he had rented a house, furnished.

In this delightful spot he hoped that a few weeks' rest would give to Emily and Hilda, and especially Mole, health and strength.

This expectation was fully shared by Mr. Mole and Harvey.

They formed a very pleasant family party.

There was riding, driving, and shooting, as well as fishing, and with a fine autumn, they contrived to enjoy themselves very well.

For the time they dismissed all thoughts of their cruel enemies.

What had become of Hunston and Toro, they did not know.

The days glided away happily and quickly, in their pleasant country house.

Occasionally the ladies drove into New York, and did some shopping.

When there was a new piece at any of

the theatres they all went into the city to see it.

Meanwhile the enmity which had always existed between the rival niggers, as they got to be called by the other servants, increased rather than diminished.

To make matters worse, it happened that Sunday fell in love with the cook.

She was a middle-aged woman, plump and buxom, who had saved hundreds of dollars.

As she continually talked about being well-to-do, and showed her bank-book, she was regarded as an heiress.

Many a dark-hued Strephon made up to her.

But she was hard to please, and did not encourage anybody in particular.

Sunday was very anxious to get into her good graces.

Aunt Lucy, as she was named, seemed to prefer the society of Monday.

We are sorry to state that though he had a wife, who was left in New York, Monday was base enough to flirt with the cook.

This made Sunday's blood boil with a jealous fire.

He could frequently have stabbed his hated rival to the heart.

Only the fear of the law restrained him.

Besides, Sunday was not fond of fighting, and rather fancied that Monday would prove more than a match for him in a stand-up encounter.

To be beaten in a bout of fisticuffs before his inamorata would have been a great blow to his pride.

So he laid out his wages in fine clothes, bought a gold-headed cane, and strutted about like the winner of a cake walk.

One morning he and Monday met in the garden.

There was in a certain spot a late rose bush.

Each had, from a window of the house, perceived a rose growing on it.

At that time of the year a rose was a rarity.

In an evil moment they both conceived the idea of plucking and presenting it to Aunt Lucy.

Monday was a little in front, and when he heard footsteps behind him, he quickened his pace.

So did Sunday, who began to run. An example which Monday quickly followed.

It was a race now for the rose.

Sunday was heavily handicapped by wearing a pair of very shiny patent leather boots.

To impress Aunt Lucy with the idea that he had a little foot, he had the boots made a size too small for him.

There is a French saying, that you must suffer to be beautiful.

The ex-porter of the Boston Hotel was no exception to the rule.

As he ran he did suffer, if the expression of agony on his ebony countenance was a fair guide.

He felt as if his feet were compressed in a vice.

His misery was complete when he saw Monday reach the tree, twenty yards ahead of him.

The rose was plucked and held aloft in triumph.

Like a racehorse, Monday had just romped in, pulling double, and won the coveted prize.

"Dat ar rose ain't worth nuffin!" exclaimed Sunday.

"What you run after um for?" asked Monday.

"I guess I was running after one ob them big butterflies for to give young massa."

"One lie's about as good as another."

"What, sah!" cried Sunday, "do you mean to insinervate that I done gone tole a lie?"

"Yes, and a big one," retorted Monday.

"That am most 'strornary thing to say, and I put you down as a very ornery sort ob cuss."

"Don't you call um names."

"What you do, hey?"

"Pull um nose. It am a modest retiring kind ob nasal organ, and wants bringing forward."

"Is that so?" asked Sunday "You's not the man ter do it."

"Oh, yes, I am. Doan't you make any beefsteak—I mean mistake, 'bout that."

"You don't dare try it on."

"Go on," cried Monday. "When I was in England, I was appointed nose puller to the Queen and Royal Family.

Get out of um sight or I'll hab your nose."

Sunday conquered his ill temper for the time.

"Mr. Monday," he began, with suavity in his tone and manner.

"That's me," replied the Limbian.

"I don't wish to quarrel with a pusson ob your distinction, becos anyone can see you's a coloured gentleman."

"So I am, and so's my brother, and my father ; it runs in the family."

"If it's not a himperent question, sah, what will you take for that flower ?"

"Money can't buy um, unless you's got twenty million billion dollars."

"What you gwine ter do with it ?"

"Present it as an offering from um heart, to Aunt Lucy, who's the nicest, smartest, and prettiest lump of humanity in all America."

Sunday drew himself up.

"I want yer ter know, sah, that I's making up to that lady," he exclaimed, indignantly.

"You're no good," replied Monday. "She don't take no stock in you. I could have 'um hand to-morrow, if I asked for it."

"Jerusalem the golden !"

"It's a fac'," grinned Monday, tantalisingly.

"You shall never have her."

"Who's to stop me ?"

"I will," cried Sunday. "By heaven, I'll carve you with a razor, sooner than you should make lub to Aunt Lucy."

"Oh, you poor silly nigger, get your wool cut. Be off from here, or I'll have to move you."

This threat of Monday's only served to further infuriate Sunday.

"You'd better look out, you stupid darky, when you talk of lub," he said.

"I'm only talking of a mild flirtation, brudder."

"That's jes' as bad."

"Why is it ?"

"Do yer want to be a bigamy ?"

"Now you're goin' a little too fast. What's my private 'fairs got to do with you ?"

"Who's you ? Only a coloured pusson like me, and we've got to obey the laws same as a white man," said Sunday.

"I'm superior to um common niggers," retorted Monday.

"But you's a nigger."

"A dandy nigger, sah. I 'tract all de females on Sixth Avenue on a Sunday afternoon parade."

"You'd like to wash yourself white, I guess, but you can't change your skin."

"Yah ! What's the use ob wasting um breath on you ?"

"I'll tell Aunt Lucy all 'bout your wife."

"If you do, I'll make pulp ob you. A squashed banana won't be in it with you."

"We shall see. I'm all there, and don't you forget it, sah."

The rivals glared fiercely at one another.

They even went so far as to shake their clenched fists in one another's faces.

Then Monday sought the house and walked into the kitchen by the back way.

Emily and Hilda were upstairs reading. Mr. Mole was in the smoking-room, indulging in Havana cigars and Sante Cruz rum.

Jack, his son, and Harvey were out shooting quail and rabbits.

Jack believed in bringing the boy up to be a lover of outdoor sports.

He did not wish him to be a book-worm, though he and Mole took care that he should devote a part of each day to learning.

Aunt Lucy was cooking some chickens for the ladies' lunch, and was frying them with mushrooms and butter, they being cut up in pieces.

A savoury odour arose, which tickled Monday's olfactory nerves.

"'Scuse my freedom in taking um liberty, ma'am, to come into your kitchen," exclaimed Monday.

Aunt Lucy looked at him with her large black lustrous eyes.

"Don't you make no 'pology, Mister Monday," she replied.

"But I didn't ought to done it, when you's busy."

"You's jes' as welcome as the flowers in May. What's that you got in your hand ?"

"The las' rose ob um summer, ma'am, which I shall feel very proud if you'll kindly accept as a gift from your devoted admirer."

"Oh, Mister Monday, you are such an interesting man."

"Me berry glad you think so. I'm sure you's berry enchanting woman."

Aunt Lucy turned her head away and simpered.

She, however, held out her hand for the flower, raised it to her face to inhale its fragrance, and pinned it in her dress.

"I don't know how to thank you," she said.

"Wear it all day and jes' give a thought to the one who gib it you as um token."

"Ob what?"

"Why, ob lub, ob course."

"Oh, Mister Monday," laughed Aunt Lucy, "you quite decompose me. I—I feel half ashamed to accept it."

"It's yours, my dear; and if you've got a kiss to bestow on the most ardent ob your—"

"Please don't. I know I shall faint right away," Aunt Lucy interrupted.

"My arm will hold you up, ma'am. If you won't gib um kiss, I's got to take it."

"Oh! you bold bad man."

"I's all that," replied Monday; "but you'll hab to 'scuse me, as I tole you before. In the presence ob so much lubliness, what am a poor man to do?"

Aunt Lucy stirred up the chicken fricassee.

"You hab um berry nice smell around here, ma'am," continued Monday.

"Dem am chickens done in French fashion for the ladies' lunch. There am four in the pan. Can I offer you one, sah?" answered the cook.

"Will um duck swim? Dish her up, aunty. I can go um frigasee chicken all day long."

"You're welcome."

"If there's one thing this chile likes, it is chicken in the pan. Set her up lively! My mouf's beginning ter water."

She spread a snow white napkin on the table, and gave him a dish of the savoury mess, with a slice of new bread.

"Golly! this the stuff to make um hair curl," he muttered.

He quickly began to eat.

When he had half cleared his plate, Sunday, who had been listening and looking on outside the window, came to the door.

"Good-day, Maum Lucy!" he exclaimed.

She looked up in surprise.

"What you doin' heah, you man?" she demanded.

"I hope I doan' intrude; but you's gibbing chicken away."

"That's nothing to do with you. All you'll get will do you good, so I tell you. Doan' you forget it."

"I can do on the smell. It isn't that I've come 'bout."

"What then, sah? This is my kitching, and I can have who I like in it."

"That's quite right, ma'am, according to de law ob these United States."

Monday left off eating, and fixed his eyes on him.

"You git," he said. "What did I tell you jes' now?"

"Habbing bad memory, perhaps I's forgot."

"Pull um nose. Do it now, if stop too long."

"Aunt Lucy, you's bein' deceived by a false nigger," cried Sunday.

"What you gettin' at now?"

"He's a married man; got a wife in New York. Anybody tell you dat. Ask Missy Harkaway, or Missy Harvey."

The cook screamed, and leant on a chair for support.

"Oh, my heart!" she sobbed. "Am dis de trufe?"

"It same as gospel. He berry bad man. I's onnerable, I is, in my 'tentions to you."

Monday had no real design on the cook's heart, but he liked the little delicacies she bestowed upon him.

He would be deprived of these, now Sunday had exposed him.

Losing his temper, he jumped up, and rushing upon Sunday, seized him by the nose, which he pulled violently.

"Ouch! Ugh! Whoop!" yelled Sunday.

"Me gib um what for!" cried Monday.

Aunt Lucy recognised the fact, that she had really been taken in by a gay Lothario. She was indignant, and anxious for revenge.

Taking up a broom, she ran towards Monday, and belaboured him with it.

A shower of blows fell on his head and shoulders.

He was forced to relinquish his hold of Sunday's nose.

There was nothing for it, but to take refuge in ignominious flight.

Away he ran, followed by the screams of the cook, and the abuse of Sunday.

He took the direction of the garden, where he hid himself in a grove of hickory trees.

His flirtation with Aunt Lucy was surely at an end.

No longer would he be a favoured guest in the kitchen, and the recipient of tit-bits.

Sunday had got the best of him this time without any possibility of a doubt.

When Monday had beaten a retreat, Sunday seized Aunt Lucy by the hand.

He fell upon his knees and pressed the other hand on his heart.

She left off crying in a moment, and bestowed a favourable look upon him.

"I's de man for you, not dat ar Monday," he exclaimed.

"He's trifled with my 'fections," said the cook.

"I lub you like de bee lubs the honey-suckle, or de grass lubs de dew in summer."

"You take me by surprise."

"Be mine, Aunt Lucy. I make you good husban'. Oh, gib me that sweet heart ob yours."

"Take me," she replied.

He jumped up and caught her in his arms, imprinting kisses on her lips.

"Dis am a big day for me," Sunday cried. "I's the happiest darky on dis continent."

"Sit down and I gib you chicken. Oh, dat base nigger! Fancy he habbing a wife! You must help me to hab revenge on him."

"I will. Nuffin' gib me more pleasure, now you gwine to be my lubbly wife."

"Not a bit more will he hab out of dis kitching. Ebbery day I gib him something."

She took a plate, warmed it, and presented the delighted Sunday with a quantity of the fricassee .

This feast she supplemented with a bottle of lager beer.

"Now what we do with that Monday?" she asked.

"Leab him to me," answered Sunday. "Ole Uncle Pomp, the gardener, am a friend ob mine. We'll fix him together, I guess, Lucy."

"Let him know he can't play tricks on a coloured lady like me, who's got money in de bank."

"Dat's what the coon was after. The depth ob his iniquity is unfathomable. It's the 'bomination ob desolation," replied Sunday.

This speech impressed Aunt Lucy greatly, for she liked long words, though she did not understand the meaning of them.

"How well educated you was, Mister Sunday," she remarked.

"I was brought up at the normal school at my native place, which is Baltimore."

"Is that whar you was raised ? "

"Certain sure."

"Lor' sakes, how strange ! " cried Aunt Lucy. "I was raised in Baltimore, too. My father was a boatman, what worked on the Patapsco River."

"'Pears to me, Miss Lucy, dat we was borned to come closer together."

"Dat's my 'pinion, sah," replied Aunt Lucy, smiling happily.

If her face had not been so black and shining, it might have been seen suffused with blushes.

"As it's all been done gone settled among us two, ma'am, may I make so bold as to ask you to name the day ?" exclaimed Sunday.

"Oh, Mister Sunday, aren't you somewhat impatient ? "

"Not at all. It's only the natural anxiety ob a devoted lubber."

"If dat's it, I'll say this day three weeks."

"Hallelujah ! " cried Sunday. "Praise heaven, all you niggers, I's won Aunt Lucy."

"Stop dem transports for a moment, sah."

"What's in de way ob de road now, ma'am ? "

"You's got ter get me my revenge on dat false nigger Monday," answered Aunt Lucy.

"He's artful nig, but I'll try. I'll go and see Pomp, the gardener. Uncle Pomp's a lubber, and I'll talk to Gumbo, the coachman ; he's got a head on him."

"They's full ob respect for me," said Aunt Lucy.

"I guess they'd go through fire and water for a lady ob your obvious talent and undeniable beauty, ma'am; especially when you makes chicken fixings like this here."

"I know a thing or two," she replied, tossing her head proudly.

"You'll be a blessing to your husband, dat's a fac'. You represent the symmetrical rotundity of the human form divine."

"Oh! Mr. Sunday."

"I'll be going now, to see about dis revenge business. You's gwine to be my wife, and I can't stand by and see you 'sulted."

Aunt Lucy suddenly remembered that the rose Monday had so gallantly presented her with, was still in the bosom of her dress.

She took it out and threw it on the fire.

"That's what he gib me," she cried.

"To the bottom of the lowest pit with it. I'll bring him on his knees, and make him 'pologise to you, before this day is out."

"Nuffin' but dat will pacify me," said Aunt Lucy. "He is a married man; he 'sulted me by paying his addresses to me. Sakes! What did he take me for?"

"Leab it all to me."

With a polite bow, and an amorous smile, Sunday quitted the kitchen.

Going at once into the garden, he had the satisfaction of seeing Uncle Pomp.

He was digging a hole in the ground near a clump of trees, and apparently very busy.

"Say Pomp, Uncle Pomp!" exclaimed Sunday.

The old white headed negro looked up.

CHAPTER XXXVIII.

HOW MONDAY WAS MADE TO APOLOGISE TO AUNT LUCY.

"Is dat you, Sunday?" asked the gardener, resting on his spade. "What's the good word?"

"You's got to congratulate me, uncle," replied Sunday.

"How's dat come 'bout?"

"I's perposed for de lubbly hand of Aunt Lucy, and she's done gone accepted me."

"Good lands! you're a lucky man. She's got a heap ob money in de bank. If I had not a wife already, I'd have tried my chance, and so I's heard Gumbo, de coachman, say, when we's been smoking a pipe together."

"Aunt Lucy's a gen'ral favourite, I guess. She'll soon be Mrs. Sunday, and folks'll hev ter keep at a distance."

As he spoke, Sunday tried to look ferocious.

He did not succeed very well, for his expression was naturally a mild one.

"I hope, sah, as you don't allude to me or Mister Gumbo," said Uncle Pomp.

"No, I don't. My animadversions appertain to a different pusson altogether."

"Who may that be? But I reckon I can tell. Isn't it that foreign nigger dey call Monday?"

"Dat's de berry man I's leading up to!" cried Sunday. "He's no gentleman ob African 'scent, like ourselves."

"He's got rather hykey, top sawyer, bossing ways with him."

"Pshaw! He's nuffin' but a intruding impostor."

"What's he been doin' now?" enquired Uncle Pomp, who was becoming interested.

"Dat false, conceited, ambitious nigger, made lub to Aunt Lucy, leadin' her to beleab dat he was single, when he's a married man, with a wife and little children in New York."

Oh, the wickedness ob some folks!" cried Uncle Pomp.

"Ain't it awful! But I's done gone exposed him, and got de gal for myself."

"Bully for you!" exclaimed the

gardener. "If I was you, though, I shouldn't let de matter stop there."

"I don't intend to, Uncle Pomp."

"Monday's insulted de lady what's gwine to compliment you by being your partner for life."

"That's so, and I say he's got to 'pologise to the lady."

"He keeps rather a stiff upper lip, and he's a sassy nigger," added the gardener, musingly.

"That's jes' why I want you to help me bring him low down," said Sunday.

"It's his pride what wants to be lowered, and we'll do it. Jes' listen to me."

"I's a taking it all in, uncle."

"You see I's diggin' a hole alongside this ole hollow tree."

"What's that for?"

"There's a skunk a hidin' in that tree trunk. Massa Harkaway smell the skunk this morning. He can't bear to hev a skunk round the house, so he tell me to get rid ob him."

"They're mighty hard things ter get out. How's you gwine to gib him notice?"

"I's got one ob them Fourth of July firework things, dey calls torpedoes, and I'll blow de ole skunk to glory," said Uncle Pomp.

"Whar's de torpedo?" enquired Sunday.

"In de ground. I's planted him. Don't you see I's filling in de hole I's dug? Dat thing on de grass, what looks like bit ob tape extending to behind de ole tree, is de fuse."

"Golly! dat good scheme. You git away to be safe from de 'splosion—light de fuse, and de darned old skunk is gone up," replied Sunday.

"'Xactly, brudder Sunday! It's what I call a practical feat of engineering."

"It's no use telling you to take de cake, you deserve de entire bakery."

"I accept your compliments with the pleasure that a word from a wise man always brings," said Uncle Pomp.

He again handled his spade, and filled up the hole which contained the torpedo.

This was a large tin containing detonating powder, which, in addition to making a loud noise, had what the negroes call a 'hysting' or hoisting capacity of no mean power.

If anyone stood incautiously on the top of it, he would be raised several feet and sent flying in some direction a distance off.

"I guess dat ar skunk 'll feel mighty sick when you light de fuse, Uncle Pomp," remarked Sunday.

"You bet that he only hab time to order his funeral," answered the gardener.

Everything was soon ready for dislodging the skunk from his domicile and destroying him.

The skunk is a noisome little animal, about the size of a woodlark, and is in the habit of emitting a dark fluid, which produces an awful and lasting stench.

It makes the ground, a tree, or a hole offensive for many days, and if it falls on clothes, it cannot be eradicated; the clothes must be buried deep in the earth.

Thus it can readily be understood that people have a strong objection to being "skunked," as it is termed.

When it is reported that there is a skunk around, every effort is made to destroy it as soon as possible.

At this moment, Gumbo, the coachman, came upon the scene, leading a mule by a long rein.

"Can I tie this here critter up to a tree, so that he'll hev a feed ob grass, gardener?" he asked.

"You may do that, coachman," replied Uncle Pomp; "but I guess I'd advise you to take him a little furder off."

"What's your reason? De grass is nice and rich 'bout this pertickler spot."

"It's undermined with a torpedo. I's gwine ter blow a she skunk out ob dat ar tree."

"That's good enough for me," said Gumbo. "I'll take de mule a few yards away."

He did so, and made the animal fast to a tree at a safe distance.

The mule, unsuspicious of danger, began to crop the herbage with avidity, and playfully kicked out, as some flies settled on his tail.

"I knowed there was a skunk around, because I smelled him in the stable yard," he remarked.

"Long Island's a fearful place for de varmints," replied Uncle Pomp.

"It ain't half as bad as New Jersey,

whar I lived with my last boss; but, lor' sakes, skunks is p'ison everywhere."

"Mister Gumbo," exclaimed Sunday, "there's two-legged skunks in dis world."

"What am your meaning, Mister Sunday? Has I ever done you any hurt?"

"Not you, sah. I call you a gentleman, by profession and education. De human skunk I's talking of is de coloured man from foreign parts."

"You are designating Mister Harkaway's servant, Monday?"

"You's hit de bull's-eye de very fust time."

"Has he been offending of you?"

"Wait till I tell you," rejoined Sunday. "His conduct is quite astonishin'."

Sunday proceeded to relate the story of Monday's perfidy, as he had done to Uncle Pomp.

The intelligence made Gumbo as indignant as the gardener had become, and for more than one reason.

Monday had assumed an air of superiority over the other servants, considering himself better than they.

"It's bad to flirt," remarked the coachman. "I won't say as I ain't done it myself, but it's bad."

"Not since you've been married," put in Uncle Pomp. "You's a church member ob the First Methodist Episcopal Church, and been a deacon."

"Can't help that. I's had my flirtations with the choir gals and school teachers; still, it's wrong, and I quite agree with de resolution passed by dis meeting, dat Monday ought to 'pologise right here to Aunt Lucy."

"I seconds dat motion," replied Pomp.

"It am carried," said Sunday.

"Clear the way, den; we'll hab one skunk fust."

"Dat's right. Step on one side."

The three negroes retreated to a safe distance.

Uncle Pomp produced a box of matches, and sitting on the grass, took the fuse in his hand.

Behind him was Sunday and Gumbo.

Striking a match, he set light to the fire, which began to fizzle slowly.

It would take about five minutes before it reached the torpedo, which was to blow up the skunk, supposed to be lurking in a hole among the roots of the hollow tree, close by.

"She's a-goin'. Hear her," exclaimed uncle Pomp.

"Let her rip!" answered Gumbo, "look out for de pieces."

As he spoke, the dark agile form of Monday appeared upon the scene.

He was walking moodily along, munching some apples he had gathered from a tree.

It was not until he was close upon the three negroes, that he became aware of their presence.

He had been rather annoyed at Sunday's interference between Aunt Lucy and himself.

Not that he cared a snap of the fingers about the cook's affections, but he had liked the run of the kitchen.

It was the good things she bestowed upon him that he cared for.

"Hullo!" he exclaimed, stopping short, "you folks holding um convention?"

He had halted just over the exact place where the torpedo had been laid in the earth. Not the least idea had he that such was the case.

"We's been talking 'bout you," replied Sunday. "There must be no more foolin' with the cook."

"I should think you've got plenty to say," retorted Monday. "Did you ebber talk anyone to deff?"

"Maum Lucy has consented, sah, to be my wife in three weeks' time. You will approach her again at your peril."

"Going to be um wife to you?"

"Yes, sah; and you've got to 'pologise for your 'frontery dis morning."

"Me do what?"

"Make de humble 'pology on your bended knees to Aunt Lucy. Ain't dat right, brudders?"

Uncle Pomp and Gumbo both agreed that it was so.

They added that they had determined they would see it done.

Monday burst out into a fit of loud derisive laughter.

"Ha, ha! yah, yah!" he cried. "You poor ignorant coons. Whar was you raised?"

"In these United States. We didn't come from where de mean niggers like you grow," retorted Sunday.

"Me am a prince in um own country. Ebber so much better than you. I's higher—ten times higher—"

Monday's utterances were cut short abruptly.

The fire of the fuse had reached the torpedo over which he was standing.

He had only time to yell, "Ouch! Oh!" when he was forced violently into the air.

There was no doubt that he was higher—very much higher, than the others in a few seconds.

He certainly ascended at least ten feet, in a cloud of earth and dust.

Then he turned a somersault, and fell down on his back half-stunned and half-dazed.

He did not know whether it was an earthquake, or the side of a house fallen in.

What was patent, was that he had gone up like a rocket.

Yet, as so many boasters do, he had come down like the stick.

The shock disturbed the roots of the old tree, and also the skunk.

As Uncle Pomp imagined, the animal was hiding in a hole hard by.

He was jerked out on the top of Monday.

The first thing he did was to squirt his offensive secretion over the Prince of Limbi.

This unfortunate member of a distant and little known, if ancient, royal family, had his clothes completely saturated.

Having accomplished this feat, the skunk sought fresh fields and pastures new.

It was in vain that Uncle Pomp threw sticks at him, that Sunday shouted, and that Gumbo discharged a pistol.

The skunk was proof against all that.

He succeeded in getting safely away, but the fact of his having been present remained.

The three negroes put their fingers to their noses.

"Him gone," said Sunday.

"But him hab left um card behind," replied Uncle Pomp.

"That sassy nigger got badly skunked. What we do with him?" exclaimed Gumbo.

"Put him on de mule and ride him out ob de grounds," suggested Uncle Pomp.

"Dat good idea. He'll hab to bury um clothes, for suah, somewhar."

By this time Monday had slightly recovered himself.

He sat up, and looked stupidly about him.

His impression of things in general was rather confused than otherwise.

"Come on, boys! Face de music!" cried Sunday.

Uncle Pomp was by his side in a moment.

They took Monday up by the feet and shoulders between them, and lifted him onto the mule's back.

Whether intentionally or not, they placed him with his face to the tail.

"Tie his legs under de belly," said Gumbo. "Eh! how will that do?"

"Fust-rate," replied Sunday.

Gumbo produced his pruning knife, and, cutting the rope that held the mule, fastened Monday's legs together.

He was unable to get off the beast now.

Nor could the mule get rid of him, if he kicked and backed ever so much.

The explosion had not improved the temper of the half-bred brute.

He began to rear, put back his ears, and hump his back.

"Whoa!" cried Monday. "What game you call this, boys? Let um get down."

"Not much, you won't," answered Uncle Pomp.

"Oh, no! Not if these childern knows it," said Sunday.

"Is dis um circus?" enquired Monday.

"It's a camp meetin'," replied Gumbo. "You's got to say your prayers for your sins, and 'pologise to Aunt Lucy."

"Hold on a bit!" exclaimed Monday. "What hysted me? Was it a earthquake?"

"Nebber mind what it was. Something comed out ob de earth and sent yer flying for yer sins, I tell yer."

"I thought it was de end ob um world."

"That's so. De day ob judgment am comed for you, and you'd better consent to 'pologise. We's all respectable law-'biding niggers heah."

"Ain't thar a funny kind ob smell 'bout?" queried Monday. "I's half choked."

"Dat's de sulphur out ob de earth. It won't go till you is made de 'pology."

"I ain't no fool," said Monday. "It was only a joke with the ole gal. You cut me loose, or I'll tell Mast' Harkaway, and he gib you all de sack, quick!"

"De debble am after you for 'sulting of Aunt Lucy. Dat what made de ground blow up. Your hair am all singed, and you smell bad of de sulphur."

Monday began to get frightened. He could not account for what had taken place.

Nothing about the torpedo was known to him, and he could not make out what caused the peculiar stench.

Still, he did not like to humiliate himself before the three negroes.

The mule had been long growing impatient.

Finding that he could not throw the burden off his back, he started at a gallop.

Instinct seemed to direct him towards the kitchen, for he went to the back of the house.

The negroes followed as fast as they could.

"Hi, yi!" they holloaed at the top of their voices. "Ain't dis a picnic! Yah, yah!"

The mule reached the yard in the rear, whence there was no exit, save by the way he had entered.

He was unable to retreat, because the negroes were pressing and shouting behind him.

It being a warm afternoon, the kitchen door was standing invitingly open.

Aunt Lucy had dished up the fricassee chicken with mashed potatoes, placing the tempting mess on the table.

All at once she heard a strange noise, and, looking up, saw the mule enter with Monday on his back.

"Oh, lor'!" she cried, "what am dis? Shoo, you brute! Git! Shoo, I tell yer!"

The mule ran against the table and fell down, kicking violently.

In a minute the table was upset, and the plates and dishes crashed on the floor.

Monday struggled to get free.

The rope broke; he was liberated, and ran into a corner, but not before he had received a kick from the mule on the knee, which made him limp and howl with pain.

Aunt Lucy jumped upon a chair. The mule turned and made for the door.

He met Sunday, Uncle Pomp, and Gumbo, rolling the trio over, and treading on them as he made his escape.

Monday was groaning, the cook crying, and the negroes gave vent to language not suited to polite ears.

Presently the smell of the skunk filled the kitchen, and Aunt Lucy raised her hand to her nose.

"What you men doing?" she demanded. "This ain't no place for foolin'."

"We's brought the malefactor to 'pologise," replied Sunday; "dat's what's he's got ter do."

"I'll do anything," answered Monday. "Oh, um poor knee. Dat mule am an experienced kicker, brudders."

"Make de 'pology," cried Uncle Pomp.

"I's very sorry for flirting," exclaimed Monday. "It is de fust time, and it shall be de last. Accept my ample 'pology, and I'll give you um pair of gloves for de weddin'."

"Dat's good; we's satisfied," replied Sunday.

"Sakes alive," said Aunt Lucy, "what you been doin' to him?"

"He am been skunked, ma'am," answered Gumbo.

"Take him away. I'll nebber be able to use dis kitchen no more. Run him out. You Pomp, get him a suit ob clothes and 'tend to him in de garden; he'll p'ison de hull house."

Uncle Pomp grasped Monday by the arm, and led him into the garden as fast as his injured leg would allow him to go.

They did not stop until they were under some trees, a good distance from the mansion.

Close by was a small hut, where the gardener kept his tools, and also a bottle of whisky.

With this he was wont to refresh himself during the heat of the day.

Good-naturedly he brought out his old rye and a glass, asking Monday to partake of it.

This the latter was not at all loath to do.

When they had pledged one another, Uncle Pomp incautiously explained all that had happened.

That which had been mysterious was made clear.

Monday found that he had been blown up by a torpedo and badly skunked.

That accounted for the evil odour which was half stifling him.

He became very angry.

Drawing a pistol from his pocket, he presented it at the friendly gardener.

"Sah," he exclaimed, "jes' you strip."

"What you mean by dat?" asked Uncle Pomp.

"You's played it low down on me. I's been blowed up, skunked, and made to 'pologise to Aunt Lucy, and been kicked by um ole mule."

"Dat not all my fault, Mr. Monday, sah."

"You was in it. Golly, I'll pay you. Bet you a red cent, you'll not forget this day."

"If you shoot me, you'll be hanged."

"I don't care a continental for dat. If you don't want de lead in your body, take off dem clothes. I want de coat, vest and pants," replied Monday.

"You can't hab 'em."

"Den I'm bound to shoot and take um off you."

"I's not a rich man. Dis is de only suit of store clothes I's got for week days and de Sabbath."

"Off with um."

Monday's manner became so threatening, that Uncle Pomp was dreadfully alarmed.

He promptly stripped to his drawers and shirt, while Monday did the same.

They were about the same height and size; and if the gardener's clothes were not so good as his, they were clean and sweet.

Monday rapidly invested himself in the other's garments.

"Oh, de good lord!" whined Uncle Pomp "I can't go home like this; if I do, I'll have ter stop in bed till I can buy a new suit of clothes. What'll my wife say?"

"I don't want to be hard on you; here's a twenty dollar bill to buy some more. Now beg um pardon."

The man did so.

Monday threw the paper money towards him, and walked away.

The gardener sneaked off to his cottage, feeling very much ashamed of himself.

"Dat's one ob 'em," muttered Monday.

He proceeded to the stable yard, where, as he had expected, he found Gumbo at work.

The coachman was whipping the mule into his stable, that obstinate animal having become unruly.

Gumbo no sooner saw Monday, than he put his fingers to his nose.

"Bad smell around somewhere," he said.

Monday snatched the whip from him and knocked him down, using his fists as he had seen Jack do.

Then he lashed him over the back and loins to his heart's content.

"Let up on me," cried Gumbo. "I didn't mean nuffin'."

"Beg um pardon, for um cheek," shouted Monday.

"Yes, sah—Mister Monday, sah."

"Are you sorry for what you hab done?"

"I is, sah. Nebber will I do so no more. You's a gentleman nigger, ebbery inch ob you."

"All right. That will do for you."

He next sought Sunday, to exact what he termed satisfaction from him.

Sunday had been complimented by Aunt Lucy on the promptness and cleverness he had displayed in making his rival apologise for his rudeness and presumption.

Very much pleased with himself, he had gone into the pantry, where wine and spirits were kept, to indulge himself in a little refreshment.

This was Monday's apartment. He was in charge of the cellar and the pantry.

As a rule, he locked the door and put the key in his pocket.

To-day he had omitted to do so, and having passed by, Sunday was aware of the fact.

Monday had an idea that Sunday would be in his pantry, and went there at once.

The negro's back was turned towards the door, and as Monday trod lightly, he was unaware of his presence.

"OH, EMMERSON, DO NOT KILL ME! CRIED GARGIA."

He had opened the cupboard, on the shelves of which stood several bottles.

Their contents were labelled on them.

"Sherry, champagne, port," mused Sunday, "brandy, whisky, gin, rum. What 'll I hab? Rum for choice. Oh, ain't dis jolly? Git aboard, little chillun, we're goin' ter hab a day off."

He laughed till his sides shook.

Then he took up the bottle of rum.

"Drop it!" roared Monday. "Dat rum am Mast' Harkaway's, and you'll not taste a drop."

Sunday had no right to be in the pantry, helping himself to what was his master's; and fearful lest he should be locked up, he fell on his knees.

"Forgive me dis time, sah," he said.

"If I do, will you keep your mouf shut 'bout my flirtation with Aunt Lucy?"

"Certain suah, I will!"

"Not a word to my wife 'bout um cook?"

"No, sah. Me be as dumb as a oyster," replied Sunday.

"Get up, then, and shake hands. I think we're square on the deal. If you've euchred me, I think I hab you."

Sunday rose to his feet.

"Now," added Monday, "we'll hab a boss drink together."

They did so, and afterwards shook hands cordially.

This little episode, instead of estranging them, made them better friends.

But Sunday did not marry Aunt Lucy.

That very day Jack received a message from New York, which occasioned him to return to the city on the morrow, with all his party.

Important events were looming in the distance.

The establishment on Long Island was broken up, and Aunt Lucy obtained another situation, where she soon forgot the wooing of Sunday.

We must now deal with stirring events in the chief city in the Empire State.

CHAPTER XXXIX.

HUNTING THE VILLAINS.

THE Bowery gang yet contrived to exist and to flourish, in spite of the utmost vigilance exercised by the authorities.

Yet a snare was being spread for them.

Untiring in the task of hunting them down were Daniel Pike and Nabley, the detectives.

Emmerson had taken the life, under the most brutal and cowardly circumstances, of Pike's most valued friend and comrade, Nabley's elder brother.

Nabley himself, as you have seen, had been nearly done to death by the same gang. And now an accumulated store of hatred had been piled up, which must inevitably bear fruit.

The Bowery gang was doomed.

The only question was how that doom was to be accomplished.

Oliver Girdwood sought to exterminate them root and branch.

But to the two detectives, Nabley and Daniel Pike, this did not suffice.

They wanted to take them living.

"Death," said Nabley to Noll Gird-wood—"death, my boy, is too good for these villains and murderers. Death would be rest. No, they must know what the living death of a convict's life is."

The boy shivered.

Hate as fiercely as he did the murderers of his beloved brother, he could not grapple with such revenge as this.

"These men are no cowards," said Nabley, "whatever faults they may have."

"Evidently not."

"Why, then, to shoot them down, or to let them die facing their enemy, would be elevating them to the dignity of warriors. They would be glorified and spoken of as heroes, instead of the miserable vermin that they are. Their last moments would be of triumph, and ten to one but the public would look upon them as bold and daring adventurers, while we should be stigmatised as bloodhounds."

There was certainly something in that.

"No," pursued the detective, "we must do better than that"

"What do you propose?"

"Take them alive."

"How?"

"That is to be seen."

"It is impossible, I fear," said Oliver.

"There must be no such word as impossible in this case."

Meanwhile, a watch was mounted night and day upon the haunt of the Bowery gang.

When Protean Bob returned to his haunt, doubly disguised, as you will remember, he took with him a whole store of food—sufficient to victual the fortress for many days.

We use the word fortress advisedly.

It was, in fact, a stronghold.

It was well-nigh impossible to storm it, to take those bold and desperate ruffians, without sacrificing human life.

In that place they could defend themselves against a small army.

"I have got the way to get them out," said Oliver Girdwood, one day, to Pike.

"You have?"

"Yes."

The detective smiled.

"You are about to offer some wild and impracticable plan ; but I must humour you by listening."

"What is it?" asked Nabley.

"I have found out that we can hire the basement of the adjoining house."

"For what purpose?"

"To effect a communication," replied the boy.

"Tell us more," said Daniel Pike, smiling doubtfully.

"I don't propose to make a large opening; I only suggest boring two fissures in the wall."

"How?"

"Easily enough. Use a centrebit where the wall is hard—complete it with the long gimlets such as bellhangers use——"

"And then?"

"Funk them out."

"What do you mean?"

"Blow noxious gases through the holes."

There was a bit of a notion in this, and it caught his hearers' attention in spite of themselves.

Pike and Nabley consulted together.

"Explain your plan fully," said Nabley ; "give us the details——"

"I will—it is this. I would set to work to bore four or five holes into their cellar—at least four should be made before we begin the last part of the work."

"Next?"

"Next I would start a number of pots of something of a stifling character."

"Charcoal."

"Or sulphur."

"Sulphur for preference," said Oliver Girdwood.

"Yes, yes," said Pike, eagerly.

"Then, when all was prepared, I would set to work upon all the places at once, and having a lot prepared in advance, blow the sulphur smoke through the holes."

Nabley found one objection to it.

"They would easily stop up the holes as soon as they discovered whence the sulphur came."

"But they would not."

"It is doubtful."

"I am sure not."

"How would you propose to prevent it?"

"By working in the dead of the night—by having our instruments oiled so thoroughly that not a sound should be heard.

"In one night we could fill every crack—every square foot, of their lurking place with noxious vapours, and they would either have to die stifled in their hole like rats in a sewer, or fly into the arms of the police for bare life."

"By jingo!" ejaculated Pike, "it sounds right."

"It does," added his companion, much struck, "yet it may be opposed by the police authorities here."

"On what points?"

"It still exposes the men waiting for them to great danger."

"Scarcely that."

"They would fight like wild beasts," suggested Pike.

"They would be more than half helpless," said Oliver Girdwood; "the stifling of the sulphur would act partly as a narcotic, and they would not be able to offer anything like a resistance. Our measures could be taken in consequence."

"What further measures would you propose?"

"I would spread nets for them—snare them as wild beasts are caught—have network or ropes waiting to entangle them as they rush madly out of their den, and so overpower them successively as they come forth."

The two detectives were singularly struck with the boldness and originality of this scheme.

Moreover, they set to work without delay to put it into execution.

The implements were brought, the place adjoining the Bowery gang's den was taken, and the lawful conspirators set to work against their lawless enemies.

One night's work was accomplished.

The utmost caution was observed in the carrying out of Oliver Girdwood's plans.

The boy inventor of the ingenious plan conducted the operations.

With him were the two English detectives, and an officer of note of the New York police, besides two workmen of great experience and skill, upon whose discretion the utmost reliance could be placed.

This completed the working staff.

The watch without comprised all our friends.

Notably amongst the watchers were young Jack and his father, Dick Harvey, Mr. Jefferson, and his little friend the dwarf.

Besides these there were several policemen.

Oliver's suggestions had been carried out.

They were provided with appliances which were certainly novel for thief taking.

Now, towards two in the morning, the door of the basement den was opened cautiously.

Young Jack pinched his father's arm to call his attention to it.

"See, dad?"

"Yes, I see."

"Hush! are they on the look-out, do you think?"

"Yes."

In fact they were.

As the door opened, three dark forms, hiding in different places, were seen to move.

One was Mr. Jefferson.

His huge form towered up in a doorway close by the gate which had just opened.

The young Kentuckian looked more like a colossal statue than a man.

A head was put out.

Two glistening eyes peered about in all directions.

Then a figure crept stealthily out.

It was nothing very formidable to look at now that it was out, this figure.

A poor old man, with white hair, and bent nearly double with age or rheumatism, or both, who could only make very slow progress as he hobbled along on a stick.

Jefferson stepped out after him.

He trod very lightly for such a big man, and in two strides he overhauled him.

Then, clapping a heavy hand upon his shoulder, he pulled him up.

"Stop! I arrest you."

"On what charge?"

"Murder."

The old man shivered from head to foot.

"Murder?"

"Murder amongst other trifles," said Mr. Jefferson.

The old man struggled, but he was powerless in the hands of the burly Kentuckian.

"You are sure that there is no mistake, sir?" said one of the policemen, in a whisper.

"We'll risk that," said Mr. Jefferson. "Anyhow, I don't mean to let go."

"It's an awkward thing to land an innocent man."

"He's the man," said young Jack; "it is Emmerson!"

"Ha!"

The prisoner renewed his struggles for liberty.

"Emmerson! Impossible. How do you know?"

"Noll followed him dressed like that," replied young Jack, quickly.

A muttered curse escaped the prisoner.

"Besides, it is just the get-up that Saul Garcia described."

"Saul Garcia the traitor!" ejaculated the prisoner, involuntarily.

He could have bitten his tongue off the next moment, but it was too late to recall his words.

Robert Emmerson was bound and handcuffed.

He tried to cry out and warn his friends and comrades in villany, but at the first word Mr. Jefferson clapped his hand over his mouth.

It was not a gentle touch.

In fact that dab loosened his teeth, and

it warned Protean Bob that he had better remain quiet, at least while he was in the clutches of Mr. Jefferson.

And so, foaming with rage, Robert Emmerson was dragged off prisonwards.

They got a cab a little way on, and the prisoner was thrust in.

Beside him sat Mr. Jefferson, and opposite were two officers.

Small chance of escape for you now, Protean Bob! He felt that too.

Yet his heart did not sink.

He sat back silent—silent and thoughtful. He was calculating the chances.

"If ever I get a chance," he muttered between his fast-set teeth, "it shall go hard with Saul Garcia. I'll have his life if I lose my own the next hour!"

CHAPTER XL.

THEIR way lay through the most unsavoury and most ill-paved quarter of the town.

The streets near the waterside were all more or less irregular—dangerous for vehicles and for horses.

Jolt, jolt, jolt—bump, bump!

Suddenly there was a jerk, a crack!

The cab rocked to and fro.

Then over it went, with a mighty crash and a smash!

Next moment the occupants of the cab were scrambling about at the bottom of the cab, struggling, kicking, and crying out.

With some difficulty Mr. Jefferson contrived to get free from the scramble, and he proceeded to help his companions out of their difficulty.

The prisoner was heard to give a hollow groan.

"Are you hurt?" asked Mr. Jefferson.

"My arm is broken, I think," replied Emmerson.

They lifted him out.

One of his arms was evidently badly hurt, for he supported it with difficulty with the other.

At the same time his groans told that he was suffering most acute pain.

Now, scoundrel as he was, it touched them to see him suffering, and so thoroughly helpless.

"Remove the handcuffs," said Mr. Jefferson.

The policeman obeyed, and Emmerson gave a groan of relief.

"Which is the one that is hurt?" they asked.

"The right."

"No bones broken?"

"It is, I am sure."

He limped a bit as he answered them.

"Have you hurt your legs?" asked one of the policemen.

"One of them," returned Emmerson. "I don't think I can walk."

They stooped down to examine his hurts; and, lo! he was cured instantaneously.

Before they could say Jack Robinson, Protean Bob gave them a desperate blow, right and left, which sent them sprawling; and then, ere an eye could wink, he bounded off like a deer.

The next moment he was lost in the night.

"Blarm you!" ejaculated the big Kentuckian, "for a couple of fools."

Off he ran in pursuit.

But Protean Bob was wonderfully fleet of foot, and fear lent him wings.

Moreover, the darkness favoured his flight, and pursuit looked hopeless.

However, Mr. Jefferson would not give it up without a trial.

On he ran for twenty paces or more, when, being at fault, he paused to listen.

His hearing was singularly keen; long habits of forest and prairie life had sharpened it, and he heard a footstep in an adjoining street.

Turning, then, sharply round, his perseverance was rewarded by a sight of Emmerson in full flight.

"Now I have you," said the Kentuckian, dashing off.

In spite of his huge size, he was as active as the slimmest lad, and he made the running very hot indeed for the fugitive.

Step by step he cut down the distance between them. Step by step he was gaining on the prisoner.

Emmerson's liberty promised to be but short-lived.

And now not thirty feet separated them, when all of a sudden the escaped prisoner vanished.

There was a cry.

A splash.

Then all was silent.

Jefferson was running so hard that, before he could fairly realise what had taken place, he found himself upon the spot where Emmerson had disappeared.

On the water's edge!

So near, so fatally close was he, that it was little less than marvellous how he contrived to draw himself up short upon the brink.

The shock made his flesh creep—his hair stand on end.

"Pheugh!" said the Kentuckian, "that was a precious narrow squeak."

He looked down.

The dark waters splashed against the woodwork below, and the wind howled dismally enough.

But there was no sign of Emmerson.

Had the English murderer escaped after all?

"I thought that that cuss had never been born to be drowned," he said to himself. "I'll never believe that old saying again."

He turned to retrace his steps, and before he had gone far he met the two policemen coming towards him.

"Got him?" asked one.

"No."

"He has got clear off?"

"Yes."

"Hang him!"

"No fear of that," retorted the Kentuckian, grimly. "You'll never hang Robert Emmerson."

"Why not?"

"Because he's drowned."

"Drowned!"

"Yes."

They hurried back to the brink of the water and looked about, but not a vestige—not a sign—was there of the notorious criminal.

"That's the end of Protean Bob," said one of the constables. "He didn't know, I suppose, that there was no thoroughfare here; but at any rate, there would be small chance of escape. As it is, with the present high tides, the best swimmer that ever lived would be done for there!"

* * * * *

They little knew Robert Emmerson, however, or they would have paused before coming to the conclusion that he was drowned, for in a short time a man might have been seen fighting his way from the dark waters; and, on reaching the shore, kneeling down and clenching his hands tightly, he exclaimed through his hard-set teeth—

"Saul Garcia, you have betrayed me. I swore I would have your life for it, and by Heaven I will!"

CHAPTER XLI.

THE gang now claims a passing mention at our hands.

So well was Oliver Girdwood's plan carried out that not a sound was heard in the haunt of the Bowery gang, and yet their cellar was slowly but surely filling with deathly vapours, which must put a speedy end to their villanous career.

When the first faint streaks of the morning light struggled through the grating of their cellar, and played across Toro's eyes, he aroused himself with considerable difficulty.

His first sensations were of a painful burning about the eyes, a swelling of the tongue and throat.

He could hardly see.

He coughed and shook himself, and rubbed his eyes.

"Something wrong here," said the giant to himself.

Do what he would, he could not shake off the unpleasant sensations.

By degrees it began to alarm him, and then he awakened Hunston.

The latter now experienced just the same sensations as Toro had on awakening.

Smarting of the eyes, swelling of the tongue and throat, and difficulty of articulating.

What could it be?

It fairly puzzled them.

"There is only one way of accounting for it," said Hunston.

"What is that?"

"We have been stived up here so long that the air has got foul."

"I suppose it is that," said Toro. "But the remedy?"

"That is more difficult to discover than the cause."

"Something must be done," said the giant.

"Of course."

"And speedily."

"Just my opinion. But what?"

Toro scratched his shaggy locks for an idea.

"We had better wake them all up and consult with them about it."

"Very well."

They set to work to arouse their sleeping comrades, and as they woke up one by one, it was remarked that they all appeared to suffer in some degree from the same symptoms as Hunston and Toro.

Some more, some less.

It was observed, too, that one man, who slept with a handkerchief over his face, had been scarcely inconvenienced by it.

The reason of it was apparent enough.

The sleeper breathed through his handkerchief, which acted as a species of respirator for him.

Now this man was naturally in a better position than his comrades to judge of the nature of the complaint which troubled them all.

"I can smell sulphur very strong," he said, with a sniff.

"Sulphur!" ejaculated the gang, in a breath.

"Yes."

"Impossible."

"Or charcoal."

"But how? Where can it come from?" said Toro.

"That I can't say; but still I have a notion."

"What is it?"

"What if they were trying to funk us out?"

"Funk us out?"

"Yes."

"What do you mean?"

"How?"

"Smoke us out, I mean."

It was a pretty shrewd guess, and it was so very likely that it made Hunston look thoughtful.

"It would almost seem like it," he said, "yet I don't see where it could come from."

"Nor I."

"The door."

"No—the grating"

"Impossible!"

"Why?"

"The grating is always clear enough."

Now, while this discussion was going forward, the sun came out and shot a powerful ray into the cellar, along which they could see the noxious vapours playing, curling, and dancing in their struggles to get to the air.

One of the gang was a mysterious German in spectacles.

He pointed to the fumes wriggling their tortuous course along the sunbeam.

"Zee dere," he cried.

"I do."

"Ve shall be chokit," said the German, in the most cheerful manner, as though he were announcing a bit of the best luck imaginable.

"Choked!"

"Ja wohl," he said, nodding.

"But how do you propose getting over the trouble?"

The German thought for awhile, and then replied—

"Make a hole, und greeb out."

"Where?" asked Hunston, eagerly; "in the wall?"

"Nein."

"In the floor?"

"Nein."

"Where then?"

"In der zeiling."

"Why there?"

"Because dey haf examine der haus, und dey haf disgover dat dere is no door —no gommunigation, und dey not on der watch dere."

"You're right, Fritz, you're right," ejaculated Hunston. "Fritz is the man to save us."

The work had to be proceeded with briskly.

And this is the way they set about it.

Herr Fritz Von Koppenhaagen was hoisted on Toro's shoulders, where, armed with different pointed instruments, he proceeded to loosen the plaster and masonry.

In this way they escaped their present dilemma—but only just in time.

The great difficulty was that the nearer the roof, the denser the fumes of sulphur, and Von Koppenhaagen had some trouble to keep at his work.

However, he was relieved presently, and the work was accomplished in this way—that is, by turn and turn about.

"I am zo glad than I can tell," said Fritz, "to zee der hole is droo. Und now I will go droo der hole. Dat ist zer goot; it make me larfs."

The French have a saying about beleaguered towns which proved to be very true during the war—

"*Ville assiégée—ville prise.*" "A town besieged is a taken town."

The inventors of that proverb were shrewd observers.

It is invariably the case.

Nor was this any exception to the rule, only, thanks to the sagacity of Herr Fritz Von Koppenhaagen, the besieged managed to sneak off and leave their fortress in the hands of the enemy.

And so it came to pass that, when three days were gone by, the besiegers resolved to effect a breach and push into the fortress.

The garrison, they concluded, would be very harmless now, thanks to Oliver Girdwood's fumigators.

The utter silence of the place convinced them that the sulphur fumes had reduced the gang to an utter state of helplessness, and that they would be discovered as dry as a fly in a spider's web.

Great was their humiliation, therefore, when they came down the cellar with endless precautions to guard against surprise, and found that the birds had flown.

They examined the house above, but found it was utterly deserted now.

Upon making inquiries, they learnt from the police authorities that the owner of the house was a suspicious customer, whose movements had long brought him under the eye of the excise people.

He was reported to have made money during the war in blockade running, and now that that was over, he appeared to turn his hand to anything which might be termed a kindred trade.

Some people said he smuggled.

Others said, with more apparent reason, that he earned a risky livelihood by serving the rebel Cubans.

This was exceedingly risky, as many poor fellows have since found out.

This rumour caught the attention of Daniel Pike, and he pushed his inquiries further in that direction.

And, after some days, they discovered that Captain Clemmans had just embarked, having got his crew completed.

The Spanish consul had ascertained beyond doubt that the "Will o' the Wisp" was engaged in a desperate venture—the transport of arms to the Cuban insurgents—and he set to work to take the necessary steps to prevent the vessel from starting.

The Harkaways were very much interested in this, for Pike and Nabley had been actively engaged in raking up evidence themselves, and with this notable result.

They had, beyond all manner of doubt, traced some members of the Bowery gang on board the "Will o' the Wisp."

This settled, they had to obtain a search warrant.

Every possible facility was granted them in this matter.

But certain formalities had to be gone through.

In the meantime certain events had occurred which must come in their proper order.

These must be given in another chapter.

CHAPTER XLII.

THEY could not get over Mr. Mole's betrothal.

The Harkaways made sure that it had been brought about by young Jack.

Little Emily, Harvey and Hilda's daughter, had now quite recovered from her long illness, and once more became the playmate of young Jack.

She was indeed a most beautiful girl, and our young friend Jack seemed at all times pleased to be in her charming company.

Little Emily believed that young Jack was the cause of Chloe selecting Mr. Mole for her husband.

But young Jack protested stoutly that he knew nothing about it.

Nor, in point of fact, did he.

"After all, Em'," said he, slily, "what's the odds? Black or white have hearts alike."

"Of course they have."

"And Chloe is a very good and kind girl."

"That she is," replied little Emily, with warmth.

"And if she loves Mr. Mole, I am very glad that she is going to have him. And I'm glad for him, too. I don't like to see people sighing and dying for each other, and not able to marry because one happens to be a dip or two darker than the other."

The sentiment caught little Emily on her soft side.

"But do you think you would like a black wife, Jack dear?" she asked, archly.

"Not I," replied her youthful champion; "but I'd marry her if I were a man, and she loved me."

"Would you, indeed, sir?" said Emily, with a toss of her flaxen curls.

"Of course."

"Then you had better go and look for your black sweetheart," said she, flouncing out of the room.

But young Jack caught her before she could get fairly away, and gave her a kiss that you might have heard in the next room.

"Well, I'm sure," said the little lady, reddening; "you're very impudent, Master Jack."

"You don't think so," said young Jack, saucily.

"Indeed I do."

"Then give it me back."

And then there ensued a chase, and young Jack let himself be caught after a very little dodging, and held up his cheek to be punished.

She lifted her little hand, but dropped it again as he stood his ground firmly, and did not flinch.

"What!" exclaimed young Jack, "you won't, Em'?"

"Not this time."

"Then give me back mine."

"Your what?" asked the young lady, demurely.

She learned the art of coquetry at a very early age, you see.

"My smack," explained young Jack, grinning.

"Don't be silly, sir," replied Emily, who could not pretend to misunderstand any longer.

"Very well," said young Jack, "I know why you won't."

"Why?"

"Oh! you know."

"I'm sure I do not."

"Noll Girdwood wouldn't have to ask you twice."

Emily coloured up at this insinuation.

"There, there," cried the mischievous boy, "you're blushing—that tells."

"I'm sure I'm not," retorted little Emily.

But as she spoke, the colour on her fair cheeks deepened to a rich purple.

"I knew you cared a deal more for Noll than you do for me," said young Jack, in that tone of voice which is called "half joke, whole earnest." "Well, I don't mind if you really like poor Noll best; only don't you flirt with him, and then give him turnips."

"That's very vulgar, sir," retorted the little beauty, "and it isn't true."

"Oh, isn't it?"

"No."

"Why, you used to be ever so fond of me."

"Well, what then?"

"Why, you're not now."

"Who says so?"

"I do."

"You're a wicked, ungrateful boy."

"I don't believe you would have cared much if Hunston and Toro had done for me. I don't believe you'd have shed a tear after me."

"Oh, Jack!"

This was too much for her, and she burst into tears.

Then young Jack was melted too, and he hastened to dry her eyes with his pocket-handkerchief, and what remained of them he kissed away as tenderly as you please.

But she sobbed away in great distress.

"You say I don't care for you," she

said; "but you don't care for me, of course."

"Indeed I do."

"You don't."

He protested stoutly, but she would not allow it.

"You wouldn't try to distress your friends so, if you did really care for them," she said.

"I was not to know that they cared enough for me," urged young Jack.

"But some of them must care for you, and if you cared for them, you would never go running into all kinds of danger for no purpose but to make us all unhappy."

"Oh, indeed!"

"No, sir," she added, with flashing eyes, and changing her tone, "but I don't admire it, I don't think it brave after all. You have no need to run after danger in that way, just to show that you are courageous."

"Is that what I do?" said young Jack, humbly; "well, I won't do it any more."

"You promise?"

"I do."

"There's a dear, good Jack," she said, clapping her hands with glee. "But you'll forget unless I give you something to remind you."

"No, I won't."

"Oh, you will. Now what shall I give you? Let me see."

"One of your curls."

"Oh, no; you'd throw that away soon, I know. Here's a box of chocolates I have just bought. Now, whenever you feel inclined to do anything too harum-scarum, look at this, and remember your promise."

"I will."

And then he sought for a gift for her.

He had nothing at that moment but his little necktie; this he took off his neck, and gave her, and she kept it for many a long year as a love gift.

Her gift to Jack was, however, destined to prove a very valuable one indeed to him. And that ere long.

CHAPTER XLIII.

MR. MOLE'S wedding was the one topic of conversation amongst our friends the Harkaways and party.

As soon as it was settled, Dick Harvey was full of his mischief.

Nothing would do, but he must organise visits of congratulation on rather an elaborate scale.

These visits were to be carried out with a deal of ceremony.

Harvey himself led the way in these congratulatory calls.

Young Jack was with him on that auspicious occasion.

You can guess how they enjoyed themselves.

"Mr. Mole," said Harvey, with the greatest gravity, "accept my warmest congratulations."

Mr. Mole winced.

"Yes, thank you, Harvey," he said; "I am much better."

"Of course you are."

"No pain now."

"Pain!" exclaimed Harvey, with an extravagant sigh and a leer of great sig-

nificance; "young fellows in your condition are insensible to pain."

"In my condition?" said Mole, glancing at his wooden leg.

"Yes."

"What condition?"

"Betrothed."

"Ugh!"

"Under sentence of matrimony," sighed Harvey. "Ah, sir, you're a lucky dog."

"Harvey," said Mr. Mole, "I can't stand it. I'm not used to it—that is, not used to it of late."

"Of course not," replied the irrepressible Dick, "but as it makes your third wife——"

Mole groaned.

"Your third black wife, I may say."

"Harvey."

"Sir."

"Unless you wish to turn my stomach, you will make no allusion whatever to the past."

"If you wish it, sir."

"I do."

" Very good, then."

" The present is quite painful enough."

" The present!" said Harvey, with a stupid, stolid look. " Who has made you a present?"

" Tut, tut, tut!" quoth Mr. Mole, impatiently. " You're a sad tease, Harvey. I mean the present time."

Harvey pretended to look serious.

" I hope that your approaching nuptials do not cause you any anxiety."

Mr. Mole groaned.

" Of course a man in your position feels anxious," pursued Dick Harvey, pitilessly, " but it exalts you in our estimation, Mr. Mole."

Here were crumbs of comfort for the tutor.

He grabbed at them eagerly enough, too.

" How?"

" We recognise in it your strength of mind, Mr. Mole. We see how superior you are to vulgar prejudice. You have no weak-minded prejudice in favour of fair faces."

" Oh!"

" Or flaxen hair."

" Oh, Harvey, but I have!"

" Or blue eyes."

" Don't, Harvey, don't!" groaned the unhappy tutor.

" You care little about the skin of your innamorata being a dip more or less inky."

" Harvey!" almost shrieked the tutor, " stop!"

" Ah," said Dick, looking up at the ceiling in rapt admiration of Mr. Mole, " that's where we recognise the strong-minded, large-hearted Isaac Mole.

" Yes, Mr. Mole, when we consider that you are about taking to your heart and home your third wife, and she, like your two first, beautiful and black, we must, in justice to you, my dear sir, say you are a man of undoubted courage."

And, apparently too much overcome for more words, he wrung Mr. Mole earnestly by the hand.

Mr. Mole could scarcely reply, but he made a very wry face.

" I hope the future Mrs. Mole is quite well, sir," said young Jack.

" Who?"

" The future Mrs. Mole."

" It is scarcely customary to speak in those terms, Jack," said Harvey.

" Oh, I'm very sorry," said young Jack, looking confused, in order to cover his laughter; " I thought I was in order."

" You mean the bride."

" The fair bride?"

Mr. Mole could not repress a groan.

" She's quite well, but I hope, Harvey, that you have not brought Jack here for the purpose of making any unseemly fun of his tutor."

" Dear me, Mr. Mole," said Harvey, with a grieved expression. " I am exceedingly sorry to find that you should attribute such motives to me."

He touched his eyes with his handkerchief.

Mr. Mole was melted.

" Come, come, Harvey," he said, " I don't mean anything, only you were always such a devil in your fun."

" All right, sir," said Harvey, winking at young Jack behind his handkerchief.

" But don't congratulate me any more about the future Mrs.—faugh!"

" What is the lady's present name, then?" asked Harvey.

" Chloe."

" Yes, I know."

" What then?"

" Why, I could never presume to speak of her as Chloe."

" Why not?"

" What!" said young Jack, looking shocked. " The future Mrs. Mole——"

" I don't know her other name."

" What an odd thing."

There was a knock at the door, and Sunday entered.

" Morning, Massa Mole," said the darkey, with his accustomed cheery grin.

" Good morning, Sunday."

" Hope you bery well dis morning, Brudder Mole."

" What?"

" Hope you bery well."

" But did I understand you to call me brother?"

" Yes, Brudder Mole, I call you brudder."

" Then, you black doll, don't learn to take liberties."

" Liberties!"

He burst into a boisterous fit of laughter at this.

The word tickled Sunday mightily.

" D'yar tink I want to kiss yar, Massa brudder?"

Jack and Harvey could not refrain from joining in the merriment at this, whereupon Mr. Mole grew violent in his language.

"Why, you impudent sweep!" he cried, "you block of coal! you black idol! you—you——"

"Go on, Brudder Mole," said Sunday, laughing. "Do you know, Massa Jack, I never look at Brudder Mole without thinking of that pusson who was took poorly at the funeral of his fifth wife."

Young Jack tipped the wink to Harvey.

"What was that?"

"Why, he was a-gwine to faint off, when someone says—

"'Let him alone; he'll soon re-wive.' Yah, yah, yah!"

Mole was furious.

"Stop your hideous joking here, Sunday," he cried, "or else leave the room."

"I 'peal to dese gemmen," said Sunday, with a merry twinkle in his eye; "am I not a man and a brudder?"

"Of course."

"Certainly," said young Jack. "Of course you are."

"And Mr. Mole," said Harvey, "will be the first to admit it."

"In a poetical sense," said Mr. Mole.

"Precisely."

"And shan't I be more his brudder than ever?"

"Why?"

"Cos he's gwine to spouse a lady ob colour."

Young Jack and Harvey assented at once.

"No doubt of it."

"I wish you would keep your remarks to yourself, you animated black pudding."

Sunday replied—

"All right, Brudder Mole."

And then busied himself about the room.

He appeared greatly absorbed in dusting about, and as he went on he sang to himself *sotto voce.*

It was a medley song, and he had a good idea of tunes, so that it did not jar upon the ear at all.

But when he got to a very old English ditty, called "Let us haste to the wedding," Mr. Mole's feelings got the better of him, and he began to use bad language to Sunday.

"Don't like music, Brudder Mole?"

"Not that tune."

"Bery good."

He changed it, rattled off a variety, and concluded his selection with a bar or two of "Old King Cole."

This was full of more painful reminiscences than the other, so he stopped it quickly.

"If you must sing, you black tulip," cried the irate Mole, "let it be something less jiggy and singsongy; I hate such muck."

"Summat stately sorter, Brudder Mole?"

"Yes, hang you."

Sunday changed his time, tune, and manner at once, and strutted up and down in his dusting, to the imposing strains of Mendelssohn's "Wedding March."

This was too much for Mr. Mole.

With a violent expletive, he threw the first thing to hand at Sunday, who caught it dexterously and tossed it back *à la* cricketer, crying—"Play!"

Mr. Mole found it anything but play, for the book he threw at Sunday, being rather heavy, and on its return passage catching Mr. Mole on the side of the head, made him feel at that moment as though he should like to exterminate every nigger in the world.

"Well, Mr. Mole," said Harvey, as he left the apartment, "I trust, when I see you again, you will inform me when the happy day will be fixed for your marriage."

CHAPTER XLIV.

SAUL GARCIA slept badly on the night that Emmerson leaped into the river and escaped from the American and English detectives.

He was full of nervous fancies, and when he dozed off, it was to dream horribly.

He got up twice and went downstairs to look to the fastenings of the house.

Then he went up again to his room,

and endeavoured to compose himself for sleep.

He tossed about upon his pillow; he groaned and moaned, and woke up with a start of terror.

"How awful!" he murmured to himself; "how awful!"

He was not altogether a superstitious man, but yet his dreams had impressed him to an alarming extent.

Thrice had he dreamed the same thing.

Thrice had an awful dream-drama been enacted before him—a drama in which there were only two actors.

One was himself.

The other was his sometime patron, Robert Emmerson.

He had gone to bed full of thoughts of Protean Bob and of his threats.

The recollection of having taken blood money from the detectives was ever before him, and although he did not repent him of it any more than he did of his many means of adding to his ill-gotten gains, he lived in continual terror lest Emmerson should foil his pursuers, and by some means hear of his (Garcia's) treachery.

Three times, as the old Jew slept that night, Emmerson the murderer rose up before him.

And each time, to the Jew's fancy, so plain, so vivid, so lifelike.

He had a peculiar look about him that the Jew could not understand.

His head and clothes were drenched and dripping with water, like one who has narrowly escaped from a watery grave.

His face was white and pallid, his lips blue, and his eyes flashed with fierce menace.

And this horrible figure, in each successive vision, glided on to the Jew, who seemed to know intuitively that his own doom was sealed.

And yet he could not move.

Could not lift hand or foot to help himself.

He tried to shake off the horrible nightmare and cry for help.

But in vain.

Again and again the dreadful vision returned to the Jew.

At length, when he had seen to the downstairs fastenings for a second time, he grew quieter and calmer, and he returned to his bed to rest.

"My supper has disagreed with me," he said to himself, "or why should the shadowy form of Emmerson haunt me so to-night?"

And mumbling to himself, he turned on his side and slept again.

* * * * *

All is quiet.

Yet hark!

There was a faint, creaking noise on the stairs.

The door was softly tried.

At first it resisted.

But a patient hand was there to force it, and with a warning creak it opened slowly.

And then there appeared a strange dark figure in the doorway.

A man of ghastly mien, with pallid cheeks and damp, matted hair; with clothes which clung to his form as though they had been saturated with water.

The figure paused.

Then the eyes rested upon the sleeping form of the old Jew, and the dark figure smiled in a peculiar way.

"He's mine," said this spectral-looking visitor—"yes, mine."

The Jew slightly moved, mumbled something indistinctly in his sleep, and then he repeated the groans and the stifled cries which he had gone through before in each successive phase of this hideous nightmare.

"Mercy, mercy!"

"He must be thinking of me," said the figure, crouching by the Jew's bedside. "He'll think more of me before I've done with him, the treacherous hound."

He took off his coat.

Then he turned up his wristbands with great deliberation, and advanced to the side of the bed.

The Jew slept like a cat.

The faint creaking of the visitor's boots aroused him, and he opened his eyes.

His glance fell on the visitor at once.

The effect was electrical.

The Jew's eyes dilated, and his jaw dropped with terror indescribable.

Death seemed before him.

His fate was there.

Yes, the chief actor in that horrible dream-drama which had so disturbed his rest—the hideous nightmare which was so fearfully realistic, was near him.

Here he was in the flesh.

" Emmerson !"

The sound came softly from the parched lips of the Jew.

The visitor nodded.

" What do you want here, Emmerson?" faintly came again from the old man.

Emmerson stood looking sternly, but spoke not.

" So late," faltered Garcia ; " so very late."

Emmerson seemed to glide towards him.

" You know what I've come for, Saul," he said presently.

" No, indeed, my dear Emmerson."

" Oh, yes, you do. I made you a promise once; I've come to redeem it."

" Ugh !"

An involuntary shudder escaped the Jew.

" I told you, Saul Garcia," said Emmerson, with fatal deliberation, " I warned you that if you played fast and loose with me, you——"

" Never !"

" You have."

" Never, I swear !"

" You have! I have proof positive of your treachery. So, Saul Garcia, I have come to fulfil my part of the contract."

" What do you mean?"

" Murder."

" Oh, no, no, no !" gasped the Jew.

" I do ; I am here for that purpose."

" You are mistaken, Emmerson ; you are, I swear, as Heaven is my witness!"

" Don't forswear yourself at such a time," said Emmerson.

" I don't, I don't !" said the Jew, eagerly. " Let that be the proof; I would not forswear myself if there was any danger."

" You are getting prudent, Saul," said Emmerson, with a laugh. " But you have betrayed me, you miserable old fool, and now your end is near."

" No, no," cried the Jew, " my end cannot—shall not be near."

" It is."

" Mercy !"

" I want to feel your throat in my fingers—to feel the life slowly going out of you as my grip tightens."

" Ha !" cried the Jew, starting up in his bed.

" What now ?" he glanced around him, fearing interruption.

" I know it is a dream," said Garcia ; " I know now. The same words as I heard before in my dream. Oh, shall I never wake—can I never shake off this horrible nightmare ?"

Emmerson laughed sardonically at this.

" I'll shake off the nightmare for you," he said ; " I'll send you out of the land of dreams altogether."

And he rolled up his shirt sleeves above his elbows.

" Help !" cried Garcia, wildly, as he sat up ; " help, murder ! Oh, Emmerson, do not kill me ; spare me, spare me, good Emmerson."

He made two strides forward and seized the Jew by the throat.

He fought and struggled, but oh, so feebly !

He was an old man, and at best he could have made but a very poor resistance to the enemy.

As it was, the fear deprived him of such little strength as he possessed.

The dreams of that dread night had paralysed him for the time being.

It was a poor look-out for him if he had to count upon his own efforts now for his salvation.

Unfortunately for himself he had.

But it was not to be very soon over.

Emmerson was a master in refined torture ; a staunch hater, too, and he had resolved to feast himself to satiety with vengeance.

So he dallied with his victim.

And he watched with keen enjoyment the wretched old man's deadly fear, and every phase in this black deed was invested with a triple charm to the ruffian.

" Now, Saul Garcia," said he, " you have sold me to the dectectives, have you ? Now, my friend, you have not ten minutes to live."

The horrible deliberation with which he spoke these words produced the full effect that was expected.

The old Jew seemed to gain strength suddenly, however, and then there occurred a desperate fight between them.

With a jerk and an effort which for him appeared something more than human, he freed himself from his enemy's grip.

Then he bounded off to the other side of the bed.

Emmerson crawled after him, seized him by his scant grey hair, and tugged a handful out.

With a muttered imprecation, the assassin grabbed again at his victim, and once more securing a hold upon his scraggy throat, he dragged himself over the bed to him.

Saul Garcia fought madly with his open hands in self-defence, and his assailant's skin suffered in consequence.

His long, snake-like fingers were tipped with nails, that cut into the assassin's flesh, and scored long channels of scratches, which were of too serious a nature to be easily effaced.

They remained there as evidences of his crime for many a long day.

And the smarting of these wounds frustrated in some measure the murderer's purpose, for it goaded him to greater fury, and he fought the wretched old man with all his brutal strength.

The old Jew battled as only one can that fights for dear life.

The assassin's face was red with blood.

The victim's was white with the pangs of death.

But the livid look of his face did not stay Emmerson's hand.

He relaxed his hold for a moment, it is true, but not because his pity was excited for his victim.

No, far from that.

His own words told his feelings upon the matter more eloquently than words of ours can describe them.

"I'm over hasty with him," he said to himself, "like the fool that I am. He mustn't go off as easily as that. Saul!"

No answer.

The wretched old man was apparently past speech.

"Saul, Saul!"

He shook him, but not a sound escaped his victim.

His work was done but too effectually.

"Hasty fool that I am," muttered he. "I have foiled myself; but now I must look after his dollars, and make sure of all that I can."

He rummaged about the room for the miser's hoard.

From time to time he glanced up at the bed to see how the victim fared.

But Saul Garcia never moved hand or foot, never quivered lip or eyelid.

His search was in some measure productive; but it did not come up to his expectations, for he guessed shrewdly that the murdered man was rich. and he hoped to light upon the hoard.

But this was no easy task.

Every now and again he paused in his search to glance at the bed, but all was still there.

"I was a fool to be so hasty," he said to himself; "I ought to have frightened him into telling me where it was hidden. It would have been rare sport to make him know that I was about to inherit all his hard earnings before I had killed him."

He paused.

"What was that?"

A serious expression of alarm shot across his countenance.

"It sounded like something moving downstairs."

He was right.

There certainly was a noise below, just as though the street door was being tried.

He listened at the door for a moment to assure himself that his suspicions were well founded.

"I was right; someone is at the street door," he murmured, looking very stolid.

He did not get flustered at all, but put on his coat with great deliberation, and, with a glance about the room, he stepped downstairs.

Gaining the passage with a hasty, yet not flurried step, he was not a little startled to hear a key in the street door lock.

But even now his consummate self-possession did not desert him.

He paused a moment to consider what he should do—a moment—no longer.

Indeed, had he taken more, he would scarcely have had time to get safe, for he had barely got up to the door when it yielded to the pressure from without.

Emmerson stepped up behind the door as it opened, and then he stood motionless as a statue.

Two men passed hurriedly in.

"I'll stay here," said a voice that sounded familiar to Emmerson.

"It is scarcely necessary," returned another voice, which he knew as well; "there is small chance of his being here."

"Indeed, I look upon it as a certainty."

Emmerson felt a little bit anxious now, as you may suppose.

"TOBO SPRANG FORWARD AND STRUCK MONDAY A FEARFUL BLOW."

"I'll wait here," said the positive speaker, who was no other than the sturdy Kentuckian, Mr. Jefferson.

Emmerson shrank as it were into a nutshell.

The door opened wide and hid him fairly from view, and the two passed upstairs.

Emmerson paused awhile to consider.

His decision, however, was quickly made.

He turned up the collar of his coat, stepped half way up the passage, and then said, in tones sufficiently loud to be heard outside—

"All right, I'll tell Mr. Jefferson."

Then he stepped out.

"I'm off for more police," he said, hurriedly. "They want you upstairs. There is something amiss there."

It was the work of a second.

Before Jefferson had time to think even, the murderer passed by and disappeared in the night.

CHAPTER XLV.

"Who could that be?"

He little thought that that flitting figure was the object of their search.

He was taken thoroughly by surprise, and Emmerson was gone before he made the reflection to himself just recorded.

Then, in obedience to the wish supposed to come from there, the Kentuckian stepped upstairs.

He gained the top just in time to follow his two comrades into the old Jew's room.

"Here I am," said Jefferson. "What do you want?"

"You here, sir?" said one of the officers, in surprise.

"Of course."

"But you said——"

"That I would stay on guard downstairs. Yes, I know."

"What have you come up, then, for, sir?"

An exclamation of impatience escaped Mr. Jefferson.

"Didn't you send for me?"

"No."

"No?"

"How could we? Here we are, both of us."

"But that man you sent down to me?"

"Man—sent!" iterated the puzzled officers.

"By Heaven!" thundered the Kentuckian, "you will drive me mad. Did you, or did you not, send a man downstairs to me, to ask me to come up?"

"No."

"You did not? Then who could he have been?"

"Who?—perhaps the man we have come to trap—Bob Emmerson himself?"

"Confound him!" cried Mr. Jefferson. "Then he has fooled me by his readiness after all."

He stepped back towards the stairs with the intention of following him.

"You may as well give it up as a bad job to-night," said one of the officers. "Emmerson will never be trapped to-night. He runs like a deer, and half as much start as that would serve him to get clear off."

Just then a low, hollow groan reached them.

They started.

"What was that?"

The sound was repeated.

Now it was distinctly from the bed, and Mr. Jefferson drew back the sheet which the assassin, in his flight, had thrown hastily over his victim.

He had left Saul Garcia for dead, surely enough.

But the wretched old man was hard to kill.

Dead to all appearance he had been for some time, but the cruel usage he had received had produced exhaustion, and a species of trance only.

Still it was not possible that that withered old frame could survive such a shock.

The marks of violence were too apparent to render any explanation necessary.

He opened his eyes and stared at them.

Twice or thrice he essayed to speak, but he was some considerable time in getting his breath again.

"Have you got him?" at last he asked, eagerly.

"Who?"

"The murderer."

"Who is that?"

"Emmerson."

"No."

"Ugh!" growled the old man, "you were too late. He will dodge you all yet and escape."

"No, he won't," said the Kentuckian, bluntly; "not if I have to spend my life in catching him and bringing him to justice."

The old man's eyes glistened at this.

"Do you say so?" he exclaimed; "that's brave."

He fought again for breath for some moments, and then he beckoned them all to draw nearer to him about the bed.

"On that shelf," he said, "you'll find some whisky in a bottle; give me some; it will give me strength to last out what I have to say, and then I can die in peace."

They obeyed.

And as the spirit trickled down his poor, maimed old throat, he appeared to revive somewhat.

The deadly pallor faded momentarily from his cheeks, and his eyes brightened.

"Now hearken all," he said. "I have no time to make a will, but I leave all my property to you."

He pointed his finger at Mr. Jefferson as he said this.

"All to you."

"To me?"

"Yes."

"Why, what for?"

"In trust."

"For whom?"

"Myself."

They exchanged looks at this.

His mind must be wandering, they all thought.

But they were wrong.

"You will spend it to the last cent in hunting this Emmerson—this murderer down. I am rich," he added, "rich! richer than they dream of. Spend it all, spend it like water; there's plenty to do that. Offer rewards so big that his best and truest pals will sell him. See here."

He struggled for something under his pillow, and after much difficulty he produced a small brass-handled key.

"Take this," he said, speaking with greater difficulty than ever now. "It is the key of the iron safe; you will find an iron ring under the mat in the shop. Lift up the trap. The iron box is there. Take all, all the house holds, use it all as I say; and until you lay him by the heels, I'll haunt you. D'ye hear?"

And he fixed his glassy eyes on the giant American.

He sank back.

They thought he was dead.

But he opened his eyes, and fixing his glance once more on Mr. Jefferson, he made one last effort to articulate.

It was one solitary word that he uttered, and was only just audible.

"Remember!"

And so he died with thoughts of vengeance on his mind, and vows of vengeance upon his lips.

His eyes, fixed in death, rested upon Jefferson, as if to give more force to his dying injunction.

* * * * *

They were not to say squeamish.

They were indeed all used to scenes of violence, but it made them shudder to witness such a deathbed.

They closed his eyes, and once more threw the sheet gently over him.

And then they left, but Jefferson fancied he could still hear the old Jew's voice repeat that single word—

"Remember!"

CHAPTER XLVI.

THE STRING AND THE HOOK.

"NOT quite so much noise there, if you please."

These words were addressed by Mr. Harkaway to his son Jack, who was playing with Nero at one end of the room, whilst he sat writing at the other.

"All right, dad," cried Jack; "we'll be quiet."

But the noise still continued.

The monkey had purloined some of his young master's property, which he refused to give up.

And he was now scampering about the apartment.

Springing from chair to chair in the liveliest possible manner, young Jack, with a switch in his hand, was pursuing him.

"It's this great thief, Nero, dad," returned young Jack; "he's been cabbaging my string and won't give it up."

The monkey had perched himself on the top of a cabinet in the room.

"I'll soon put a stop to that," said Mr. Harkaway.

As he spoke he picked up a pair of slippers, and launched them at the monkey's head.

They were not hard enough to hurt, but just sufficient to dislodge Master Nero from his perch.

Down he came with a bang to the ground.

"Now I've got you," cried young Jack, as he sprang upon him.

Harkaway then, as the shortest way of keeping Nero quiet, shut him up, for the present, in the cupboard.

Young Jack, in the meantime, was carefully winding the string upon a small piece of stick.

At the end of the string was a moderate-sized hook.

"What's that?" asked Mr. Harkaway of his son, with a smile glimmering on his features. "It means mischief, I think, doesn't it?"

He remembered his own boyish peculiarities, and fancied the hook looked a little suspicious.

"Oh, no, dad," answered Jack.

"Are you sure—quite sure that that hook is not intended for some respectable gentleman's hat, or unsuspecting old lady's bonnet?"

"Quite, dad, and I don't think you'd ever guess what this is from."

"Indeed!"

"No."

"Suppose you tell me, then?"

"It's a memorial."

"A memorial!" echoed his father, with a smile. "Of what?"

There was a slight pause.

Then Jack said—

"You remember the night of the fire, dad?"

Mr. Harkaway was serious in a moment.

"Do I remember it! Shall I ever forget it?" he murmured, fervently.

"I never shall," said our young hero.

"No, my brave boy," warmly returned his father. "I shall never forget your brave conduct on that dreadful night."

"Well, on that night," continued Jack, "as I was helping to steady the ladder for you to descend, one of the hooks caught in my boot, and fixed itself so firmly that I was obliged to cut the hook away from the rope, and now I keep it in remembrance of your escape."

"I understand you, my dear child," returned his parent, with emotion, "and the feeling does you honour. Keep it, then, and in years to come, long after your parents are in their graves, that simple memorial will recall the night when you hazarded you own life to save them from a cruel and terrible fate."

Having said this, he kissed Jack's rosy cheeks, and then, having finished the letter he was writing, he took his hat and went out.

Young Jack sat thoughtfully and in silence—a very unusual thing for him—for some little time after his parent's departure.

At last Jack started up, saying—

"Dad's gone out; I don't see why I should not go too."

The monkey, who was imprisoned in the cupboard, seemed to be of the same way of thinking, for he rattled the door and chirped vociferously.

"Ah! there's Nero wants to come," thought Jack; "I mustn't leave him behind."

So he went to the cupboard, and said—

"I suppose you're sorry for what you've done, ain't you?"

The monkey gave a penitent chirp.

"Very sorry, eh?"

"Chirp, chirp."

Jack turned the key and opened the door.

Out sprang Nero, and immediately evinced his contrition by tumbling head over heels and walking round the room on his hands.

"That'll do," said his young master; "you can drop that hanky panky now and be quiet."

Nero appeared to understand and

squatted down quietly on the hearthrug, where he became absorbed in hunting his fleas.

Jack rang the bell.

Monday answered it.

"Are you particularly busy to-day?"

"Well, not particular, Massa Jack," answered Monday; "um got few little odd jobs, that's all."

"And how long will it take you to do these 'little odd jobs?'"

"Something like about half an hour. Why you ask?"

"Well, I was thinking of going out for a good long ramble, and if you had done your work, I should take you with me," replied our hero, condescendingly.

"Take this child wid you, Massa Jack! Golly, him cut along with de jobs like winking."

And away he hurried in a state of great exhilaration.

The Limbian, in the pride of his heart, went straight to where his comrade, Sunday, was busily engaged in polishing a pair of boots.

"What you tink, old Sun?" he said, his ebony countenance glistening with satisfaction.

"What?"

"Dis child have jess received a very kind invitation."

"Where from?"

"Massa Jack Harkaway."

"To go where?"

"Out along with him for big spree."

Sunday dropped the boot he was polishing.

"Massa Jack might have asked dis child to go as well."

"What he want you out with him for, um like to know? Massa Jack only like de society of gentlemans," Monday replied, as he stuck out his chest and cocked his nose in the air conceitedly.

"You mean to say dis child not gentleman, den?" inquired the African, in an aggravated tone.

"Um mean to say," returned the other, "you not got de polish of dis child."

This was too much for Sunday's endurance.

"Take that, you impudent nigger!" he shouted, as, snatching up the boot, he threw it at his comrade, who caught it cleverly in his hand.

"Take it yourself, you black fellow!" cried Monday, as he threw it back.

Sunday also caught it—on his nose.

"There now, you've got the polish as well as me, yah! yah!" grinned Monday.

The African rushed after his comrade.

The latter dodged him nimbly.

"Phew! it's no good running after you, you too quick for me," muttered Sunday, breathlessly, as he came to a standstill, and prepared to continue his labours.

"What you get in a passion for?" asked his comrade at length.

"Him not in a passion," Sunday answered.

"Am you prepared to forget and forgive?"

"Of course."

"Shake hands, den."

"Dere's mine," said the African, magnanimously, as he extended his hand.

"And dere's mine," returned the Limbian, as he took it.

"Now we friends ag'in."

It may seem strange that Sunday should have so suddenly forgiven his comrade.

But he had a plan of retribution in his head, which will presently appear.

"Well, now, den, him get on wid him lilly jobs," said Monday at length, "cos Massa Jack is waiting."

He was about to turn away when his comrade called him back.

"I say, Mon," he said, confidentially.

"What you say, Sun?"

"Tink you could drink lilly drop ob rale Jamaikey, if you got some?"

Monday opened his eyes and licked his lips longingly.

"Tink him jess could," he replied. "Am dere any?"

His comrade went through some very expressive pantomime, and eventually pointed to a door at a short distance.

It was where the coals were kept.

"Coal cellar rum place keep rum in, ain't it?" remarked Monday.

"Jess de proper place," replied his brother nigger, winking and putting his finger knowingly to the side of his nose; "keep um safe. No one 'xpect find rum in de coal cellar."

"Dat true," admitted Monday, with a grin; "dat bery good idea."

"Fuss rate, I tink," grinned Sunday.

"Whar'bouts de bottle?" asked his comrade, as he approached the cellar.

"You find um standing on de shelf lilly way in on de left side," Sunday explained.

Monday, licking his lips, eagerly opened the door and went in.

No sooner did he disappear than the African stepped quietly after him, and listened, chirruping to himself intensely.

After a moment or two, Monday called out from the interior—

"Um can't find no rum."

"Good reason why; dere none to find. Yah, yah, yah!" grinned Sunday in reply, as he turned the key in the lock.

Monday heard the click.

"What dat you do?" he asked, rather suspiciously.

"Lock you in, dat's all," returned the African, with immense complacency. "Yah, yah, yah!"

Monday sprang to the door.

But he was too late. It was fast.

In vain he raved and threatened and kicked at the door.

His comrade only laughed at him.

At this juncture a bell from upstairs rang loudly.

"Dere Massa Jack's bell," shouted Monday through the keyhole.

"Nebber mind de bell," replied Sunday, consolingly, as he took his departure; "dis chile answer um. You hab big spree wid de rats all by yourself among de coals. Yah, yah, yah!"

"Where's Monday?" asked Jack, as the African answered his summons.

"Monday gone out, Massa Jack," replied the latter, without turning white at the fib.

"Gone out?" exclaimed our hero, in surprise.

"Yes, Massa Jack. Him gone out hab big spree."

"Um," muttered our hero to himself, "the silly fellow must have misunderstood me. No matter, I suppose I shall find him waiting outside."

"That's all, Sunday," he said, aloud, to the African.

"Want me to go wid you instead, Massa Jack?" urged the latter, modestly.

"No, thank you," answered our hero. "Nero and I will be company for each other."

Sunday made his exit rather ruefully.

He was disappointed, and his conscience pricked him into the bargain.

"Dat de punishment for not telling de truf," he muttered as he went downstairs.

"Come, old fellow," cried Jack to the monkey, as the door closed, "we may as well be off."

Up sprang Nero in an instant to follow his master.

The latter had reached the door, but suddenly he turned back.

He had forgotten his hook and string.

"I mustn't leave you behind," he exclaimed, as he took them from the table and put them in his pocket; "you may be useful to me some day. Who knows?"

Who knows?

Who does know, when he leaves his home, what may happen to him before he returns?

CHAPTER XLVII.

NERO GETS INTO A SCRAPE, AND JACK GETS HIM OUT OF IT.

"Come along, Nero; keep close to me, and mind how you behave yourself."

These words were addressed by our young hero to his dumb companion as he stepped from the door of the hotel into the street.

Jack was in the most buoyant spirits.

Rejoicing in the beautiful day, he strode along with heart as light as the sky above his head.

Nero went hopping along by his young master's side in a very quiet and orderly manner for a monkey, only pausing occasionally to catch a tormenting flea.

Jack kept a very wide awake look-out as he went along after Monday, whom he fully expected to find either lounging against a lamppost waiting for him, or strutting along some of the thoroughfares as he passed on.

But no Monday came in sight.

This seemed strange to our hero, although it is not so to our readers, who know he is safely locked up in the coal-hole of the hotel.

Jack and his comrade went on for some distance, until they approached one of the quays, beyond which the bright waters of the Hudson appeared in sight, sparkling in the sunshine.

Again he looked out across the water.

The more he looked, the more intense grew his desire to take a boat and to be gliding along its bosom.

"I'll have a boat; here goes. And Nero shall come with me; here, Nero, Nero!"

As he called, he turned to look for his companion.

He was no longer in sight.

"The rascal, to give me the slip like this," he murmured, fretfully; "I must go and see after him."

But ere he could leave the spot on which he stood, loud shouts reached his ear.

And the next moment Nero came in sight, bounding over the ground in fine style with some light-looking article in his paw, pursued by the owner of the article, and followed by a yelling crowd.

The monkey, hissing and chattering, came straight up to where Jack was standing.

The crowd followed.

"What have you been up to now, eh, sir?" demanded his young master, as Nero reached him.

The monkey, who appeared vexed himself, grinned rather angrily and held up the article he had secured.

It was a mass of light flaxen hair.

"Good gracious! what have you been stealing now?" exclaimed Jack. "Give it to me directly."

But Nero was obstinate, and refused to part with his treasure.

"Give it me, I say," repeated our hero.

The monkey, instead of obeying, hopped away and put it on his own head instead.

In spite of the vexation he felt, young Jack could scarcely refrain from laughing at the comical appearance the animal presented.

He looked like a dried-up specimen of some ancient judge.

But before he had time to take any further steps, the crowd had reached him.

Foremost amongst the multitude was a very tall young gentleman of the swell order, in a raving state of excitement.

He appeared certainly to have been pretty well mauled.

His light coat was torn to ribbons.

His dicky (for he wore a false one) hung by a tape and fluttered in the wind.

One of his moustaches had disappeared.

And his head was as bald as a badger.

"I demand the life of that venomous brute!" raved the young gentleman, breathlessly, as he arrived at the spot.

Nero had wisely taken shelter behind his master, where he sat winking and blinking and chattering, with his eyes fixed sharply on his denouncer.

"Why do you demand his life?" asked Jack, quietly.

"Why?" shrieked the indignant speaker, in a shrill tone; "because I do, and I'll have it too!"

"Will you?" thought our hero; "not if I know it."

And then he asked again—

"What has he done?"

"What?" shouted the young gentleman, fiercely; "look at me. What do I look like, eh?"

"Something between a Guy Fawkes and a scarecrow," returned Jack, who could not restrain the impulse to joke.

The crowd laughed unanimously, and our hero felt he had, at all events, made his first point.

"If I am a scarecrow," exclaimed the sufferer, passionately, "it's all through that infernal monkey. Let me get at him."

"You'd better mind," counselled Jack.

But the young gentleman was deaf to expostulations and wouldn't mind.

He made a frantic rush at Nero, for the purpose of annihilating him on the spot.

Instead of which, Nero astonished him by a terrific snap at his fingers with his sharp teeth.

At which the young gentleman roared lustily.

"I told you you'd better mind," said Jack, coolly.

"I insist upon that darned vicious brute being destroyed instantly!" shouted

"MR. MOLE, MADE HAPPY ONCE MORE."

the youth. "Knock its brains out. Will anybody oblige me?"

He looked round at the crowd, but no one responded to this appeal.

"Why don't you knock them out yourself, if you're so anxious?" suggested Jack here.

"Because he's afraid," cried a voice from the crowd.

Our hero could see, from the expression of the faces that surrounded him, that the crowd was rather for than against him.

This gave him confidence, and he replied, in a bantering tone—

"I beg your pardon, Mr.—Mr.—what's your name?"

"His name is Norval," cried an English actor from the crowd; "on the Grampian Hills his father feeds his flocks."

"It's a darned lie!" shouted the young gentleman; "my name is Long—Lanky Long, and my father doesn't feed any flock."

"Bravo, Lanky!" and a laugh from the crowd.

"Very well, then, Mr. Long, Nero is considered a very handsome specimen of the monkey tribe, and I cannot have him injured."

"Ugh! the diabolical wretch," growled the young gentleman; "he ought to be skewered, roasted, boiled, hung, drawn and quartered, the darned object."

"I don't see that he has done any harm," said Jack, coolly.

"No harm!" almost shrieked the long young gentleman; "my coat torn to ribbons——"

"Never mind," laughed our hero, cheerfully, "it'll make it good for trade. Buy another."

A laugh from the crowd, and "Bravos!" from three tailors.

"My shirt front——"

"Dicky, you mean," from Jack.

"Torn to shreds; my moustache dragged out by the roots."

"You should have glued it on stronger."

Another roar from the crowd.

"All my hair plucked off my head."

"What can you expect if you wear a wig?"

Again the crowd yelled with delight at Jack's daring rejoinders.

"Yes," continued our hero, addressing the bystanders on behalf of his dumb companion, "this sagacious creature can't bear to be poked with a cane, as it always gives him the collywobbles in his pandenoodles, and then no one can manage him."

This last speech brought the affair to a crisis with a roar.

Jack contrived to get Mr. Long's property out of Nero's clutches and restore it to its owner.

And the dishevelled young gentleman, amid the derisive laughter of the multitude, sneaked away with his wig on the wrong side foremost.

A few moments more, and Jack and Nero were once more alone.

"There, I've got you out of that mess," said the former, as he looked down upon the monkey, who was squatted at his feet; "and now we're going on the river. Do you understand?"

The chimpanzee grinned and nodded, as much as to say, "Perfectly."

"Come on, then; and mind, no more tricks for to-day. Forward, to the river."

As they retreated, two men stepped from behind a projection that had previously concealed them from view, and looked hatefully after them.

Unnoticed and unsuspected, Hunston and Toro, disguised, had separated from the rest of Emmerson's gang; they had mingled with the crowd, and heard all that had passed, and had received a tolerably good specimen of the coolness of the boy.

It seemed to suggest that, if he lived to be a man, he would be as hard a nut to crack as his father.

"Is it worth while following him?" said Toro, moodily, as our hero disappeared.

"It may be," returned his companion.

"We can't do much in broad daylight," muttered the giant, regretfully.

"No, curse it! Fortune seems to go against us with this young whelp," exclaimed Hunston, petulantly.

"Yes. But the wheel will be reversed before long, perhaps, and then it will be our turn."

"This brat seems to have the luck of his father," remarked Toro.

"Yes, and he's the image of him," admitted Hunston, surlily.

"And he's got his father's bulldog

pluck besides, and that's worse," grumbled Toro.

"*Corpo di Baccho!* Did you hear the young bantam cackling to the crowd?"

"Of course I did. I felt as though I should have liked to have strangled him as he spoke."

"And that infernal grinning chimpanzee, too," said the Italian, vindictively; "I shall never be satisfied till I've knocked the ugly brute's brains out."

"Never mind him; he has no tongue, and can say nothing against us."

"But he has nails, and he can scratch," exclaimed Toro, with a very wry face.

"I can vouch for that," said Hunston, "and I'll pay him off for old scores some day for what he's done; but now never mind him; let us think of the boy."

"He is going to take a boat."

"Most likely; he's fond of the water."

"But come," exclaimed Hunston at length; "while we are talking, our prey is moving away from us. Let us move on."

"I'm ready."

"Be cautious, and keep as much out of sight as possible. This precocious imp has sharp eyes."

"Our disguise is perfect; not even the detectives could recognise us as we are dressed," said Toro.

The two accomplices walked forward, and reached the quay just in time to behold one of the steam passenger boats that plied from one side of the river to the other, leaving the pier with its living freight.

On the deck of this boat stood young Jack and Nero the monkey.

Hunston and Toro looked significantly at each other.

"What do you understand by the young pup being on board the ferry boat?" asked the former.

"He is crossing, perhaps, for a walk up the country, or a ramble in the wood —anything," Toro replied.

These words acted like a spark of fire to gunpowder. Hunston's eyes suddenly blazed up with a fierce glare.

"A ramble in the woods," he repeated with intense vehemence; "fiends grant he may."

"I see; you would still follow him."

"I would, I would," exclaimed the malignant Hunston, desperately, "follow him into the dim shadows of those giant trees. Once there, my prey should not escape me; I'd torture him."

"I'd help you."

"Kill him piecemeal, Indian fashion."

"Bleed him slowly, drop by drop."

"Oh! that we may have the chance oh! that we may."

"Now let us go and have a cigar and a brandy smash; we will there arrange our plans."

Arm in arm, the two ruffians walked towards a drinking bar, to drink brandy and plot murder of the most horrible and atrocious character.

CHAPTER XLVIII.

ON THE TRACK.

HUNSTON and his companion hurried down to the water's edge.

Mingling with the crowd, but taking care to keep as much out of sight as possible.

The brandy they had drunk had not destroyed their caution.

It had only added fire to their vindictive passions.

The passenger boat had returned.

Eagerly did the two accomplices watch the passengers as they disembarked.

Our hero and his companion were not amongst them.

"Good! good!" muttered Hunston, as the last one stepped ashore; "they remain on the other side."

"Good for us; bad for them!" remarked Toro, significantly.

"Ye—es," thoughtfully replied his comrade, with an evil glitter in his eyes. "I think fortune is going to favour us at last."

"Well, and what are you going to do now?"

"Cross over by the next boat."

"And go after them, eh, as we arranged?"

"Yes, after the boy," growled Hunston, emphatically, between his teeth; "d——n the monkey. I take no notice of him."

"I mean to square accounts with the brute by knocking his brains out," grinned the brigand.

"With all my heart. Now let us go on board."

In a few moments the partners in villany were smoking their cigars on the deck.

Having received its complement of passengers, the boat was about to leave the pier.

Suddenly a voice was heard shouting vociferously—

"Stop de ship; dis chile goin' across!"

It was our sable friend Monday, who had just reached the spot, and came hurrying along at a good speed for a negro.

As the vessel had not yet begun to move, there was no occasion for it to stop.

Monday had time to get on before it started.

It will be remembered that he had been somewhat treacherously consigned to the quiet seclusion of the coal cellar.

But on getting out, he started to look after young Jack.

And by dint of asking everyone he met if they had " seen anything of Massa Jack and his monkey," he was guided to the quay.

But those he sought were not to be found there, from the fact that they were already on the other side of the river.

Monday was informed of this circumstance by the loiterers at the pier, who had seen them depart.

And he said to himself—

"Dey gone across, dis chile go arter 'em."

Accordingly, after them he went.

And was now aboard a ferry boat, straining his eyes anxiously towards the opposite shore.

Trying hard, but failing to catch a glimpse of his young master and Nero.

But while thus engaged, he was not aware that he was closely watched by two of the passengers.

Hunston and Toro, who were scrutinising the negro with scowling brow.

"That darkey belongs to Harkaway. I know the brute well," remarked Hunston at length, in an undertone.

"What the devil does he want here?"

"It's pretty clear what. Look how the black rascal rolls his eyes across the water. He is going after the boy, I suppose," Hunston muttered to himself, growlingly.

"That's it," briefly returned the brigand.

"Let him go on. He'll go too far for himself if he doesn't take care. I have a trifle or two to settle with him."

"And he will find some trouble in getting back again, perhaps," grinned Toro.

Hunston remained silent and thoughtful for a moment.

Then he said, reflectively—

"This Monday is likely to be very much in our way."

"Unless we put him out of it," replied his companion, coolly.

"Then we will put him out of it," said Hunston, in a tone of determination.

"There won't be much difficulty about that," Toro continued. "It's nice and quiet on the opposite side."

"True; a death cry or the report of a popper would scarcely be heard."

"No, especially a mile or so up the river."

"And how do you propose getting rid of the black?"

"I should be guided by circumstances," replied the Italian, with a cool shrug of his shoulders.

"How do you mean?"

"If the spot was retired, we might knock his brains out with a bludgeon."

"Psha! niggers have no brains."

"Well, then, we could give him a leaden pill between his ribs."

"That's better."

"Or send him flying from the path into the river, and fire at him from the bank."

"That would be the best sport," muttered Hunston, gloatingly.

Whilst this interesting conversation was terminated by the arrival of the boat at the opposite pier, the passengers disembarked.

Monday, eager to continue his search after his young master, was amongst the first to leave the vessel.

Hunston and Toro were the very last.

It was their policy to let Monday go on ahead.

Whilst they kept him in sight and followed at a distance.

The black, on stepping ashore, made his way at once to the footpath that ran along by the river's bank.

Here instinctively he began to examine the ground with scrutinising attention.

In his own country, he had often traced a friend or a foe by their footprints.

He had not searched more than a few seconds, when he uttered an exclamation of joy.

"Here dey am," he cried; "here de marks ob de monkey's paws. Dey gone dis way."

For some distance, he continued his course in this manner.

But never thinking, in his eagerness, of once looking behind him.

Gradually the city on the opposite bank was left in the rear.

The path grew more solitary.

The footmarks had ceased to continue in a line with the path.

Monday came to a halt.

The sun was shining hotly down upon his head.

"Him tink him jess hab lilly drop of rum 'fore him go on again," he soliloquised.

Taking a flask from his pocket, he took what he called a little—but which some might have thought a tolerably large drop.

As he was replacing the cork, some sound seemed to strike upon his quick ears, for he suddenly assumed an attitude of Indian caution, and listened.

"What dat?" he muttered to himself, in a low, suspicious tone.

Hastily thrusting the bottle into his pocket, he looked back along the road he had just traversed. No one was in sight.

Nothing was visible but nature, smiling in the bright sunlight of that lovely day.

But this did not allay Monday's suspicions.

He could not believe his ears had deceived him.

"Him almost take him oath him hear footsteps," he exclaimed, thoughtfully.

And then he stretched himself full length along the path, and placing his ear close to the ground, remained in that position listening for several moments.

When he again raised his head, there was no longer any doubt in the expression of his face.

His dark eyes flashed with certainty as he directed their gaze towards the river's bank.

And Monday looked, as of old, a brave and cautious Indian.

"Whoever dey am, dey dere," he ejaculated, as he pointed in that direction.

At a short distance from where he stood, the river wound into a sort of creek. It was upon this spot his eyes were fastened.

But he did not long remain inactive.

With a step as wary as that of some wild animal approaching the river's bank to slake its thirst, Monday drew near the edge of the creek.

As he came on, the murmuring of voices caught his ear and made him pause.

They were the voices of Hunston and his comrade.

The bank was high, and the vindictive pursuers, having advanced thus far unsuspected, had concealed themselves there the better to watch the direction the black was taking, feeling confident that to follow him would be the readiest means of finding young Jack.

It was as they ran hastily up and plunged into this retreat that their footsteps had first become audible to Monday.

Throwing himself once more flat upon the ground, he approached the edge of the creek, with the writhing, snake-like motion of an Indian on the war trail.

Having proceeded in this manner to the utmost limit that prudence permitted, he stopped and listened, trying to hear what those below were saying.

In this he was successful.

He could hear distinctly.

The conversation, too, at that moment, was particularly interesting, the subject being himself.

"Ha, ha!" he heard one of the speakers say, with a laugh, "the black beggar's stopping to consider which path to take next."

"Yes, and to have a suck at his flask. *Corpo di Baccho!* how fond these niggers are of rum."

It was Toro who had just spoken.

His words rather tickled the "black beggar," who was listening above.

"Dat true enough," he admitted to himself, with a grin; "darkies like ole Jamaikey; dat am a fact."

Hunston then continued—

" I am inclined to think, from the way in which the negro examined the grass, that Master Jack Harkaway must have branched off about this spot across the country."

" Very likely; all the better if he has," returned Toro.

" We must keep close upon Monday, and it's hard if we can't settle him between us."

" A pull of a trigger, or a stab with one of our knives, will get rid of the carrion," said Hunston, with contemptuous indifference, "and then there will only remain the boy to dispose of."

" And the monkey," suggested Toro.

" I leave the beast to you," returned his companion, in a tone of disgust.

" I'll attend to him."

As Monday listened to the foregoing ominous words, the smile died out of his face His eyes glared fiercely.

His broad chest heaved up and down like a wave of the sea.

Not with fear, but excitement, mingled with horror.

The negro. although he had not seen the speakers, had formed a pretty correct conception who they were.

His honest heart was filled with indignation.

" Dey tink dis chile lead 'em whar de dear young massa gone, do dey?" he murmured inwardly to himself. " Him be shot twenty times ober fuss, and den him wouldn't, de dam skunks!"

Monday, in his wrath, felt strongly inclined to thrust his head over the edge of the bank, and tell the lurking villains what he thought of them.

But prudence held him back.

He was unarmed.

His young master was ahead, on this solitary side of the river.

Unsuspicious of danger, he would certainly return the same way he went.

Nothing could prevent him from falling into the hands of the wretches who waited for him, thirsting like savage tigers for his innocent blood.

Nothing—but one thing.

That was forcing the murderers to retrace their steps.

But how was this to be accomplished ? His foes were two to one.

Armed, too, to the teeth, whilst he had no weapon of any kind.

Not that he would have feared even these odds in defence of his master's child.

But he felt strongly that the life of that child depended now upon his own.

" If dis child get shot, him not much good certainly," he argued to himself; " but what poor Massa Jack do ?"

This somewhat complicated list of thoughts has taken some little time to embody in words.

But they rushed through Monday's excited brain with the rapidity of lightning.

He was in a most embarrassing position.

But just at this moment, to his dismay, he heard one of the men below say—

" I wonder what that infernal nigger's up to by this time? Look out; it is time."

" I will," returned Toro, to whom the words were addressed.

As he spoke the giant slowly raised his head above the upper ridge of the bank.

" Hullo !"

He found himself confronted by a black face, a pair of gleaming eyes, and a set of very white teeth, clenched desperately together.

The noses of the negro and the Italian almost touched each other.

No wonder the latter was astonished.

" Diavolo !" he ejaculated, in a startled tone, and seemed inclined to bob his head down again.

But Monday never stirred.

He kept his large brown eyes fixed and glaring at Toro.

Toro glared at him.

For a few seconds not a word was spoken.

At length Toro, having recovered from the slight start he had received, growled out, very emphatically—

" Who, in the devil's name, are you ?"

" Dat de identical question dis chile war going to ax youself," was Monday's reply.

" We're gentlemen," exclaimed Hunston, in a contemptuous tone, showing his face above the bank for the first time.

"Dis child gen'leman too," returned the negro, rising to his knees, and looking down upon those he addressed.

"And what do you want here, prying about, eh?" Hunston inquired.

"Tell dis child what you want fust, den him tell you what him wants," was the equitable answer he received.

This at once roused Hunston's inflammable temper to an ungovernable pitch, and, throwing aside all self control, he shouted, fiercely—

"I'm here to take the life of that young cub, Jack Harkaway, you black son of Satan! Do you understand that, eh?"

Monday's broad features became convulsed at these words.

His lips quivered, and his eyes rolled ominously, as he replied—

"No, him don't; but him tell you why dis child here. Him here to save de life of Massa Jack from you two white debbils. You understand dat, eh?"

An ironical burst of malignant laughter answered this appeal.

"You save his life!" exclaimed Hunston, mockingly. "You! Put a bullet into him, Toro," he shouted.

"With pleasure," returned the brigand, readily, as he thrust his hand into his pocket in quest of his weapon.

It was a critical moment for our friend Monday.

But, just at that instant, he was inspired with a brilliant thought, and, before Toro could produce his revolver, his negro opponent drew forth his weapon, and levelled it at the head of his adversary.

This formidable implement was, after all, only his rum flask.

Bu. s he concealed the body of the bottle in his large hand, the neck, which protruded, represented the barrel very effectively.

"Now, den," he cried, determinedly, to Toro, "de minnit you take your hand out of your pocket, dat minnit I pull dis trigger, and blow you to mortal smash."

The Italian kept his hand where it was; but Hunston, whose patience was rapidly becoming exhausted, quickly detected the imposition.

"What are you afraid of?" he shouted. "Don't you see it is only a liquor flask?"

This restored the brigand's self-possession, and he sprang up the bank, and opposed his giant bulk against the stalwart but less formidable proportions of the Limbian.

At the same time he drew his revolver from his pocket, and cocked it.

Another moment and it would have been probably pointed at Monday's head.

But Hunston checked him.

A better idea had taken possession of his mind.

"Hold!" he exclaimed, as he laid his hand upon his comrade's arm.

"Hold!—for why?" asked Toro.

Hunston answered, in a low tone—

"He must first serve our turn; after that, kill him as soon as you please."

"Right," returned the brigand, as he lowered the hammer of his weapon, and placed it in a belt which he wore round his waist.

Monday's quick eyes noticed this.

His quick ears, too, had caught the remark made by Hunston.

In an instant he had decided upon his course of action; and, with a tremendous bound, he sprang forward, and, with one determined wrench, dragged the revolver from the resting place to which Toro had just consigned it.

The giant fairly staggered at this daring feat, and then he recoiled several paces in dismay.

Hunston strode forward with a threatening gesture.

But it was only to find the six barrels pointed at his face, and looking at him like so many angry eyes.

It was now Monday's turn to crow.

"Now, den," he cried, exultingly, "de best thing you two fellahs to do am jess to turn round and go back same way as you come. If not, sure as this chile's name Monday, him gib both ob you more pills dan you like to take."

Hunston turned pale, and bit his lips till the blood started.

Toro glared moodily from under his thick eyebrows at the sable hero.

"We'd better make a move, or pretend to do so," he muttered, in an undertone, to his comrade. "I'll drop upon the black devil in a minute."

At the same moment he glided his hand into his pocket, and brought forth something, which he concealed in the palm of his hand.

This something was a thick elastic

"I AM BEING ASSASSINATED!' YELLED MOLE, FALLING."

ring, which he presently slipped upon his left wrist, where it was concealed by the sleeve of his coat.

"Come, move on, you white debbils!" cried Monday, impatiently. "You know the way—straight ahead."

As he spoke, he pointed imperatively forward with the weapon he grasped.

The two accomplices slowly commenced their retreat.

Toro whispered a few words to his companion as they went.

Hunston nodded in reply, and asked, in a low tone—

"When?"

"As soon as we reach the other side of the creek," was Toro's answer.

In a few seconds they had reached this spot, Monday, like a faithful custodian, following almost close behind them, with the revolver pointed and ready for immediate use.

"Now's the time," whispered the Italian, hurriedly.

Hunston suddenly stopped, and looked behind him.

"There he is!" he exclaimed, with assumed eagerness, as he pointed over the negro's shoulder.

"Massa Jack!" cried Monday, with vivid excitement, thrown off his guard, and looking quickly round.

Quick as thought, Hunston bounded forward and gripped the revolver.

Monday turned with a startled yell.

But ere any struggle could take place, Toro crept quietly behind, and took from his wrist the elastic ring.

Then, by an effort of his immense strength, having expanded it sufficiently, he slipped it dexterously over the head and shoulders of the negro.

The strong contractive power of the ligature acted like a vice.

Poor Monday was completely fettered.

His arms were fixed to his side as though they had been glued there.

Taking advantage of his embarrassment, Hunston wrenched the revolver from his grip, and battered him cruelly with the stock about the face and head.

The burly Toro punched him with his massive fists.

Monday, from the helpless condition of his hands, was quite unable to defend himself.

Step by step he drew back, stunned and bewildered by the sudden and ferocious attack.

He neared the edge of the creek.

Toro saw his advantage, and with a yell of demoniac triumph, he sprang forward, just as Hunston fired, and struck the negro a tremendous final blow on the forehead with his clenched fist.

It was severe enough to have felled an ox, and it sent Monday flying backwards into the middle of the creek, with a loud splash.

The black was usually a splendid swimmer, but he was now stunned and helpless.

Accordingly, after the first commotion had subsided, the waters closed over him.

Only a few bubbles rising to the surface revealed what was going on beneath.

The ruffians shouted with fiendish glee at the success of their plan.

"Let's give him a bullet for luck!" cried Toro, brutally.

Bang went a revolver.

"There's mine," exclaimed Hunston, with a sardonic laugh. Bang again.

"And there's one more," grinned the giant.

A few more bubbles, and some streaks of blood floating up and reddening the surface, proved that the shots had taken effect.

"Good bye, Monday," cried Hunston, with a mocking sneer; "now I have paid you for your services to Jack Harkaway."

"To the devil with you, you black brute!" growled Toro.

"And now for the boy, Jack Harkaway."

Having said this, Hunston turned from the spot, followed by his comrade.

A few moments later they were hastening across the country in search of a fresh victim, whilst in the river creek, close under the bank, lay a dark body, washed ashore by the tide.

It was the body of the hapless negro Monday.

And poor young Jack was to be Hunston's and the giant Toro's next victim.

CHAPTER XLIX.

IN THE TOILS.

TEMPTED by the beauty of the day, and little thinking of the great danger that followed him, our young hero wandered on till he reached a spot where the trees began to grow thicker and closer.

"A wood!" he exclaimed, joyously; "that's jolly, I like woods. Come on, Nero, old boy, we shall have some fun here."

Nero grinned and chattered, clambering up one tree and down another, and swinging himself from branch to branch in a reckless manner, that proved him to be perfectly at home in such acrobatic feats.

Jack had taken the precaution to bring a packet of sandwiches.

And having arrived at a convenient spot, he resolved to halt there and have dinner.

Nero also had his enjoyment at the same time, which consisted of seizing upon the table-napkin and mounting with it up to some neighbouring branch, where he sat looking down with his round, cunning eyes at his master, and gibbering a strange *patois*, which, if translated from the monkey dialect, would probably have been—

"Catch me if you can."

"Bring down my napkin directly, sir!" cried young Jack, laughing, as he shook his fist at the robber. "Do you hear?"

Nero heard, and replied by flourishing the piece of damask, and exclaiming—

"Chirp, chirp!"

Which evidently meant—

"Don't you wish you may get it?"

"Will you come down?" shouted our hero.

"Chirp, chirp!" and a shake of the head from Nero.

"Very well, sir; then I shall come up after you, and pull you down by your tail."

Our young hero, for his age, was an expert climber, and as fearless as he was expert.

As he was climbing, he could just catch an indistinct view of the monkey at a considerable height above him.

A few more moments of hard work brought Jack within reach of Nero's tail.

"Now I've got you!" he cried, as he made a grasp at that useful member.

But the monkey, quick as thought, sprang into the branches of the tree adjoining.

This feat, though perfectly easy to a monkey, was utterly impossible for a boy to perform.

And there Nero sat, mischievously nibbling the napkin with his sharp teeth.

"Drop it, you aggravating rascal, do!" cried our hero; "if you don't, I'll——"

Without waiting to hear his sentence pronounced, the monkey suddenly uttered a shrill squeak, and dropping the napkin, made a wild spring into the adjacent branches, and was soon out of sight.

The napkin had fluttered to the ground, and Jack thought the sooner he followed it the better.

Accordingly he began to descend.

"I wonder what dad would say if he could only see me now," he said to himself, as he went on, "and Monday, dear old Monday! I wish he was——"

He broke off suddenly, for he fancied he heard a subdued laugh beneath.

"It must be Monday," he said to himself, "who has followed us. I hope it is."

He continued his descent, calling as he did so—

"Is that you, Mon, old fellow?"

"Come down and see," replied a voice from below.

It was not the honest voice of his friend, however, that reached his ear, but the stern, cold tones that chilled his blood, he remembered only too well; he had heard them before.

Clinging to the branch that supported him, he looked down.

Beneath the tree stood Hunston and his gigantic companion Toro.

The deadliest enemies of his father and himself.

Their eyes were fixed upon him.

He could almost read their intentions in their looks.

And these seemed to be summed up in one awful word—

" Death."

Death without mercy, in that silent, secluded wood.

For a moment, as if fascinated, our hero remained gazing at his foes beneath, and they at him.

At length, from the lips of Hunston, oozed forth the imperative command—

" Come down !"

" No, thank you," coolly replied Jack, who, in spite of his position, had all his wits about him.

" Come down, I say," Hunston repeated, in a louder tone.

" I shan't," returned our hero, with something like a smile of defiance glimmering in his eyes ; " I think I'm better where I am."

" I order you to come down !"

" What do you want with me ?" asked Jack.

" I'll tell you when you reach the ground," Hunston replied.

" I'm not coming to the ground ; I can't trust you," replied our hero. " If you've anything to tell me, tell me here."

Hunston bit his lip with rage.

" If you don't come down this instant, you whelp, I'll fetch you down in double quick time."

" Will you ? You'll not find it quite so easy as you think to climb this tree."

His listeners, in spite of their aggravation, uttered a hoarse laugh at this innocent idea, and Hunston asked, in a sneering tone—

" Who's going to climb the tree, eh ?"

" Didn't you say, if I wouldn't come down, you'd fetch me down in double quick time ?" Jack replied.

" I did, and so I will," growled his enemy.

" I don't see how you can do that without climbing," returned our hero, in a quiet tone of assurance.

The ruffians below laughed again.

" You young idiot !" exclaimed Hunston. " There are ways of bringing down a refractory boy without climbing after him."

As he spoke, he drew from his pocket a revolver.

Toro did the same.

" Do you see this ?" cried Hunston, as he held up his weapon.

" And this ?" asked his companion, as he displayed his.

Poor Jack saw both too plainly, and felt that he had but little chance.

" It's all over with me," he murmured to himself.

" These are the messengers we intend to send up the tree after you," continued Hunston ; " they're capital climbers."

Toro laughed loudly.

" Now, then, are you coming down ?" Hunston inquired.

" No, I'm not," returned Jack, determinately ; " if you mean to shoot me, I'd just as soon be shot up here as on the ground."

" It won't be good for you if you remain where you are another minute," growled Hunston. " Stop your chatter and come down."

But far from obeying, the young climber only shook his head, and clung more firmly to the branch that sustained him.

A muttered oath burst from Hunston's lips, and he conferred for an instant with his companion.

The brief conference over, they cocked their revolvers, and levelled them towards himself.

It was an awful moment.

Our hero felt his heart throbbing like a giant hammer against his ribs.

" Pray God help me, and bless my dear father and mother, and little Emily," was his simple prayer.

Then he quietly closed his eyes, and waited for his deathstroke.

Bang—crash !

Bang—crash !

The two revolvers had been discharged.

" Strange," thought young Jack, " I am not touched."

The bullets had buried themselves in the branch to which he was clinging, instead of his body.

" Will you descend ?"

" No !"

Again the weapons were levelled.

Again their report rang out through the wood.

Bang--crash!

Bang--crash!

Still he was unwounded.

The bullets had pierced the branch as before.

What did it mean?

The men who were firing at him were good shots.

It was hardly likely they would miss their aim.

Once more the revolvers were discharged, but without any harm to him.

Were they only trying to frighten him?

He almost began to think it must be so, when again and again the weapons belched forth their contents.

Suddenly the mystery was explained.

At the last shots the branch, which had been repeatedly pierced by bullets, creaked for a moment, and then, assisted by the weight of the body attached to it, broke short off.

Our hero had no time to save himself.

Down he came headlong, crashing through the branches, and now lay prostrate on the ground at the very feet of his foes.

The branches of the tree had broken Jack's fall, but he felt giddy and shaken by the tumble he had had.

When he opened his eyes, the first objects he saw were the forms of Hunston and the giant Toro bending over him.

"You see I have brought you down, my sprightly youth," grinned the former, mockingly.

"And now you've brought me down, what are you going to do with me?" asked the plucky boy, boldly.

"We'll soon let you know what, you impudent pup!" growled Toro; "I know what I will do with you."

Then he thrust his hand into his pocket and produced a piece of cord.

"Now, then," he cried to Jack, as he held it up before him, "do you know what this is for?"

"No, I don't; nor do I want to know," returned our hero, doggedly.

"I'll tell you, then," replied Toro, with a demoniac grin; "it's to tie your feet together."

Our hero sprang up from the ground.

"I won't be tied," he exclaimed, defiantly, making a bolt at the same time.

"Won't you?" cried the Italian, mock-

ingly, as he swooped down upon him like a vulture, and held him fast.

"No, I won't," returned the prisoner, still struggling vainly to get free.

"Oh, yes, you will," continued Toro, "and be hung up by the heels."

"Let me go!" cried Jack, excitedly, as he struck out with his clenched fists, and kicked with all his might.

"We'll soon stop your kicking," snarled Hunston, as, by a sweep of his foot, he knocked our hero off his legs.

Toro pounced on him in a moment and wound the cord tightly round and round his ankles, as an enormous spider might have wound up a hapless fly in his web.

"Now, then, pinion his arms; quick!" cried Hunston, gloatingly, as he watched the proceedings. Toro felt in his pocket.

But he had no more cord.

"Take this," said his comrade, as he threw him Jack's damask napkin, which, in his eager excitement, he had twisted into a wisp.

"The very thing," grinned Toro, as he caught it.

Resistance was useless.

What could one poor boy do against two powerful men?

Young Jack Harkaway was perfectly helpless in the power of his remorseless assailants.

"Up with him," shouted Hunston; "I long to see the young cub hanging."

"Ha, ha! with his head downwards," added Toro, with a ferocious chuckle.

As he spoke, the brigand took up his helpless victim with one hand, as though he had been a bundle of wood or wool, and carried him to a tree, from which a branch projected about six feet from the ground.

"I shall want something to tie him up with," said Toro, as he stood carelessly swinging his human bundle to and fro.

"Anything will do," returned Hunston, hastily; "here, use my silk handkerchief."

As he spoke, he dragged his silk handkerchief from his pocket, and thrust it into Toro's hand.

"That will do. Now then, *amico mio*, perhaps you'll hold our sprightly young friend whilst I tie him up by the heels."

"I will," replied Hunston, readily, as he made a step towards the helpless prisoner.

But ere he could reach him, a very unexpected incident took place.

A violent agitation was perceptible amongst the branches above, and a heavy body came plunging down upon Hunston's head.

Hunston found his hat suddenly knocked over his eyes, and himself hurled to the ground.

The heavy body was no other than Nero the monkey.

The sagacity of the animal on his return at once recognised Hunston and Toro as dangerous customers.

Instinctively he seemed to divine that they meditated evil to Jack, and that under the circumstances strong measures ought to be adopted.

Accordingly, he commenced, as we have described, by dropping upon Hunston, and, having floored his foe, he went to work with his teeth and nails in true monkey fashion.

Hunston's hair was tugged out by handfuls.

His nose was pulled till he hardly knew whether he had any nose at all.

His face was riddled with scratches, like the bars of a gridiron.

In vain he struck out wildly, and strove to escape from his assailant.

The monkey was immensely strong.

Each time he made a blow, Nero retaliated by a bite or a scratch.

When he strove to escape, the monkey pulled him back by the leg, and rolled over and over with him, each time doing Hunston some injury.

Hunston, bruised and breathless, and unable either to conquer or fly, became desperate.

" Help, help, Toro !" he gasped, wildly ; " this infernal brute's knocking the life out of me."

" I'll be down upon him," answered the brigand, as he drew his knife.

As he approached the spot, however, where the struggle was continuing, a new idea suggested itself.

Nero's tail was towards him.

The giant brigand, seeing Hunston getting the worst of the fight, sprang forward and seized the monkey with both hands by his tail.

Nero uttered a tremendous squeal at finding himself thus assaulted.

But before he could take any steps for his deliverance, he was being whirled round and round in the air with tremendous rapidity by the strong arms of the giant.

Poor Nero was quite helpless.

And his captor having swung him in this manner until (monkey though he was) his brains were completely turned, he dashed his head with tremendous force against the trunk of the tree.

This was a settler for poor, helpless Nero.

The last blow was a cruel one, and the poor, faithful monkey lay on the ground lifeless, motionless.

It was with a sickening sensation our young hero watched these dreadful proceedings.

The only friend who could have helped him was now past helping even himself.

His cruel foes were upon him in a moment.

Hunston smarting from his wounds, and more deadly and implacable than ever.

" Now then," he hissed between his teeth, savagely, " string the boy up."

As he spoke, he stooped down and dragged his fettered victim roughly up by his heels.

He could only protest against the brutal treatment he was receiving, whilst Toro was performing his hangman's office.

" You'll be punished for this, both of you," cried Jack.

"Psha !" growled Hunston.

" You are sure to be found out."

" Ha, ha ! Who's to find us ? "

" My father will," returned our hero, with strong confidence.

" Your father be ——! " burst out the malignant Hunston ; " he's nothing but a lying, boasting braggart."

" My father's a gentleman, and never told a lie in his life," boldly retorted young Jack ; " that's more than you can say."

" Chatter away, you young whelp ! " Hunston hissed between his teeth ; " your magpie tongue will soon be quiet enough, and then your bold father shall know where you are, and it shall go hard with us if we do not serve him in the same way ; how do you like our plan, you young beast ? "

" Wait till the blood begins to run into

his head, and then he can inform us. Ho! ho!" shouted Toro.

"Wretches!" murmured the poor boy, at these horrible words. "My father will avenge me."

"Ha, ha, ha!" shouted Hunston, mockingly. "Let him do his worst; I defy him."

"Father, father, where are you? Am I to perish like this? Oh, do come," and the brave boy strained his eyes anxiously around, as if half expecting to see his parent hurrying to the spot.

But, alas! he came not.

He was far away at that moment, entirely ignorant of the deadly peril that threatened his darling son.

"Ah! you may look, but no help will reach you here," said the villain Hunston.

"Poor dad will never know my fate," murmured Jack, mournfully; "I hope he won't."

"Oh, yes, he will," hissed Hunston between his teeth, "he shall."

"I pray not; it would break his heart."

"Aye! break his heart, that's what I desire," roared Hunston.

"I'll take care he shall know your fate," he continued; "I'll take care he shall come here, here to this very spot, here to find you, his pretty sailor boy, his darling pet, dangling by the heels from this branch dead, and to learn that I, Hunston, was his executioner. Ha, ha! this will be revenge indeed. Jack Harkaway's son and heir hung like a cur. Ha, ha, ha!"

And a fiendish laugh burst from the wretch's throat.

"Now, my boy, try how it feels," grinned Toro. "You can let him go."

Hunston threw young Jack from him with brutal violence, and the poor boy was swinging to and fro, suspended from the branch by his heels with his head downwards, there to die a horrible death, whilst his murderers stood by, eager to gloat over his expiring agonies.

Young Jack, as our readers well know, was no coward.

He was his father—Jack Harkaway—over again, staunch to the backbone.

But his present awful position might have appalled the stoutest heart.

And the poor boy, if the truth must be told, felt inclined to give in and plead for mercy.

"But what would be the use? No," he thought, "I won't ask."

Even then his spirit triumphed.

"If I must die, I must," he murmured to himself, and prepared himself to meet his coming fate.

For a short time he strove to bear up against the sensations that began to steal over him.

But as the blood rushed from his body into his head, the horrible sense of pressure on the overcharged brain became almost too great for endurance.

It was horrible, as the pressure increased, to hear the sound as of raging waters thundering in his ears.

Then his breathing became oppressed.

He writhed with agony.

"He feels it now," remarked Toro, in a tone of intense interest.

"Yes, yes," returned Hunston, whose eyes were fixed upon his victim's face. "Oh, how I wish I had his father and Harvey bound the same way; then would my revenge be complete."

Poor young Jack! His eyes, widely open, seemed to be starting from their sockets.

He gasped terribly for breath.

His face was purple.

The veins in his neck and forehead swollen almost to bursting.

The blood flowed from his nose and ears.

A stifled cry of agony burst from the tortured lips of young Jack Harkaway.

Soon all would be over.

Stay!

Hark!

Was it fancy?

Or did a shout at a short distance off answer the poor boy's cry?

Toro and Hunston seemed to think so.

For they started and looked suspiciously at one another.

Again the young sufferer shrieked wildly.

A quick and loud shout came sounding in reply through the wood.

"Hullo!"

This time there could be no doubt there was help at hand.

"Dat young Massa Jack's voice!" was shouted, in familiar tones.

And the next moment, crashing through the undergrowth, his eyes glaring wildly with terrible excitement, the dark features of Monday came in sight.

"MR. MOLE GAVE A LOUD CRY OF ALARM."

CHAPTER L.

THE BEGINNING OF THE END.

HE was dripping with wet, and his clothes were stained with blood.

But it was dear old Monday still, and not his ghost.

Monday alive, and ready to do battle against any odds in defence of the boy he loved.

He saw at a glance the two murderers and then the deadly peril of his young master, and he cried, as he advanced, in a voice hoarse with horror and indignation—

"You big villains! you dam big cruel 'fernal villains!"

But he did not attack them.

He rushed straight up to him who most needed his assistance.

"Massa Jack! dear Massa Jack!" he wailed, piteously, with the tears in his eyes; "are you alive?"

"Ye-es," murmured the poor boy; "cut me down quickly."

"Dis minit," replied the delighted negro, as he dragged his knife from his pocket; "I save you, dear boy."

The blade flashed in the air.

Another instant and our hero would have been released from his awful position, but ere this could be accomplished, the report of a revolver was heard.

Then a cry of mingled pain and despair.

And the brave negro fell backwards on the ground, pierced by a bullet from Hunston's weapon.

"The idea of that nigger having the d——d impudence to be alive after the pummelling and the cold bath we gave him," remarked Hunston, coolly, as he restored his smoking revolver to its place in his belt.

"Nothing but lead will quiet these black beggars."

"He's quiet enough now," said Toro, giving the motionless body of the prostrate negro a contemptuous kick as he spoke

"And so is Master Jack Harkaway," continued his comrade, as he approached the branch from which our hapless hero was suspended and contemplated his murderous work with satisfaction.

"Yes," assented Toro; "there's no doubt about that. His account's settled for this world. Our next victim shall be Jack Harkaway, his hated father."

Poor young Jack hung there perfectly still and motionless.

Not a limb stirred. Not a feature quivered.

The purple hue had died out from his face, and he had become pale as death itself.

"I'm quite satisfied," exclaimed Hunston, in a cold-blooded, deliberate tone, as he turned to depart.

"Shall I put a bullet in his heart before leaving?" inquired the brigand. "That would make certain that the boy will trouble us no more."

"No, that would spoil my revenge; his father must know he perished slowly. I will let Harkaway know the exact spot where he will find his dead son."

With these words the accomplices plunged into the thicket and disappeared.

Hardly were they out of sight, when the supposed lifeless body of our hero began to stir convulsively.

Suddenly he opened his eyes and glared wildly around him.

Young Jack, in spite of the vindictive malice of his enemies, was not dead yet.

Providence had watched over him.

The blood he had lost, instead of hastening his end, had relieved the pressure from his brain and saved his life.

But he was in a terribly critical position.

And though conscious of his danger, he was too weak to rescue himself.

"Monday, help me," he murmured, in scarcely audible accents; "Mon——"

His voice ceased abruptly.

He had no power to finish the word.

Poor Monday.

He, alas! was unconscious.

What was to be done?

The helpless boy cast up his eyes despairingly, as if imploring Heaven to help him.

His eyes fastened on the branch over his head.

If he could only raise himself so as to grasp that, he might still be preserved, he thought.

He had no strength.

Suddenly, as if by a gleam of inspiration, a thought flashed across him.

The coil of string with the hook.

Might not that assist him?

Undoubtedly, if he only had the power to use it.

But, so far from that, he could not even get at it.

But the desire for life was strong within him.

As he pressed his arm against his side, he could feel the hook resting in his jacket pocket.

This inspired him, and he resolved to make an effort to draw it forth.

Cramped and pinioned as he was, he endeavoured, by means of his left arm and hand, to coax that part of the jacket where the pocket was placed more over his breast.

In a few moments, he was able to grasp the lappel of the coat with his right hand.

An instant more, and he had possessed himself of his coil of string and hook.

A thrill of joy passed through him as he grasped it.

But there was not much cause for exultation at present.

He had yet to fix the hook in the branch over his head.

"I can never—never do it," he wailed, piteously.

But the thought of his desperate situation quickly aroused him.

"I must try," he murmured; "it is my only chance for life. Please, God, help me!"

Having uttered this simple prayer, he began to unwind the string to which the hook was attached.

Then, with a sudden jerk, he tried to swing the string over the branch from which he was suspended.

It fell short, and he had to commence the operation over again.

Again he made the attempt.

Again a failure.

A cry of disappointment burst from his lips.

He was growing dreadfully exhausted and faint.

His lips and throat were parched with thirst, and his old sensations were beginning to return.

The pressure on the brain, the strange sounds in his ears, and a strange bewilderment in his thoughts.

"I shall die, I shall die," he groaned, despairingly; "I have no hope."

"Have hope, Jack," a soft voice seemed to whisper in his ear; "courage, try again."

"I will," cried our hero, stimulated by the voice he fancied he had heard, "I will try once more; but if I fail this time, it will be the last. I have no more strength."

By an intense effort of determination, he once more set the string in motion.

"One, two, three," he cried, as, with one last remaining effort, he swung it up with all his strength.

The attempt was successful.

God had helped him.

With a bold curve, the cord flew clean over the branch, and twisted round it, the hook fastening itself in a projecting knot.

When our hero drew in the cord, and pulled against it, it was quite firm and tight.

The heart of the poor boy bounded with renewed hope at the success of his exertions.

"If I can only pull myself up," he thought.

And without waiting to indulge in further surmise, he began at once to make the attempt.

This he found the hardest work of all.

He dared not make any violent effort, for fear of breaking the cord, which was thin.

He was obliged to twist it round each hand in turn, to raise himself slowly, cautiously, inch by inch.

The cord cut into his flesh almost like a knife.

It was a struggle for life, and that nerved our brave young hero for endurance.

Gradually his body assumes a horizontal position.

He is approaching the branch slowly but surely.

One more effort, and he will be able to clutch it.

Again he breathed a short prayer, and once more he thought he heard a small voice say—

"Courage, courage, Jack. Keep on."

Again the cord is wound round his swollen hands, then, by one more effort, he rolls himself over full length upon the branch, where he lies panting but rejoicing.

The monster—death—is foiled of his prey.

* * * * *

For some time our hero lay with his eyes closed, but fervently breathing a prayer of thanks for his escape from the villain Hunston and the brigand Toro.

Whilst Jack is recovering himself, we will turn our attention to another of our characters, poor Monday, who was now stretched upon the ground, wounded and insensible.

Our readers will naturally be anxious to know how, after being at the bottom of the river, the faithful negro could ever have lived to be shot.

The mystery is, nevertheless, simple enough when explained.

When Monday was, by the iron hand of the giant Toro, knocked backwards into the creek, he was not drowned.

The water, which would have speedily destroyed any ordinary individual, had a contrary effect upon our sable friend.

It only revived him and brought him to his senses.

From his infancy he had been accustomed to live almost as much in the water as out of it.

When, therefore, he found the waters of the creek close over him, he was not alarmed, as most people who could not swim (and many who could) would have been.

On the contrary, he congratulated himself on his position, his reasoning being somewhat as follows—

"In de fust place, being at de bottom ob de creek, him out ob de reach ob Massa Hunston and Toro : dat one good ting.

"In de next place, if I don't come up again, dey tink me dead ; dat anoder good ting. Let dem tink so.

"Den, when dey gone, I get out and follow the darned rattlesnakes—look arter Massa Jack. Dat de best ting ob all."

These arguments passed through the negro's brain in the twinkling of an eye, and determined him to keep where he was.

Although his arms were fettered, his legs were free.

With these he had sufficient power over the elastic element to keep himself beneath the surface, and at the same time to remove to a safer distance, whilst his experience as a diver enabled him to hold his breath until his enemies had departed.

Hardly had they turned their backs, ere a woolley head and a black face rose slowly out of the river, looked after them, took a deep gulp of air into his mouth, and slowly disappeared again beneath the surface.

"De boy, de dear boy !" thought Monday, as the water closed over him.

The idea of his young master's danger gave him the strength of a giant.

With one sudden and mighty effort of his strong arms, he burst asunder the elastic ring that confined his arms.

Then, swift as an arrow from a bow, still, however, keeping beneath the surface, he darted towards the bank.

His grazed shoulder bled profusely, for Toro's shot had taken effect, and his jacket was deluged with blood.

Anyone looking at him as he lay there would have certainly pronounced him dead.

But in a few moments more he was on his feet, and, though feeling rather faint and giddy from his exertions, and the continued bleeding of his wound, following on the track of Hunston and Toro.

How he arrived at a most momentous crisis, what he said and did, and the fate he experienced, is already know to the reader.

Now he lay prostrate on the ground, the pulses of his faithful heart beating slowly, his strong limbs, feeble as those of an infant, bleeding, dying perhaps.

The Continuation of "HARKAWAY AND HIS SON'S ADVENTURES ROUND THE WORLD" Next Week (Tuesday), One Halfpenny.

Those who have followed the adventures of our hero,

JACK HARKAWAY,

thus far, will probably be pleased to know that this series :—

JACK HARKAWAY

AND HIS SON'S

Adventures Round the World,

will extend to two volumes.

At the termination of the Second Volume we shall follow our Heroic Friend through China, Greece, and Australia, and conclude the English series with,

Harkaway and His Boy, Tinker.

Published Every Tuesday - - -
ONE HALFPENNY.

Office: 173, Fleet Street, London, E.C.

www.ingramcontent.com/pod-product-compliance
Lightning Source LLC
Chambersburg PA
CBHW080826250626
47160CB00008B/2863